Campaign Widows

a novel

AIMEE AGRESTI

GRAYDON
HOUSE

**GRAYDON
HOUSE**

Recycling programs
for this product may
not exist in your area.

ISBN-13: 978-1-525-80426-7

Campaign Widows

BookClubbish.com
GraydonHouseBooks.com

Printed in U.S.A.

For my family

"Campaign behavior for wives: Always be on time.
Do as little talking as humanly possible. Lean back
in the parade car so everybody can see the president."

—ELEANOR ROOSEVELT

CAMPAIGN SEASON KICKS OFF AS RUMOR MILL CHURNS: IS GRAMMY WINNER HAZE MULLING PRESIDENTIAL BID?

By Sky Vasquez, Staff Writer, *The Queue*

The Iowa Caucus—the official start to the presidential campaign season—is just days away with no fewer than two dozen candidates already in the race.

Among the very early favorites, according to recent polls: Vice President John Arnold; billionaire businessman Hank Goodfellow; and freshman Congressman Carter Thompson.

But sources say yet another contender may soon enter the ring: Grammy-winning hip-hop artist Rocky Haze. Yes, you read that right.

A source at the Federal Election Commission confirms paperwork has been filed on behalf of the star. "Primary ballots in New Hampshire, Haze's home state, are being printed as we speak—her name is on there," says another source. "She does things her own way, no one would be surprised if she sat out the Iowa Caucus and got in the game later."

Whatever her plans, she's playing it close to the vest. Haze, a United Nations High Commissioner for Refugees, who has penned articles for *Foreign Policy* magazine, has yet to publicly declare her candidacy.

Reps for Haze did not return calls.

PART I

PRIMARY EDUCATION

1

THIS IS TOTALLY THE AMERICAN DREAM

★

January

One look at that endless spiral staircase and Cady knew this just wasn't going to work in heels. She craned her neck, following that epic skyward coil leading presumably to the Capitol Dome, as she slipped off her pumps and stowed them in her satchel. This called for pragmatism. "So, how many—"

"Twenty-six stories, give or take," the buzz cut Capitol police officer said, pulling shut the door onto the rotunda. Twilight descending from the windows above, tourists and lawmakers cleared out for the day, the grand, airy rotunda had been so Zen-like at this hour. With the creak of the door, though, they were now sealed inside the stark and claustrophobic hidden passageway of the staircase. "No elevators."

"Okay then," she said, squeezing the bouquet of glorious red roses in her hand. "Let's do this."

The plan had been a quiet dinner in Dupont Circle, near Jackson's place—their place now, *their place*—to celebrate her first day of work, but instead a sleek black sedan had arrived outside her office and whisked her here, to this officer bestowing flowers with a note that said only, "See you at the top. Love, Jackson."

She wondered why the sudden change. Jackson had said nothing in his texts, going silent after instructing her to get into the car. The officer led the way, and Cady began the climb in her tights. To keep pace, she hummed that quick, steady drumbeat of Rocky Haze's "Constitutional Rite," the catchy song that had been playing *everywhere* for weeks.

About eighteen stories up, her legs burning, she caught her breath: the twisting, turning path opened to a narrow catwalk, allowing her to glimpse the bottom of the rotunda, nearly making her queasy, before another passage sent them up again, deep into the webbed architecture of the dome. Metal beams and trusses extended out at all angles across the empty space in a way that appeared almost delicate. She didn't mind this long journey up, circuitous as it felt. Two days earlier, she had completed a similar odyssey and equally stunning feat: making the leap from New York to Washington…and to Jackson. The months apart had felt as arduous as this climb, so much scheduling, traveling week after week unsure of where the relationship was headed but with the vague hope of reaching a summit at some point. And at long last, it had all culminated in her move to his city.

She replayed that moment in his apartment, trying now, as she had that day, not to be concerned. He just hadn't gotten around to making room, he'd said, he'd been "slammed" with work, when she arrived to find not a single drawer vacated nor any welcoming windows created among his dozen navy and black suits, his vast array of button-down shirts. No room anywhere, really, for anything of hers. But there would be time for the proper melding of the things, she'd comforted herself. And so she had simply, joyfully shoved her boxes and suitcases along the periphery of the one bedroom apartment like sidelined players waiting to be let into a game.

The time was right, pure and simple: she couldn't take it anymore, the distance, being away from him, shuttling along Amtrak's Northeast Corridor or worse, along I-95 in those cheap buses with the reckless drivers that dumped you at

Union Station or Penn Station or Chinatown—just to see him for a brief weekend. The more time she spent with him, the more she wanted. She ached for a full-time relationship, but it had been up to her to make it happen. As a Capitol Hill staffer, Jackson was firmly entrenched in DC now, and as a TV producer, she had more options, and Washington was still a great market, after all. She began looking sooner than she had admitted—these things took time—and finally she had gotten the job, which was a good one with a good title—Senior Producer at the local morning show *Best Day DC*—a step up.

Except for the pay cut.

She stopped and stood on her toes for a second, straining to spot the top, but it was too dark and winding to see anything other than more and more stairs.

She sighed and continued her ascent. She had fought hard, but the pockets just weren't as deep as they had been at *New in New York*. Her new boss, Jeff —who seemed just a few years older than her but dressed as though heading a tech start-up (hoodie, jeans, sneakers)—had promised to "reevaluate" once ratings improved. "There's no question you deserve more," he told her. "But between you and me, we just *rebranded*—aka *cheated death*—and things are a bit…capped…until we see the expected…growth. You know? But we will, especially with a producer of your caliber."

That was another thing. The show wasn't quite the *number one* local morning show. *Best Day DC* might be two on a good day…or possibly three. But she had felt sufficiently flattered by her new boss's confidence in her. So Jackson didn't need to know her salary details, or any of the reservations she had about leaving her old job and old life behind. From what she heard everyone had some kind of dirty little secret in Washington, so this could be hers.

Three hundred steps later, they finally reached their desti-

nation. She paused to catch her breath, smooth her long brunette bob, slip her shoes back on. When the officer pushed
open the door to the viewing deck, the aggressive January
wind roaring at them, she found Jackson across the way, leaning over the railing. At the sounds of their arrival, he spun
around, cleared his throat.

"Hi! Hey!" he said, rattled, like he'd been caught shop-
lifting. "That was fast!" He ran his fingers through his short
blond hair, then smiled *that smile*, the one she had fallen in
love with. The one that got her every time. Even after three
years together, Jackson Winfield still reminded her of that
universally beautiful male model whose photo accompanied
stories in glossy women's magazines advising "How to Get
THAT Guy!"

"This is— Wow!" She took a step forward and scanned the
backdrop: all of Washington twinkled below.

"That's the idea," Jackson said. "Okay…so…Cady…" He
tested the words as though rehearsing and hopped up and
down like he was gearing up for something.

"You okay?" she asked gently. He seemed unusually nervous, jittery even.

"Yes, better than okay." He nodded, definitive, ready, and
smiled that gleaming smile again. "Okay, so—" he started,
then stopped again. "Oh, hang on." He dug his phone from his
suit breast pocket and handed it to the cop, who began filming.

Finally Jackson reached for her, setting the flowers on the
ground and taking her hands in his warm palms. He looked
deep into her eyes in an *important, vital* way, not just a *should-
we-go-to-Lauriol-Plaza-or-Kramer-Books-for-dinner?* way. The
Washington Monument shone behind him in the distance.
"I had a whole speech I was working on, but I'm no speechwriter. So… I love you… Will you be my running mate?"

"Your…what?"

"You know, my running mate…in life? Marry me?" he asked, kneeling now. His face stony, serious, aqua eyes glittering.

She stood there, hands to her mouth in pleasant shock, possibly having an out of body experience.

"Soooo—" he prompted her.

A gust of wind whooshed past, waking her up. "Oh! Sorry!" She shook her head, brain activity flickering again. "Yes! Of course! Yes!"

He kissed her in that perfect way of every film and book she had ever seen or read. And then he gently swept a lock of hair away from her face and sighed. "Now, just a couple quick things—"

"Oh?" she asked with a nervous laugh.

"No big deal—just, if anyone asks, we're supposed to say Carter was here with us," he explained. "It's, more or less, well, *illegal* to be up here without a member of Congress but—"

"But then what could be more fitting for us?" she interrupted, smiling as she recalled the last time they were up on a roof overlooking the city. "Breaking the rules is kind of our thing now." When she had been offered the job, they had celebrated by crashing a party at the Hay-Adams Hotel, sneaking onto the terrace to gaze at the White House and breathe in the night air of the city they would take on together.

"Rule breaking, for better or worse." He grinned. "That's why I love you. So anyway, Carter would've been here but he's in Iowa—"

"Obviously." She smiled, then thought about it. "Ohhh…"

"Yeah, and so I'm flying out tomorrow, just a few days, you know how it goes… I'm sorry. You know I'd rather be here celebrating with you."

"C'mon, you know you're thinking *this is totally the Amer-*

ican dream," she teased. "Being indispensable. Staffing your boss, who happens to be a *presidential* candidate, on his first big campaign trip."

For a flash it seemed like he might object, brows furrowing, but then he dropped the facade. "I know!"

"Congratulations," she said and meant it, shaking his arm, the proverbial pieces all falling into place for them both, and so swiftly. "It's something to celebrate, another thing to celebrate."

He kissed her. "Thank you, I'm glad you feel that way," he exhaled. "Because there's one last thing that's not the greatest but it'll be okay—" He paused for too long.

"You're kind of worrying me now—"

"I don't have your ring," he blurted. He sheepishly glanced toward the ledge and back at her: "Actually. It…fell. Down…there…somewhere."

"It…wait…it what?" She ran to the ledge, peering over as though she would be able to spot a lost diamond nearly thirty stories down. Instead, a postcard-perfect panorama of Washington winked back at her.

2

WASN'T THAT JUST THE AMERICAN DREAM?

★

If Reagan didn't wash her hair, she could shower in ninety-five seconds and dress in two-and-a-half minutes. As she tore off her plaid pajama pants and beat-up Georgetown sweatshirt, two identical wailing cries pierced the air, their pitches perfectly matched as only twins— or exceptionally gifted, though grating, a cappella singers—could. The girls shouldn't expect to see Reagan for another eight minutes; they were just trying their luck. (She nuzzled Natasha's and Daisy's matching halos of raven curls and whispered, "Good morning, lovelies!" at precisely 6:37 a.m. every day.) Ted's flight didn't leave until noon, probably later with the weather: just a confectioner's-sugar dusting of snow, nothing so remarkable for January, but enough to cripple Washington. He had plenty of time. He could greet the girls this morning.

Reagan bounded into the telephone-booth-sized shower stall, fast, fast, yanking the glass door shut with enough force to shake its frame, and pulled on the faucet. Old pipes squealing, no time to let the hot water crank, it felt like walking into an ice storm naked. "Mother*fucker*!" she shouted. As though in response, her phone began blasting that new Rocky Haze song, the one in which she rapped the Constitution. Reagan had forgotten to turn off her alarm. Why did she still set her alarm when the twins woke her daily at 6:24 anyway? As she pushed the door to step out, the cries crescendoing once more, the glass wouldn't budge. She shook it, again, again, and it was as though she had been vacuum-packed in there: the seal around the door's frame, which had been peeling for months—and which Ted kept promising to repair and she kept refusing to do herself on principle, one of the many things falling apart in their home—had gobbed up and gotten lodged. If she pushed too hard, the whole thing would likely shatter, it was that old.

"Fuck this motherfucking house!" she said to herself, not expecting to be heard. She couldn't even bang her fists against the glass, so she started to shout, "TED! TED! I'm trapped! In the shower! Trapped!" She imagined him singularly focused, returning emails over breakfast, reading headlines, making calls and finally whistling as he packed his bag and hopped in the cab that would pull up to the house right on time, no matter the snow, to whisk him to the airport and possibly to his place in history helping to elect the next president— well, now, wasn't that just the American Dream?—all while the children cried and she stood imprisoned in their shower. If all else failed, she told herself, she had been a black belt in high school for God's sake and could sidekick the hell out of that door if she wanted. But then she would just have to clean up all that damn glass. She just didn't have time today. They had a My Gym class to get to and it was the girls' favorite— "Music and Motion"—and she was *not* going to let them miss it. "TED!" she yelled again.

She didn't have the energy or patience for this. She'd stayed up all night writing a column and had sent it in minutes ago without bothering to reread. "Ugh," she grunted, then chanted to herself, head against the glass door, "Perfect is the enemy of the good, perfect is the enemy of the good." And who had said that? Besides Voltaire? Bill Clinton, right? Why couldn't she come up with lines that good? Work, parenting, she was doing everything wrong. The only part of motherhood she was completely acing was the constant guilt. Even her own mother had no patience for her self-flagellation. At least three times a week, her mother, a nurse, would FaceTime her at the end of her shift and tell her, always in Korean because she knew Reagan never spoke it otherwise, "You need some mom friends! You need a group of women supporting you!" To which Reagan would reply some variation of, "Ugggghhh, enough with you," in Korean and then usually tune out yet another of her mom's diatribes about the power of sisterhood.

Actually, now that she thought about it, kicking the door down could be kind of fun. Her heart revved up considering, the slightest adrenaline surge—or was that nausea? (She couldn't pull all-nighters like she used to.) Ted had clearly forgotten she could *do* stuff like that. She would show him what happened when home repairs weren't made in a timely manner. She was warming up to the idea when the bathroom door flew open. Ted strutted in like a chipper kangaroo, a grinning Natasha snuggled against his chest in one baby carrier and a giggling Daisy loaded onto his back in the other. He still wore his black track pants and hoodie from his early jog in the bracing cold, Bluetooth in ear, ice-blue eyes bright: the image of work-life balanced bliss.

"Daddy to the rescue!" he called out, galloping like a horse. "What do we have here? Well, you've gone and got yourself into quite a pickle, haven't you?" He laughed. "Look at Mommy!"

She waved. "Good morning, lovelies."

The girls squealed and cheered, contentedly attached to Ted, as he fiddled with the door, inspecting the seal, picking at it, and jiggling the whole thing in its frame. (Somehow, observing this effort felt worse than just kicking the thing down.) The non-sleep-deprived Reagan would've already been laughing at the whole episode, but this one—the cold, tired, wet, naked one—put her hands on her hips and sighed. "Give me your cold, your tired, your naked. Give me a towel." With a *pop*, the door unstuck and Ted opened it proudly, the girls clapping as he tossed a towel at her.

"So I'm gonna need that ride to the airport, after all."

The mailman arrived at the same time as the sitter, Stacy, their favorite My Gym teacher, fresh out of college but seemingly even younger. Reagan kissed Natasha's and Daisy's soft curls, snuggled their necks in that way that always made them both giggle, then left them playing with Stacy in their bubblegum-pink bedroom.

She stole away to her room and tossed the much-anticipated package on the unmade bed. She lived a mile from the shops at Friendship Heights, two miles from Bethesda Row, and four miles from Georgetown, but damned if she knew when she was supposed to have time for shopping. She hoped one of these rented cocktail dresses fit. At least she hadn't eaten in the twenty-four hours since being freed from the shower—too busy—though it wasn't like her. She feared she might be on the verge of another bout of the Norovirus. She barely slept, and her immune system had been shot since having the twins.

Reagan sat at her desk, fired up her laptop and began reading—today was as much an indulgence as it was a necessity. She had until about 6:00 p.m. to get through the *New York Times*, the *Wall Street Journal, Politico, The Queue,* the *Washington Post*, the *Economist*, the *New Yorker*, the *Atlantic, Financial Times*, the *Los Angeles Times*, and then for extra color, *Us Weekly, People, Vogue, Vanity Fair.* Everything she no longer had time to read on a regular basis; everything she needed to feel prepared for a Birdie Brandywine cocktail party.

She flipped on the TV to CNN and poured a 5-Hour Energy shot into her hot coffee, stirred it with her finger—

"Ow! Fuck!"—and took a big swig before shooting off a quick text to Jay, her best friend, who was currently in the throes of a romantic upheaval: It isn't chickening out, if you DON'T do something that would've been a mistake. You're suffering from a case of good judgment. Kudos. xo. With a deep breath, she began speed-reading. As she consumed the words, and the caffeine, she felt herself metamorphosing into her alter ego: a sociable person capable of discussing an array of topics beyond just the eating and sleeping habits of tiny humans. Politics, news, government had once been her lifeblood. She was reminded again—as she had been with the karate—that she had all sorts of skill sets that weren't being utilized on a regular basis.

3

THIS IS IT, AMERICAN DREAM STUFF RIGHT HERE

★

Just as Jay shrugged off his coat and the first snowflakes of January, and pulled up the email, which had arrived right on time, the phone rang. "Shit, Helena," he said out loud when the executive editor's name popped up. She never called Arts & Culture; too much legit news needed attention, especially this election season. There was a reason *The Queue* had become the fastest-growing internet magazine/news aggregator/ online forum/digital powerhouse/whatever-the-marketing-team-was-branding-it-as-this-week since Helena came on board. He ran his hand through his short black hair and answered, too peppy, "Hey there, Helena!"

A flat "Pop by, Jorge" was all he got in return. Helena was the only person besides his mother who used his full name. And that construction was her trademark: "*Pop by*, you're fired." "*Pop by*, you're short-listed for the Pulitzer." Whether good or bad news, it didn't matter. And at a site where each story was ranked by traffic—hence "the queue"—it was too easy to see which editors were delivering and which weren't.

"Absolutely, on my way!" He hoped he wasn't getting fired. To be honest, he always felt the place was probably a little fast and a little competitive for him, not really his scene—and that's what he told himself anytime he got harsh feedback on a story he edited or had ideas shot down.

He grabbed his iPhone, tucked a pen behind his ear and bolted out of his office, bringing up the email he had just begun reading on his computer: Happy Monoday, J! Here you go... He overlooked the typo. Classic Reagan, she had probably pulled an all-nighter. She'd always loved the thrill of the deadline, ever since he'd met her at Georgetown, back when she would start studying for a final the night before and ace it. Write a ten-page paper the morning it was due and see it go on to be published in the *Georgetown Law Journal*...as a freshman, and which undergrads couldn't even submit to. She had even caught the eye of Alexandra Arnold, then a visiting professor and senator on her way to becoming the Secretary of the Treasury. That was Reagan, and she always acted like it was all no big deal.

Jay skimmed the column quickly enough to gauge that there were no major problems (of course) and, still walking, tapped out a speedy response just so Reagan wouldn't worry (because she would if she didn't hear from him promptly enough). Thanks, doll. Fab as always. More soon, running! As he strode past the reporters' labyrinth of cubicles, a tall, lean body fell in line with him. A notepad tapped the small of his back, then came a nervous whisper.

"Shit. Helena," Sky said.

"I know." Jay looked up from his phone as they walked together. And now Jay *did* know: he wasn't getting fired. But a whole new set of fears crashed over him. He tried to be cool, always a struggle.

"Is this about my tip?" Sky whispered. "Gotta be, right?"

When Sky had brought the news to him, Jay had been the one to get the Politics desk on it and to keep Sky looped in, not let it get passed to some other reporter just because Sky was Arts & Culture. There was always a bit of a Cold War between the news and features departments at *The Queue*.

"Yeah, could be, absolutely, I mean. Yeah," Jay said.

"Then, what next?" he asked quietly. Sky was asking if he was up to the challenge.

"Then, this is it, American dream stuff right here," Jay said, managing some reassurance, but he couldn't help feeling a twinge of dread in his gut. If Helena went for this, then things would change. But, of course, he wanted this for Sky. He deserved it.

Eyes straight ahead, Jay dug his hand into his pocket and pulled out Sky's watch. Without a word, Sky fastened it on his bare wrist. He had left Jay's U Street condo that morning, in his lululemon sweats and earbuds, looking like a paparazzo shot of a celebrity out in the wild: gorgeous without even trying, as he returned to his own studio on H Street in Northeast. He forgot his watch, his phone, some vital personal item, three out of five days a week, but they maintained the somewhat inconvenient arrangement all to avoid walking into the office together. It was a habit that had started after their first night together—floated by Jay, playing the role of the older and wiser of the two—and continued now, mostly because things had been going so well and Jay dreaded boat-rocking of any kind.

"My source was solid. Like, better than solid, know what I mean?" Sky whispered, barely making eye contact as they wove around a pair of Capitol Hill reporters pulling on gloves and hats to go cover hearings, editors returning from their morning coffee breaks and a trio of writers ducking into *The Queue*'s own yoga studio. The site had been doing so well in the five years since its inception that their three-floor office in Columbia Heights had begun to resemble a mini Palo Alto tech campus.

"Washington Ballet review coming to you at ten," said Sophie, the long-limbed freelance dance critic, who spent more time in the office availing herself of its amenities than people who were actually on staff.

"Great," Jay said, knowing full well that it wouldn't be in until noon but would be good enough that he could let it slide.

"Hey, Sky, great interview with José Andrés." Sophie petted the long waves of her ponytail, so thick it looked like doll's hair. "Jaleo is totally, like, my favorite restaurant. Or, second to Bar Mini maybe."

"Thanks, Soph," Sky said, patting his abs. "Put on a few on that one. His new place is killer." He appeared not to realize that she was flirting with him. Jay had gotten used to this, *everyone* flirted with Sky. Boy, girl, animal, vegetable, mineral.

As soon as they set foot in Helena's office, they knew. Jay raised his eyebrows at Sky, who looked like he might be sick. He didn't get called into the executive editor's office often or ever. Rocky Haze played on Helena's laptop. She clicked the keys feverishly, pausing only to signal they should close the door and to push her blunt black bangs out of her face.

"Did you know Haze raps a huge chunk of the Constitution on here?" she said to her screen. "I mean, almost in its entirety? I suddenly have a newfound respect for the American people that they're into this. They may learn something." She was Canadian and enjoyed a minor superiority complex about it.

"Haze is actually a pretty smart lady, beneath the tats," Jay said, jittery. Sky looked too nervous to speak.

"She writes two articles for *Foreign Policy* magazine and suddenly she's qualified to be president." Helena shook her head.

"It's two more articles than Hank Goodfellow has ever written," Jay said under his breath, skewering the most popular and least qualified of candidates in the race so far.

"Well, she's a UNHCR Special Envoy," Sky said, hesitantly. "United Nations High Commissioner for Refugees, you know? She's pretty up on what's happening in Syria and stuff—"

"Save it for the copy," Helena cut him off.

Sky straightened his posture beside Jay, optimism now ricocheting between them.

"So, I thought you were crazy when you said she cut off her hair extensions because she was running for president, but hat tip to you," she said. "As you may know, there are literally twenty-seven people running for president at the moment, so we are tapped out. You guys are now moonlighting on the political team."

Jay and Sky looked at each other, a mix of fear and shock reflected in one another's eyes.

Helena continued. "Travel is hooking you up, check in with them and tell Haze we want some exclusives at the presser since she came to us first."

"Wow, this is, wow." Jay dabbed his perspiring brow, trying to smile.

"Thank you, Helena," Sky said, though she was preoccupied with her screen. "This is, you won't regret—"

"Yeah, yeah, yeah." She clicked her laptop keys. "I'm forwarding some files to you." She looked at Jay. "You'll start getting all the poli team threads. Off you go."

Jay wanted to go home. Now. He had to find that velvet box hidden in his sock drawer. That brushed platinum ring he had purchased two months ago, while battling a rare case of overconfidence, from Tiny Jewel Box in Dupont Circle. He realized he had spaced out and missed the cue to vacate when she repeated, "Off you go."

Just before he closed the door, she barked, "Hey! Where are we on Birdie Brandywine?"

Jay peeked back in, making an effort to appear less deer-in-the-headlights than he felt. Birdie Brandywine was the queen bee of Georgetown; she threw the best parties—and also happened to be one of Washington's most successful political fund-raisers. That story was the last thing on his mind now. "Brandywine. Right. Big Iowa caucus viewing party is tomorrow night, of course. I'm nearly done with the piece. Dropping in colorful anecdotes of the last-minute preparations tomorrow morning. Going back with the photographer then. Flowers arriving. Caterers. But the phone pre-interview is all done." He spoke in bullet points, expecting to be cut off anytime. Jay generally didn't have the time to write these days; editing a daily portal left him creatively spent and in need of a generous glass of wine at the end of each day. But for the great Birdie Brandywine, he would make an exception. He felt they were kindred spirits, even though he had only actually spoken to her once. His fantasies revolved around someday presiding over his own *salon*, like hers, and being the consummate Washington host.

From the corner of his eye, he saw Sky—that cobalt-fuschia-striped shirt beneath his slate sweater-vest—already halfway down the hall, a spring in his step. Jay needed to follow him, needed to know what Travel would say, how soon he'd be going. He could barely remember what the newsroom felt like before Sky walked into it—and into his life—a year ago.

"We'll need the piece by noon tomorrow. Pics too," Helena said, shaking him from his thoughts. "And make sure there's a Buck quote." She looked him in the eye, firm.

"Of course," he said, lying. Buck Brandywine was notoriously reticent when it came to his wife's business.

As soon as the door closed, he pulled his phone from his pocket, finished his rambling message to Birdie just as he reached Sky's cubicle.

"I'm on the first flight out tomorrow!" Sky said, eyes wide, giddy. "Can you believe? Granite State, here I come!"

Jay threw a Hail Mary. "We're celebrating—Rose's Luxury, 7:00 p.m. Last supper before you embed."

"Seriously? Do we have time to wait in that line?"

"7:00 p.m.!" Jay said over his shoulder. Thinking, thinking: should he do it tonight? Yes? No?

The next morning, Jay settled into a firm, ivory sofa and quietly studied Birdie Brandywine's living room. He couldn't help but gawk at the larger-than-life photo of a very young Birdie, golden hair blowing in the wind, and youngish Buchanan "Buck" Brandywine in jeans and plaid button-downs, sitting stately atop a horse like some kind of throwback Ralph Lauren ad. Together, the toast of Washington and pride of their native Great Plains.

A triple-shot latte from Leopold's Kafe sat untouched on the glass coffee table. This was Birdie's regular order from her favorite coffee shop: Jay had done his research. He had gotten one for himself too, which he now regretted, having nervously guzzled it on the chilly walk through Georgetown to her historic brick, Federal-style mansion on tony, tree-lined N Street. By the time he had reached her charming emerald-painted door, he'd been a sickly, jittery combination of hungover and overcaffeinated. Not the way he'd wished to arrive at the Brandywine home, but at least he had been on time.

Though he was excited to meet Birdie in person for the first time, Jay couldn't stop thinking about Sky. Their celebratory dinner the night before had been near-perfect and yet, ultimately, a failure, hadn't it? It would have been a brilliant send-off too, if not for that one unasked question of Jay's. What was wrong with him?

That couple in front of them in the endless line outside hadn't helped matters: they had just gotten engaged, and Jay didn't need that kind of pressure when he himself had a vel-

vet box in his pocket, like a concealed weapon he was too
terrified to actually wield. Of course Sky had made friends
with them, and they'd found out that the guy had somehow
dropped the ring off the top of the Capitol just before what
should've been an epic proposal. While waiting in line for their
table, the editor in Jay had sprung into action and posted the
guy's video of the proposal on *The Queue*, with a call to help
find the diamond. By morning the story was ranked No. 3.

His heart sped. He already missed Sky, who would be at
the airport by the time the interview ended and wouldn't be
back until next week. He wouldn't be there to duck out for
dinner after work, or at Jay's place when he woke up, forget-
ting his watch on the night table. Jay's thumb hovered over
Sky's name on his speed dial. Their union felt so dependent
upon proximity and momentum, like certain laws of physics
or, for instance, Hank Goodfellow's current poll numbers, and
he needed to hear his voice. Jay was about to push the screen
when a familiar voice came from the doorway. He recognized
it from years of news programs.

"You must be from *The Queue*." Buck Brandywine strode
in after thirty minutes, wearing jeans and a flannel shirt.

Jay stood to shake his hand, speechless in the presence of a
Society Pages unicorn.

"Buck Brandywine. Welcome." Skin the color of leather,
hair the shade of straw. He seemed far younger than his fifty-
six years, and looked like he belonged on a ranch, which, of
course, was exactly where he had famously grown up before
arriving in Washington to work for a senator, jumping to the
White House, and henceforth becoming a political legend.

"Yes! Jay. Hi! Mr. Brandywine, sir," he found his words at
last. "Great to meet you. Thank you for having me today, it's
an honor. Your home is stunning."

"Thank you. I know my wife is looking forward to show-

ing you around." Buck perched on the arm of the sofa, mo-
tioning for Jay to have a seat. "She's the brains of this act, you
know. I wish I knew how she did it. For me, getting a party of
this magnitude off the ground is like trying to launch a rocket
from a lily pad. But she just loves it. We get all these folks in
here, ambassadors, cabinet secretaries, administration types,
and they never want to leave. Here's a story for you, Birdie
would have my hide for telling it, but I once woke up the
morning after her Iowa party in—what was it, '96?—to find
the CIA director passed out on the couch, wearing nothing
but his skivvies. His wife got fed up early in the party, went
home. He was drinking whisky all night, fell in the pool, got
hauled out by the ambassador of Paraguay. I made him hair of
the dog, loaned him some clothes and drove him home myself. Lived over an hour away, all the way out in Middleburg,
Virginia, horse country." He shook his head.

"Amazing," Jay whispered, feeling as though they were at
a campfire in the middle of Wyoming and Buck had a guitar
and a canteen of Jack Daniel's to share. A door smacked open
in a distant room, the sound of street traffic resounding with it.

Buck straightened. "Anyway, no one ever knew—till now.
And you can quote me on that." He winked and backed away,
then, just before leaving, added, "Birdie would never tell you
that, but she would tell you the first thing she says when
she wakes up the morning of her Hawkeye party every four
years…" Jay leaned forward, listening.

4

I LOVE THE SMELL OF BUNTING
IN THE MORNING

★

Every morning, as the flat screen TV in their bedroom flipped on, the electronic shades rose, and the coffee machine downstairs buzzed alive all at the same expertly programmed moment, Buck Brandywine greeted Birdie with the same four words: "Good morning, pretty girl."

Birdie was *well* past girlishness—a meticulously preserved fifty-three, but who was counting? Not her—yet in spirit, she felt far younger, certainly. She made sure of it: everything about her was cultivated and deliberate, from her smooth, preternaturally firm skin to her flaxen hair (not too long but absolutely not too short), the fringy bangs obscuring just enough to shave off a few years, all lovingly maintained by Georgetown's most exclusive salon; from her willowy physique and lean legs sculpted by daily early-morning sessions at the SoulCycle blocks from their home to her very name, *Birdie*.

Buck had woken her with these words every dawn since their first night together decades, *decades*, ago, and hearing them first thing in the morning—before the precious cosmetics, layers of expensive creams and serums, or the luscious clothes and heels—had taken on new meaning with each passing year. She absorbed his words like a kind of nourishment.

Except today. During election season.

Just as January flexed its muscles outside her window, the year's first snow swirling in a bitter wind, something equally wintry raged within her. The midterm elections didn't affect her the same way. But when the presidential campaigns began, she felt her battle armor slip on. She couldn't help it; it was a reflex. Just as she couldn't bring herself to perform the same quiet acts of kindness for him that she could the rest of the year. She couldn't bear, for instance, to leave love notes in his office or to make his favorite fresh-squeezed orange juice every morning, a process that she'd otherwise enjoyed since acquiring that fantastic juicer, which had cost more than her first car.

Buck had cheated.

Years ago.

While on his first presidential campaign.

Out on the trail. Overworked, underpaid, sleep-deprived, thrilled by it all, loving every minute of it, as any true political junkie would. But, impassioned by the job, engrossed in the frenetic energy, and far from home, he had slipped up. He'd confessed to her immediately, with true tears and proper pleading, and as gutted as she had felt, she loved him too much, so she had stayed. But her heart had scarred, her healing never quite complete. For some reason, she could not just forget it all, and every presidential election cycle, those stubborn memories came barreling back, steamrolling over her life. So she hardened her shell and kept extraordinarily busy. She had a ridiculously successful political fund-raising and event-planning firm to run, after all.

And so Birdie Brandywine's day, the eve of the true kickoff of the campaign season, had been an appropriate whirlwind: meetings, interviews, phone calls, confirming the timeline of tomorrow's events, dishing details about her all-star guest list, fielding décor questions. For her, there was nothing more electrifying, except for the fete itself. The next day's party wouldn't be in full swing until at least eight o'clock, but the preparations would begin at dawn with deliveries, and her veins would already be humming with adrenaline. Coordinating, planning.

Trying to ignore the memories. No matter how lovingly Buck had greeted her this morning.

The eve of an Iowa party was also absolutely not a night to turn in early. And so even after a long day, even as the sky began to darken, evening setting in, the temperature falling enough to freeze a thin layer of ice on the wet pavement, she had one more meeting.

The elevator doors opened onto the top of the W Hotel, music spilling out to greet her and lure new patrons—that song everyone was listening to by Rocky Haze. Her cultural tastes still skewed plenty young, thank God. She would never permit herself to become the least bit "out of touch," there could be no worse fate, as she saw it. Career suicide, to be sure. People came to her for vibrance, and she delivered.

She strode into the sleek lounge, phone to her ear as she listened to a voice message left half an hour ago—when she had intentionally declined the caller: Buck. Walls of windows faced the Treasury Building, that statue of Alexander Hamilton presiding proudly over the columned fortress, and in the distance the White House aglow. "Guess I missed you, just got home." Buck's easy twang. "Anyway, it's a no-go on the remote hit. MSNBC is doing the panel, after all. I'll have to head out to Des Moines tomorrow morning. Sorry, Bird…" In other words, he would not be making even so much as a cameo at her Iowa Caucus viewing party tomorrow evening.

She rolled her eyes and hung up just as a helicopter buzzed past the windows, chopping at the navy sky loud enough to sound like an extra percussion line in the Rocky Haze track. Marine One en route home to 1600 Pennsylvania. The lounge patrons collectively hushed, craning necks and pointing for a moment, gawking, before sitting back in their plush banquettes again, remembering to play it cool. Birdie refocused too, scanning the room for her 7:30 p.m. appointment. So many dapper twenty- and thirtyish men in their slim-cut suits with splashy candy-colored ties and thick-framed glasses, you could just tell they were hipsters on the weekend. Their female counterparts in structured knee-length sheath dresses, heeled boots, bags that cost more than Hill staffers ought to be able to afford—Birdie loved it all. They made her feel enlivened instead of decrepit. If only Washington had been more like this when she was coming up. Of course, she told herself, she helped it *become* this, hadn't she?

She had truly grasped it, how this city operated, for the first time in her twenties when she watched a gaggle of her contemporaries—all gorgeous, leggy, the kind who could get any man—huddle around a balding, chubby, middle-aged White House press secretary at a downtown cigar bar like he was the sixth member of Duran Duran. She *got it* then, and it gave her comfort: this was a town that ran on power and proximity to power, not looks, not even money—though looks and money never hurt.

As she made her way around the bustling bar, she could feel those many sets of eyes shift to *her* now. She pretended not to notice getting noticed, but felt her posture straighten, her stride lengthen as though she were walking a runway. And she reveled in looking the part: collar of her crisp white shirt popped, just enough buttons undone to show she wasn't in government, glittering chunky necklace peeking out, her jacquard pencil skirt giving way to toned legs. She was glad she hadn't caved and put on the stockings. She *never* wore stockings, even in winter, though she had almost made an exception today, what with the snow. At her age she considered stockings a white flag of surrender, one stilettoed foot in the coffin. She would flaunt what she had as long as she could. In her five-inch heels tonight, she entered the room at a glamazon six foot one, which pleased her, and she enjoyed her view: she had earned those eyes on her.

She spotted him at the very back of the room, on a low, cushy couch with the best sight line to the White House. Nose buried in his phone, he glanced up and, seeing her, stood and buttoned his suit jacket, grinning. Tall, dark, handsome, early thirties and baby-faced.

"Hope you weren't waiting long," she said, having planned to arrive exactly seven minutes late.

"Hi, oh, no, not at all. I was immersed in the new Madison Goodfellow interview." He flashed his phone. It was the top story on *The Queue,* a sneak of the next *Us Weekly* cover featuring the first-lady hopeful. Birdie had already seen it. "Thank God I don't want her husband to win."

"I know! The sound bites are horrifying," she said, her hand on his arm as though about to tell a secret. "I have *got* to meet this woman."

He laughed; she did too. But she had meant it. Birdie had a gut feeling that, politics aside, she and Madison were cut from the same cloth: both stealthily scrappy. She had, naturally, made sure an invitation to her Iowa party had found its way to Madison.

"Well." He shook his head as though starting over. "I have got to meet *this* woman." He gestured to Birdie. "The whole room just watched you walk in, and they're wondering how I got so lucky that you're here with me." He said it sweetly, holding out his hand. "Cole Cleaver. Honored. And delighted, Ms. Brandywine. Obviously."

She took his hand and leaned in, turned his formal greeting into a kiss on her cheek, so much better for their audience. "Well, there's certainly a reason you're a lobbyist." Even though she knew charm was a prerequisite for his work, she still appreciated a man who could flirt.

"Tell that to Senator Bronson," he said with a laugh.

As she took her seat beside him, the bartender appeared without her having to signal him, and set her usual dirty martini on the table.

"You got it." She held up her glass in a toast and took a sip. "He and I go back a long way, you know."

"I do. I might've heard some stories about you," he teased, a mischievous glint in his eye. "Something about House and Senate ethics rules being changed because of some over-the-top birthday party you threw for Bronson."

"Guilty," she demurred, swirling the olive in her drink. It was indeed true, her old firm's lavish party for the senator fifteen years earlier had caused quite the stir. She had secretly loved the attention. And recalling this to her now, with just the right amount of reverence and awe, was the quickest way to her heart. She felt an instant pull to him. "Well, don't you just know all my secrets? Bob—Senator Bronson—*did* promise me you were the best and brightest." He would have to be for her to agree to meet with him instead of the senator himself.

"He's very kind. I'm probably not fit to even shine his shoes." He smiled.

"Or ghostwrite his Twitter feed," she quipped.

He laughed at that. "Exactly! And I've done that too, but, honestly…it freaks me out."

"As it should." She glanced at her vibrating phone—a text from Buck—turned it facedown and pulled her iPad from her handbag, firing up her proposals for the Arnold fund-raiser.

"Although, I guess I'm doing something right if they're letting me take this meeting," he said, just enough earnest self-deprecation to fully win her over. "The senator says hi, and that money is no object."

"Excellent. Always liked that guy." Senator Bob Bronson had been her first boss, and she was proud to call him a life-long friend now. He had recently left the Senate and launched a lobby shop. His first order of business: getting Vice President John Arnold elected president. "So! Bronson has got himself a new firm and wants a party full of the fabulous people and deep pockets to rake in cash for Arnold and put him in good when Arnold wins the presidency."

Cole nodded, taking a drink. "In a nutshell."

"He told me last week," she went on. "He wants young turks on the guest list, press in the right places, image-building, buzz. No problem, love."

"He said you would make this easy." He drained his glass.

"That's what I do."

"His words—'Just make it not stuffy, not like another one of those parties thrown by retired senators who started a lobby shop. *Fun!* Arnold needs young voters.'" He mimicked the man's deep, grumpy-sounding voice.

"We'll have the details done before you finish your next drink." She signaled for the bartender.

He suddenly looked embarrassed. "Can I tell you: I was a little nervous. To meet you."

"Who, me?" She smiled. "I love that about you."

She would be out all night. It was decided.

The sun rose into a pink-hued early-morning sky over the Capitol dome as Birdie breathed in the brisk air, clearing her lungs. It had been a long time since she had smoked weed, or whatever the kids were calling it these days. But it was legal here now, and though it may have felt even better when it *wasn't*, she forgot how much she liked it. Still in her skirt and now-rumpled button-down from the night before, she wandered up the center of Pennsylvania Avenue, her stilettos dangling from her fingertips. Early risers zipped past in cars, zooming up to the Hill and down to the surrounding agencies: Labor,

Justice, IRS, FBI. She just wanted to walk a few more blissful blocks here at the center of the world. Today was the day she had been waiting for, much like the way athletes ticked down the years and months until the next Olympics.

She was so fixated on time in its *grand* sense, that she had lost track of it in the more immediate: When had she said she would meet *The Queue* guy? She checked her watch. *Now.* She ran down a cab whizzing past the Newseum and once inside freshened up her makeup, spritzed Chanel N° 5 and chomped a handful of Altoids.

Birdie emailed her assistant from the cab—on my way. phone out of juice. keep everyone happy pls. be there soon. thx.—and arrived to a nervous Abbie pacing by the front door, an interviewer in the sitting room and decorators on hand transforming her home into its own bipartisan campaign headquarters. Those iconic half-moons of red, white and blue draped her mansion and the one next door, which she and Buck used as their offices. The vintage posters had been hauled out from the storage room in the basement: "I Like Ike" and "Keep Cool and Keep Coolidge" and "All the Way With LBJ" now replaced some of the more obscure artwork usually displayed (though the Banksys and the Shepard Faireys were, of course, still prominently on view). Extra flat screens had been brought in, enabling guests to watch the caucus returns in nearly every room.

Birdie barely paid attention as Abbie ran through the checklist on her iPad. She was too focused on Buck's voice coming from the sitting room, her ears pricking up: What was he *doing*? They had long had an agreement that he was to stay out of her business. It got her wondering what act of sabotage he might be committing, just how ruffled his feathers might be by her staying out, ignoring his calls. She tossed her bag and shoes on an antique brocade chair and headed in his direction.

She reached the room just as Buck said, "Birdie usually wakes up on Iowa Caucus day and says to me—"

"I love the smell of bunting in the morning!" Birdie finished his thought, strutting in barefoot in wrinkled clothes, but with that luminous smile.

"Speak of the devil," Buck said. "Ears burning, were they, Bird?"

"Shouldn't you be on a plane to Des Moines instead of hijacking my interview, darling?" she asked in her most flirtatious tone, giving him a peck on the cheek.

"Weren't you wearing that yesterday?" Buck smirked.

"Oh, Buck! Your suits all look alike to me too," she volleyed, upbeat. She knew what he was doing, could tell from the flinty set of his eyes that he was angry. She turned her attention to Jay, who stood, extending his hand. "Buck wouldn't know a Derek Lam skirt if it bit him in the ass," she said saucily. "So terribly sorry to keep you waiting, Jay." She kissed him on the cheek.

"No problem at all, I—"

"Just putting out some late-breaking fires, as you can imagine," she cut him off.

With an "I'll leave you to it," Buck let himself out.

Birdie turned to Jay, throwing her arm around him. "The flowers have just arrived and I have so much to show you. Shall we get started?"

5

WHAT A WINNING IDEA!

★

Madison Goodfellow was the only one paying attention as Hank's new press secretary, Mike *Something*, sat in a corner of their suite at the Des Lux Hotel a day before the Iowa caucus, quietly apoplectic as he read from his smartphone. "Ohhhh, boy. Ohboyohboyohboyohboy. Not good. Not. Good," he said.

Madison looked up for a moment, just in time to make eye contact from across the room, where she sat on a chaise by the window. She gave her best poker face: a blank canvas. She could guess what he might be reading.

No one else seemed to notice. Room service tables, with the remnants of dinner, sat in the middle of the room. Outside, the dusk rush hour began to overtake downtown Des Moines, and on TV a buxom blonde news anchor gave a rundown of everyone's Iowa odds: Hank still came out the favorite. Madison hated that picture they always used. He looked so much more presidential when he smiled without showing his teeth (perfect as they were—veneers, naturally), not that anyone had bothered asking her opinion. She had never loved watching the news, but there was *so much of it* on every hour of the day on *so many channels* that it was unavoidable. And it had become a new brand of torture watching clip after clip of Hank shouting from so many podiums in so many states. Her husband had undergone some sort of lobotomy since declaring his candidacy. In every public appearance he was sounding more and more like he did at cocktail parties when he'd had too much bourbon: "What's the big deal? I could fix this whole goddamn mess. Washington just needs a kick in the ass and lemme tell ya, I can kick." Except he wasn't drinking. And every day brought new challenges as she learned to coexist with this Frankenstein in expertly tailored suits. She missed the old Hank. The one who used to skinny-dip in their pool in the Hamptons at all hours of the day.

Madison curled her long legs beneath her, sipped her cappuccino and scrolled through her own emails. The most interesting among them: an invitation from Birdie Brandywine. She knew the name. She had read Birdie's decorating and entertaining book when Hank first started talking about a presidential run nearly a year ago, in an effort to wrap her head around what Washington was about. She realizes you'll likely be in Iowa, but even so… the email from Madison's assistant had read, with a photo of Birdie's very flattering FedExed handwritten note calling Madison a "tastemaker" and "powerful woman in her own right." Madison so wished she could go to the Iowa viewing party at Birdie's undoubtedly stunning Georgetown home.

She gazed out the window again. She had no problem with this city itself, it was lovely. The fields and farms they'd passed on the way from their rally by the airport reminded her of home in Alabama. She and Hank spent the majority of their time in New York now, ever since Hank had bought that basketball team. His oil company could run itself at this point. Hank preferred New York to anywhere, and that was certainly all right with her. Her true priority was just to keep her family unit as intact as possible on a daily basis. Or three out of four of them, with Henry, their oldest just a train ride away at boarding school. So New York worked.

Their six-year-old daughter, Gemma, was back in New York with her nanny now, and Madison missed her dearly.

Earlier in the day, she had managed to break away from the Hank Machine—as she dubbed the handlers traveling with them 24/7 now—to wander the sculpture park just blocks from the hotel, and had texted Gemma a picture of one piece, the bunny "thinker" sitting on a rock. Madison had sat beneath the spindly branches of the white enamel tree sculpture until she got too cold, yearning for the pinecones Gemma would bring home in her lunch box after weekly nature walks through Central Park with her school class. Though she missed their old life, she actually enjoyed seeing all these towns with Hank. She met so many kind people who wanted to take a picture with her, who held her hands and told her how hard their lives were and how much they needed to believe in someone. Hearing the stories of struggling families, the tears welled in Madison's own eyes. It was bad out there. They *did* need someone to believe in. She just wasn't quite sure her husband was the one for the job.

Madison heard Mike sigh, and from the corner of her eye, watched as he vigorously shook his prematurely balding head, like a dog trying to shimmy water off his coat. She fluffed up her ginger hair and reached into her purse for lip gloss and her Chanel glasses—she just felt she should be wearing glasses for this.

Mike sighed again, ran his fingers through his hair.

"I can hear ya, Wilson," Hank said flatly, his back to the man as his longtime makeup artist, Penny, spackled a spot on his left cheekbone.

Wilson, Madison thought, *that* was his name.

"What's goin' *on* over there?"

"Nothing, Bomb," he said unconvincingly.

Hank liked to be called this, as in "H-Bomb." It had started in high school when he was a football star who could blaze through any obstacle, and he saw no reason to discontinue it now, in his late forties, after making himself into a billionaire oil man/basketball *and* baseball team owner/stock market-playing champ.

Mike went on. "It's just, that, well. Madison—?"

Here it came, she thought. She looked up. Ready. "Hmm?" She smiled innocently.

"We just got a PDF of the interview from *Us Weekly*. Madison's cover."

"Maddy, hear that?" Hank asked.

"I saw! We look divine!" she said, bubbly. The photo of the four of them—Henry, had even come in from Andover—really was frameable. She looked much younger than forty-four and wondered how much—if any—Photoshopping had been done. Not that she minded. Just the opposite; she would've liked to know who to thank.

"Yes, Bomb, it's a handsome photo shoot." Mike gave Madison the side-eye. "But I'm afraid we're going to need them to issue some major corrections, sir."

"You don't say?" Hank looked over now.

"I mean, I was there. For the interview. But. This is. I don't know. This is...ridiculous," Mike stammered.

"What's he talking about, Magnolia? Someone show this thing to me," Hank said, still seated.

Madison looked on from behind her spectacles and her cappuccino, pleasantly confused. "What exactly is the problem, Mike?" she asked in her sweetest, most honey-coated voice.

"Madison."

Mike stood now, taking a few steps in her direction, eyes on his phone. "I was sitting *in* on this interview. I don't remember ninety percent of this."

She wished he would just stop talking, wished, for instance, that there was a ladylike way to punch him in the face. Instead, she just smiled.

"How can anyone make that much up? Get 'em on the horn!" Hank said, angry now.

"Relax, dear, you'll mess up your makeup," Madison said calmly.

"She's right," Penny agreed under her breath.

"When did you *say* these things?" Mike pushed.

"What things? I thought it was a delightful interview."

"'Delightful,'" Mike repeated. "Things like, 'My husband would look soooo handsome in the Oval Office. He certainly looks better in a suit than any of his opponents seeking the nomination. Attractive people are good at getting what they want and that would be good for the American people, in terms of foreign policy and so forth.'"

"Right. You've got to admit that's true." She grinned. It did happen to be true. At forty-eight, Hank still had a boyishness about him, a full head of blond hair (with wisps of distinguished gray mixed in), a trim physique and that Southern charm. Anyone with eyes would have to agree. And she thought she had spoken well. She had always liked how you could add "and so forth" to any statement to give it an air of authority, as though there was so much more you could add but you were giving people just the most salient points. It was an old pageant interview trick. She had scored under just Miss New York in the interview component, way back when.

"She's got a point, Mike," Hank considered.

"Well, I'm not sure voters will find it encouraging to hear you say—" he began to read again "—'Hank knows that I know him better than anyone, better than he even knows himself sometimes, so I'm probably his most trusted adviser, always have been—except those few years when we were divorced, before getting back together again—but otherwise, always have been, always will.' There's so much wrong there, besides it being a run-on sentence."

"These are lovely things to say, aren't they? I felt like I didn't give the reporter enough, you know, what would you call it? *Meat.* During the interview at the house—"

"Meat," Mike repeated.

"And I wanted to be super—what's your word, Mike?— *approachable.*"

"Approachable," he parroted.

"So I called her back, and we talked a little more," she said lightly, with a shrug, taking a sip of her cappuccino.

"Of course you did. Okay, well, maybe *never* do that again." Mike threw his hands in the air.

"I don't think I love how you're talking to me." She softened her words with a flutter of her lashes.

"You two, get along already," Hank ordered them from the vanity across the bedroom, tissues in his collar, as Penny airbrushed on his sun-kissed glow. "Hey! Whiplash!" he called out, loud enough to reach the living room, where a handful of trusted advisers could be heard gaming out his Iowa victory rally a day early. His deputy chief of staff, who had started as his driver on the oil company payroll and worked his way up, poked his head in the door. "Where are we on getting this thing tonight moved inside? What kind of idiot books a rally outside in Iowa in January? Gonna be a blizzard tonight."

"Working on it, Bomb," Whiplash said, managing not to add that Hank himself had been the idiot. "John is on the phone now with…"

Hank, lost in a status update, had moved on.

"Look, this was supposed to be your big introduction to the American people," Mike said, sitting on a desk as though he wanted to appear like he was trying to reason.

Madison wasn't impressed. She chuckled. "The American people already know me."

"No offense, but Miss Fifty States was…a while ago," he

said, cautious. "They need to be *reintroduced* to you. And saying things like…" He looked at his phone again, reading in that disapproving tone, "'Honestly, it's all a bit stressful. My husband was more fun before the campaign, and I think he spent more time helping people. He used to give away millions of dollars anonymously every year, and now it's all going to the campaign. I can understand the need for campaign finance law reform. It shouldn't cost so much to compete for a job. Although, this *is* the American dream, isn't it?'" He shook his phone. "Saying this is not the way to do it. I don't think the American people want to hear about campaign finance reform from you, with all due respect. That's not your…function…in our *unit* here."

"Oh, I'm sorry." She offered that "who, me?" smile again. "Of course. Won't happen again. I was just trying to bring something more to the table."

"Next time, just bring, I don't know, flowers. From your garden in the Hamptons," he said. "That would actually be a great idea, and very FLOTUS of you. You know, the White House has a garden."

"What a winning idea!" She nodded enthusiastically.

"Mike, I need ya. You guys done throwin' mud?" Hank said lightly, winking at Madison. "Bottom line, Maddy, muzzle it up."

"Oh, Hank, you're such a sweet talker." She laughed it off, not taking any of it seriously, and sipped her cappuccino as she reread Birdie Brandywine's note. This campaign was going to get ugly.

6

AWWW, HONEY, YOU'RE A
CAMPAIGN WIDOW

★

Mere hours to go until Birdie's grand Iowa soiree and the Brandywine home was nearly ready: it had been transformed into a veritable greenhouse of peonies, calla lilies and French tulips, just enough without appearing overcrowded or worse, gauche. A fleet of chafing dishes sat on the sharp-edged marble dining-room table just waiting to be laid with a buffet of delicacies. Florists, caterers, decorators, so many bodies working all afternoon as one well-oiled machine to ensure the quadrennial festivities would go off without a hitch. Only two hiccups had contributed to Birdie's need to dip into that secret Valium stash in her lingerie drawer.

The first: Buck. He should've been long gone by the time she'd arrived this morning. And then ambushing her writer? She had been only forty minutes late and had shown her interviewer such a pithy-quotable good time, what did it matter really?

The second: the forks and knives sparkling under her $30,000 Lalique chandelier. She'd spotted them while ushering out *The Queue* reporter. "No, no, no!" she'd barked, brandishing a silver dinner knife at a trio of cater waiters like it was a switchblade in a particularly well-appointed street fight. "We can*not* serve anything resembling a main course. Everything bite-sized! Or I'll have ethics committees from every branch of government up my…" Deep breath. "Do you know how many elected officials are coming tonight? Where's

Michael? He should be here. Check the original order—
bamboo sticks, cocktail forks, shot glasses with those tiny
spoons. This is a huge f—" She'd caught herself, remembering to be polite lest she should wind up in the gossip blogs for
the wrong reasons…again. "Foul up. Many thanks, loves."

By the time the TV crew knocked at the door, the music
boomed out of the built-in Bose sound system throughout the
house, her hair and makeup team had come and gone, and she
had slipped into that splashy red, white and blue Jason Wu
cocktail dress (made just for her). She felt that hum of antici-
pation (sweetly muted by the tranquilizer) in her veins. Still, it
nagged at her just enough that she couldn't help but wonder:
How much had that writer, Jay, picked up on? Had he read
the chill in the room when she'd arrived? Caught her peeking at her phone after their tour to find that text from Buck,
who'd departed for the airport without a proper goodbye:
Didn't want to interrupt interview, he wrote. Not sure what to
think. You can spin me when I'm back. See you in a few days.

She greeted the grizzled cameraman she recognized from
four years ago and a young woman she had never met. "Ah, so
Gracie finally decided to sit one out," Birdie said to the young
woman and cameraman standing on her doorstep.

"Well, really, I just wanted to see your beautiful home for
myself. Cady Davenport, senior producer, *Best Day DC*. I'm
new to the show and having too much fun to share the good
assignments. But Gracie sends her best."

"I'm sure she does." Birdie laughed. "But as Madeleine Al-
bright once said, 'There's a special place in hell for women
who bring cheap wine and cheaper morals to other women's
dinner parties.'"

Tour and interview complete—and perfect Birdie-isms dutifully captured, among them Cady's favorite on the matter of

updating the historical home—"I caught some flak for making changes, but, you know, we can *respect* the past without having to actually *live* in it."—Cady and Max, her cameraman, camped out in the news van, editing the segment so all that remained would be to drop in scenes from the party itself. From the moment she had set foot in that house, Cady was grateful she'd had the good sense to let Gracie Garfield off the hook. The show's longtime host—six feet tall, blonde, fifty-something and accustomed to getting what she asked for—had cornered Cady after the morning meeting and informed her with the frosty, formal tone, "I need to respectfully withdraw from this assignment. I don't feel I am best suited for such an undertaking." Cady had sensed she could bank points by giving in, no questions asked, and doing the segment herself.

By 7:30 that evening, the sun had set and the lights from a constant stream of sedans and limos lit up N Street, discharging so many familiar, cocktail-attired partygoers. As she and Max made their way back inside, Cady felt the electricity: the buzz of weighty conversation (Iraq, China, Wall Street, Senate hearings, polls) spoken in the impassioned tones usually reserved for matters of the heart or the arts, the clink of crystal stemware, the glow of flat screens mounted in every room set to news coverage on every network. She had covered her share of parties but had never seen so many truly powerful names clustered under one roof: cabinet secretaries, senators, an ex-president or two, a few Hollywood stars, and of course, a retinue of reporters and news anchors. If anything happened to the president and vice president, then the nation could ably be run by the people in this house, and there would be plenty of press to keep everyone informed of it all.

They were given exactly twenty minutes to shoot the party, and she and Max set to work circulating, capturing snippets of spirited cocktail chatter, giving socialites the chance to twirl and preen, and catching cameos of the big names. They followed Birdie, rolling tape as she welcomed guests with air-kisses and witticisms. When she came upon that chiseled, charming CNN anchor Grant Foxhall, she told him with a laugh, "Just because Buck is on MSNBC tonight doesn't mean we actually have to watch!" and then flipped the channel. In fact, Cady noticed, she did that in every room they passed through.

As soon as their time was up, Birdie clapped her hands, three loud staccato claps, instantly gaining the attention of the entire first floor: "Okay, everyone say good night to *Best Day DC*. The camera crew is leaving," she announced. "We're off the record now. Commence raucous caucusing!" A cheer erupted, and the conversation returned to its roar.

"Thank you, darlings, it was a pleasure," she said. "And, of course, feel free to linger in the capacity of guests. You just have to check *that thing* at the door." She pointed at the camera as though it were emitting an unsavory scent. "I won't get any of the good dirt otherwise, and that really is the whole point of having a party in the first place, isn't it?"

Cady couldn't resist. She was instantly glad she had worn her favorite black sheath and quickly doffed her blazer, folding it over her satchel.

"My kind of girl," Birdie said in approval, plucking two champagne flutes from a waiter's tray while nodding and waving to revelers sashaying past. *"Salud!"* she toasted Cady. "So this airs tomorrow morning?" She sipped, then grabbed the remote control from inside an urn on the table beside them.

"Absolutely. The segment will actually run two or three times over the course of the—"

"So tell me," Birdie cut her off. "You're new you said. You came from…?"

"New York. The city's number one morning show called—"

"How are you enjoying it? Here? Working with Gracie?" Birdie asked, pointing the remote toward the flat screen carefully, like it was target practice.

Glancing at the TV to avoid eye contact, Cady formulated a neutral response. "I, of course, don't know her well, but I know her work and she seems to be well respected. She certainly knows…" She trailed off, a figure on screen catching her eye, just behind the MSNBC reporter's live shot from a crowded hotel ballroom in Des Moines. "Wait a minute! Don't!" Cady blurted out, grabbing Birdie's arm reflexively to keep her from switching channels again. The chyron read Carter Thompson Headquarters.

"That's my boyfriend! Fiancé!" She shook her head, something to get used to. "I mean, yeah, that's him, Jackson." She pointed to the screen, where Jackson smiled as he chatted on his phone in the background. Cady spotted a few of Jackson's colleagues and Carter, of course, high-fiving supporters. Late forties, slim suit, freshly shined shoes, expertly gelled hair, Representative Carter Thompson looked like he could be Jackson's big brother, which had been a large part of their instant bond in the mayor's office. Cady had known Carter as the New York City mayor's chief of staff before he had quickly become one of DC's hottest freshman congressmen and most eligible bachelors.

"That one in the back?" Birdie asked, sizing Jackson up. "He's cute. So is Jackson a save-the-world type or a power junkie?"

"Hmm? I'm sorry?" Cady didn't understand the question.

"Everyone here is one or the other," Birdie explained. "He's with Thompson?"

"They worked together in New York. Mayor's office." She was distracted by the projected returns, so many percentages, so many precincts. Her heart swelled with pride for Jackson, to be there in the middle of this excitement, have a hand in this win.

"Isn't Thompson just everyone's favorite these days? I'm not sure if it's the cheekbones or the kumbaya bipartisan talk," Birdie said.

"Probably the cheekbones," Cady joked, making Birdie smile. "But he's got the right sort of superhero origin story, right?"

"I suppose there's some passion balancing out the playboy antics," Birdie quipped.

"A guy moves home to Iowa to care for dying parents who pass within weeks of each other, then, out of loneliness, spends sleepless nights at those endless city council meetings and starts heading up citizen action groups, helping at-risk teens, cleaning up litter-strewn parks, until he jumps into the race for his local seat on a whim? I'd say so," Cady recalled. It was true, Carter had never expected to win. Jackson had been among the first he'd recruited when it came time to staff up.

"It's pretty saintly lore, perfect for politics, I'll grant you that," Birdie said. "That's why he can get away with dating Victoria's Secret models and socialites."

"I think the most recent was a foreign correspondent," Cady said, offering a mild defense.

"Speaking of traveling, your fiancé must be on the road quite a bit these days."

"Jackson was out there a couple weeks ago and he's there now, but, you know, he's back tomorrow, so, it's not so bad." Still focused on the TV, Cady realized she was rambling.

"Awww, honey," Birdie said, grabbing Cady's shoulder, nestling her head against Cady's. "You're a campaign widow."

7

THESE PARTIES ARE LIKE WATERBOARDING

★

Reagan loved Birdie, *loved her*, but she really hoped Birdie wouldn't fish for any Alex Arnold gossip tonight.

"Jay, darling, so glad you could make it," Birdie cooed, dispensing air-kisses, as they walked into Birdie's living room where a rollicking party was already in full swing. "Your story was brilliant, not just saying that because it was about me."

"Total objective opinion," Reagan, at Jay's side, quipped as she and Birdie embraced.

"And Reagan! Love! Didn't you *just* have a baby?" She looked her up and down, nodding.

"Two, actually. But fifteen months ago," she clarified.

"Well, you look like you could be the hot nanny, not the mama."

"Thanks, that's what I was going for." Reagan smiled, curtsying in appreciation. This was the best compliment she had received in ages, and precisely why she adored Birdie.

Birdie waved over a waiter with more champagne cocktails. "I was just thinking of you," she said and held Reagan's hand. "Buck and I were at the Alfalfa Dinner the other night and you know, your speech for Vandercamp is still the *best* I've *ever* heard there. Hi*lari*ous. Miller *so* needed you. That man is missing a funny bone."

"And a spine too, from what I hear," Reagan said. "That *Economist* story on his party-switching shenanigans was brutal." She had read the piece hours before, thankfully.

"Sure, sure, but now what about tonight? Iowa? Have you been in touch with Alexandra Arnold?" Birdie segued, as expected.

"Yes." Reagan smiled kindly, taking a glass, volunteering nothing. She was fiercely protective of Alex, Birdie knew that, the mentor who had hired Reagan fresh out of college and later helped shepherd Reagan to her Dream Job, even though it was elsewhere. But Reagan couldn't blame Birdie for trying.

"And how are they *feeling* over there? In the Arnold camp?" Birdie prodded. "Do they think Iowa will go their way?"

"They're confident, but they're aware that it could be tight and you just never know," Reagan said, calm and easy but hoping to wrap up the conversation. "We'll see."

Birdie waited a beat, as though hoping for more, and then said, "We certainly will," seemingly giving up and changing course. "And what *are* you up to these days?"

"Well, I'm writing a parenting column for this guy." Reagan elbowed Jay. She hated explaining why she had willingly left the Dream Job at the city's top boutique speechwriting shop to which everyone from members of Congress to CEOs to the president outsourced their humorous remarks.

"Major traffic for this one, off-the-charts page views," Jay said, covering for her as only a best friend could. "Fastest growing column on *The Queue*."

Reagan had told her this at least twice in her six months on the column, but Birdie tended to tune out any information that felt useless to her and/or involved children, so this was two strikes.

"That's right, of course," Birdie said, uninterested.

"Necessity is the mother of invention, and motherhood necessitates reinvention." Reagan shrugged. She felt no regret about having left her job; she just didn't like thinking about that time in her life: the twins had been born just a little early, about a month. They were fine now, of course, *fine*, and she was grateful every minute of the day. Still, when it came time to return to work, she'd thought of those early days and couldn't quite bring herself to do it.

"Is that the name of your column?" asked a young woman Reagan hadn't noticed before.

"Nope, that was too brainy," Jay answered.

"It's called Motherfucker," Reagan said.

"I've read that and I'm not even a mom!" the woman said. "'Every mom has a Motherfucker! moment,'" she quoted the tagline.

"A what?" Birdie stepped back in.

"That moment when you feel like you've totally fucked up or you're just totally unprepared for what life throws you as a parent," the woman explained. "You're fantastic! You should be on my show."

"You're very nice," Reagan said. Maybe she really should get out more often.

"Hey, you're my viral star!" Jay said.

"The one from Rose's? You mean the proposal?" Reagan hadn't actually clicked on that video.

"I do," Jay said, grabbing the woman's bare left hand as she smiled shyly.

"Congratulations!" Reagan said.

"We'll find that sucker," Jay said, squeezing her hand. "And when we do, I want a follow-up."

"Bling is overrated," Reagan said.

"On that we shall agree to disagree," Birdie mumbled, swiping another drink from a passing tray as Abbie materialized, whispering in her ear. "In the koi pond? Already?" Birdie questioned. "Who? It's far too early to be that drunk even at one of my parties," she said to the girl, then addressed the group, "Must go. But so nice you all know each other. Makes my job easier. So *this*—" she held the woman's shoulders "—is Cady. She's our newest widow, loves. Be kind."

"My condolences," Reagan kidded.

"OMG, I'm one too!" Jay blurted out, reaching for her hand again.

"Listen," Birdie said, still squeezing Cady's shoulders. "It's totally what you make of it, widowhood." She winked. "Have fun, all!" And with that she allowed herself to be lapped up by the many guests no doubt waiting for their moment with her.

"Thanks, but I'm not really a—" Cady started.

"I'm in semidenial about it too. It's okay," Jay cut her off. "Reagan's the real pro."

"Guilty," Reagan said, raising her palm.

Somewhere within their little circle, a muffled version of that Rocky Haze song started. Jay smacked at the pocket of his suit jacket, fished out his phone. "Sorry, gotta take this." He answered, "Hey! Miss me already?" as he slipped away from the ladies.

Reagan watched him, concerned. It was probably Sky. She hoped, for Jay's sake, that Haze would get knocked out of the primaries instantly. She turned her attention back to Cady. "It's not so bad," she offered, without much feeling as she scanned the room.

Grant Foxhall, the square-jawed CNN anchor, drink in hand, at the center of a group of familiar reporters near the white baby grand piano, caught her eye and nodded a hello.

She simply nodded back.

"...And so we could use some real, relatable parenting personalities on the show, you know what I mean? Instead of the usual know-it-all types—" Cady finally turned to Reagan, but she was gone. How long had Cady been talking to herself? She had been too busy gabbing on autopilot while observing the room's boldface names to notice.

As swiftly as Cady had been engulfed, she had been abandoned, left alone with the ideas they'd put in her head. What was the big deal? Wasn't a campaign just like any other business trip? She knocked back her cocktail, found a spot out of the way beside the bookcases and pulled out her phone, snapping a pic of the room and tapping out a text to Jackson, from whom she had heard nothing since he'd landed in Des Moines that morning. *Just another*, she started typing, but something bumped into her shoulder, pushing her into the bookcase, and she hit "send" too early. "Hey!" she said, looking up.

A white-jacketed cater waiter turned around after backing into her. "Shit, didn't see you there, hi, sorry, want one-a these?" he asked, not looking at her but circling so that he could see the room over her shoulder.

"No, thanks," she said, anxious to amend her text. She typed *another day* but, then—

"Please?" He shook the tray, which held a dozen sliders on fluffy mini-brioche buns with a fancy sauce oozing.

"What? No, I'm good," she said again, slightly annoyed. She typed *at the office* —

"It's a veggie burger slider. More specifically, a barbecued cauliflower slider. Just an experiment," he added as though apologizing.

At this plea, she finally looked up. He had a few days' scruff, deep brown eyes and messy dark hair, and appeared to have misbuttoned his white chef's coat uniform.

"It's okay," he added in a whisper. "I'm trying to look busy too."

"Excuse me?" She laughed.

"No, I just mean, if you're just trying to look busy anyway, then you could have one and tell me what you think." He had that kind of wide, wild smile that couldn't be contained.

"Maybe I actually *am* super busy and I'm not just trying to *look* busy." She normally would have been mildly offended, but for some reason, she wasn't, and found herself smiling. Maybe it was the cocktail, which had been sweet and fruity, like so many of the most lethal ones.

"Well, are you?" he asked.

He seemed so disarming and friendly, unlike the chilly partygoers orbiting them, that she tossed her phone into her bag and sighed. "Actually, no."

"Yeah, I'm like that too. These people sorta freak me out, but you looked less scary than the rest of 'em."

"Thanks, I get that all the time."

"No, I meant that as a compliment." He laughed. "These kind of parties are like my version of waterboarding, when I'm not working...like this. At least when I've got props—" he gestured with the tray and a slider tumbled to the floor but he didn't seem to notice "—and a clear purpose it's less painful. So, have one already—"

"A clear purpose?"

"One of these. Jeez, you're a handful." He held out the tray in one hand, his stack of Brandywine-monogrammed cocktail napkins in the other.

Cady grabbed a slider, studied it and took a bite as he stepped around her so she had a view of the party again.

"Not bad," she said with her mouth full.

"Told you."

"And traditionally I don't love cauliflower."

"I'm honored, then. It's underappreciated as vegetables go."

"Veggie burgers in general tend to make promises of heartiness they can't deliver on," she went on, chewing. "But what

could be more election-appropriate than overblown promises, right?"

"Hoping to change the world one slider at a time." He
sighed. "Okay, is the coast clear yet?"

"What?" She finished her slider and helped herself to another.

"Those guys." He cocked his head in the direction of the bar.

"Which?" She had to stand on her toes, crane her neck to
see over his shoulder.

"Don't look—"

"Well, then, how—"

"The one with the pocket-square thing. *Them*."

She glanced over his shoulder again, scanning. "Ohhh.
Yeah. They're walking over here."

"Fuck. Are you kidding?"

"Why would I bother to—"

"Parker! My man!" The pocket-squared guy sidled up, slapping Parker on the shoulder, his two slim-suited cronies close
behind. He looked like he played lacrosse at a prep school,
summered in Nantucket and dated every society girl between
here and there. Probably simultaneously.

Backed into the corner, Cady couldn't escape and simply
sipped her drink and fixed her eyes on the flat screen where
Hank Goodfellow stood at a podium in a park in Iowa, wife
Madison by his side. Was she *frowning*?

"Brock," Parker said, grinning and faking it well enough.
"Hey, man, how ya been?"

"What're you—fuck, man, Melanie lets you outta the house
like that?" He smacked Parker's chef's coat. "You *working* this
party? This is what you left the Hill to do?"

"Long story. Bore you with it another time."

"Shit, man, even answering constituent mail is better than
this, am I right?" Brock laughed, slapping his buddies on the arm.

Without thinking, Cady jumped in. "He's my star reporter actually," she said. "Cady Davenport, *Best Day DC*. We're doing an investigative piece on how people treat catering staff. You weren't the nicest getting that gin and tonic over there. That's a camera." She pointed to a gargoyle-type statue perched on the highest bookshelf, then dug her hand into her purse. "Can you just sign this release so we can include you in our segment?" As she pulled out a folded piece of paper, the three men backed away, hands up like she was about to spray them with mace.

"Whoa, whoa, whoa," Brock said. "Hey, man, great to see you. Let you get back to it."

Parker waved and when they'd disappeared, leaned in. "So, I could be all, 'Hey, I don't need your help, I got this,' but, thanks, seriously."

"Nice friends." She raised her eyebrows.

"Yeah, they're assholes," he said. "Hey, so you're with that show?"

She nodded. "But, no hidden cameras." She unfolded the paper, which was really just a map: "This is actually just, like, directions to get here."

"Nice." He laughed. "So my girlfriend and I are opening a restaurant—" Parker patted at his pockets, pulling out a crumpled business card, and looked around the room before handing it over. "That's me. Not open for a couple weeks, but we'd appreciate any press. And by 'appreciate' I mean, we're prepared to bribe you with free booze for life."

"Sounds like a good deal," she joked. The card read "Preamble" in a font reminiscent of the Constitution and "Parker Appleton, Owner."

"Cute name," she said.

"Oh, uh, thanks." He shrugged. "I was named after a suffragist, a dude actually, Parker Pillsbury?"

"No, I mean, 'Preamble.'" She laughed.

"Oh! Right. Thanks."

"But me too, actually—Liz Cady Stanton?"

"Seriously? Sure, she was a boss."

"Pride of Johnstown, New York." She pulled out her own card, handed it over. "That's me." She felt a hand on her arm. A droopy-eyed Reagan, arms folded, body slightly hunched.

"Reagan, this is—"

"Have you seen Jay?" Reagan whispered with effort.

"No, actually—hey, you okay?" Cady asked.

"I just don't feel so good," Reagan said.

"Shit, my boss. Okay, back to the huddled, hungry masses," Parker said, saluting them.

"Wait," Cady said. "Do you need something to eat?"

Parker turned around.

"Ohmagod, I can't look at those." Reagan buried her head in Cady's shoulder as though she'd just witnessed a violent crime. "No offense!"

As Parker slipped away into the crowd, Reagan bolted, running out the nearest door.

Cady followed and found her vomiting into a planter of French tulips on the back porch. "Those champagne cocktails will get you," she comforted, hand on Reagan's slim back. She noticed the zipper to Reagan's dress had buckled, a small "o" from strain interrupting the track.

"I didn't drink a thing," Reagan choked out.

8

SHE'S THE LIFE OF THE PARTY, JUST SHOW THAT

★

"Are you just determined to get me out of my first Birdie Brandywine party?" Jay joked. He had left Birdie's Iowa caucus party as soon as he got the call. Sky had been invited to Rocky Haze's rehearsal unexpectedly, and he knew this was it, a gift in the form of an exclusive and a chance to own the story until the official all-media press conference the next evening.

"I don't know where to start with this, to write this. I don't know what to do," Sky said, panicked, as though he had never written before. "There's an NBC van out in front of the hotel, aaaahhhh. And I just passed by a dude from *60 Minutes*—"

"When do you watch—?" he started to ask.

"Nana. Jay?" Sky cut him off, aggravated.

"Right, sorry." Of course, Sky had been known to watch the news program with his grandmother in Miami whenever he was home. It was her favorite.

"These are, like, real reporters, you know? Not even reporters but legit *journalists*. What am I doing here? I can't do this." As Jay listened on speaker, he ordered an Uber, only one minute away.

"She's a different kind of candidate, so she requires a different kind of writer. You got this, Sky. We'll do it together." Jay, already outside Birdie's house, jumped in a black sedan as a woman wearing a dime-sized congressional pin on her black dress stepped out—he wished he could've remembered the congresswoman's name, but Sky's anxiety had now gotten him flustered too. He took the car straight home, grilling Sky about everything he'd seen and heard, the quotes he'd gotten. He hardly ever saw Sky this unsure of himself, but he seemed to be in the throes of some sort of block. Helena had spooked him, was all.

Once home, Jay loosened his tie, sat down at his laptop and punched out an outline so complete it'd practically be just a game of Mad Libs for Sky, filling in the anecdotes and quotes.

"She's the life of the party, said it herself, so just show that and it'll write itself," he coached. It was kind of nice to feel needed; it energized him and made his heart swell for Sky even more.

And so Jay settled in for a long night, firing up the beloved espresso machine they'd bought together for the holidays, which, luckily, lived at Jay's apartment since it was where the duo spent the vast majority of their time. ("The Ferrari of espresso machines," Jay had called it, while Sky declared it "so much better than getting, like, a puppy or something.") Jay even stayed on FaceTime to write the story with Sky. They sent the text back and forth to each other at least a dozen times—smoothing the language, checking with Haze's people for permission to publish her lyrics—until 3:00 a.m. when Jay, after much prodding from Helena (who actually made Sky ask about Rocky's hair extensions, despite the pushback), finally sent in the edited version. A half hour later it went live.

When the story posted, Jay again FaceTimed Sky, who wearily asked if Jay could read the piece to him instead. As Jay began, Sky closed his eyes, as though it were a bedtime story, "'Life of the Party: Rocky Haze Wants to Be Your Next President. By Sky Vasquez, Staff Writer, *The Queue*.'"

On a blustery January night with caucuses in full swing in Iowa, primary season at last under way, Rocky Haze steps up to the podium outside the dilapidated Sound Inc recording studio in Manchester, New Hampshire. "Man-chest-er! How y'all feelin' tonight?" she shouts to the near-empty parking lot. It was here that Haze worked through high school and cut her first demo, and she has now come back to rehearse. But not for any concert tour. In less than twenty-four hours the multiplatinum rapper will do the unthinkable: she will enter a presidential race already littered with more than two dozen candidates.

It's okay, she expects to not be taken seriously. She's almost looking forward to it—after all, she won a Grammy for her ode to underdogs, "The Quiet Ones."

And though her timing may not be ideal—her home state's primary is less than a week away—she's always been game for a challenge. "Yeah, sure, it's crazy!" she admits. "But you say I'm late to the party? I say, I'm the LIFE of this party!" Which party might that be? "Look, man, I define my party affiliation same as my sexuality—fluid." (She's on the ballot in NH as a Democrat but an insider says she isn't above a switch depending on "how things shake out." "You'd be surprised at how fiscally conservative she is," says the source.) It's that kind of open-mindedness and rejection of labels that she's hoping will swing voters ready for serious change this November. That's exactly what she'll be telling supporters at her announcement rally, where she's slated to be introduced—and formally endorsed—by New Hampshire Governor Frank Fisher.

"I don't like what I'm seeing out there," Haze says. "I don't like what I'm seeing HERE—Manchester with the drugs and the crime. Our nation living in fear of what terror might be around the corner. The differences between us dividing us, instead of enriching us and uniting us. Our lawmakers in gridlock in DC. We've got work. To. Do. Let's do it. Together. Yeah?" Indeed, as she orders in her latest No. 1 hit "Constitutional Rite": "Shut up and listen, we the people got something to say/From our Founding Fathers' time to the day of Rocky Haze."

She's certainly got the right backstory— one of bootstraps and pluck— ripe for political myth-making. Born Raquel Richard to drug-addicted parents, she was orphaned at age three and grew up in foster families until she was adopted at age eight. She credits the Hayes family (dad Harold, mom Nancy and brother Tom) of Portsmouth—who would enroll her in one of the area's finest prep schools while also nurturing her love of music—with turning her life around. "Rocky has always been a force of nature, so dedicated to what she throws herself into," Nancy says. "We just made sure that force kept steady on the right path." Dad agrees. "She has always had that deep, strong voice, that demands that you listen. She makes you believe that she is powerful and in control. She's a born leader."

Speculation began when she got political while accepting last year's Grammy for best rap album soon after attacks rocked Paris. "This record was about love. This place needs love, it needs change, it needs fresh ideas and shaking up. We got to care about the future of this world. My daughter and yours and your sons and your friends and families can't all be inheriting this fucked up place. Join me and start caring." She followed it up with…a haircut: much was made of her shearing her trademark waist-length wavy locks for the pixie she sports now. She laughs off any suggestion the style change was meant to make her appear more serious.

"Did I cut it off to look like a president? You know what I'm going to say to that?" she says, her tone cutting enough to shut it down but a smile still on her face.

We would never be talking about a man that way.

"Thank you," she says.

The Hayes clan—along with a dozen members of their extended family, an entourage of handlers and, of course, Rocky's husband, R&B powerhouse Alchemy, and their three-year-old daughter, Harmony, who's up past her bedtime—are on hand outside the recording studio, cheering through the cold at the many applause lines in her speech. After delivering her passionate remarks, which feel winningly off-the-cuff—not a teleprompter in sight—she breaks into song. It's a new single she's penned just for the occasion called "All In," which will serve as her campaign anthem. (Proceeds from its purchase go directly to her Super PAC.) The music track cues up—her pal DJ Downbeat will do the honors at the official event—and Rocky pulls the mic from the podium, strutting as she raps:

"They're all droppin' the ball, so I'm droppin' the mic,

This country ain't going down without a fight,

The system was there for me, came through when I needed it,

Now I'm giving back my heart and soul, not sitting out, talkin' shit,

Got my one-way ticket booked nonstop to Washington,

Gonna stay, play nice, pray, work night and day, till the job is done…"

At the very least, she is sure to have the best rally song of any candidate running. Shut up and listen, indeed.

By the time Jay made it into the office, the story was already No. 1 on *The Queue,* four networks had requested interviews with Sky and he had done his first hit, ever, for *The Today Show.*

The story was so good, in fact, that even Helena had summoned Jay to her office to ask: "Why did *we* get this exclusive?"

"Remember when Rocky Haze dropped her last album two years ago with no advance warning in the middle of the night? And it became one of the top five biggest selling records of all-time?" Jay had recounted. "That had been Sky's idea. He said it as a joke during their first interview together. Haze tried it before anyone else, and she always felt like she owed Sky."

The last of Birdie's party guests—the former ambassador to Sweden and her husband, dear old friends—left at dawn, and Birdie walked to the kitchen, ignoring the mess: the occasional overturned armchair, pile of broken glass, hunks of star-spangled cupcake on the floor, abandoned drinks lurking behind sofa cushions like Easter eggs, and who knew what had happened inside one of her rare nineteenth-century Imari porcelain urns—like it was all just wallpaper. She had given Abbie the morning off, but thankfully the cleanup crew would be arriving soon. She sliced two thick wheels of cucumber, returned to her bedroom and lay down, still in her gown. Cucumbers on her eyes, she drifted off to sleep amid

CNN's commentary on the Iowa results, a snarky aside about Madison Goodfellow headlined "WTF with the RBF?" (as in the resting bitch face, which Birdie too, had noticed and been fascinated by) and some tease about Rocky Haze that she was too exhausted to make sense of.

When her alarm went off, she pulled the cucumbers from her eyes and switched the channel to that local show just in time. The house, the gown, the interview: all perfection. She couldn't help but smile.

Cady barely made it to work in time to finish editing the segment on Birdie. She had dozed off at Reagan's house, a three-bedroom, one-and-a-half bath bungalow just over the Maryland line. Despite the fact that it was literally across the street—somewhere called Western Avenue, to be exact—from the District, it felt So Far Away and so oddly suburban. Not in the way of her childhood home in Johnstown, New York, but still. She was surprised at how peaceful it was, none of the street traffic she was so used to, the buzz at the center of the city. She knew Reagan must've been pretty sick to ask a stranger (her) to stay the night, and she had secretly been dreading going back to Jackson's empty apartment anyway.

She'd stayed awake for a while, flipping through news channels for more Carter Thompson victory party footage—he had actually *won* the Iowa caucus; she called and texted obsessively but had yet to reach Jackson—and Googling some of the people she had met, these other "widows."

Before dawn, awakened by Reagan's screaming twin girls, she cabbed home and then raced to work, where the segment on Birdie's party came together in record time, because it had to. A message popped up in her email inbox immediately after the show wrapped, as though timed to a T.

Cady,
Nice meeting you, thanks again for the save.
Here's some lowdown on our place, opening soon. Come by
anytime!
Your humble star reporter,
Parker (and Melanie)

She opened the first attachment, a press release, and skimmed.

Preamble aims to become the ultimate after-work haunt. The
first place you go when you leave the office. The gathering
place for a drink before dinner. The start to your night. And
the start of great things. It's a place for people of all political ideologies to meet, harkening back to the time when ca-
maraderie reigned supreme in our branches of government.
When progress was made, deals struck and common ground
found over distilled spirits and spirited conversation. To that
end, we even have private rooms for elected officials to talk
it out. Neutral territory. Think of it as an extension of your
office wet bar, your liquor cabinet away from the workplace.

It did have a catchy gimmick. She read further.

Co-owners Parker Appleton, a former Senate staffer, and Melanie Harper, a former House legislative director, are from
different sides of the aisle (and chambers in the Capitol) but
share a belief in bipartisan imbibing...

And then: The co-owners are also engaged to be married
in November.
The second attachment included a collection of photos of the

bar itself—more "of the people" and divey than she expected, complete with vibrant splashes of graffiti on the walls, and finally a shot of Parker on a bar stool with a pretty brunette on his lap, playful and sweetly smiling. It looked as if it could double as an engagement photo. Cady stopped reading, feeling jittery all of a sudden, her heart beating faster. She tapped out a text.

Hi! Me again! Should we be doing engagement photos???

The extra question marks were manic and aggressive, but she couldn't hold back. She had actually begun making a list of wedding-related things to tend to, but had gotten quickly overwhelmed: she had actual work to do, new job, a move, their lease would be up soon and they hoped to buy. She couldn't flip through eight hundred pictures of gowns on brides.com right now. She couldn't even string together the minutes to research wedding planners to do it for her. And she wanted to *enjoy* doing that stuff. She just didn't know when she could clear the decks enough to focus on it.

Jackson would probably be at the airport now, and she shouldn't annoy him about the wedding at a time like this. But her phone began flashing a response in process and then this appeared: Coming up for air. Thanks! Exciting here. Heading to New Hampshire with Carter for a couple days now! More speeches. See you on the other side.

She began typing but her phone buzzed again with yet another text: photos? today? what?

no, in general, should we do them? she typed, feeling bad for bringing it up now.

i don't know cady I don't even know what time zone i'm in

you're in central. Then she wrote again, never mind. go,

enjoy, congratulations, tell me when you arrive. good luck in the granite state! She'd had to Google that one; she wasn't so up on her New Hampshire trivia.

Reagan woke up late and had to wait until the twins' morning nap before sequestering herself in the dank, dungeon-like storage room in their basement. The musty space, illuminated with a lone yellow light bulb, teemed with boxes of stuff they never used, didn't need, forgot existed, but hadn't had time to officially get rid of. It was scary. The box she needed was, naturally, beneath the one she least wanted to see—a banker's box crammed with Ted Campion for Congress lawn placards, "Campion Is Your Champion" bumper stickers and matching buttons, detritus from Ted's failed run just before the twins were born. It felt like a lifetime ago. She had still been working at the firm and moonlighting as Ted's speechwriter too. Such hope and passion and adrenaline, enough to propel her to do two jobs—and do them well—while growing two human beings in her belly, a feat of multitasking she was still proud of. Now she barely had the brainpower to construct a cogent text message.

As if on cue, her phone buzzed. She expected it to be Ted, whom she had tried to comfort earlier: Iowa doesn't always predict the nom, it was wrong at least 6 times for GOP and twice for Dems, she had typed, but she could picture him brooding nonetheless.

Instead, it was Cady, short and very sweet: Hope you're feeling better!

She vowed to send along a thank-you gift of some sort. It was so unlike Reagan to feel like she needed someone with her, but she had sent Stacy home too hastily, experienced another bout of sickness and worried that the twins might wake up and that she'd be too depleted to handle them.

Reagan tucked her phone in her pocket, then shoved the box—and its memories—out of the way too. It hadn't quite occurred to either of them then that Ted might not win. She burrowed through a box of maternity clothes and "What to Expect" books until she found it. Only a true pack rat like her would have saved the package. It had been a five-pack and, shockingly, the expiration date was still a month away. Just staring at the three remaining pregnancy tests, she felt like she might be sick again.

9

DEMOCRACY AT WORK IS A BEAUTIFUL THING

★

Birdie hadn't seen Buck for a week. He had remained on the road after Iowa, needing to "soak in as much color as I can for the book before class starts," or so he'd claimed in his messages to Birdie. As a special guest star for a class at Georgetown this semester called "The Modern American Campaign," he would be rooted in town more than usual this campaign season, which, theoretically, she should have been excited about. But the class didn't begin for another two weeks, and she could tell Buck was really just avoiding her.

So when she heard his twang, her ears so conditioned as to pick it out even on a TV on very low volume, even with Rocky Haze's "All In" playing on a loop in her airy Lucite, teal and zebra-printed office suite, even with Abbie in the adjacent room chattering on the phone, she perked up. It was the morning of the New Hampshire Primary, and Buck sat at a roundtable on MSNBC in a sport coat, no tie.

"Look," Buck said. "Haze is someone who already knows how to connect with an audience, that's eighty percent of this job. We could all be very surprised come tomorrow mornin'."

This morning he had informed Birdie in a terse text that he would be home the following afternoon. Only 10:00 a.m. and she already needed her painkillers.

It was some sort of interplanetary law, something about inverse and opposite reactions, that a truly dire head-under-the-covers, don't-bother-getting-out-of-bed day came so soon after a stellar one. In the past week she had hosted two congressional fund-raisers that raked in over a million dollars each and had taken daily meetings lining up more events. And, of course, her Iowa party had been one for the record books: Abbie collected the hundreds of glowing press mentions, everywhere from the *Times* and *Vanity Fair* to hoards of blogs she'd never heard of that posted photos of all the charming details from chocolates in the shape of four of the front-runners to the starred-and-striped Georgetown Cupcakes adorned with tiny pennants reading "Happy Primary Season! Patriotically yours, Birdie & Buck Brandywine." (She always gave Buck near-equal billing on party favors.)

But now the universe was evening things out: Bob Bronson, the former senator, was proving to be more prickly and micromanaging than she had anticipated when she signed on to plan his fund-raiser for Vice President Arnold. She had dodged Bronson's gorgeous associate Cole all week, no use seeing him if Buck wasn't around to notice. (Though she still didn't understand how *Cole* had been the one to end up in the koi pond at her Iowa party. The incident gave the fish—who had settled at the bottom for winter, plenty snuggly thanks to her aeration system—quite the scare.) At any rate, it was Bronson himself who called her regarding the upcoming Arnold fete:

"Second thoughts on the location. Sorry, Birdie," he told her before she'd even finished her morning coffee. "Think outside the box."

"Oh you, flip-flopping again," she joked of his indecision. She didn't ask what prompted the switch: when people like him, used to getting their way, changed their minds on something, it didn't matter *why*. You just had to find a way to give them whatever it was they *did* want.

So she begrudgingly began amassing a new list of potential

party locations. But, still, she couldn't stop thinking about tomorrow. About Buck's return.

Reagan was certain that if Dante Alighieri had been a woman, one of the circles of hell would have involved being trapped at a lady-doctor appointment with two wild toddlers. But there she was, an unfortunate detour on the way to My Gym. She had strapped them firmly into their Bugaboo double stroller as they arched their backs and kicked their legs and screamed, both always preferring to be running than sitting still, and gave them her iPhone and iPad, immediately inciting a grabbing-tugging match as each battled to secure whichever device the other had. Then she managed to shove the wide stroller through the narrow lavatory doorway so she could pee in a cup and confirm what the three sticks at home and her intense nausea had already told her. Afterward, she piled them back into the car: "Okay, mommy had her fun and now you guys get to have your fun," she promised, as they squealed.

Having to follow traffic laws felt overwhelming at a time like this, her mind already working so hard to wrap itself around this latest development. Like when they had just moved to the house, before the kids, back when they needed to establish residency in a nearby district with a potentially competitive congressional race, and she had accidentally run over a squirrel. It had been her first day of work at the speechwriting firm, the Dream Job, and she was too focused on her excitement to notice the little fucker dart into the driveway as she backed out.

She ran a stop sign now, a car swerving around her, honking. "Motherfucker. Focus," she said aloud. Then with her bounciest pep, "Sorry, babies!" She looked in the mirror to view yet another mirror, this one reflecting those two smiling faces in their rear-facing car seats. She patted her belly, hand shaking.

It was amazing knock-you-out sort of news, a kind of off-the-charts sublime surprise. But also, totally not part of The Plan. She hoped the twins would be okay. She suspected they would love having someone tiny and new to let into their circle and boss around, another competitor to wrestle with in the manner of the baby mixed-martial-arts games they already played, rolling and jumping and tackling each other. They'd adapt fine, she knew in her heart. But Ted. He was the wild card. She would tell him tonight if they won New Hampshire. And if not, well…she just wouldn't think about that yet.

At the gym, she took a rare deep breath and vowed to enjoy the relative nirvana that came with being able to let her two little animals loose. Stacy sat at the center of the circle of children, singing some song about animals that called for hand motions. Reagan was relieved it was a Stacy class. She claimed to enjoy the twins' "energy," as she called it, and never minded if they ran off midclass to climb up the slide or jump off some cushioned structure not intended as a launch pad.

Luckily it was hard to get hurt there, so Reagan zoned out, even managing to ignore the occasional side-eye from other moms seemingly wondering when she would step in and control her kids. *Never,* she wanted to tell these women. *It's called being a free spirit. Which, despite what you may have heard, is actually a good thing. Good luck to you when your perfectly regimented and repressed little angels turn into drug dealers in ten years.* She hated other moms sometimes. Then she hated herself for feeling that way. But it seemed the vast majority were judgy at best and self-righteous at worst. *Maybe I'm just some kind of misanthrope?* she wondered. Or more likely, just severely sleep-deprived.

But, Ted. *Fuck,* she thought. He had threatened to get a vasectomy during one particularly bad night several months earlier with two screaming children, four teeth being cut and no one sleeping. His schedule ultimately had been too packed, and he hadn't gotten around to rescheduling his appointment.

As Daisy and Natasha bonked each other on the head with foam jousting spears, she typed: Hey T! How's NH? I'm knocked up! Talk soon! then erased it, shook her head and started a new message, this one for Cady. Thanks again for the help the other night. Can the girls and I repay the favor and treat you to milk and cookies? She pressed Send and opened her Notes app, keying in some thoughts for her next column, grateful for these blissful thirty minutes of freedom.

HAZE TAKES NEW HAMPSHIRE, SETS SIGHTS ON SUPER TUESDAY

By Sky Vasquez, Staff Writer, *The Queue*

"Even I'm in shock," Rocky Haze says as her mother sets a cup of hot chocolate, extra marshmallows, before her. She's seated in the kitchen of her parents' home in the suburbs of Manchester at four in the morning after clinching her first primary win just a week after entering the race for the White House. "I am humbled and grateful that the people of New Hampshire can feel my fire, that they are willing to take a chance on me. Man, tonight I just needed to reflect on this, you know?" she says, shaking her head, a tear in her eye as her love, Alchemy, perched on the arm of her chair, pats her back. "Needed to rest my head on the pillow where my dreams began."

It's been a busy night for the Grammy-winning candidate. After watching the confetti fall and delivering a stirring speech at her victory party attended by Governor Frank Fisher and

Senator Shep Bishop, where she thanked voters for "their open-mindedness, their ability to recognize passion and to see that the change our country needs could come in a form they didn't expect," she made an appearance at her campaign headquarters here—a bed-and-breakfast where she spent summers busing dishes—surprising volunteers who had gathered to watch election returns en masse. "Their support and faith in me gets me through my sleepless nights," she says. Then she called up Mom and Dad.

"We were just honored to be celebrating at the party, but to have her here on such an important night." Mom Nancy Hayes tears up. "She is already a winner."

Helena materialized outside Jay's door just as he arrived, his coat still on, cold fingers clutching his morning coffee— a Venti. He'd been up late, but he had the glow that emanated from the inside out whenever he felt he'd helped usher a good story into the world. Sky filed two that night, the one with the shocking basics—somehow Haze had actually *won* the New Hampshire Primary—and the other, when Haze's assistant called Sky at 3:30 a.m. and told him to get in the Escalade.

"FUUUCK!!! Jay! Help!" Sky had called, frantic all over again. "What do I do with this?"

"You go and you make note of everything, and we file a follow-up with all the personal details. Text ASAP and let me know who else is there, media-wise."

Half an hour later Jay received: OMG, just me here. At her parents' house, Alchemy, Harmony, her bro.

On the ride back to the hotel, Sky typed up the email that Jay helped shape into the story, and an hour later it posted and had been firmly atop *The Queue* ever since.

"I'm kind of in love with this family," Helena said by way of greeting as she opened Jay's door herself, flipped on the light and plunked down in Jay's chair. "The mom is so cute. Haze actually might be the most normal, least fucked-up of all these clowns running."

"Democracy at work is a beautiful thing," Jay said, firing up his laptop.

"Just emailed you guys. Sky has hits on Bloomberg, Fox and CNN at 9:30, 10:15 and 11:00. They'll come to him. And tell him to keep the exclusives coming. Let's get some more on the nuclear family, Alchemy, the kid—"

"Alchemy seems to be on hiatus. Sky said he's pushing back his next album release."

"Fascinating. He's clearing the decks for her."

"I know, right? Not how he usually rolls," Jay said. But then his impression, from what he'd read and observed purely as a fan, was that Haze was a diva in the greatest, take-no-prisoners sense.

"She's in it at least through Super Tuesday now. We'll keep Sky on the trail till then," she said, typing on her phone as she rose to leave. "Keep him filing as much as he can."

Jay nodded and flipped on the TV to catch Sky's latest spot, but they were still showing a roundup of the previous night. Jay found it equal parts puzzling and hilarious that Madison Goodfellow looked so happy after watching her husband lose. She stood by his side at a podium in New Hampshire, grinning as broadly as she should have after they'd won Iowa.

Jay shook his head. He just didn't get these Goodfellow folks.

Cady had to say something; she couldn't just let this go, so she cornered Jeff in his office before the morning meeting. No greeting, just a knock on the open door.

"So I can't help but notice that Rocky Haze—Rocky.

Haze!—has won New Hampshire." She dropped her jaw for effect. "We've gotta do something, anything, maybe talk to the *Foreign Policy* editors who've worked with her? Or I've been doing some digging, and there's a guy in the UN office here who accompanied her on a trip to Darfur once," she said, selling it, though he was giving her that kind smile and head nod that said, *Love your attitude but the answer's still no.* "It's kind of a big deal."

"Cady, Cady, Cady…" Jeff smiled, shaking his head as he leaned back in his chair. "What did I tell you on your first day?"

"Right, know your audience, I know, but—"

"The trick here is *less* politics," he said, perfectly jovial. "Remember? No religion or politics, like at any good party, am I right?"

"Good one," she said, unconvinced.

"We've been over this. We let the big dogs do that, plenty of national news shows with national-news-show resources."

"I get that," she said. "But, shouldn't we be, if not a *big* dog, then *some* dog, or, like, *at* the dog park at least?"

"We're really just a…a…" He struggled. "I had cats, I don't know—a Shih Tzu? Or whatever dog is a little ball of fluff."

"No bite, got it." She exhaled in a grand, highly disappointed way.

"I know, I know, but trust me, we did focus groups. People aren't coming to us for that. We rebranded to the point that we're counterprogramming to all that news now. Like I mentioned in your interview, your sound bites at *New in New York* from Andrew Cuomo about Sandra Lee's best meals at home? That was a winner."

"And, also, vaguely political," she pointed out cheekily.

"Almost too political." He laughed. "No one wants you to be Woodward or Bernstein here. C'mon, meeting time."

★ ★ ★

Much to Reagan's chagrin, the twins, as though sensing daddy's boss had lost in New Hampshire, had awakened at eleven o'clock last night and every two hours like clockwork until morning. After Arnold's dulled concession speech ("We have only just begun our fight," the vice president said, audibly sighing), she'd tried to call Ted but had to settle with a text: so sorry. i still say haze is flash in pan right? will all sort out super tuesday. meantime get them writing more upbeat stuff, he sounds so defeatist/old/status quo/blah. loosen his tie— metaphorical & literal. Tash and D awake, sending kisses. and crying bloody murder xo.

It was morning now, and Ted still hadn't written back. She worried he was taking this hard, too hard. It was too early to be that upset.

MSNBC had a panel for morning after quarterbacking, and she was about to switch to Grant Foxhall's show on CNN when she spotted Buck. "I warned you all!" Buck laughed. "People on both sides—on *both* sides, mind you—are gonna need to take Haze seriously. As an antiestablishment candidate, she's persuasive. But she's got this loyal following. She knows how to tap into people's emotions with her music. She's already part of their lives, their good days and bad, comfort and joy. My wife listens to that song all day long." The panel laughed. Reagan too, in spite of herself.

Buck and Birdie were such a team. Reagan knew bits of their history, the gossip. But they seemed so rock solid. Meanwhile, she felt like a barefoot, pregnant, bedraggled single mom. She tapped out an email to Birdie, in a Birdie-esque tone to be all the more pleasing, and copyedited it three times.

Dearest Birdie, Wonderful to see you last week, no one throws a Hawkeye State Soiree like you. Watching Buck on MSNBC now:

nice shout-out! Full disclosure: I'm equally obsessed with that song. All in, Reagan

A cool stream of thick, organic mango yogurt squirted across her cheek. She looked up from her phone. "Who did that?" Natasha giggled wildly, kicking her legs against the high chair. Reagan wiggled her fingers and crept over. "You're getting tickles for that! Gotcha gotcha gotcha!" She tickled her daughter's chubby arms and belly and legs, and Daisy, seated beside her sister in her own high chair, burst into matching chuckles before shooting her yogurt pouch at Reagan too, this time missing. "Uh-oh, you're next, lady!" Reagan said, lunging to give the same treatment while Natasha smacked her tray happily and swept bananas and Cheerios in every direction.

Despite the mayhem and destruction that came with each meal, Reagan still found these times peaceful, since the girls were strapped in and contained. She caught her breath, wiped her face and set to work cleaning the mess from the floor just as the phone rang. The girls squealed at each other, communicating in their own language, then chanting, "Da!-da!-da!-da!-da!" They always assumed every call was Dad, though they were wrong most of the time. Especially now that campaign season was under way.

"Hey, Jay! Great Sky piece. Did you get—" she started, but he jumped in.

"Um, is there something you want to tell me, Rea?" he asked. "Because I'm editing your column—"

Natasha began kicking and screaming, Daisy copying her a split second later; they hated when she was on the phone for longer than fifteen seconds.

"Ohhhh, yeah, I figured you might—" she said, unhooking Natasha from the chair.

"Mmm-hmm, one of these letters is very curious. Let's just read it aloud, shall we?"

"Sure, okay." She pulled a piece of smushed banana off Natasha's plump thigh and ate it, then caught herself and shook her head in disgust, plopping the girl into the pack-and-play. Sometimes she made full meals of the food picked off her children's bodies, and she wasn't proud of it. She was so desocialized, she was practically a primate at this point.

"'Question: Is it ever appropriate to *email* your husband—rather than tell him in person—that you're expecting another child?'" Jay read in a flat tone.

Reagan unbuckled Daisy, who smiled sweetly and clung to her like a koala bear when she tried to put her beside her sister in the playard. She kissed her on the head as she peeled Daisy's grippy limbs from her body, careful that the girl didn't kick her belly.

Jay continued. "'It's his! Phew! No worries there, but he's traveling on business for weeks, stressed out, it's hard to catch him on the phone and he seldom has much privacy or time. We have two kids already, so this one is just a bonus (aka: surprise!) anyway. Please advise.'"

"Ohhhh, that. Right," Reagan said, washing the dishes from last night's meal while cradling the phone in her neck. "So what did you think of the answer?"

"You mean, 'We live in modern times and what could be better than to receive such lovely news via email? Congrats?'" He read it all as a question.

"Yeah?"

"No."

"Okay. So, I fucked up my birth control," she launched in, shutting the water and wiping her hands. She tossed a few stray board books into the playard, then made her way upstairs to the hamper in the girls' room. "I always wondered who the idiots were who couldn't remember to take a pill at the same damn time every day—but mystery solved, it's me, I'm the idiot."

"You and probably a lot of other extremely busy people. Not idiots at all," Jay comforted.

"Not idiots at all," she repeated. "Apologies all around. Clearing out any bad chakras here."

"Oooh, can I be *the godfather* again?" Jay asked, doing his best Marlon Brando, which wasn't good at all.

"Sure. You're hired." She hustled downstairs to the basement with the overflowing laundry basket.

"This is awesome, Rea! You guys make supercute kids. How're you feeling? Need me to Uber you some pickles and ice cream?"

"Thanks. No, yeah, crazy and exhausted and overwhelmed. So the usual, except with someone else leasing office space in my body." She laughed, pausing and pensive before tossing the laundry in, then said seriously, "But, you know what? Happy actually. Nauseous and happy."

"Good! You should be! Happy, I mean. Despite the other stuff, you know?" he said, glossing over. He had been her confidant during the vasectomy talk; he knew it all.

"Right. So, any other edits?"

"Ted?" Jay asked gingerly.

"Yep," she said knowingly.

"Sorry, but speaking as your editor, gotta change that answer, girl."

"I know," she said.

"Gotta do it in person or at least on the phone. At least."

"Yep."

"Give him a chance to have the right response. And then if he doesn't, well—"

"We'll do a follow-up column."

They both laughed.

10

I DON'T LECTURE ANYONE FOR LESS THAN $25,000

★

"Thought it might be nice to stay in. I'm sick of being out," Buck said, plating the juicy burgers—procured from their favorite eatery, Martin's Tavern—on their gleaming white china and setting them on opposite ends of the dining table while Birdie opened a bottle of red wine. He had done hits on MSNBC much of the day, breaking down the New Hampshire results, then hopped on a train and made it back in time to pick up dinner. Birdie poured generously and gulped down her wine through their sunny small talk about New Hampshire, Iowa, Rocky Haze's entrance into the campaign and Buck's travels.

"There's this new place everyone's staying at. It was fine. I woulda preferred that bed-and-breakfast where we stayed that one year, remember that? But— "

"Haze's people took it over." She pointed to the flat screen in the corner set to Bloomberg, where a dapper reporter for *The Queue* answered questions at a coffee shop Haze had visited earlier in the day. "Whoever their people are. Seems she's being staffed entirely by record label executives—which, come to think of it, might not be any worse than all you so-called strategists." She smiled.

"Prob'ly true!" He laughed, sincerely. Then sighed. "Who really knows anyway? Whole lotta luck involved in this game."

"So that's what they pay you the big bucks to hear," she said, taking a swig.

"Even I can't explain Hank Goodfellow."

"And how much do I love that Madison? It's like she read the Spouse Handbook but got it all fouled up. Don't look overjoyed when he loses and—"

"Like you're having intestinal discomfort when he wins." Buck laughed. "Someone needs to tell her the camera is always on and—"

"—and the world is always looking for this week's next great GIF," Birdie said, though she suspected there was more to Madison than what she was showing them all. "Bless her and Rocky too, for making this all more interesting than it usually is."

"Sure thing. But you know the real question on everyone's minds this election season?" Buck asked, perfectly congenial, sitting back in his chair with his wineglass as he looked her in the eye across the table. "Is my wife cheating on me this cycle?"

The jab came out of nowhere, Buck's specialty. And it was why he made an excellent living prepping candidates for debate.

"I don't think that's on *everyone's* minds. I'm a far more discreet person than that." She laughed, trying to sound as though they were talking about something trivial. Inwardly, she felt every muscle tense.

"Well, then, for argument's sake, let's say it's on *my* mind," he said, stretching his arms and resting them behind his head as though lounging on a hammock.

His open body language meant to disarm her; she knew how his mind worked. Her veins ran icy. They had never had this conversation before; she had begun to think they might never have it. Which would have disappointed her actually. "What makes you think—" she began with calculated ease, leaning back in her own chair.

"Roberta—" he said sharply, cutting her off.

"Hey—" she snapped back in reflex, as though she'd been called some sort of slur. Her own name sounded so foreign and chilly to her. She had not been "Roberta" in decades, not since arriving in Washington, when she had quickly taken on the more pleasing, precious "Bertie" and then finally "Birdie" while working as an assistant for Bronson. She was proud of who she had fashioned herself into. Back then, when she had met Buck—Bronson's chief of staff at the time—he had said the nickname suited her delicate bones, that she looked like she could take flight. Her crush on him had been instant—everyone had a crush on Buck, he was that kind of guy. It had been a true shock when he kissed her that one spring night after working late and walking the entire length of the Mall together, lost in conversation. It had been ages since she'd thought of that night; she suppressed it all once more.

"Of course, Birdie, doyenne of Georgetown. Or whatever they call you. Who uses each election as a yearlong hall pass—"

She wanted to say, *So you noticed*, for shock value but stopped herself. She thought of telling him that nothing had happened with Cole—because it truly hadn't—but instead she chose to say, "Why? Because I'm *busy*? Because I have work to do and I'm not *around* enough? This is my season, love. The campaign hath begun." Her smile remained, with great effort. "And *campaigning* is all that's being done."

"Look, this was once *my* season, so I don't need a lecture about professional commitments—"

"*Look*, darling, that's not my intention at all," she chirped. "I don't lecture anyone for less than $25,000. My point is—"

"*My* point is, this feels personal, not professional. I don't wanna know what you've been doing or who you've been doing it with. I just want you to know I'm not gonna be made a fool of—"

"Like I was," she cut him off, frosty. "You won't be made a fool of *like I was*." What she had resented most in the end, those years ago, was being made into a cliché. She was so much more interesting than that.

He froze, as though sucker punched, and she could feel him curse himself for walking into that one. After a beat, he collected himself. "I made a mistake. Many years ago. For which the statute of limitations will apparently never expire."

"Oh, yes, I forgot this is *my* problem. It's *my* problem that I haven't managed my response to *your* problems better. Sincerest apologies." She said it calmly, smirking. It was exactly what she might have expected from him, what he would've counseled his clients to do: give a pat answer.

"When you want to truly talk instead of trade barbs, lemme know. But this? This, artificial act, this Birdie caricature, I can't talk to." Yes, there it was, the pivot. Rendering this conversation wholly unsatisfying and not worth the air to respond. He continued even so. "I thought it was for the papers—" he sounded so old when he said "the papers" "—and the gossips, for the circus. But if it's for me too, if that's what I come home to at night then—"

She wanted to say it wasn't artifice, it was a shell encasing her body so she couldn't be taken down again. She would always be that shy, nose-to-the grindstone Hill staffer who had come to Washington—on her first airplane flight ever—to work for her congressman so long ago. A very expensive therapist had told her this and it was true, though she had already figured that out on her own.

Buck tossed his napkin onto his half-eaten burger, grabbed his empty glass.

"You like *Roberta* more than *Birdie*? Well, *Roberta* is the one who gets pissed off and holds grudges. She's human." She kept her tone perfectly steady, light even.

"Well, if you see her, tell her I am too." He grabbed his plate and pointed at her now. "And that she should decide if she still wants to be in this thing with me."

He had to have noticed the shock flicker across her face. She recovered quickly and asked in a dull tone, "Are you going to storm out now? Or do I get to?"

"I'm serious, Birdie. I'll be next door until November 9, lemme know then."

November 9. The day after the election. She had too much pride to ask the other details, the parameters of this setup, or to show any passion, throw her glass or her plate, to make noise or to scream. Or even to bother defending herself by telling what little had really gone on with her and Cole or any of those men. She felt as numb as that day Buck had first confessed about Gracie. The emptiness colonized her heart, then crept out to her extremities. She felt unsure of who or what to fill up that space with. So she stood there, watching the flat screen, as she heard a door slam. Then, realizing her office was next door, in the town house he declared he would have custody of until November 9, she calmly took out her phone and plopped onto the sofa. If he was serious about this arrangement, she would at the very least demand access to her office from 9 to 5 daily. But for now, this would have to suffice. She had work to do.

Madison lay wide-awake as Hank, nestled into the lush thread counts of their Upper East Side bed, snored peacefully beside her. He never was one to lose sleep over anything, she marveled, not even, apparently, a New Hampshire Primary loss. After the sting of coming in second to "that nitwit," as he called his competitor in an interview on CNN, he had ordered the jet back to New York.

Madison had been so convinced that this was it, the end to

this experiment or whatever it was, that she'd had trouble suppressing the joy during his speech, literally biting her tongue to keep from grinning. But instead, Hank had stormed back to their hotel suite with the rest of the Machine, looked in the mirror and shouted, "Someone gimme a goddamn tie! Someone! Anyone! Whiplash, hand it over." Madison had watched from the corner of the room as her husband snapped his fingers to his young staffer, "C'mon, c'mon," and Whiplash untied his own tie (a horrid plaid) and handed it over. Hank looped it around his neck, for the first time in decades, and the room fell silent. Madison had sighed, understanding: this was his version of doubling down. Not only would he stay in the race, he would be more determined than ever. And sure enough, Hank looked at his reflection and a smile crept slowly over his face. "Yes, that's it." He nodded. "Get me more-a these!"

It had been harrowing to say the least. As she lay there, staring at the ceiling, Madison flashed back to those days when they'd attend gala after gala, so many organizations always wanting to honor Hank for the money he gave, and he and Madison would break away, drinks in hand, and watch the room. "Kill me if I ever take myself too damn serious, will you?" he would whisper, nodding to all the puffed-up chests beneath the starched shirts and suffocating ties. He wore an open collar to everything from business meetings to black tie affairs. "They need more of us here, more of this. They need more small town, dirt road, big heart types."

That was the Hank she loved, the semi-iconoclast who brought something to New York that hadn't been there before, not this egomaniac the election had unleashed.

Not the Hank who, at the victory rally in Iowa, had barked at the crowd from a stage in the sculpture garden in Des Moines, so impassioned his voice grew hoarse: "I will stand out in the cold for you! To make your world a better place! I will fight whoever I have to! And invade whatever country I have to! I AM YOUR NEW LEADER!"

She hoped New Hampshire meant the tide was now turning. And she prayed she would never have to hear that terrible slogan of his—which sounded so much like words spoken by an alien on one of their son Henry's favorite sci-fi shows—ever again.

11

IN RETROSPECT, THAT COULD'VE BEEN
A LOT WORSE

★

Cady and Cameraman Max drove past the bare trees and bleak gray landscape of mid-February to the address on the Hill. Their show was, she had discovered, perpetually short-staffed so she'd decided she might as well just go herself to interview Parker. Plus, it was nice to get out of the office and begin to find her way around the city, now that it was really hers too and not just a place to visit on weekends. She fidgeted, tapped her fingers the whole way there, occasionally glancing at that *thing* on her ring finger: her long-lost engagement ring.

Jackson had texted the day before, something about a surprise, and she'd arrived home to the 3-carat asscher cut set in platinum. "Some guy dropped it off in an envelope at the office early in the morning," he'd explained, presenting it to Cady on bended knee in the living room of their apartment. "Left it on Michelle's desk out front and walked away without a word. He was gone before she put together what was going on."

"Yay and also, that kind of creeps me out," Cady had admitted. "I wonder where he found it and when and how long he had it."

"Well, we had promised no questions asked if it was returned, right?" He shrugged.

"Not the easiest concession for someone in the news business, but I'll take it." Cady laughed. Then it dawned on her: "Hey, we've gotta tell Jay!"

"Why?" he asked flatly.

"Why?" she asked rhetorically. Was he kidding? "He'll be so excited! Remember, he said he wanted a follow-up story if—"

"Do we really need to do that?" Jackson asked.

"Define *need*," she said.

"I just think it's a little much is all," Jackson said, tentative, with a sigh. "We've got the ring. The whole world doesn't need to know how we got it back."

"I'm kind of…confused." She shook her head. "I thought you liked Jay."

"I do." A hint of frustration crept into his voice. "I just don't think we need to be the subject of any more articles."

She didn't understand, but she let it go for the moment, not wanting to ruin one of the rare nights when he wasn't traveling. It was actually proving harder to have him away now that they were living together—she missed him even more. Somehow she had already forgotten how to be in a long-distance relationship. So they opened a bottle of wine celebrating the ring's return and she secretly vowed to email Jay before too long.

She was anxious for any excuse to keep close to these new acquaintances she had been fortunate enough to make, and she wasn't about to miss this opportunity. She had somehow happened upon this group that felt at the epicenter of the city, and they had, for some reason, welcomed her into their circle. To a transplant like Cady, still navigating her new position, new city, searching for some social life beyond just friends of Jackson's, meeting these people seemed like an incredible gift.

Cady stole quick glances at the ring now as she and Max reached the building. The sparkly bauble made her whole hand look like it didn't belong to her. But even if it didn't quite feel right yet, it was undeniably gorgeous.

The bar occupied the ground floor of a row house, just a

stone's throw from the Hart Senate office building. The sign reading PREAMBLE was up, but the windows still appeared papered from the inside, concealing what she expected was still a construction site. Finding the door locked, she worried she had missed an email. Parker had written that morning attempting to cancel, then changing his mind *again* and telling them to come by in the afternoon. She imagined he just had a lot to do and was in crunch time before opening—she was still hazy on their official grand opening date. The bar's website promised simply: Opening Soon! She had optimistically slated the piece to air this week as part of a package previewing upcoming openings and she didn't feel like scrounging for a replacement.

Eventually Parker unlocked the door:

"Sorry, I'm all over the place today, not so much geographically as just mentally," he said, the words pouring out.

"Hey." Cady held out her hand to shake his. "You're about to open a restaurant, that's kind of major, thanks for making time." She introduced Max, and he began setting up. "Glad you were free, we'll make it fast."

"No, yeah, no problem." He ran his hand through his hair, agitated. "I just, I wasn't going to today because it's not the best day or whatever."

"Oh, sorry, if there's a better—"

"But then I couldn't imagine a *good* time—" he just kept talking "—like, ever, anytime soon. So, yeah. Sorry. Great to see you, this is the place." He nervously turned his watch around and around on his wrist as he spoke.

"It's really...nice," she said, wondering if they should go, how messy it might be to pull the interview from the show's lineup. Parker had seemed fun, chatty, easygoing at Birdie's party. In short, he had seemed like he would make for good TV. "This is a great location," she went on.

"Yeahhhh, I know, it's really, really expensive. I'm freaking out a little bit," he said.

"I kinda sense that," she said gently. Worst-case scenario, they could edit it choppily to mask his discomfort, right? "But, you know, nothing wrong with that. Being...genuine...works great on camera...most of the time. Let's get you some bar patrons with this, right? Pay that rent!"

She wandered around the dim space. Max was tinkering with the lighting and camera near a red vinyl booth in the back.

"Love the graffiti," she offered, pointing to the phrases adorning the walls, among them "life, liberty and the pursuit of happiness."

"An artist friend did that. I did the bar though." He slapped his hand against the mahogany bar covered in penknife carvings.

"All of this?" She bent down to study some of the designs, names, dates, hearts with couples' names, swirls, peace signs, four-leaf clovers. "How did you do this?"

"Little bit every day. It's pretty much my only talent." He smiled.

"Well, it's a good one," she said. "I bet you messed up a lot of desks in high school."

He chuckled once. "I wanted the place to look lived in and, loved, you know?" he said, lost in his thoughts. He walked over to the center of the bar, traced a carving with his fingertip, then slapped a napkin on it as though killing an ant.

"But hey, you guys need drinks, what's your poison?"

"Well, we're working so—" Cady started.

"What's on tap?" Max piped up.

Parker set down drinks for the three of them at the booth— a Diet Coke for her, beers for him and Max—and while Max miked him up, Cady reviewed the list of questions on her phone once more, slowly sipping her Diet Coke. When she looked up, she noticed Parker intently watching her hand that held the glass. The left one.

"Hey, so that's nice," he said somewhat bitterly, nodding. "What's that three carats, cushion cut? No, asscher?" He knocked back the rest of his beer.

"A man who knows his diamonds," she said. "Yeah, asscher." She studied it herself. Wow, it was weird to have a rock like that.

"That's awesome," he said flatly. "Can you take it off?"

She thought he was kidding, but he looked too agitated. "This?" She laughed, a single unsure laugh. "Really? Should I, like, put it in the dish with the nuts?"

"Is that an option?" He held up the bowl. "Yes? Wait—" he dumped the nuts out onto the table "—maybe?"

"Uhhh..." She looked at Max, who appeared to be taping already.

"No, sorry, that's...never mind... I just." He took a deep breath, hung his head. "So, yeah, Melanie broke up with me. And gave me back the ring and all, not unlike that one, and I'm not sure if I can get my money back or what. I guess it's good she gave it back, but now I have to deal with it. Hell, I could probably upgrade the bar stools or something with what I paid for that sucker. And this place, what the fuck? It's like she left me with our kid—this bar—and ran away, and I don't know how the fuck to raise it." It all came out like one long sentence.

"Wow. Okay." Cady nodded. She looked back at Max and made a motion to stop rolling.

"Yeah. Sorry. I tend to just expel...stuff... Am I talking too much? Still freshly wounded here. My filter is off. Way off."

"Yeah, no, no, I get that. I'm really sorry. That's awful. Okay, first." She slipped off her ring, held it up for inspection and made a show of tucking it into her bag, nestling it into a small, zippered pocket.

He exhaled. "Thank you."

"Next, total unemotional, fact-gathering question. What's the deal legally with the bar? Any kind of joint custody situation or really you're a single dad to it?"

"Single dad. Bought this place with my money. We were just gonna run it together." He said it wistfully, and she felt for him.

"Okay, so let's do this thing." She clapped once, like a coach. "You just need an angle on this."

"Right," he said. And a second later, "What?"

"You know, do you want to go into the whole…thing… about what happened with Melanie? Go for, like, the sympathy vote to get people here?"

He was expressionless.

She was glad. "Because if I might make a suggestion…?"

He nodded.

"Let's just rewrite history now. This is the first press you've done?"

"Yep."

"Good. Pull down what's on the website and write your own story, right now. New start." She sensed this was going to take more work than anticipated and settled in for the long haul. As she spoke, she wound her hair into a bun and secured it with her pen, then nestled back into the booth. "Edit her out. Tell me why you, Parker—just Parker, not Parker of 'Parker and Melanie'—wanted to start this place. Why does DC need another bar?"

He nodded as she spoke, looked into her eyes as though for hope, like he was getting revved up to play a game his team wasn't expected to win, but he would sure try to beat the odds.

Parker took a deep breath and said, "This town needs a

place for people to remember we're all in this together, to make this country a better place. Right? Gotta remember the core values that got us all here." He pointed to the graffiti on the walls, and Cady eyed Max, signaling to start taping again. "Get back to the time when folks who might not have entirely agreed, could still throw down some drinks and hammer out some deals. Congress is broken, right? Let's fix it one drink at a time."

Half an hour later, Cady had everything she needed, but she inadvertently kept Parker talking just because it was so easy. He leaned back in the booth like it was just the two of them, answered her questions with stories, a dream interview subject. He squinted when he was telling a good story or when he was listening, as though trying to figure it all out right then and there, unrehearsed. Her original instinct *had* been right.

"Growing up in Wilmette, Illinois, I was always that kid setting up lemonade stands, like way past the point of it being cool, my friends were practically driving over when I finally stopped." He laughed at himself. "I just liked providing a service, something folks needed, being useful. And then in high school, I started interning for my local congressman. So this was in a way born out of all that work experience."

"That's perfect. And I think we're actually all—" She was about to wrap up when she realized. "There's just one thing. So you've taken a big gamble on this. Was it hard to leave the Hill? You said you loved it there, working for Senator Welling."

"I'm an all-or-nothing kind of guy. I like to devote myself to one thing and do it really well. I loved working on the Hill. There are days I wish I hadn't left. I still watch C-SPAN late at night when I can't sleep. Not because it's boring, but because it's comforting to me. That's the official answer. But, between you and me?"

"Sure." She nodded.

"I just needed a break. It's hard. It weighs on your soul when you feel like not enough is getting done. It's all-consuming work, and sometimes it feels like you're running in place, running really hard, like a marathon, in place. I was the intelligence committee guy, homeland security, weapons, those were my issues…"

"Heavy stuff, not the kind of thing you leave at the office at the end of the day," she said.

"Yeah, so…" He began to darken.

"Maybe if you had a place like this to go at the end of the day…"

"Exactly, see, you get it. Make sure to tell everyone, half-price drinks if you bring someone with you from a different political party."

"You just did. I guess you need an ID and voter registration to get in?"

"Now that's a great idea, can I steal that?" he asked seriously.

"Sure, my consulting services are free of charge. I think we're good here, thanks, Max." She turned around to wave. "And thank you."

"Yeah, sure, sorry for the…therapy session."

"Just put the check in the mail," she joked. "All we need now is some B-roll, you know, you walking down the street, arriving to work. Pouring drinks or something."

"I have an awesome idea, just got this thing," he said, smacking the table, excited, and disappeared into a back room. He returned with a hoverboard.

In no time they were set up outside the bar, dusk falling on the chilly evening, Massachusetts Avenue illuminated by car lights. Before he climbed aboard, Parker explained, off camera, that he had envisioned being that cool neighborhood business owner who rode to work on his new hoverboard. He had broken down and Amazoned one just hours after Melanie left. When the camera started rolling, he glided ten feet then the board shot a spark and bucked him off. He landed with a thump against the sidewalk pavement.

Cady gasped and ran over.

"Are you—?"

"I'm fine," he said from the ground in a growling tone that suggested otherwise.

She gave him her hand. A few pedestrians leaving work veered around them, with pained expressions. "In retrospect, that could've been a lot worse," she offered. "You could've, you know, totally gone up in flames."

"Hard to tell, but I was actually a kick-ass skateboarder back in the day," he said, massaging his elbow. He picked up the board. "Clearly this should be filed somewhere between 'cry for help' and 'early midlife crisis.'"

"Good to get that outta the way early." She laughed. "Maybe try that again, just walking in this time?"

"You have *got* to come, Rea! I am dying—*dying!*—of loneliness!" Jay pleaded into his phone.

"I don't think, medically speaking, you can actually die of loneliness." Reagan laughed, and in the background, Jay could hear the twins screaming joyfully. "Fuck. Guys, stop! Sorry," she said to Jay.

"I have some case studies from respected medical journals I can send you," Jay went on. He had attempted to keep every evening busy and bustling with dinners, plays, concerts, cocktails; he had never been so attentive to his wide circle of friends. Anything to keep from missing Sky in such a debilitating, annihilating way. So when he got Cady's email about finding the ring, it seemed a perfect way to pass the evening hours. "Come on, you know you could use a night out. I need a writer for this story, you need—" More screaming came from the other end. "I'll add babysitting expenses and cab fare into your fee. Or we can even meet at your place first." He wasn't above paying people to come out on a school night.

He knew it was self-serving. He could easily have assigned this to another writer, had it done over the phone, but he selfishly wanted to talk to Reagan about Sky, *again*, and have her set his mind at ease. Again.

"I'm in." Reagan laughed. "You had me at babysitting expenses."

Cady, Reagan and Jay, had already commandeered a leather booth at 2 Birds 1 Stone, the tucked-away basement bar in Logan Circle, when Jackson breezed in, five minutes late. It had taken so much convincing to get Jackson to agree to this, so Cady had been anxious. But as he greeted Cady with a kiss and them with a wide smile and warm handshakes, all her nerves fell away.

It didn't hurt that Reagan introduced herself with, "I'm Reagan and you're fantastic. Stellar job on the bling."

"Stellar," Jay repeated sincerely. He had grabbed Cady's hand the moment he saw her, before even saying hello, to inspect it. "Check that out, power of the press, baby!" Then he'd added wistfully, "Awww, it's really pretty."

Cady noticed Jackson instantly ease up. "Thanks, relieved to have it back," he said to Reagan. "You're the one with the twins." He snapped his fingers, as though putting it all together.

"That's me. And I'm equally grateful you've got your ring, it means this one—" she nodded to Jay "—is subsidizing a rare night out for me to update your story."

"Oh my God, I'm terrible, how are you feeling?" Cady

asked now. She had been honored to be among the first Reagan had told about her pregnancy.

"Fine, fine," she said, not completely selling it.

Cady gave her a questioning look, but Reagan only repeated herself, slightly more convincing this time.

"Congratulations," Jackson said. "I can't even imagine three kids."

Cady shot him a look.

"I mean, right now, you know."

"No, I know, believe me." Reagan laughed. "Your fiancée, here, is my hero, by the way." She nodded toward Cady.

"Yeah, she can be pretty heroic." He grinned.

"Seriously, how many girls would say yes without a ring? *Hello*," Jay joked. "So let's hear it all. Go, go, go!"

Nestled in their cozy booth, Cady recounted the story of the ring's return, amping up the drama as best she could. Jackson sat back, arm around her, polishing off two beers and offering only little nuggets. "Nope, no idea who the guy was"; "Yep, it was in perfect condition."

At the end of the evening, before hopping in her cab, Reagan—who had only had to excuse herself to throw up once all night—pulled Cady by the arm, whispering, "Love him, he's supercute!"

Cady was glad for the positive review. Jackson had actually been a bit quiet as the night wore on, and she felt like she'd done all the talking.

As they walked home in the chilly air, they held hands, and when they reached the apartment, Cady threw her arms around him. "Thank you, they love you. And so do I. And this thing ain't so bad either," she said, holding out her hand, admiring the diamond again. She could get used to the ring, she'd decided.

"You're welcome. And you're welcome," he said, kissing her twice.

Reagan's story posted the very next morning and reached No. 2 on *The Queue*.

"Someone is certainly getting grumpy in his old age," Birdie cooed into the phone, sounding perfectly upbeat though quietly seething. This was no way to start the day. She hung her head over the back of her desk chair. She had at least worked out a time-share with Buck, allowing her to use her beloved home office from nine to five while he was over at Georgetown.

"You know me, Birdie, I always like to keep everyone guessing." Bronson laughed on the other end. "Arnold needs to bring in young voters. Let's have the kind of party they would like."

"Well, that would be a cheap party. Maybe you'd like to lower the threshold for getting in the door?" She was kidding; it was a fund-raiser for God's sake.

"We're getting there. I like that! Done," he said. "Now pick a place to match. The fat wallets will still come. Talk tomorrow."

She threw her phone across the room, instantly regretting it. She missed landlines sometimes; it was so much more satisfying to slam a handset into its cradle.

She was beginning to feel like she'd lost her touch. Was Bronson just being prickly, as perhaps he always could be (and she was just usually not on the receiving end of it), or was it *her*? Buck leaving had set her off balance. She didn't like this cold war that had settled between them, but she particularly didn't appreciate that he had been the one to initiate it. It made her furious. This was a busy time for her, an exciting time for her business, and she didn't have the time to be consumed with any personal drama.

She had been the one originally wronged; it wasn't fair that the power balance had shifted this way. Though she could monitor his comings and goings and could easily declare a truce, all she wanted was for him to be bothered by this new arrangement. Really, all she wanted was to be *missed* and *needed* and *wanted*.

She turned the volume back up on the TV and flipped through the channels to clear her head. She passed the local news network and paused, recognizing the voice: that woman who had interviewed her, Cady. She'd always admired the crisp, clear tones of those who worked in broadcasting. When she was just starting out, Birdie herself had hired a speech therapist to mimic this intonation before deciding that there was something disarming about her drawl.

As the camera panned a dive bar, zooming in on quotations from the Declaration of Independence, a photo of Mount Rushmore with the presidents donning Ray-Ban Wayfarers, Birdie pulled up an old email and found the phone number. "Cady, love, it's Birdie Brandywine…" As she spoke, Birdie kept one eye on the TV and another on her laptop, conducting a quick search and finding a new, freshly posted story on *The Queue* of Cady with her fiancé. "Hi! So I'm watching you, as we speak, and I have a question for you…"

12

SUPER TUESDAY SHIII-SHUFFLE

★

Dallas evenings could be surprisingly chilly, even in March, so no one would bat an eye at Madison's trench coat. She remembered this from that year she spent as a Dallas Cowboys Cheerleader after college (graduated a year early from Alabama, Crimson Tide pride!) and before Miss Fifty States, back when they were at that stadium with the big hole in the middle of the roof, like a donut. She would've been a lifer there, on the team until they pried the pompoms from her old, arthritic hands, if not for the pageant. The Cowboys games had been a thrill though, those performances with the music blaring, the crowd roaring, her hot-rollered hair whipping as she clomped in white boots.

There was no way the football players worked half as hard as those girls: they never had time to sit on the sidelines, they didn't *rest* during *halftime*. She and the girls were Ginger Rogers in heels and hot pants, doing everything better and backward, wasn't that the line? She couldn't quite remember. But no, they didn't have time to slap each other's asses, congratulating each other after every good play; they were in *constant motion*. Like most women she knew growing up and the one she was raised by, and the woman she believed she actually was deep in her heart: in constant motion, doing a million different things at once, children, jobs, husbands, while the guys did one or two things and then talked about how great they were.

She tossed her boxy decoy dress, which she had worn all evening, onto the bed. Buttoned her suit jacket, smoothed out the fine wool and tied the scarf around her neck. She nodded at her reflection in the mirror. Applied a bit of fashion tape to her suit jacket, smoothing it against her chest.

In the lounge of their presidential suite at the Dallas Four Seasons, Madison could hear the celebration kicking into high gear thanks to some favorable Super Tuesday returns from Fox News. Men who barely knew what they were doing, let's be honest, and who had just gotten lucky at this whole thing, were slapping each other on the back, clapping, chanting, "Tex-as! Tex-as! Tex-as!" as though at a sporting event, clinking glasses, opening up more bottles from Hank's personal collection, which he'd actually seen fit to bring along. Texas now sat firmly in the victory column with Oklahoma, Virginia, Alabama and Arkansas. And those were just the ones the networks had already projected. There could be...*more*. If this winning kept up, their wine cellar would run dry.

None of this sat right with her. And not just because she had a sluggish foundation to fund. It didn't help that she was away with him all time instead of drumming up more humanitarians to donate. The Madison Goodfellow Foundation had been chugging along all these years as Hank made his billions, but she never asked him for a cent. He gave some money now and then, as he gave generously to many causes, a staggering number of them, really. In high school Hank used to say, "I want to make millions so then I can give tons of it away." It was what she had loved most about him. Until all this election nonsense began. He wasn't doing any good anymore. That's what angered her.

Someone rattled the doorknob and knocked. "Maddy? Mike told me to tell you, we're rolling out in five," Kimberly,

Mike's assistant and one of the very few women in the Hank Machine, called. "Think you'll be ready?"

"Absolutely!" she called out, perky as ever.

Madison slipped on her Burberry trench for the ride to AT&T Stadium, and kept it firmly fastened as Hank's Traveling Roadshow, as she referred to it, waited to take its place on the stage—at the center of the stadium. Then, seconds before climbing the steps, she peeled it off, tossing the coat at Kimberly, whose eyes seemed to bug at her plunging neckline. "Um, Maddy!" she said, but Madison just kept walking, pretending not to hear. She smoothed her suit jacket, tightened her scarf and patted herself to be sure everything was in place; no need to be fined by the FCC, after all. Fashion tape wasn't quite made for heavy suiting fabrics, but it seemed to be doing its job.

As Hank settled in at the podium, she stood beside him, waving wildly at the crowd—just enough motion to create the slightest concern that she might flash a national television audience.

She smiled warmly at Hank throughout his speech, ever the perfect wife.

HAZE CAPTURES THREE STATES IN SUPER TUESDAY SHOCKER

By Sky Vasquez, Staff Writer, *The Queue*

Rocky Haze took to the stage in Boston to declare victory in three states—Massachusetts, Vermont and Colorado—on Super Tuesday. Energized and secure, she made it clear to the crowd of hundreds assembled in Boston Common that she's not backing down anytime soon.

"To all the voters out there who cast their ballots for me,

thank you, from the bottom of my heart. You are bold and courageous to stand with me and say, we can do better for this country and we can do it together. As long as you keep having faith in me, I'll keep forging ahead," she told them. "And to those who didn't vote for me this time, I still love ya! I've got until November to show you what I can do for ya!"

Those inside the Haze camp, and the woman herself, say they always planned to use today as a barometer. "This means we can push on, there are enough people out there who feel we are speaking to them," Haze told *The Queue*.

Those outside Team Haze have taken notice too. "Three states for this kind of outlier candidate is significant," says a strategist for one of Haze's opponents, speaking under anonymity. "She can't be discounted as a total fluke."

Following her moving remarks, she was joined on stage by R&B-star husband, Alchemy, and daughter, Harmony, to debut a new rally song: "Onward, Together."

"We got ourselves a race, turned this game on its face

Shuttin' down the haters, standing strong in this place

We got plans and demands, making fans, shaking hands across this land

Gonna allay fears with fresh ideas, lend us your ears, hold your jeers

Onward together, peace, love, joy, cheer…"

"I'm beginning to think you don't need me anymore," Jay said, instantly regretting his choice of language. "You know what I mean." Maybe it was a Freudian slip; how obvious was it that he was just waiting to be left behind?

"Thanks, no, I know, I feel like maybe I'm getting my

groove now," Sky said. "Or at least, today. Tomorrow, who knows, right?"

"You're killing it, be proud," Jay said. He wanted so badly to say how much he missed Sky. How empty his apartment now felt. How dull the office had become. How he had been filling his endless nighttime hours making a Shutterfly photo album of the two of them like a teen with a secret crush. (It would be arriving in three days. He'd opted for rush delivery.) But Jay wanted Sky's mind clear of personal stresses, free to do the best work he could, to shine, so he kept it to himself.

"Nah, I've got a great editor," Sky said, as he always did when anyone complimented his writing.

"You wrote so fast tonight, you've got all this time on your hands now." Jay was fishing, of course.

"Yeah, it's perfect. Paz found a great honky-tonk bar out here, so we're going line dancing with a few others once they file their stories," he said, perky.

"Honky-tonk in Boston?" Jay felt out of step.

"I know, right? It's literally the only one here. It's kind of an inside joke, we didn't get to go when we were in Nashville," he went on. "So, you know, Paz found this place, she loves a challenge."

"Of course she does."

Several other news outlets had now stationed reporters on the trail with Haze, and Sky would talk about getting a drink with Kat or Johnny or Paz or Steve after the day's events. Jay vowed to become versed in these new names and vital stats, asking about them, laughing at the recaps of their hijinks, reading their stories too (which were never as good and never boasted such open access as Sky's, nor did these reporters get the TV hits Sky did). Some were music journalists, some were serious newshounds getting their first big break; all were young. Younger than Jay, who had never felt even remotely old until he had begun dating Sky.

Still, Sky would loyally call Jay each night after returning from whatever event or rally Rocky might have held, after cocktails, after getting off the tour bus, one of Rocky's own, outfitted with video games, stocked with snacks and treats and a traveling gym. Sometimes it would be quite late and Jay would already be asleep, but he would awaken and stay on the phone as Sky dozed off.

"Hope you packed your cowboy boots," Jay said, trying but failing to match Sky's tone.

"Always!" Sky laughed.

Birdie had surrounded herself on the sofa with files, her laptop and two cups of coffee, working as she watched the Super Tuesday coverage on CNN. This election was just getting weirder and weirder. Haze had an absurdly strong showing with three states and still a shot at a fourth. And Goodfellow had practically swept for his party. His competitors were a decidedly lackluster bunch, a couple of them managing to win their home states, but no one putting together enough victories to represent a serious threat. His wife, though, had truly stolen the show wearing a megawatt smile and a chic, slim gray suit nearly identical to her husband's, a scarf fashioned into a bow at her neck and with the same pattern and cornflower blue hue as his tie, and no blouse whatsoever. This Madison had some fire to her. Even if it was just about as un-FLOTUS a look as one could imagine, she had the figure to pull it off. Birdie wished she had thought of it first; the outfit would've been *perfect* for the Arnold fund-raiser, but now of course, she couldn't wear it.

Even so, the show that mattered more to Birdie was the one taking place outside her window. She had kept a quiet lookout all evening, peeking next door, and now at last Buck was arriving home, accompanied by three other men in their forties and fifties, laughing and talking spiritedly as though he was joining some kind of old-guy fraternity, and one woman, late thirties, pretty in that sexy librarian way (which some are into, sure, but not Buck, to her knowledge). *Ugh, already a groupie*, Birdie thought to herself. She imagined these were probably fellow university pals. They'd likely had a grand old time watching the returns at one of the bars on M Street and all insisted on walking Buck home even if it was out of their way, because they knew they were lucky to get that kind of time with him, hoped maybe they could make him their queen bee.

He looked up now as though sensing her thoughts, and she flung the curtain shut again. She didn't have time for any more distractions. Back to work.

Back in their Dallas hotel suite as Hank celebrated—with his circle of advisers, a glass of his favorite twenty-year-old Pappy Van Winkle bourbon and a cigar—Kimberly materialized. Mike, still meeting with reporters in another room, hardly ever entrusted Kimberly with any assignments besides rounding up Starbucks orders, so Madison took great pleasure in knowing her ensemble must have at least succeeded in making Mike, personally, uncomfortable tonight. Her own quick scan of the major news outlets had found mentions in passing of her "questionable attire," "suit better suited for an awards show red carpet," and "costume of a kinder, gentler Hank Goodfellow," while another accused her of "nearly upstaging the main event."

"I was just looking for you! Great news. Mike says there's room in the budget for a stylist," Kimberly said with forced enthusiasm, probably recognizing this was a suicide mission.

"We've got it narrowed down to two. Can I photograph your closet to send to our top recruits and see what—"

"Oh, how thoughtful!" Madison said, smiling, as she took out her chandelier earrings. "But I wouldn't dream of taking money from the campaign just to put clothes on my back. But tell him thank you!" She managed to sound perfectly cheery and hospitable as she closed the door on Kimberly.

Two hours later, Madison would be shocked to discover that *Vogue*—in a post entitled, "Reconsidered: How Madison Goodfellow Turned Our Heads"—had "endorsed" her for first lady based entirely on her ensemble (but with the caveat that they did *not* support her husband).

"Say hi to Daddy!" Reagan instructed the girls, fumbling as she put the phone on speaker. They had awakened way too early the morning after Super Tuesday, and though it was just 6:00 a.m., they were already dressed and breakfasting. It had to be bad if Ted was actually calling *her*.

"How are you doing?" she asked gently but with hope, as you might someone after a root canal.

"It's a mess here, Rea. A total shitshow. A Super Tuesday Shi—"

"Wait, you're still on speaker—"

"Shitshow!" Natasha blurted out.

"No, no, no sweetie! Super Tuesday Shhh…uffle! Super Tuesday Sassafras!"

"Shitshow!" Daisy smiled sweetly.

13

WHAT ARE YOU SO WORRIED ABOUT?

★

Cady arrived early at Momofuku Milk Bar, located among a glittering enclave of posh stores downtown: Louis Vuitton, Hermes, Zadig & Voltaire. It was nearly April, but the air still held that deep chill of winter and a perpetual gray hung in the sky, threatening snow. She ordered a latte and found a seat in the front window, placing her two pink gift bags on the counter. Jackson had gotten home late the night before, without warning, only to inform her that he'd be working all weekend to catch up: Arizona, Utah, New York, Connecticut, she had lost track of where he'd been and where he'd be going next. To Cady all that just translated to another weekend on her own, so she had texted Reagan to take her up on her offer.

Nothing wrong with a day off, Cady told herself, not totally believing it. Like Jackson, she had been working every weekend too, covering events, restaurant openings, concerts, plays, boutique openings (like the one in Georgetown by the local designer who made Madison Goodfellow's killer suit from Super Tuesday), the kinds of assignments newbie reporters might handle, but she had time on her hands and with Jackson away so much, she was glad to keep busy. Besides, she enjoyed getting to know the city this way. She pulled out her phone now and scrolled through the sea of rejection that was her email; she had been tasked with securing potential tablemates for the White House Correspondents' Dinner to no avail.

"You're aiming too high," Jeff kept telling her. "We need to fill seats, just get somebody, anybody, who is famous enough that it won't be embarrassing to us."

Their parent company had bought a pair of tables and offered a few seats to the show, provided she and Jeff could come up with a name bold enough. Otherwise their bosses would just bring more advertisers. Cady had reached out to every presidential candidate and FLOTUS-hopeful, stars with upcoming movies, stars with DC-centric shows. She wanted to deliver on this. As she waited for Reagan, she brainstormed some more, checking out the supporting players from a few moderately popular basic cable shows. But she quickly lost interest and switched to *The Queue*, where she found Sky Vasquez's story at the top: Haze had taken Idaho.

Farther down the rankings she found a story about restructuring within the Arnold campaign and skimmed for Reagan's husband. A handful of staffers had been canned, and it seemed he was getting a promotion to fill the new void. Someone knocked on the window, and she looked up to find Reagan with her double stroller, the twins munching away on matching Baggies of Cheerios. "Hey, come on in!" Cady said through the glass, then glanced around realizing they needed a table with more space.

"You shouldn't have—we should be buying stuffed animals for *you*," Reagan joked, setting a Compost Cookie on each of the girls' stroller trays as the twins bonked each other on the head with the matching plush puppies Cady had gifted them.

"No, I should've brought *three*! How are you feeling?" Cady asked.

"I'm fine, still puking but that'll end soon." She shrugged. "So, bon appetit." She set down a cookie and a fresh latte before Cady. "These are to die for. This is the girls' favorite place. Oh! Here, for Jackson." She handed over a bag filled with treats.

"Wow! Thanks! Though I may eat these myself before he gets home." Cady laughed, taking a bite.

"Is he still in Thompson's house office or has he been officially swallowed up into the campaign yet?" Reagan asked as Natasha threw pieces of her cookie on the floor.

"Not swallowed up yet," Cady said, a hint of trepidation. He was already working so much, if he officially joined the campaign she would surely never see him. She imagined he would be on the road all the time or might even be stationed full-time in an office in another state. But she was proud of him, so of course she wanted these things if he wanted them.

"*Yet* being the operative word, right?" Reagan laughed and Cady smiled the gritted teeth smile of Reagan's favorite and most-used emoji. "What are you worried about? It's all good! It's going to be good for him." Reagan picked up the piece of cookie from the floor and ate it. "Thompson's totally racking up the delegates. He's running a great race. Jackson is in the right place at the right time."

"Yeah, it could definitely be worse." Cady smiled again.

Daisy threw her cookie now and Reagan, chugging her coffee, caught it midair with one hand, nonchalant.

"I just didn't realize we'd actually see less of each other when I moved here. I feel like I'm maybe not part of his world enough."

"Well, you're always welcome to come museum-hopping with us on weekends Jackson's not around." Reagan was afraid she was being too aggressive; she didn't have many adults to hang out with. Most of her friends who were now moms were still working and seemed so much better at juggling everything that being around them made her feel inadequate, made her second-guess having left her job. And the other stay-at-home moms were all the make-your-own-organic-baby-food types that made her feel like she was sucking at mommying. Hence, no adult friends.

"That's right, how was Air and Space?"

"Ugh, my exercise for the day," Reagan said, cleaning up a sippy cup spill on Natasha's tray with the sleeve of her dove gray sweater. "They love to run in opposite directions, and that museum is always a clusterfuck. But amazing too! Have you been?" Something banged against the window. The twins shrieked, and the women turned to find Jay outside, agitated, holding up a color printout of what appeared to be a *New York Times* story. "Oh! Jay's having some kind of meltdown so I invited him too..." Reagan explained as Jay elbowed through the crowd that had amassed, holding the printouts up in the air.

"Ohmagod, have you seen this from tomorrow's *Times*?" he launched in.

"Um, hi, greetings from the future?" Reagan waved her phone and pulled out the chair beside her, setting out a cookie and cup of tea. "Nope, haven't seen it. You okay, there?"

"He sent it. Sky did. Front page. Styles section. Tomorrow. Gonna be." He placed it in front of Reagan, not speaking in complete sentences.

"Ohhkay, Yoda, say hello to Cady," she said, shaking her head and grabbing the printout.

"Hi!" Cady waved.

"Hi! Hey! Sorry! I'm all over the place today. But how fabulous was Rea's story, right?"

"Number 2 on *The Queue*, we're very honored," Cady said.

"Jay, this is awesome!" Reagan said, shaking the paper. A photo of Sky graced the lead story: The New Campaign Trail." He wore a vibrant paisley-patterned button-down, slim navy suit, turquoise tie, immaculate sneakers. Notebook and pen in hand, seated at a Haze press conference.

"He belongs to the world now," Jay said, sighing.

"I'm emailing him right now." Reagan began typing on her phone as Natasha contorted herself and arched her back, trying to escape the straps of her stroller. "And you know he's only there because you pushed for him to get to go." Daisy tugged at her straps and kicked her legs, whimpering.

"We would love to have him on the show next time he's in town," Cady said, reading along now.

"That Helena woman wanted to send her political people," Reagan explained, cleaning up the table. "He must be so grateful. And if I know Sky, I bet he is."

"Why are you always so good at this?" Jay said, taking out his phone. "Now I have to show you this."

As he thumbed through his phone, Reagan stood, shimmying on her coat. "I think they want me to get back to chauffeuring them around." She nodded to the girls. "Up for a walk?"

On their three-block walk to the Portrait Gallery ("I like it because the kids can run amok in the chic fountain in the indoor courtyard while I get the stink eye from snack bar patrons."), Jay shared his note from Sky: All this is because of you. Wish we were reading this together tomorrow morning over omelettes at Busboys and Poets. Love you. XX #TeamSkay.

"Skay! Like, Sky and Jay?! I have hashtag envy," Cady said as they found a table closest to the fountain, which trickled along the courtyard's stone floor.

"Seriously, you two are so frigging cute," Reagan said, unhooking the girls from their stroller seats. Her phone rattled in the cup holder, pinging a text. It was from Ted. "See, in contrast, these are the romantic texts I get." She flashed her phone at Jay as Natasha and Daisy ran off, holding hands. The screen read: Wyoming caucus may go to Thompson, too early but still, looking bad… Followed by the red angry emoji. Another loss for Arnold, Ted might be coming home soon, after all.

14

THIS? THIS IS NOTHING

★

The night of the Arnold fund-raiser arrived, and Birdie welcomed the all-encompassing distraction: she could get lost in so many details, logistics, so much to be done, so much to orchestrate, and forget about Buck and Cole and any of the current snags in her life's tapestry. Her feelings didn't matter; she had an event to host.

It had certainly taken a lot to get to this point. The planning process had sent Birdie running to her painkillers drawer *again*. For one thing, she'd had to circulate the invitations without the party location determined, which had *never* happened in all her years of event planning and fund-raising. She had simply typed "RSVP for the secret location," spinning her failure into something exciting and exotic. Bronson had shot down twenty-two places—and frankly, was beginning to piss her off—when finally, with just a week until the party, she'd pitched something so far outside the box it was almost laughable: the dive bar from Cady's *Best Day DC* segment. "Just what I was looking for," Bronson had shocked her. "The kind of place I used to go when I was a young staffer."

Unfortunately, Cole had been dispatched to tour it with her.

"I was wondering when I would get to see you again," Cole had greeted her with warm eyes as he hopped out of a cab.

She had been out front smoking a cigarette, a vile habit she had resurrected during this *hiatus*—she dared not call it a separation—from Buck. It was still the safest of her go-to vices.

As they'd roamed the space with the familiar-looking owner, Birdie caught Cole studying her, as though trying to gauge whether he had just imagined that spark that had kept her at his apartment until dawn the night of their first meeting, smoking from his secret weed stash and admiring his record collection like they were courting in the seventies. Since then, with the exception of dropping by her party, it had been strictly business-related emails. He had called, but she had not returned.

She hoped to avoid him tonight.

The red and blue klieg lights blazed out front now, the balloons jerking around in an oddly fierce April wind. She had hired scores of extra bartenders and servers, not leaving anything to chance. Inside the bar, the drinks flowed, the small plates streamed out from the kitchen, a photographer snapped for the society pages, the reporters circled, and the guest list of senators, congressmen, industry titans, lobbyists and even a celebrity or two seemed to be enjoying themselves. Young donors flowed in, so many that the room became too crowded, a line forming outside. They brought new life to the proceedings.

She kept one eye on Arnold at all times, to be sure he was happy, cared for, feeling like a king. But otherwise, this was the time in any event when she could breathe a sigh, shift into her version of autopilot and have a glass of champagne. Sure, there was still plenty to do to keep it running smoothly, but she always felt a slight easing when she saw the star of the show was pleased, the guests were joyous, the libations were flowing, the food plentiful. She had set the fete in motion and now it could nearly propel itself, like an aircraft at cruising altitude in clear skies. She loved her work.

Jay's phone pinged as he and Sky got dressed for a long-overdue night out: You sure you guys don't want to at least pop by? Don't make me play the pregnancy card #Rather-BeHomeInSweatpants #FriendsDontLetFriendsGoToBoring-Fund-raisersAlone, Reagan had texted.

Jay would've loved to join her, actually, but it wasn't up to him: I wish. Have ceded control of evening to oligarchy comprised of paz, kat and johnny or steve or johnny and steve. Who knows. I'm an eighth wheel #GottaKeepMyMan.

With Rocky campaigning in Maryland ahead of the primary, the Haze media pool was enjoying some time back home in DC, and Jay was determined to be his best self: easy, breezy, affable, the perfect totally supportive and unthreatened boyfriend. He realized this role would require acting chops he just might not have. The very idea of having to share Sky tonight made Jay downright sulky. He'd dreamed of ordering in from their favorite Thai place, talking all night, curling up in bed, silencing their phones until Sky had to be back on the trail in another two days.

Instead, they caught a cab to Sax nightclub, DC's answer to the Moulin Rouge with its burlesque performers set amid a luxe gold-and-burgundy palette. Paz, earthy-beautiful in that Coachella way, had reserved a table. ("She knows a friend of a friend of a friend to get us all in for free," Sky had informed Jay, making Jay feel even less cool than he already felt.) Their group soon ballooned to a dozen as they all got drunk on bottle service and danced into the wee hours.

Before the night's end, an overserved, self-medicating Jay lay on the velvet couch, head pleasantly spinning. "I love them all," he said. "You all, I love you all. Why are you so much fun? Why can't you all be dull and boring?"

"So you're really going to this?" Jackson asked, disappointed.

"I'm sorry, it's just one of those things, it's work," Cady said, pulling on her black Narciso Rodriguez cocktail dress.

Reagan had turned her on to the joys of renting party attire: *"It's what you do when you're on a Hill salary, or, you know, in any non-lobbyist job in this town,"* she'd informed Cady. No need to admit to Jackson that she thought it might be kind of fun to dress up and mill around a party with a presidential contender— who also happened to be the current vice president—and two hundred of his closest and most well-to-do friends. She'd never been to a fund-raiser before, and this one promised some star power. And a possible POTUS sighting.

"I just mean, I'm home tonight. I thought we could actually hang out," he said, flopping on the bed.

"I know, I would've loved that—zip me?" She turned around, and he sighed as he yanked the zipper, then returned to the bed, sulky.

"If you had told me even twenty-four hours ago, then I could've lined up a replacement," she explained. Though honestly it would've been tough. One of their three reporters had been laid off this week, concerning on many levels, though Jeff claimed there was no reason to worry. "But this is where we are now. I have to cover it." She eyed herself in the full-length mirror, fluffed her hair. "I'll try to make it fast at least." She and Max had a good shorthand now; this probably wouldn't take long. But why should she have to rush anyway? She was more than a little irked that Jackson was dictating how she should do her work. Why couldn't he just sit back and let her do her job? She had a nagging feeling the answer was that he just didn't attach the same value and respect to her job as to his own.

"Whatever. I still don't get—what do you like to call it? The 'news value'—" he said it like "news" was the nasty kind of four-letter word "—in going to someone else's fund-raiser. I'm kind of offended, you know?"

"Look, when you invite *Best Day DC* to cover one of Carter

Thompson's, I'll be there too," she said, buckling her strappy black stilettos. Birdie had said she envisioned making this event the talk of the town and had therefore lined up plenty of press, but promised Cady the exclusive on video. (Probably because she believed no one watched the show, so it wouldn't irritate her guests. But Cady didn't mind; she would take what she could get.) Jeff had humored her. *"Cady, you're hearing me but not hearing me,"* he said whenever she snuck in anything campaign-related to their broadcast. But she liked the idea of incorporating some of the primary season razzle-dazzle, and she didn't think she was the only one excited by it. Their viewership had already begun to see the slightest uptick. Why shouldn't their show get to cover these things and have a little fun? It seemed absurd to outsource it all to the networks, no matter what some focus group said.

"That's not fair," he said, sounding hurt. "I think you're... betraying me. It's like you're sleeping with the enemy or something."

He almost, *almost* seemed vulnerable and because of that, she bit her tongue, took a deep breath. She thought he was being awfully dramatic, but was she possibly being insensitive? She started to feel guilty now. "It's just a work assignment," she said finally. "Be back before the Caps win, okay?" She spritzed her perfume—Birdie had gifted her a bottle of Chanel N° 5—and kissed him goodbye.

When Cady arrived, the party was already in full swing, music thumping, red, white and blue lights dancing. The dive had been transformed into a club. She spotted Max roaming, capturing the revelry, and Reagan stationed at the center of it beside Ted—who she recognized from the photos on the walls of their home. Beside them, Vice President Arnold himself. Reagan was always so ho-hum when talking about him that it was easy to forget he was the second-most-powerful guy in this town. Six feet tall, mild-mannered, the lean, gray-haired sixty-something had been dubbed a "silver fox" in *People* magazine's Sexiest People issue, in the early days of the administration. Now he seemed a little battered by the years and the campaign, some of the sparkle gone. This might have been why Carter Thompson, fourteen years his junior, had taken up the mantle as the sexy young upstart, sucking up all the sexy young votes.

Reagan nodded in Cady's direction now, bobbing her head at the talk, talk, talking she was being subjected to, as though she had heard it before many times. When Arnold got pulled away, she beelined for Cady.

"You look so pretty," Cady said, adding in a whisper, "and I still can't tell…"

"Neither can he," she said, eyes on Ted. "I'm telling him this weekend. He's home for a few days." Then, in her best soap-opera-bad-acting voice, "I can't live a lie anymore! Kidding. Want a sound bite with Arnold?"

In no time, Reagan whisked Cady and Max over, made introductions, and delivered this from the man of the hour:

"You know what is the greatest joy?" Arnold said, looking around the room, then in Cady's eyes, sincerely. "Mixing old friends with so many young supporters here tonight. You don't often see that at these kinds of events. It was important to me to lower the threshold to allow this new guard in the door," he said, grinning. "I treasure the support of all our voters."

After that coup, they needed only one last sweep with the camera to be sure they had footage of the major stars, and then they'd be all set.

Across the way, Cady spotted Parker in dark jeans and a gray Henley beneath a tuxedo jacket. When he raised his arm to wave, she saw his sleeve was rolled up and a red cast with blue stars encased his right arm. He must've noticed her confusion; he shook his head and smiled, looking embarrassed.

While Max finished up, Reagan provided her own off camera running commentary on the party attendees. "Don't get that one talking," she whispered, pointing to a woman in a pantsuit. "It's like listening to a C-SPAN call-in show. She's a Hill lifer, a superwonk—which I totally respect—I'm just, frankly, not up on all the minutiae of the bills going through Congress at the moment and not in the mood to smile and nod." Reagan paused to drink her club soda. "This hottie over here with the rest of the press—" she gestured toward a leggy blonde in a black cut-out sheath sipping wine in a group of young suits and twentysomething ladies in knee-length cocktail dresses "—she's a gossip reporter for which one, *Capitol Report*? I think some of those are *Politico, Axios,* some are *The Hill,* a *Postie* or two, *Roll Call...*"

Cady felt a tap on her shoulder and turned around to find Parker standing behind her.

"Hey! Pretty good bash," he said.

"Ohmagod, what—?" On reflex she took his arm, cradling it like a baby bird.

"This? This is nothing." He laughed. "Yeah, a broken heart *and* a broken arm in the same week. What are the odds?"

"That sounds like a pretty lousy week," Reagan said.

"You remember Reagan," Cady reintroduced her.

"Oh, hey! My sliders made you sick at Birdie Brandywine's house."

"Actually, you're off the hook. Wasn't you, it was my husband's fault."

"Oh?" he said. "Well, I changed the recipe anyway. They were too spicy."

"Maybe a little." Cady laughed.

One of Arnold's beleaguered body men appeared, summoning Reagan back to one of the VIP rooms, just as the music cranked up even louder.

"So what happened here?" Cady had to lean more closely into him to be heard now. "Kitchen injury?"

"Yeeeeahhh, no." He ruffled his hair with his good hand, looking away before turning back to her. "Actually, I had a little hoverboard mishap. You were right, those things *are* dangerous."

"Who knew?" She feigned surprise.

"Who knew?" he repeated.

"Consumer Products Safety Commission?"

"Consumer Products Safety Commission, yes. This guy—" he gestured to himself "—no."

She laughed and threw her hands up.

"I kinda blame you, though." He smiled, leaning closer. "If you must know."

She tucked her hair behind her ear to hear above the pulse of the music. "Me? What did I do?" Her phone buzzed in her clutch, and she peeked at a text from Jackson: when U coming home? He sounded like a caveman. She hoped he was kidding.

"This was on your watch. After the interview?"

She thought of him completely wiping out that day and began to laugh, then put her hands over her mouth.

"Yeah, yeah, yeah, go ahead, kick a guy when he's down."

"I'm sorry!" She patted his arm, still trying to stifle her giggles.

"Yup, went to the emergency room as soon as you left. Made sure you and the camera dude were already back in the truck and driving away, at least. But, yeah."

"This is a totally inappropriate response, but for some reason, I can't help it." She abruptly stopped laughing. "Wait, are you gonna sue us? Because the show isn't doing so great, we probably don't have the cash to pay you…"

"I'll let it go this time. The free press was kind of helpful." He looked around the packed room.

"Well, you're welcome, then," she said. "But this is kind of embarrassing." She gestured to the cast. "No one has signed this?"

"Are people still supposed to do that when you're older than the age of ten?"

"Absolutely." She pulled a felt-tip pen from her bag, good enough, and then started scribbling. Her phone buzzed again.

"Injuries aside, I do owe you. Have you noticed there are some super important people here, besides ourselves, of course," Parker went on.

"Of course," Cady said. Her phone buzzed again, another text. She finished writing. "There you go."

"This is great, now there isn't even room for anyone else to write." He read her message and laughed out loud. "'The things some people will do to get on TV! Just kidding. And sorry!!—Cady & your pals at *Best Day DC*.'"

"Glad to help," she said. "And that's an old-fashioned emoji. It's called a sketch." She pointed out the small TV she'd drawn.

"Ohhh," he said, joking. "That is definitely old-school."

"Hey, you should get Arnold to sign." She wasn't serious.

"I met him!" he said, like a kid. "I wasn't very cool."

"Well, you look pretty calm."

"Nope, I'm pretty much never calm. It's a social anxiety disorder thing, self diagnosed. But I try. Fake it till you make it, right? Hey, isn't that a TV thing?"

"You're ready for your close-up now!" Her phone started ringing, easy enough to silence, but she was annoyed and had to put an end to this. "Sorry, mind if I—?"

He put his hands up. "Go, I've gotta go play darts with

the VP," he joked. "Even with this—" he held up his hand
"—I'm pretty killer."

She nodded and picked up her phone as he slipped away.
"Still working. What's up?" she launched right in, just curt
enough, rolling her eyes.

"I've thought about it, and I don't want you at this fund-
raiser." Jackson slurred his words like he'd been drinking. "I
don't like the optics."

"Are you serious right now?"

"Yeah, I'm serious. You've gotta pick a side."

"I'm not writing any checks here. What's the big deal?
There are probably plenty of reasons to fight with me, but
honestly this one doesn't seem like such a big deal."

"I could go out too. There's a lot I could be doing, with
a lot of people. You're making a choice not to be here." His
words came out garbled.

"What? I can't even understand you." She stopped in her
tracks, then started pushing through the crowd toward the
door. "Why are you turning this into a thing? Have you been
drinking? Alone?"

Reagan had that feeling again. For some reason it flared
when she was wearing heels and a cocktail dress, as though
her body was allergic to anything not made out of Lycra and
intended for use at the gym. She instantly wished she had just
told Ted weeks ago.

From the corner of one of the private rooms, where Arnold
was shooting pool with George Clooney, she scoped an escape
route to avoid people she knew: too bad she knew *everyone*
here. It was a minefield. Ted was speaking with some of the
big money around the billiard table, and Reagan pulled out her
phone, pretending to read an important text before stepping
up and touching his arm with a bright smile. "I'm so sorry to

interrupt. Natasha has a fever so I'm going to have to sneak out for a moment, call our sitter." She nodded and pushed through the main room, packed wall-to-wall with people under thirty, finally making it outside and breathing in the cool night air.

Ted followed close behind. "You're not leaving are you? Can't Stacy just give her some Tylenol and then let us know when the temp goes down?"

"Um," She kept walking to the curb, bringing up her Uber app.

"I'd like you to be here to circulate. Arnold likes having you here. He likes a team effort, shows the campaign is about family values, blah blah, you know."

"Yeah, yeah, I got it, look, I'm sorry," she said, struggling. "I just don't feel so good."

"Can't you just hang in for, like, two more hours?"

"Honestly? No. I can't."

"One more hour? Just something. A little longer."

"I wish I—"

"This is a make or break night. We need you here. You've gotta understand that."

"I *do* understand that," she snapped, then reminded herself it wasn't his fault. He didn't know she had a baby on board.

"Then come on, help me here." His voice grew louder than it should have, his tone harsh.

A dozen young donors still in line to get in pretended not to watch them. She ordered her car.

"What's going on with you?"

"We can talk about it later," she said in a whisper, hoping he would lower his voice too. "Now's not the time. I've just gotta go, okay? See you at home."

"This is RIDICULOUS." He was angry now. "All I'm ASKING is to not have to explain to Arnold where you are when—"

He caught her arm before she could get away, and by then it was too late to stop it: she vomited, all over his shoes. A handful of the guests in line noticed and then looked away.

"I'm pregnant," she said, depleted. "Yay."

"Are you kidding?"

"Yeah," she said flatly. "This is all an elaborate ruse designed to get me home early on one of the rare nights I'm out of the house after 5:00 p.m. and dressed like an adult."

A black SUV pulled up to the curb. She thought it was hers and walked over as fast as she could manage, but when the door opened, a woman floated out in a sparkling emerald dress beneath a luscious black coat. She breezed right by them, an air of importance and urgency, past the guests waiting in line, past the doorkeepers.

Ted froze. "What is Madison Goodfellow doing at an Arnold fund-raiser?" he said out loud, watching her disappear into Preamble.

But Reagan was already storming away into her own arriving sedan.

Enraged and unable to hear a damn thing over the music, Cady stomped toward the door, barking into the phone. "Why are you doing this *now*? Can't we fight about this later? I don't call *you* in the middle of Cedar Rapids to yell at you for being no help planning this engagement party we're supposed to be having in six weeks." Jackson's parents had set the date for June and put them in charge of finding a location, which she had yet to secure. It just kept falling to the bottom of her list below so much work—work that she actually preferred over party planning.

"Well, maybe that is more important than what you're doing." He threw down the gauntlet.

"Ohhhh, okay, right..." She tried to sound tough but felt

ill. They didn't usually fight, so when they did it cut deeply, unmooring her. "Look, I'm not appreciating—" she started. Not paying attention to where she was going, she ran up the steps to the building's front door and collided with a tall, sequined, late-arriving guest. Cady stumbled backward but caught her balance.

"I'm so sorry, all my fault," Madison Goodfellow said, beaming.

"No, no problem at all, my apologies, hi." Realizing her good fortune, Cady hung up on Jackson immediately.

15

YOU'RE MY KIND OF GIRL

★

So far the only good thing that had come of Hank running for president—besides Madison getting to meet so many truly nice people, who continued to send her cards and bring her flowers—was the condo Hank had bought at the Ritz. Tucked in a neighborhood called the West End, it was near Georgetown but quieter and had a lovely gym (with an instructor who taught her parkour, which she liked so much better than yoga or pilates) and a delicious restaurant on the ground floor that used to be their friend Eric Ripert's but was still quite good. Hank knew she loved it there, so she felt confident he wouldn't be suspicious when she said she'd be spending a long weekend there. "I just need a break from the campaigning. It doesn't come as naturally to me as it does to you." She knew the Machine would be glad not to have to babysit her during their visit to Pennsylvania.

Over the past few months, Birdie Brandywine had invited her to three bipartisan events but not this John Arnold fundraiser—obviously—which was why it made the most sense to Madison that *this* would actually be the one to attend. A switch had flipped in her after Super Tuesday, and she wondered what she might be able to get away with. She couldn't avoid hearing the campaign press and had the feeling that people liked her.

So she poured herself into her most vivacious dress—it had to be the sparkly green, always the green, if that one could talk, the stories it would tell!—and took a car to someplace on Capitol Hill that looked a little rough around the edges for such a function, but what did she know. Her goal: to be noticed. But if she met a donor or two, with the right open-mindedness, that could also be enormously useful to her.

She breezed in the door, red-lipped smile plastered on her face, ready to charm.

Cady launched into Cheerful Crisis Mode. She flagged down Abbie at the door—"Hey! Wanna grab Birdie?"—then made use of the seconds before Birdie's arrival.

"Cady Davenport. I'm a producer with the fastest-growing local show in DC," she said, figuring it could possibly be true. "We'd love to have you on, hear about your unique perspective on the campaign trail. I reached out to Mike—" She pulled out her business card.

"You know what," Madison cut her off. "I'll give you this back." She took the card and plucked a monogrammed gold pen from her tiny gold envelope purse. "This is my email address," she said, scribbling on the back of the card: *MissAlabamaForTheWin@madisonfoundation.com*. "My regular account was hacked." She shook her head.

Cady nodded, sensing there was a story there.

In seconds, Birdie appeared. "Darling! What a totally delightful surprise. And I do mean surprise!" Birdie looked as though she were trying to control the deer-in-the-headlights reflex sweeping her face. "Birdie Brandywine," she introduced herself. "Thrilled to meet at last."

The women shook hands, traded air-kisses, looked as though they might be sisters: same tall, lean figures, long legs, aura of glamour.

"Maddy Goodfellow," she said.

"I had no idea you were—"

"Hope you don't mind. I was in town with nothing to do."

"You do realize you're at a fund-raiser for Vice President Arnold," Birdie said through her smile, barely moving her lips.

Madison laughed. "Oh, yes, details, details."

Birdie seemed concerned, perplexed. "Did you pay the $20K entry, or are you merely crashing?"

"I'm on a fact-finding mission?" Madison said it as a question, as though she was unsure of the terminology.

"Sure, okay, what facts are you finding?" Birdie asked.

"On the record or off?" Madison laughed.

"I think you're my kind of girl!" Birdie threw her arm around Madison.

As Cady slunk away, Birdie gave her a look of appreciation. She had caught an enormous fish and graciously turned it over to someone more skilled at reeling it in.

After trying, unsuccessfully, to find Reagan and getting no answer on her cell, Cady yanked Parker away from a conversation with a group of young, hot female donors.

"I need to talk to you!" she blurted, grabbing his arm.

"Ow! Other arm, at least, okay?"

"Sorry!" She glanced at the group he had just left. "Ohhh! Really sorry. Rebound prospects?"

"Not anymore," he said.

"You'll thank me—look who's about to put your bar on the map?" she said into his ear, pointing so he could follow her line of vision.

"No fucking way," he said. "Shouldn't she be in like Pennsylvania or something right now?"

"Go! Talk to her!" she said, giving him a shove.

He started nodding uncontrollably, looking nervous.

"I'll send the photographer over," she said, with another shove. "Go! GO!"

★ ★ ★

Reagan was already in bed asleep by the time Ted got home.

He curled up beside her and placed his hand softly on her swollen belly, whispering, "Please tell me we're due after the election."

"November 19," she said groggily, appreciating the "we."

"Cutting it close, but when have we ever been early?"

Cole hung around even after everyone had left, offering to drive Birdie home. She gave him a kiss on the cheek and said it had been such a long night, they would have to catch up another time, and he was too polite to push. She'd considered going home with him—anyone would, he was young and beautiful—but tonight she would be returning alone, to her own house. Besides, she had too much else on her mind: she still hadn't fully processed what she had heard tonight. It wasn't often that someone could completely surprise her. She had thought she'd seen it all. But Madison Goodfellow, Birdie had sensed she had a spark, and she had been right.

Birdie hadn't been able to resist asking, feeling that she may not get another chance. She'd thought she'd read something in Madison's eyes, that it hadn't been a mistake that she had chosen this event of Birdie's to attend.

"Madison, I hope you won't find this rude, but I'm sincerely curious—do you want Hank to win the nomination? The election?" She had asked when they'd had relative privacy.

Birdie watched as a prism of possible responses filtered through Madison's eyes, and then she settled on one that seemed to be the truth. A smile blooming, a secret freed. "How did I know you would understand?"

Birdie nodded. "I think I can help."

By the time Cady hopped in a cab home, she was pretty pleased with herself. She had had a good night. After all the obligatory photos and enough time sequestered in one of the VIP rooms to meet with donors, Birdie had facilitated a quote from Madison.

"Madison Goodfellow, what brings you to an Arnold fundraiser tonight?" Cady asked as Max recorded.

"Well, I came to see a new friend—" she gestured to Birdie "—but didn't realize the purpose of the event. Oops." She smiled winningly. "But I'm so glad I'm here because I need to start learning all these Washington hot spots if we're going to be living here come January." She winked into the camera.

It was enough of a coup that Cady had managed to forget all about that awful conversation with Jackson. But it came rushing back now as the taxi wound its way past the White House, lit up and gleaming in the night. She couldn't gauge who was right and who was wrong on this, and wondered if she was just being terribly blockheaded. Had it really been a criminal offense to go to this event?

As she passed Lafayette Park and then the Hay-Adams Hotel, guilt smacked her in the face. Jackson had taken her there to celebrate her job offer in December. At her second interview, she had accepted on the spot, then called Jackson on her way out of the station's headquarters. By the time she'd made it back to the apartment, he had already planned their evening. A drink at Off The Record, the Hay-Adams's famous underground lounge with its sumptuous red décor, and then dinner at the hotel's pricey and indulgent restaurant, The Lafayette, with those stunning views of the White House.

After dinner—where they polished off a bottle of wine—they had snuck up to the hotel's private top-floor event space with access to the roof terrace, crashing a law firm's holiday party. It was crowded enough—and they were dressed well-enough—that they could slink around, holding hands, without anyone questioning whether they belonged there. They'd slipped out to that glorious rooftop, gazed upon the city that would now be not just his but *theirs*, and he had wrapped his arms around her in the brisk December air, nestling his face into her neck. As if it wasn't enough, while they were there, he had gotten a call that a room had become available. They had nothing with them, but stayed anyway, which made it all the more romantic and extravagant.

She had known then, of course, that every day wouldn't be that way. That wasn't real life, it was fantasy. But she had expected something…more, now that they were finally in the same city.

When Cady arrived home after midnight, she found Jackson asleep on the couch, a few empty beer bottles on the floor, TV still on.

Cady's interview with Madison ran the following day and scored hundreds of thousands of YouTube hits.

Parker sent her an email first thing the next morning, a link to a blog post on the *New York Times'* political portal. His subject line: "rebound material?" and the body of the message: Think this'll make Hank Goodfellow jealous? Seriously though, how awesome was last night?

The post entitled "Girl About Town" opened with a photo of a smiling Madison Goodfellow beside a slightly dazed-looking Parker. She was at her most glamorous, poised and posed, clearly reveling in the attention, while he seemed like he had inadvertently wandered into her shot. Cady had to laugh. It probably wouldn't spark any romance rumors.

PART II

CONVENTIONAL WISDOM

16

WE'RE IN FUCKING SIBERIA

★

The ballroom of the Washington Hilton, all abuzz on this warm evening in late April, seemed roughly the size of a football field, and Cady and Jeff were in the equivalent of the nosebleeds. They sat in a dark, dank corner, light-years from the dais where POTUS, FLOTUS and VPOTUS would sit.

"This is unacceptable," Cady said. When they had finally secured a guest, all Cady's doing ("I don't know how the hell you pulled this thing off, but if we ever have any money, I'll give you a raise and a better desk chair," Jeff had promised), it had been far too late to lobby for better placement in the ballroom. *How bad could it be?* they'd figured. But this was bad. Some sort of air-conditioning machinery could be heard buzzing directly overhead.

"We're in fucking Siberia," Jeff moaned. "We should've just gotten a suite and watched it on TV with her."

"Is it too late for that?" Cady joked, scanning the room, hundreds of black-tie-attired politicos and journalists milling about, shaking hands, gabbing spiritedly.

Jeff checked his phone. "Fuuuuck, they're here, waiting in the red carpet line."

Cady stood up on her chair in her stilettos and her off-the-shoulder (rented) Carolina Herrera gown, hand over her eyes as though seeking a ship on the horizon.

"I'm not crazy," she said. "That table upfront is still totally empty. There should at least be some activity this close to showtime, no?" It got her thinking.

"This sucks," Jeff said. "We can't even see the jumbotrons. It's like we're at the party but we're, like, serving the punch."

"Come! I have an idea!" Cady hopped down, grabbed the number "95" at the center of their table and set off to the front of the room. "There has *got* to be someone to bribe."

"All I know is Bloomberg is sitting there," a server named Angela told them.

Apparently, as Angela had heard it, there had been some sort of backup on Connecticut Avenue, and on top of that, the Kardashians had been running *epically* late. Everyone at the news network's table would be arriving en masse, if they ever got through the traffic. For a sum of $250, all the cash that Jeff and Cady had on them, Angela agreed to look the other way while Cady swapped the table numbers. Bloomberg's table "5" would now be located at the very back of the room. Not the most genius switch of all time, but worth a try.

Cady ran out to the red carpet to intercept their bosses and the advertisers, who were all traveling as a pack. At the center of their group was Madison, who shimmered in a gold chain-mail column dress, collecting all the light in the room, so many cameras trained on her, snapping away. When she saw Cady, she stopped midinterview with *Access Hollywood* to give her a hug.

"I'm so excited to be here, and this is the woman who was kind enough to bring me," she said, linking arms with Cady.

"And how did you get Madison Goodfellow to be your guest?" the interviewer asked as though Cady was a nerd who had managed to bring the quarterback to prom.

Cady laughed. She still didn't quite know the answer to that question. "Well, I guess, I just asked nicely."

"And where is your husband tonight, Mrs. Goodfellow?"

Cady was prepared to step in, but Madison simply piped up, with that killer smile, "Oh, well, he has very serious and important things to do, meeting with voters to help secure his nomination. He felt he would be too busy for a frivolous night like this."

Reagan, seated beside Ted at a table up front, typed furiously on her phone, adding a last minute tip from Cady—involving the Kardashians, of all people—and sending her updated speech to Arnold's communications team. Then she took a deep breath to settle the butterflies she felt. It had been a long time since she had heard anyone deliver one of her speeches, and Ted wasn't exactly helping to ease her nerves. "You're sure Goodfellow is on board with all this?" he asked Reagan for the millionth time.

"You're insulting me right now. I told you, Cady has it all set with her." Reagan sighed. Cady had said Madison was surprisingly overjoyed at being included in the speech, and fully down to take a ribbing, and that she had refused to let her husband's press secretary review the speech at any point. *"Oooh,"* Reagan had said then. *"That means this is going to be even better."*

The night had already gotten off to a somewhat inauspicious start from a social standpoint, though. She and Ted were guests of MSNBC (he appeared enough on the network to warrant the invitation), and she had been seated beside Buck Brandywine. Buck informed Reagan that Birdie was too busy overseeing the *Vanity Fair* afterparty at the French ambassador's residence, but when he grabbed his brandy she noticed his ring missing. She audibly gasped, then began coughing to cover. "Uhhhh, reflux, pregnant lady thing, sorry," she said.

Honestly, Reagan almost hadn't come at all. It had taken

two failed shopping attempts and an emergency visit, with both children in tow, to Georgetown to secure a dress for the night. Her belly had popped, no mistaking it now, and she had crossed the line from looking like she'd possibly just stolen too many chicken fingers off her daughters' high chairs to looking like a new baby was due any day. Her Badgley Mischka full-length empire gown had a bit more of a plunging neckline than she would've liked for an event with the commander in chief, but its full tulle skirt was so voluminous it might have been the only garment in existence capable of making her bump appear smaller. A winner for sure.

And she deserved to be there to watch Arnold read her words. This most coveted of speechwriting gigs had fallen into her lap just four days before the dinner. She had received a frantic text from Ted on the trail:

POTUS letting Arnold speak at nerd prom: HELP??????

She hadn't wanted to let on how excited she was, even to her husband. But she had a feeling that if she was being asked—and SO late in the game—then Team Arnold had been pretty dissatisfied with the jokes provided by whichever ghostwriters they'd already hired. Ted had called immediately after receiving her response.

"Thanks," he had launched in as soon as she picked up. "So Watkins was too soft—"

"And totally saved all the best material for POTUS," she had finished his thought, knowing her former competitor firm well.

"Exactly. Arnold wants 'edgy-ish.' Safe edgy. Edgy lite."

"No problem. I'll write it at My Gym this afternoon. The girls have back-to-back classes."

And so she had whipped up a few jokes and bits on her

phone while Natasha and Daisy flung themselves around on the equipment for an hour and twenty minutes. She was so unexpectedly exhilarated to have a speechwriting gig after so long that she didn't even notice when Natasha made a break for it, running out the gym's front door only to be scooped up by Stacy and carried back in over her shoulder.

But the White House communications team had been pleased with her work. And all the moreso by Cady's tip about Madison attending the festivities.

Now she just had to wait a little while longer.

Soon after a dinner that had made her nauseous (she couldn't bear any kind of meat with this pregnancy; her baby must be a vegan), Arnold took his place at the podium. His wife, Alex, seated beside him on the dais—the slender beauty, nearly sixty, former Treasury secretary and Reagan's favorite Georgetown professor—looked down at something in her lap just a moment, then set her eyes back on to her husband, her hands returning to the tabletop. As Arnold began with a few of Reagan's easy jokes, earning chuckles, Reagan's phone vibrated.

"ALEX" popped up on Reagan's screen: never seen him so excited for a speech. thank u. fingers crossed.

glad to help, fingers dutifully crossed, she typed back. It had been nice to feel needed, in a professional capacity, again. She just hoped she had done the job well. Her ears pricked up now, listening for the part of the speech she hoped everyone would be talking about afterward: "…And Madison Goodfellow is here tonight." Arnold, poised at the podium, paused for applause. "That's right, definitely Hank Goodfellow's better half. In fact, she's here *without* her husband, proving that even *she* is sick of seeing so much of that guy." Laughter swept the room. "Seriously, you all can stop covering him anytime now. Maybe Madison figured if all of you people were here, there'd be no one left to put Hank on every news network and in every paper." More laughter. "But, you know, my sources tell me that Madison's been making some news herself tonight, stirring things up. I even heard a turf war broke out over the Bloomberg table and can't help but notice that Madison Goodfellow is now just a few feet away while the Kardashians are somewhere at the back of the room. Who's keeping up with whom, now?" He paused again for laughter for the brand-new bit Reagan had written just before dinner. "Look, though, Madison, we'd all be happy to let you sit up here on the dais with us if you just promise that you and your husband *won't* be sitting up here next year, if you know what I mean."

The crowd roared.

Madison smiled and shrugged and said nonchalantly, in on the joke, "I'll take that deal!"

"Madison says okay! All right, come on up, Mrs. Goodfellow!" Arnold called out. "See, I keep my campaign promises!"

And in her dazzling Versace gown, to considerable applause, she hoisted her chair above her head, walked up the steps on the side of the stage and wedged her seat between Arnold and Alex.

Reagan spotted Cady looking over at her, and winked in return.

A calm began to replace Reagan's nerves. As she listened to the laughter in this room full of the most powerful people in media and government, she closed her eyes for a moment to take it all in. Yes. She *was* good at this. She could still do this; the muscle could still perform as it used to.

When she opened her eyes, she found Grant Foxhall gazing at her from the CNN table, directly in her sight line. One of those local celebrities you couldn't help but know if you worked in politics long enough. He raised a brow at her as if to say, "Your handiwork?" She shrugged demurely as though

replying, "Maybe. But you didn't hear it from me." Grant nodded in recognition of her good work. His hair had been darker
when they had first met on that atrocious date eons ago. The
surest sign she was getting older (an old 34) she now often
found men with salt-and-pepper hair attractive. She hoped
the lights were dim enough that he couldn't see her blush.

The *Vanity Fair* afterparty was a zoo of beautiful, exotic
beasts, its guest list a combination of Oscar nominees, Emmy
winners and Victoria's Secret runway-show models. Reagan
ducked into room after room, all of them grand with sparkling chandeliers and lavish furnishings, weaving through
the throngs of fabulous people. She had lost track of Ted early
on, and Cady and Madison had only had time for quick victory high fives as they'd passed by. She finally wandered into
the dimly lit Empire Salon, with its lush scarlet furniture,
and leaned against the window seat, eyes set outside where
the party had spilled onto the intricately landscaped grounds.

Her phone pinged, the answer to a text she'd sent Ted a long
twenty minutes earlier: Heading to Politico party, bra bldg—
the "Bra Building" was, of course, that charming nickname
for the Institute for Peace building down on Constitution
Avenue, which featured a curved overdesigned roof vaguely
resembling an undergarment—Arnold wanted to make the
rounds. couldn't find you, meet there? It might've been helpful if he'd texted a little sooner.

Then another ping right after, this one from ALEX: you
might have single-handedly resuscitated his campaign tonight
and to thank you, we left you behind? they're all idiots. so sorry,
thought you had gone home, which you should. rest. you're not
missing anything here.

gladly taking your advice! Reagan texted back, dreaming

of ditching her heels. She was firing up her Uber app when a familiar voice refocused her attention.

"Hey, how'd you get a Plus One to this thing?" Grant said, gesturing to her bump and greeting her with a kiss on the cheek, that TV smile, a hand on her bare bicep.

"I know people." She shrugged.

"Apparently." He stood beside her, shoulder against hers, and watched the room. "Word on the street is Arnold was even better than POTUS tonight." Even with the party swirling around them, he spoke in the hushed tone of someone relaying classified information. "You might be too good."

He smelled of cedar, some kind of expensive cologne. His jaw always looked so much more angular in person, in the way of soap opera actors.

"There are worse things to be," she said, looking into her glass and then back at the room. She glanced at him a moment; his eyes were the palest blue, seawater that allowed you to see straight through to the bottom. "So what other scoops do you have?"

"A confession—security caught me looking around upstairs."

"What were you looking for?"

"Come on, what's the point of being here if you don't look in all the rooms they're trying to keep you out of?"

"You news guys, always after a story." She shook her head.

"I have a story for you." He took a swig of his drink, something amber. "'Hero Speechwriter Ignites VP's Otherwise Sluggish Campaign With Scene-stealing Nerd Prom Remarks.'"

"A little overblown, likely some factual errors there, check your reporting," she said, wishing she could have a drink now.

"No place for modesty in this town," he chided lightly. Music poured out from a piano in a nearby room, soft and sentimental, probably being played by a Grammy winner, and the salon began to clear, everyone flowing out toward the impromptu performance. "Seriously, if you want to be on the show anytime in the next couple days, you've got an open invitation." He turned to look at her now.

"Thank you, though I wouldn't be a very good ghost then, would I?" She smiled.

"You are tough, aren't you?"

"I don't know about that," she said.

"I'd say so. I've been flirting with you for years," he said, so sincerely that she almost didn't recognize his voice. "Or maybe I'm not very good at it and you haven't noticed."

She hadn't, actually. She'd just thought this was how some of these broadcaster types seemed to talk to everyone, a kind of high-octane intense charm. Before she could say a word, he turned to leave.

"Always good to see you, Reagan," he said softly, then kissed her goodbye. This time though, he missed her cheek, his lips brushing against hers, landing there only a split second. It was all just rapid enough that, to anyone watching, it would look mostly friendly. Her glossed lips had remained perfectly still. But it didn't matter; she still felt a charge that shouldn't have been there.

17

I'M ON, LIKE, EVERY TEAM

★

STARS COME OUT FOR WHCD FESTIVITIES, ARNOLD, HAZE AND GOODFELLOW (THE MISSUS!) OUTSHINE PREZ

By Sky Vasquez, Staff Writer, *The Queue*

After a dinner full of surprises—Vice President Arnold delivering the night's best laughs? Madison Goodfellow, the ultimate good sport?—the French ambassador's posh residence played host to a slew of stars and a couple of presidential nominee-hopefuls. Rocky Haze sat out the dinner itself. "I'll go when I'm seated onstage," she quipped. But the musician did appear unannounced at the must-see after-party, the annual *Vanity Fair* soiree, capping the night at the piano performing seductive, stripped-down renditions of her rally anthems (which currently occupy the top three spots on iTunes' singles chart).

With just a month left in primary season, buzz is circulating that Vice President Arnold, enjoying a bump in the polls thanks to his Correspondents' Dinner speech, is considering some out-of-the-box running mates. The hope: to lock up the nomination before the convention by getting one of his key competitors to drop out and join his ticket.

"Rocky Haze has been approached by the Arnold campaign as a possible VP pick," a Haze insider told *The Queue*. Other possibilities include another opponent, Representative Carter Thompson...

Jay held Cady's thick card stock engagement party invitation in his hand. He had waited to RSVP in the hopes of having Sky go with him, but Sky had now returned to the trail, to Haze's private jet and fleet of tour buses, to his new friends in the press pool. At least Reagan would be there. He called her.

"Separation anxiety hotline," Reagan answered, horns honking in the background.

"Hilarious," he said flatly. "And also, help."

"I know, sweetie," she said. "*A latte please?* Sorry multitasking—poorly."

He opened the box, closed it, opened it again. The hinge had almost busted at this point. "So I keep *not* doing it. I was going to before he left or after Nerd Prom, all these times. I have this stupid ring—"

"You have it with you now? At work?"

"Maybe." He snapped it shut one last time, shoved it in his pocket.

"Jay," she said gently. "Maybe cool it with the proposing and just enjoy the time you have when you guys are together? At least until Haze is out of the running? Whenever that is. Did you manage to have any fun when Sky was home?"

"I don't know," he said, grumpy. He heard police sirens blare from Reagan's end.

"No no no no," she said. "They just got to sleep. No! Fucking motorcade!" she yelled into the phone as the sirens and revving motorcycle engines grew louder.

"Where are you?"

"Pennsylvania Ave, of course. Made the mistake of stopping for coffee after our walk around the sculpture garden. I thought, hey, look, they're napping, why don't I do something crazy like stop for a coffee and sit outside."

"You're going to Cady's, right?" he asked.

"Be my date?"

"Yes, please."

Cady couldn't help but notice that Madison Goodfellow once again arrived entirely alone, just as she had weeks earlier to the Arnold fund-raiser—either she was the most down-to-earth billionaire in the history of billionaires or she didn't enjoy her husband's handlers. It didn't matter to Cady, so long as she showed up on time to the studio and the segment went well.

Cady kept waiting to hear from Madison's people, expecting the inevitable list of topics that would be off-limits to bring up. It never came though and she sure wasn't about to ask for it. In fact, Madison had been so oddly low-maintenance, she never forwarded Cady to any assistant or press secretary at all; everything went directly through Madison herself at that email address she'd scrawled on the back of Cady's card. Cady didn't want to question it, worried it would all somehow fall apart.

The show's set designer, Francine, who also handled all the props, came into the control room, ponytail askew and eyes deadly serious. "You need to see something," she told Cady, leading the way to the kitchen set.

"Madison is still in the green room?" Cady asked. She had arrived hair-and-makeup-ready, a dream interview subject.

"I know you said Madison would be bringing the ingredients with her for the segment even though that is *highly* unorthodox."

"Right, but you know—what the talent wants, right?" Cady said, nervous.

"She gave us this." The woman opened up Madison's Louis Vuitton weekender bag to reveal a refrigerated pack of ready-to-bake Toll House chocolate chip cookie dough, a Wedgewood serving platter, a silk scarf, a basket and a Tupperware container filled with cookies.

"Made these this morning," Madison said now, appearing beside them with a cup of coffee in hand. She gave Cady a hug. "Sooo excited to be on, thanks a million for having me. So, I know how you have to have some already made to taste during the segment, so there ya go!"

Cady had read that Madison had been a cheerleader before Miss Fifty States, and now she could see it. This was a side that hadn't shown up on the campaign trail, at least publicly. "Ooookay," Cady said, smiling. "Fantastic. Francine, make these all pretty and we'll be ready."

Francine looked horrified.

"I'm so happy to be on and really show the Washington area how approachable and easygoing we are as a family!" Madison bubbled over.

She was due on in five minutes. "We're so thrilled to have you. Let's do it," Cady said, upbeat.

Gracie arrived, outfitted in her apron, shaking Madison's hand as Cady slipped away.

"Scrap the 'Home Cooking,'" she said as she burst into the control room, pointing to a graphic about to air. We're calling the segment, 'Kitchen Hacks with Madison Goodfellow.' Live in five."

"I make these all the time with my daughter, Gemma," Madison said to Gracie, the items from her bag artfully laid out on the butcher-block table, cameras rolling.

"There's a photo. She is just darling," Gracie said as a picture of the smiling girl wearing aviators on what appeared to be the Goodfellow yacht filled the screen.

"Yes, we love to make these and send them to her brother, Henry, at Andover." Another photo flashed, Henry playing lacrosse.

"Very handsome, looks just like his dad," Gracie said.

"These are the easiest cookies you'll ever make," Madison promised. "First, of course we wash our hands."

"Oh, alrighty, we're really starting at the very beginning of the process here," Gracie said.

Madison washed up, then held her hands in the air as though to keep them sterile. "I like to keep them up like this, pretend I'm scrubbing in to surgery," she said.

"Isn't that charming. Got it, doc." Gracie followed her lead.

"Cookies are serious business," Madison said and smiled. "People you love are depending on you. You don't want to fuck them up." Still peppy, "Can I say fuck on here?"

"Well, you just did, twice, in fact." Gracie smiled uncomfortably at the camera. "So, water under the bridge. But, for future reference—no, please."

Madison proceeded to talk her way through cutting open the package, pulling apart the ready-made dough, placing the dough on cookie sheets, consulting the packaging for baking times and then taking the cookies out of the oven. All completely unremarkable, and uproariously funny to the entire control room, reducing grown men to tears.

Jeff whispered to Cady, "Madison Goodfellow might be the best thing that ever happened to our show. You're a genius, Cady Davenport. 'Madison's Hacks' is a recurring segment starting now."

"I'll get on it, stat," Cady said, holding up her arms, just like Madison.

"Now, this is the best part," Madison was finishing up. "Arrange them on the most expensive china you have, or maybe wrap 'em in a Hermes scarf and throw 'em in a basket. You get the idea. No one will ever know they're not entirely home-made." She flipped her bodacious fiery mane and smiled into the camera, holding out the platter in one hand and the scarf-adorned basket in the other.

Cady couldn't help but smile in the control room. She had no idea why she had gotten so lucky, but she had stumbled into gold at that fund-raiser.

By the time Madison hopped into the black sedan and headed from the studio back to the apartment at the Ritz, she was thoroughly unsurprised to find five missed calls from Mike and this testy voice mail: "You have *got* to stop sneak-ing off like this, Madison. No more going rogue, please. Es-pecially before the convention. It's a very sensitive time. And we really could use—" She didn't even bother listening to the whole message. She had a feeling her leash would soon be shortened. She was going to have to start getting creative.

But as the car crawled along Roosevelt Bridge into DC, she discovered this encouraging note in her inbox: "The orga-nization is set up. Our intern registered with the FEC today, kept your name off it. I sense your donors are enjoying your antics, so keep it up, makes them feel they're getting an early return on investment."

That was all the hope she needed to go on.

Jackson was working late again and since Cady had an inter-view at the Folger Shakespeare Library, she figured she'd say hi on the way home. They barely saw each other these days, it seemed—he traveled weekly now with Carter—and when he *was* in town, he was locked away working till midnight on the Hill. Some nights, if she was shooting a story in the neighborhood, they would meet at Preamble for a drink or a bite and then she would walk Jackson back to the office. Now that spring had set in, brightening the evening sky and lifting spirits after a harsh winter, Preamble enjoyed constant crowds. The flood of early press certainly hadn't hurt.

Parker manned the bar, sliding drinks left and right, greeting his suit-clad patrons by name. He looked so perfectly at home, she couldn't help but smile at the sight. She was happy for him.

He glanced up and made eye contact, and before she knew it, he was calling out over the chatter and blaring TVs set to the Nationals game, "There she is, patron saint of Preamble!" He pointed and grinned. His arm had healed since she'd last seen him.

A group with loosened ties and rolled sleeves toasted in her direction, "To whoever you are!" She waved, suddenly shy.

He came around the bar to greet her. "Hi there."

"You don't have to do that every time I come in here," she said, laughing.

He grinned. "Jackson's in the back. What're ya drinking tonight?"

He had remained true to his word; she had yet to pay for a single drink on all her visits there. Parker even had named a couple of cocktails after her and Jackson: The Jackson and Coke, and The Sour Suffragette, which Cady had taken mild offense to.

"Um, if alliteration is the goal, there's always The Sassy Suffragette or The Sophisticated Suffragette?" Cady had gotten carried away.

"Kind of missing the point here," Parker had said. "It's basically a glorified whisky sour, get it? Hence the 'sour.'"

"Hence," she had repeated, unconvinced.

"Good luck, man," he had joked to Jackson, who was on his phone at the time. "You've got a lifetime of this."

Cady had smacked Parker on the arm.

Tonight Jackson's Thompson pals scattered with quiet hello-goodbyes when she arrived at the table, averting eye contact as though they were thirteen-year-old girls and had all *just* been talking about her. She felt a wave of paranoia wash over her and tried to ignore it.

"They didn't have to go," she said, though she wasn't disappointed to have them gone.

"Yeah, no, they're going back to the office, you know," Jackson said, thumbs typing, typing, typing on his phone.

"Everything okay? Long day, huh?" she asked, leaning across the booth to kiss him.

Jackson made no motion to get up but kissed her back, quickly. He had a nearly empty beer glass in front of him. After a final flurry of typing, he set down his phone and looked at her. "Sorry, hi. How was the interview?"

"Oh, totally fine, just ran late because, you know, parting is such sweet sorrow," she said, shimmying off her sweater.

He looked confused.

"Shakespeare Library? A little Shakespeare humor?"

"Oh! Right!"

"Never mind." She waved it off; they had more pressing matters to discuss: their engagement party was now two weeks away. "So! I heard from the DJ today confirming, which I was superimpressed by, because, you know, I always feel like DJs are just kind of fly-by-the-seat-of-their-pants or whatever, but he sounds on top of it."

"Right, got him a song list and everything," Jackson said. Securing the music had been one of his two party-planning tasks.

"So, we're set with that and I'm good with the florist, the venue, furniture rentals, linens. So then just—"

"Are you checking up on me?" he said, the slightest bristling, before she could ask.

"Nooo, who, me? What?" she said cheerily, looking innocent.

"I told you I'd do it and I'm doing it."

"So we're all set on Occasions then." She made sure to say it as a statement and not a question. Occasions was their caterer, which Jackson had reluctantly offered to handle, but she had yet to see any emails or contracts or menus from them.

"Yeah, it's fine."

"Cheers, then," she said as a waiter brought her Sour Suffragette and set down another beer for him. She took a hearty gulp.

"Or maybe Madison Goodfellow would like to cater," he said. "Saw your cooking clip, on the *New York Times*. That one blogger is all over you guys. But I guess I see it's kind of a big deal."

"That we're the only ones who've gotten an interview with Madison Goodfellow in months? Not that I'm pumping us up here or whatever, but, pump pump, you know?" She laughed, proud. What was good for her, for the show, was also good for him, and vice versa. Wasn't their relationship at its strongest when they were both succeeding? He seemed engrossed in the condensation on his beer glass, so she just continued talking. "Can you believe her? She's a total trip! I still don't totally know what to make of her at all, she is so *not* what I expected when—"

"Listen," he cut her off, surprising her. "Don't take this the wrong way," he began. "But I'm starting to feel like you're on the other team."

"What is the right way to take that?" she asked, laughing. "I mean, I'm in TV, I'm on, like, every team. Arnold and Carter and Arnold's wife and Carter's girlfriends—plural—all have open invitations to be on the show. No one has even returned so much as an email to *reject* our offers."

"We're very busy with real—" He caught himself, stopped.

"Ohhhh, okay," she said, hands up. "Got it."

"No, I just meant…"

"I know what you meant."

"Look—"

"I get that you don't think I'm doing anything all that special. But you know what? I actually like this show, and I like the people I've met and I'm grateful to them because they're a lot less self-righteous than you are these days." She tossed back the rest of her drink. "I'm kind of wondering if you're on *my* team." Didn't he want her to do well? Just as she always took pride in his accomplishments? But she was too unsure of the answer to ask the question.

"I've just got a lot to do."

"I know, I know, congratulations," she said, annoyed. "I'll see you at home."

As she expected, the clip of Madison and her cookies made it onto every late-night talk show. Cady watched alone, flipping back and forth between them as she texted with Reagan.

18

IT TAKES A VILLAGE TO THROW A FABULOUS ENGAGEMENT PARTY

★

Marriage, Cady had been told, was about compromise. So she agreed to *not* have their engagement party site tented. The month of May had been exceedingly warm and dry, apparently creating a false sense of security among *some* as their June date approached.

"My parents and I hate tents," Jackson said when she had brought it up. *"Hate."*

"Well, *I* hate rain and the forecast is very iffy," she argued. It was the deadline for reserving a tent, their party just two days away.

"My parents won't pay for it."

"I'll pay for it."

"I'm not going if there's a tent."

Birdie had helped her book the sprawling grounds outside the Smithsonian Castle but had been unable to secure the inside space too—it was June, after all, everyone was having parties, and it had already been booked—so Cady had secretly reserved a small tent for over the adjacent Moonstone Garden. The greater expanse of the party at the picturesque, impeccably manicured Haupt Garden would be left open to any and all elements. She would simply hope for the best. Lately, everything had become a battle and she didn't understand why, but it was too exhausting to keep fighting over.

No matter, Cady was in good spirits with her pre-party playlist blasting on repeat (much of it Rocky Haze since her music wouldn't be allowed at the party itself, as per Jackson's instructions for the DJ) when the glam squad arrived at Cady's apartment right on time, a gift Birdie had insisted upon. Cady had a feeling it all had to do with helping Birdie book Preamble for that Arnold fund-raiser, which had not only brought in millions but had gotten attention for attracting so many young, new voters.

At any rate, by six, Cady pulled up to the castle, hair and makeup perfect and cut-out black Halston cocktail dress looking as though it were made for her. (Birdie had vetoed her first choice: "Look like you're the star of this show for God's sake!") Her parents had flown in earlier in the day with her brother, Sam, sister-in-law, and six-year-old nephew, Zack, the ring-bearer-to-be, supposing they ever got around to setting a wedding date.

The castle's event planner met her as soon as she flung the car door open, and walked her through everything: the DJ setting up his turntables and iPod dock, lighting technicians lining the walkways and illuminating the garden, furniture rental team creating comfy clusters of white loungey sofas and chairs and dotting the space with sleek high-top tables, florist installing tropical blooms of vibrant pink and green along every surface, lit topiaries sparkling here and there. All of her vendors present and accounted for. All except for one. "We're just waiting on the caterer," the woman said, trying not to sound concerned.

Though it was a Saturday, Jackson had gone into the office, toting his suit in a garment bag, and planned to meet her at the garden at partytime.

Cady paced, heels clicking against the stone walkway, phoning him. Above, gray clouds hung heavy, ominous.

"Am I supposed to be there already?" he launched in as soon as he picked up.

"No, it starts at seven but—"

"Then what's—"

"I need to call the caterer. They're not here yet. I need your contact, do you have a—"

"Fuck."

Her stomach dropped. He didn't need to say another word. "Are you serious right now?"

"I never finished booking it. I started, but there was paperwork I meant to do and then call back and…" he admitted.

"Ohhhhmagod." Suddenly it felt very hot outside, so much hotter than she'd realized. She pushed through the castle doors, not caring that another event, thrown by people clearly much more organized than herself, was being set up. She took a breath. "Not to get all shrill-harpy about this, but we've got 150 people on the way and no food. No drinks. No food or drinks." She couldn't snuff the panic out of her voice.

"I've had a lot on my mind. What do you want me to do about this?" He stopped, sighed. "I didn't mean it like that, I meant, what can I do about this? There's a snack bar at the castle right?"

She looked over at it now. "They sell chips and ice cream, Jackson. This isn't, like, a kid's birthday party." She was trying to think. She could call Birdie; Birdie had all the answers. But her gut told her not to return to that well too many times. Plus, Birdie was coming as a guest tonight, and Cady wished so deeply to have the woman in her new friend circle, not be one of many who probably tried to use Birdie all the time.

"I can… I don't know…" Jackson said, unhelpful.

"Forget it, I'll figure it out. See you at seven." She hung up without saying goodbye, paced some more as she Googled and found the number she was looking for.

When the line picked up, it sounded busy and energetic in the background, the hum of a full house: music playing, glasses clinking, laughter and life, voices projecting to be heard.

"Wasn't it you who once told me Washington runs on fa-vors?" she said.

"Something like that."

"I think I need to cash in."

By 7:15 p.m., music pulsed in the garden, lights glowed, friends and family stood chatting in that controlled business-like way that people do when they haven't yet had a drink and are anxious to avail themselves of the open bar they've been promised. Still, they greeted each other with hugs, told Cady how gorgeous she looked, asked for Jackson. Jeff and her friends from the show arrived together, then came some of Jackson's officemates (apparently not working that day), then her old friends from home.

It had already been the longest fifteen minutes of her life when Zack, who loved trucks of all kinds, raced toward her. "I got to honk the horn!" he yelled, then proceeded to leap for joy into the fleur-de-lis-shaped hedges before being scooped up. He and Cady's brother had been dispensed to keep lookout.

In the distance, parked outside the ornate Renwick Gates on Independence Avenue, a beacon: a food truck reading "PRE-AMBLE The start of great things…"

Parker strolled along the lit path, saluted to her, and she set off to meet him halfway. The wind picked up, billowing her satin dress, and in one fluid motion she swept her hair away from her face. She didn't notice the darkening sky anymore.

"There's the bride!" he shouted as they neared each other.

She rolled her eyes. "I have never been so excited to see anyone in my life. I need a drink."

"You look really pretty," he blurted out.

"Thanks," she said, a little embarrassed, tucking her hair back behind her ears again.

"I mean, glad to be at your service, pal." He punched her shoulder like she was in his weekend kickball league.

"Ow." She laughed.

"I've got stuff to eat and a truck full of booze." He turned around, pointing to nearly a dozen Preamble-T-shirted staffers climbing out of the truck and two burly guys lifting boxes of bottles from a van behind it. "Your pop-up dive bar has arrived."

"It's like a clown car, this is awesome," she said, watching. "You're my hero. How'd you round up everyone last minute?"

"Easy, we took our show on the road."

"Hmm?"

"We closed for the night." He shrugged, arms folded like it was no big deal, and looked away.

"Oh, no. Oh. That's really...really nice. I promise we'll cover it, charge us whatever. You're saving my life."

"Like we discussed, I owe you," he said, matter-of-fact.

"I think we're more than even." She watched him a moment, touched by his kindness, distracted by the flecks of gold lighting his eyes.

"So let's get this party started," he said finally. "Where do you want me?"

"Right, sorry, anywhere," she said, surveying the grounds. "But maybe we can get those guys liquored up first." She pointed and leaned in to whisper, "Soon-to-be in-laws."

"On it." He grinned. "Now, go. Mingle. Greet your loyal subjects." He shoved her. "Go!"

"Thank you," she said, walking backward as he walked backward to his truck.

Go! he mouthed at her again.

She smiled and headed back to her guests.

Birdie arrived half an hour late, grabbed a tasty drink advertised as the signature cocktail by the underdressed catering staff (it tasted like a whisky sour), and made a lap. She had thawed the cold war just enough to call Buck and invite his voice-mailbox to the party. Technically speaking, his name was also on the invitation, so it was the right thing to do. He had declined, of course, also via voice mail.

It took her no time to size up that the groom-to-be was MIA. Leaning against a cocktail table in a prime spot nearest the grand castle, sipping her drink, she watched Cady navigate the crowd, making excuses with a smile, administering hugs and kisses. She looked fantastic, no doubt having accepted Birdie's staff and advice. Birdie caught Cady's eye as Cady politely wrapped up with a young couple and sashayed over in her strappy gold heels.

"You and your party are equally stunning." Birdie greeted her with an air-kiss.

"Many thanks to you," Cady said, bowing.

"Please, it takes a village to throw a fabulous engagement party," she said. "And now what's going on over here?" She pointed to the food truck in the distance.

"It's the hottest new thing in event catering?" Cady said it as a question.

"Old glamour—" she gestured to their garden surroundings "—meets new convenience? I like how you do things." Birdie nodded. "So, now where is—" she began, but a gaggle of girls descended, talking *at* Cady in high-pitched chirping squeals. She gave Birdie an apologetic look, as though embarrassed by the interruption, but Birdie waved her off. "We can talk later, you're in demand, love," she said.

"I don't want to talk about this," Reagan told Jay, scanning the crowded garden for a seat.

"Too bad, start talking." Jay grabbed a cocktail from one of the Preamble waiters. "So, Grant?"

"No, 'so, Grant,' we were just chatting. I don't care what Sophie said. I didn't even see her there."

"I'm appalled—"

"Jay—"

"No, appalled that you didn't tell me this when it *happened*."

"There is no *happened*. We were talking, that's it. This is already more discussion than it deserves," she said, putting hands on either side of her belly. "Earmuffs! La la la! I don't want baby hearing any of this."

"I mean who hits on a pregnant lady?"

"I know, right? And hey, I should be offended by that." She pointed at him, then focused her attention away toward the nearest sofa. "Ugh, I'm going to glare at those people until they take pity on me and let me sit there."

"But, then, you guys do have, like, *history*," Jay mused, clearly not finished with this subject.

"Please, it was one date a million years ago. A few dates. Next topic. Moving on."

"What was the problem again? He gave you a current events quiz?"

"Yes, and I mean, I passed, *obviously*, and actually I knew way more about Afghanistan than he did."

"Not surprised."

"But he was an egomaniac and completely obnoxious."

"Of course."

"Which is why he's become so successful in cable news."

"I forget, does Ted know about your little *history*?"

"Please stop with that word."

"Does he?"

"I mean, sure, I think he's sort of repressed knowledge of it at this point. It's a small town, it happens. It wasn't a big deal." Baby kicked, as though trying to tell her, *Shut up, Mom*, and she listened.

"Well, I'll say this. I'm not surprised because you're totally rocking your maternity style," he said. "So I get it, but still, you know."

"I know," she said, annoyed, her eyes zeroing in on a waitress across the garden. "Are those fries?"

"We'll find some. But seriously, I have to live vicariously through *someone's* flirtation. Sky has been away *forever.* I can't take it anymore."

"You just had a conjugal visit a couple weeks ago," she said, relieved at the shift in conversation.

"So, I was thinking of surprising him in California."

Reagan made a face.

"What? It's romantic!" Jay argued.

"He's gonna be working, I wouldn't do it. I did that once years ago when Ted and I were actually spontaneous, impulsive, exciting people. Do you *not* remember me calling you in tears when I showed up in Austin and he sent me home on the next flight?"

"Maybe. But that was different."

"It's not. But it's your funeral."

"Can you at least do the math—like, literally—and tell me how much longer until Rocky is out of this?"

She sighed. "I'm not up on all the latest tallies, but basically Rocky has to win Cali to be in contention for the nomination."

"That's what Sky says. So if she pulls it off..."

"That's, like, a super big *if...* Yes! Quick, come sit down!" They hustled over to the low-slung couch and plopped down, and she continued, "But then again no one's got the amount they need to just secure it outright, and it could be a contested convention. But that's extremely unlikely. Don't tell Ted, but Thompson will probably take California."

"My brain hurts."

"Bottom line—I think Sky's coming home."

"Is it bad that that makes me happy?"

"Aww, no, love." Birdie alighted on the sofa beside Jay, pecking him on the cheek.

"Birdie Brandywine!"

Jay always acted as though Birdie was the sun shining on him, Reagan couldn't help but notice.

"It's far worse to *not* want them home." Birdie laughed. "Am I right?" She leaned over and kissed Reagan's cheek. "You look divine, love. There are people here, not presently growing tiny humans, who don't look even half as good as you."

"Thank you?" Reagan said. "And you're gorgeous as ever."

"Have you seen our hosts yet?" Birdie asked.

"Cady, looks like she needs saving," Jay said, nodding in Cady's direction.

On the other side of the garden, Cady exerted considerable effort to appear interested in the group of girls surrounding her.

"And Jackson?" Birdie asked.

"We're just hoping he actually, you know, shows up to his engagement party," Jay explained.

"The super weird thing," Reagan said, pointing in the distance, "is that Thompson is here."

"NO!" Jay said.

Reagan gestured toward the grand Renwick Gates, where Carter Thompson strode in hand in hand with that bombshell national news anchor everyone was calling the next Diane Sawyer.

The beauty of being the guest of honor at a party of this size—or one-half of the guests of honor—was that you didn't have to spend too much time talking to anyone. You were expected to float and flutter through the masses, spending minutes of quality time, but zero quantity time. "Exuberant, engaged efficiency," Birdie had called her strategy for circulation, during their interview before her Iowa party.

For some reason Cady found herself needing an escape from her old friends. They had come all the way from Manhattan and Johnstown and Princeton and were so excited and sincerely happy for her. They asked all sorts of questions about the wedding, for which she had not a single answer because she hadn't done any planning. They asked about Jackson and didn't seem to understand why he wasn't there yet. She wished at least one of them could have bothered to ask her about work, which actually *had* been going well. But none even knew the name of her show. She feared they had somehow outgrown each other, fallen out of sync, now that they didn't share a city or workplace or timeline for personal milestones. So when Carter arrived and the party took collective notice, all eyes glancing in his direction like a wave sweeping through, she was grateful.

"Jackson's boss, I'd better say hi," she said, sneaking away at last.

At nearly nine o'clock, a suit-clad Jackson finally materialized, practically running from his cab to plant a kiss on the top of Cady's head: "Sorrysorrysorry." His eyes sparkled, in that way that told her it was going to be okay, that he had brought his best self to this party.

She had been talking with Birdie. "Ms. Brandywine, I have heard so much about you from Cady and am so glad to meet you at last," he said, reverential, shaking her hand with both of his.

Birdie had one eyebrow cocked, as though still reserving judgment.

He went on. "I understand we have you to thank for finding a home for our party tonight. I'm so grateful. Cady might have mentioned I haven't been the most helpful of grooms." He gave Cady a bashful, apologetic look that she couldn't *not* accept. "And I'm just lucky that she's far more on top of things than I am and that she's made such true, caring friends here."

"Anything for darling Cady," Birdie said, more warmly now.

Jackson took Cady's hand and they made the rounds together—greeting her family first with hugs and smiles, friends with handshake-hugs and compliments, kisses on the cheek and sweet inquiries about children. He was *on* tonight. And when he was on, everyone around him was powerless against it. This was what she had first fallen in love with, the Jackson that could sweep you up and make you feel like you were taking flight, touching the stars.

He pulled away only when he spotted Parker, replenishing supplies at the bar they'd set up.

"The man of the hour," Parker greeted him as they walked over.

"No, man, that would be you," Jackson said, shaking his hand and giving him a pat on the shoulder. "Owe you, thanks for this."

"Anytime, not a problem, glad to do it," Parker said, nodding as he returned to the food truck. "Enjoy the party!"

At a quarter after nine, they were cutting the cake, both hands together on the knife, when she felt the first cool drop fall from the sky onto her bare shoulder. She ignored it, too happily distracted by how well the evening had recovered from such a rocky start.

After, as Jackson stood encircled by practically his entire office, an exhausted Cady stacked pieces of cake onto a Preamble tray and scurried to the food truck. Parker and two of his staffers were inside, flipping sliders and frying sweet potato slivers.

She knocked on the side of the truck and he turned around.

"What have we here?" he said, adjusting his baseball cap.

"The least we can do is provide you with a sugar rush to thank you for tonight," she said, holding out the tray.

"We should be professional and politely decline since we're working and all, but forget it, hand 'em over," Parker said, smiling. He gave the guys their slices, keeping one for himself, and leaned out the window. "And I was just saying, I should thank *you* for getting me over this way. I don't get here often enough. I used to go to the Air and Space Museum, like, monthly when I was on the Hill."

"I still haven't been," she said, embarrassed.

"You gotta go, if nothing else then for the gift shop," he said, between bites. "My complicated relationship with Astronaut Ice Cream got me into the restaurant business."

She laughed. "Seriously?"

"It's pretty good, but I felt like it should taste a little better than that. I wanted to come up with something besides that chalky stuff."

"How's that going?" she teased.

Thunder sounded in the distance.

"Turns out, not well." He laughed. "But you know, the way the space program is, I suspended that project for the time being."

"It's NASA's loss."

"Thank you, appreciate that," he said. "Now go, your people need you," he ordered. "You've only got till ten."

She took a few steps back toward the party. "Thanks again. For everything tonight, Parker," she said, and the skies opened up, sheets of rain cascading, thunder roaring. She galloped off, yelping, turning back only a moment to shout, "Is this kind of the worst night ever?" Laughing as her hair, dress, skin, instantly became soaked and the sweet rain beat down harder.

When she and Jackson finally got home that night, having left their parents drenched at the Mayflower Hotel with hugs and the promise of *indoor* brunch plans the next day, they toweled off and changed out of their wet clothes. The rain, still not letting up, crashing against their windows.

"That tent was helpful," Jackson admitted as he crawled into bed.

Indeed, the partygoers had crowded under it, finishing their drinks and remaining moderately festive while waiting for cabs to arrive.

She hung their dripping clothes in the shower. "If I don't get charged for ruining this dress, it'll be a miracle," she said, mostly to herself. She pulled some loose change from his pants pockets along with a wet glob of pulpy business cards fused together. A Willa from the *Capitol Report* newspaper. A John from the Department of Energy.

"Hey, wait, what?" she heard him say as he appeared in the bathroom doorway holding an expertly wrapped box. She forgot she had tucked that into their bed.

"An engagement gift," she said.

His hand flew to his head, a modified face-palm, sheepish. "I left yours at the office."

She shrugged and urged him to open the box. "Go on."

It was a monogrammed flask.

"Because you've been working so hard," she added. "Keep it at work. It's like I'm buying you a drink even if I'm not there."

"Thanks, I love it," he said, kissing her. "I don't actually have anything—"

She stopped him. "You don't need to." And surprisingly, she meant it. Nothing could upset her tonight. The party had been salvaged; she reveled in the sweet relief of having pulled this off, of having averted disaster. And Jackson had been so unexpectedly "on," charming their guests and, most importantly, her new friends. Tonight it seemed they were a true team again.

19

LESS CALIFORNICATION, MORE CALIFORNIA DREAMING

★

HOME IS WHERE THE VOTES ARE? ROCKY HAZE RETURNS TO CALIFORNIA, KEEPING THE DREAM ALIVE

By Sky Vasquez, Staff Writer, *The Queue*

Alchemy, attired in yoga clothes, is finishing up a morning workout with daughter Harmony in their sprawling family home in Brentwood. Harmony sings along to the track, working on her impressive downward dog. Not everyone gets to do their morning sweat session to a Grammy winner's highly anticipated new album, but this toddler already knows the words to daddy's newest tunes. *Something to the Imagination*, the follow-up to the R&B star's *Magic*, Billboard's best-selling album of 2014 (Rocky Haze's *Hazy Shade of Summer* was No. 1 a year later), was due to drop this week, reviews had already begun to post online (among them raves from *Rolling Stone*, the *New York Times* and, yes, NPR) until he pulled it at the last minute.

"Listen," he says with a smile, feeding chunks of star fruit to Harmony in their bright and airy kitchen. "Our family is focused on Rocky right now. When *Magic* came out, she stopped everything for me, everything, to allow me to tour without being away. Because I didn't want to have to leave her and our baby. We personally work better when we devote ourselves to each other's dreams." He says it easily, as though it were all obvious. "I want to be able to give my whole self to my music and right now I need to be here, part of this dream, her dream. What's good for one of us is good for all of us." Their secret to familial bliss is simple: "We just juggle. Like any family in America. We juggle. Some days better than others." And when they do need to make those tough decisions? "We just play, 'Rocky Paper Scissors,'" he jokes.

He and Harmony put on their Sunday best and pile into the awaiting Escalade to join Rocky downtown. The candidate has spent weeks canvassing the Golden State, visiting inner cities, churches, homeless shelters, prisons, meeting with young and old, big potential donors (from Hollywood producers to record label honchos) and those who have nothing. "I want to paint myself a full picture of what's going on in every state in this great nation," she says. "I want to know firsthand what people need to make their lives better. And then I want to gather the greatest minds to work with me and make those lives better."

With the primary that will decide her fate just days away, Haze has allowed herself a more lighthearted day today: a rally on Santa Monica Pier. A stage is set as though for any other concert here as fans, voters and tourists alike crowd the strip, spilling into the sand, a sea of people forming. After riding the carousel and Ferris wheel together, posing for hundreds of selfies and ditching their shoes (and her heeled booties) to dip their toes in the ocean, the family of three is ready for showtime.

"I have the best fans in the world," Haze greets the crowd. "And I have the best voters in the world! And if you're still not sure about me, that's okay too, come on up and tell me about it. I got all the time in the world." She's changed into her version of a suit: a slim, cropped blazer with jodhpurs. ("You know you'd never write what my male competitors are wearing," she warns this reporter.) She takes a seat on the edge of the stage, legs dangling. The crowd hushes, the only sound on this entire pier the crashing waves and carousel music. For the next two hours, baking in the blazing June heat, she hosts an impromptu town hall. At the end, she raps a medley of her fight songs.

On stage left, Alchemy sways to the beat, snuggling a yawning Harmony in his arms. Is this family ready for the White House? "We just follow our passion. We're ready for anything life has in store for us," he answers, his Trinidadian accent coming through. He kisses the top of his daughter's head. "Right now, we're ready for a nap."

Jay and Sky had always wished to be that thrilling couple who hopscotched the globe every few months. But both worked too hard to be away very long or very far. So what was so wrong with a splurge weekend in LA? He had always wanted to stay at Shutters on the Beach, after reading about it in a celebrity profile ages ago. He dreamed of rolling out of a fluffy bed with Sky, hitting the spa, lounging at the pool, then the beach, maybe going somewhere buzzy and sceney for dinner and drinks, because it's LA after all.

Jay had arrived Friday, planning to stay through the primary, like Sky. But after thirty-six hours of sunning poolside alone while waiting for Sky to return from an endless array of Rocky events, then editing his story in their hotel suite, he'd decided to pack it in.

"I'm too tired to have any fun anyway, I'm sorry," Sky apologized.

"Got it," he said, trying not to sound hurt. "A little less Californication, a little more California dreaming?"

Sky smiled. "Something like that. This is a rock star schedule. I get why so many musicians are on drugs, I don't know how more politicians aren't. The running around city to city, so many people, and performing—because it really is all performing, even the ones who aren't, you know, up there rapping. Anyway, so all I want to do is sleep when I'm not with Rocky. I'm not a natural at this, Jay," he admitted. "It takes every ounce of energy to try to do this well. But weirdly I love it too."

"I'm proud of you, Sky," Jay said, poised outside the cab that would take him back to LAX. "So proud of you. Keep doing what you're doing. The fun can wait until you're home."

They kissed curbside, and Sky put his forehead to Jay's to look in his eyes.

"You know how much I miss you," he whispered.

That was all Jay needed. That alone had been worth the cross-country trip.

Much to Madison's disappointment, California didn't even matter to the Hank Machine. They were a lock, everyone had dropped out, and plans were full steam ahead for the convention. At home in the Hamptons, Hank geared up for a coronation. "Why can't we just skip the convention and hold the election tomorrow so I can win?" he kept saying, puffing on his cigars, and his advisers guffawed. Madison kept busy with Gemma, making a bright summer salad with tomatoes they'd picked from the garden. Her darling girl, in her favorite Lilly Pulitzer dress, sat on the kitchen island, kicking her legs, singing a Taylor Swift song and plucking chunks of tomato from the salad bowl when she thought Madison wasn't looking. This was their game.

"Wait a minute, what happened here?" Madison tossed her salad, searching, pretending to be upset. "Who stole my tomatoes?!" Gemma smiled sneakily, her front tooth missing—Madison had been away when it had fallen out, the *first* one, she was tired of missing things. Gemma put her hand over her mouth, laughing and chewing as Madison kissed the girl's button nose. "It's a good thing we picked so many. But where are they?"

Gemma produced two new tomatoes from behind her back. "Surprise, Mommy!"

Madison would go to California. She didn't want to but she had to. On top of everything, Hank's team was playing the Lakers in the championships. They too were expected to win.

So much *winning*. She didn't know how she was going to do this, talk to him. It certainly wasn't going to happen right now. But it needed to be done.

Ted was apoplectic and overcaffeinated, among other things, not that Reagan was surprised. If he was calling her in the middle of the night, he had officially come unglued. She pretended that she had been sleeping and missed the California Primary results, even though she and the girls had been awake, together in the living room watching returns trickle in from every single precinct in the state. "All we needed was to fucking win this state, and we could have clinched it. The nomination. Now I don't know what the fuck this is going to look like."

That wasn't actually mathematically true, but it wasn't the time to correct him.

"How the fuck did Rocky Haze make it into this race?" he went on. "Thompson shouldn't even be here. He's way too green. Arnold is the only one on either side that actually seems even remotely presidential."

"Maybe—" she started, then stopped herself just as fast, but it was too late.

"Maybe what?"

She sighed. "Maybe it's changing, the idea of what is or isn't 'presidential,' I don't know."

"I can't believe I'm hearing this."

"No, I just mean... I mean... I don't know, Thompson and Haze are not bad. I don't get the idea they would be reckless or stupid, they just might have more of a learning curve. I would be okay with them."

The girls squealed in their pack-and-play, "Dadadada!" It was one of the anchors on CNN. Every time someone wearing a suit came on the screen, they thought it was Ted. They had been right once that night: early on when MSNBC interviewed him from the hotel ballroom. He had been so oddly optimistic then: "We think we'll be celebrating tonight." She cringed thinking about it now.

"I can't believe I'm hearing this from you," he said again.

"I just mean, this will be okay. As long as Goodfellow doesn't win, it's all okay, right? You know everybody in this town. You'll get another position fast without a problem, won't you?"

He was in no mood for practical matters, "It's not about that. You don't understand. Forget it." He hung up.

Jay edited Sky's story from the comfort of his U Street apartment:

ROCKY SHOCKER:
HAZE PULLS OFF CALIFORNIA WIN
RAPPER HEADED TO CONTESTED CONVENTION

He still couldn't quite believe it, no matter how many times he read the news.

★ ★ ★

Cady had left work early and made a pilgrimage to the Air and Space Museum. Jackson was away again, so she stayed longer than planned, walking through the replicas of early airliners, standing on a metal plate on the ground and pressing the button so it would shake, shake, shake her up, simulating the bumpy rides on the first commercial jets. It wasn't unlike the way she had felt since arriving here. Parts of her life—the professional parts—had been fairly smooth sailing, but the stuff she expected to have been easy, the personal part, had instead been shaky.

She ducked into the gift shop before leaving—the primary purpose for her visit—and found just what she needed. With Jackson away, she didn't know when she'd get to the bar next and she didn't want to make a big deal out of it so she mailed it from work the next day with a thank you note.

Parker emailed her a day later. Thanks for the awesome ice cream: they totally changed it, way better than it used to be. Apparently the space program doesn't need me. Happy to have helped out the other night. Glad you survived that monsoon. Cheers, P

Rocky Haze had contacted Birdie months in advance, introducing herself as though Birdie might not have heard of her, which instantly won Birdie over. If she was still in the race by July 4, Rocky planned to throw "an epic fund-raiser" at the Kennedy Center. Her friends wanted to "help out," as if pals throwing a bridal shower: Kanye, Beyonce, Jay-Z, John Legend, Alicia Keys, they'd all flown in to perform.

Even if it hadn't brought in millions for Rocky Haze, Birdie's fund-raiser still would have ranked as her personal best. They'd sold out the Kennedy Center's Opera House with a special added perk of a rooftop afterparty for big donors. The rooftop of the Kennedy Center on a warm and sticky July 4 night watching the fireworks explode in the distance? It didn't get much better, really. Even Buck couldn't resist showing up to this one.

He sidled up to Birdie on the roof, fireworks bursting in a bright kaleidoscope of red, white and blue.

"Hello, stranger," he said, watching the sky.

"Who let you up here? Clearly I need to fire someone," she said, even though she had put his name on the list, just in case. She knew him well and suspected he would be too intrigued by the zeitgeist of it all to stay away.

He cut to the chase: "Listen, how about a temporary détente for an introduction to Haze?" he asked, tossing back his brandy.

With those words, she instantly, blissfully, felt she had the upperhand. And she loved it.

20

I'M REALLY HOPING I CAN LIGHT UP THE ROOM

★

"Pack your bags," Jeff greeted Cady as she arrived at work on a hot and humid July morning. "You and Max are on the next flight to Conventionville." He said it with jazz hands.

"But Gracie—"

"Madison called me personally asking for you. And what Madison Goodfellow wants, Madison Goodfellow gets. We want you there for the segment—"

"'Madison's Delegate Style Stars,'" she said.

"Right. And then her speech tonight."

Madison had splintered off from the Machine long enough to roam the convention center with Cady, her cameraman, Max, and Mike's assistant, Kimberly. She had boldly chosen to tell Mike about the segment, as an olive branch. And a bit of a diversion. "I'll just be walking around handing out certificates to the best dressed delegates. Apparently people get all done up in buttons and hats and red, white and blue everything?" she asked innocently.

"They do." Mike sighed. "Okay, you can do it," he agreed, assigning Kimberly as her babysitter. "But just remember, you're representing Hank. He is about to be nominated by a major party for the presidency."

"Absolutely!" Madison said.

It had all been charming in that man-on-the-street, roving-reporter way. And the delegates squealed like game show contestants when they met Madison. A few cried as she handed over their certificates. Others flubbed, overcome with too much emotion to even speak, when Madison posed questions like, "Tell me, did you make this hat? It looks heavy to wear, can I try it?"

Cady and Max were the perfect companions, cheering her on, all smiles. When they wrapped the segment that afternoon, they walked her back to her hotel room for a nap before the main event, with one final question.

"How do you feel heading into tonight? What can we expect from your speech?"

"I suppose I'm a little nervous, you know, that's probably normal," she said. "It really is a crazy big crowd. But I'm really hoping I can light up the room!"

She swooshed open the hotel shower curtain to reveal her secret weapon—a thirty inch Kraskin—leaned upright against the tub, soaking in a jar of tiki torch oil, Goodfellow brand oil, of course. (Not the company's bread and butter, but a surprisingly lucrative offshoot.) One side of the baton was already finished and wrapped lovingly in aluminum foil. In all these years, Madison thought there would have been greater advances made in the world of pyrotechnics.

Her phone's alarm buzzed: forty-five minutes were up. A generous amount of time, but she could think of little more embarrassing than a flame extinguished too early. She shook off the excess oil into the tub, pulled the precut foil sheet from her bag, snuggled it around the oil-coated end, tucked the apparatus into a garbage bag and shoved it into her Balenciaga tote as cheers erupted outside the bathroom door. In the lounge of their presidential suite the Machine celebrated, as they had since the roll call earlier this evening, officially clinching the nomination.

She was scheduled to take the podium at ten, and as they all rode over together in the SUV and made their way through the back entrance to the wings of the stage, she never let her bag out of her sight.

"Don't be nervous," Mike said to her. "Everyone is pre-disposed to like you, because they like Hank."

She had slipped the music to the sound engineer that af-ternoon: "Hank made a change for my opening tonight, you know, copyright thingy," she'd said. A very believable lie. It had proved plenty hard to find a proper fight anthem. Hank had racked up primary votes, but none of those voters seemed to be chart-topping musicians willing to grant him permis-sion to use their songs.

She looked straight up. Back in the day, she had had a good arm, could toss that baton into the rafters without breaking a sweat. The ceiling height of the arena was 140 feet, give or take, so at least there would be plenty of room if she could still manage to give the baton some good air when she threw it. She had only gotten in a few practice rounds last time she was at the Hamptons home. Gemma loved to watch, but Madison only allowed it if the girl was nestled firmly in her nanny Isobel's arms—lest Gemma should rush at Madison and grab for the baton. Madison had always found, though, if she closed her eyes, visualized her routine, it all had a way of going off flawlessly.

The crowd roared for Hank. They did love him, didn't they?

"…I know, I know, I know," he was saying to them. "You're not really supposed to see me or hear from me until the last day of this big show. But you know what I say to the way things are supposed to be done? Fuck all that!" The convention center went wild. "I do things MY way. I am Hank Goodfellow! I am your new leader!" Signs all around the grand space waved at him, among them, #GoodfellowGoodForUs. "So I wasn't about to let just anyone introduce this next lady. She is special and has been special to me since we met in high school back in Tuscaloosa. Meet your next first lady, Madison Goodfellow!"

"Sweet Home Alabama" cued up, just as it was supposed to, and Hank accidentally exited stage left instead of stage right, where she waited. All the better, she thought, as she walked out smiling and waving in her sensible Mike-approved navy blazer and skirt suit and white boots, a sequined star-spangled top peeking out beneath. Many in the crowd waved tall, narrow signs reading "Mad About Maddy!"

Once at the podium, music fading, she bellowed into the microphone: "Thank you, Hank! And thank you all! Hello there! I'm Madison! And I think you've had about enough talking for one day! I thought this was supposed to be a celebration! This is how we do it where I'm from!" The new music blared now: "Hail to the Chief," a techno remix, suitable for a dance club. In one flowing motion—fast enough that no one would have time to stop her—she pulled the lighter from her pocket, flicking it on with one hand while the other reached back to pull the baton out from the hole she'd made in the lining of her oversize blazer. She lit the oil-soaked Kevlar-wick ends of the baton, slid the lighter across the floor to the backstage area, threw the flaming baton up, up, up into the air and before its descent, ripped off her blazer and skirt, tossing them into the crowd and revealing her sequined and skirted red, white and blue majorette leotard beneath.

Prancing, preening, twirling, she skipped and leaped and flipped and threw the fiery stick so high and so fast, it resembled a spinning, lit wheel. She felt her mind clear, in that zen zone of autopilot and muscle memory, ease and exhilaration.

From the corner of her eye, mid-split-leap after her final toss, she caught Mike's slack-jawed expression. He was the most dangerous of the Machine because he was, as of now, the only true legitimate political operative on the campaign. The others were just Hank's business buddies from the oil company; they didn't really know what they were doing here. But Mike did.

"They used to call it the secret weapon at Tuscaloosa High School," she told Mike backstage immediately afterward, shaking the steel case that housed her extinguishing baton. "I thought it might be nice. You know, even if the team was losing and I brought it out, the crowd revved up. Once we came back from a twenty-one-point deficit in the third quarter to win the game. And really, a good fire baton routine is worth a thousand words."

"Magnolia, that brought me *back*! Didn't know you could still do that." Hank greeted her with a kiss and wide smile.

She could see in his eyes a glimmer of the old Hank.

"It's like ridin' a bike," she said, in urgent need of a glass of rosé, and secretly relieved she hadn't set fire to anything. The crowd had been tough, silent and puzzled at the start, but then they'd more than made up for it.

Mike closed his eyes as though speaking to a toddler. "While we appreciate the artistry and spectacle, I think it's best, in the future, if you could just stand there and read the words we've written. Smile. Wave. That would be perfect."

"Sure thing. But if you change your mind..." She grinned.

"And technically," Mike continued, "we're not allowed to use that song. Yet."

"Well, I don't see why not," Hank piped up. "It's a great tune. They'll be playin' it for me soon enough anyhow."

21

THIS'LL BE A NICE MEMORY FOR
THE BABY BOOK

★

Ted had been home two days waiting to ship out to the July convention, and Reagan found herself counting the minutes until he would be gone again. He was on the phone constantly—nothing new—but jittery, nervous, dropping things, yelling, talking to himself. She had begun to worry. "This is the process, you always say that," she'd tried to console him. "Short of paying off superdelegates, I think things are out of your control at this point, right?"

"Stay out of it," he'd said.

So it had been her idea for Ted to meet up with his old buddies for drinks, let off steam. He hadn't seen them since the campaign had revved up. They had all left the Hill around the time he ran for Congress and now spent their weekends doing things like half-marathons or coaching Little League. "Uber into the city," she'd told him, "have a beer, do something fun for a night."

She almost didn't answer the phone when it rang after midnight, but it was a 202 number and she figured it was one of the guys' phones, that he had lost his, left it in a cab or a bar, that he was having too much fun.

A recording asked if she would accept charges for a call from "Ted Campion." She sat straight up in bed. "Yes, yes, yes, of course," she blurted.

"Rea. It's me," he slurred. He sounded exhausted and drunk.

"Are you okay? Are you hurt?"

"No. I'm okay."

"Then what the fuck is—"

"I was at that bar from the fund-raiser," he started in, loudly but very, very slowly, mumbling. "Pretext... Prelude... whatever... Goodfellow's asshole press secretary was there... Fuckin' hate that guy... You know who...I'm talking about?... Guess I had too much...to drink?... Maybe not enough to eat...dunno...been dehydrated...lately..."

"Yeah, yeah, what happened?"

"He was talkin' shit about Arnold and all... I landed a pretty good punch—"

"What the hell, Ted, how fucking old are you?" She pulled on yoga pants that didn't have a hole in them, a T-shirt, found her car keys and wallet, threw them in a bag.

"But there were some off-duty Capitol Hill police and the Goodfellow asshole called 911 like I'm some kind of menace..."

She was barely listening at this point. She put him on speaker, texted Jay and Cady, and was dressed and waiting by the time Cady arrived. There was no way she was dragging the twins out of bed in the middle of the night to pick up daddy at the jail.

She pulled up to the station on a quiet residential street not far from the hubbub of Eastern Market. She'd passed by restaurants with so many young patrons seated outside, sipping drinks, probably talking about the convention, maybe Madison Goodfellow's impressive agility, maybe the showdown to come between Arnold, Thompson and Rocky Haze. Or maybe they were just talking about their hot intern—because every office had one—or their friends who had made it onto *The Hill*'s 50 Most Beautiful List, which had just come out. She and Ted had been on it back in the day, featured together. They laughed about it now, but his colleagues had framed it when he left to run for Congress and gifted it to him as a gag. It now hung in their living room, beside their wedding photos.

A no-nonsense woman at the front desk looked at Reagan's belly and then at her face again.

"Hi there, I think you've got my husband here? Campion? Theodore."

The woman looked something up in her computer.

"This isn't like him at all," Reagan continued. "He's been under a lot of stress lately. But I mean, who isn't, right? Your job must be very stressful. I can't even imagine. Thank you for your service." She didn't realize she was actually saying this all out loud.

In the waiting area a disheveled man began chanting. Two girls in very short shorts sat crying, mascara running down their faces, talking about how their moms were going to kill them. "Busy night here."

The woman glared. Reagan had gotten used to enjoying some minor sympathy thanks to the small watermelon ballooning from her midsection, but this woman was not having it.

"Or not. Maybe a quiet night." Reagan was a little nervous, to be honest.

The woman said nothing until finally: "Theodore Robert Campion. Assault charge. Bail's been posted. He's free to leave but will need to report to court on the appointed date. Look for paperwork in the mail." The lady cop picked up the phone, issuing instructions to whoever was on the other end.

"Whoa, whoa, whoa, how does that work? Who paid? Him? The guys? But they wouldn't take him home? I'm confused." She was trying to make sense of it all, thinking aloud again. It was a lot to take in.

"The party wishes to remain anonymous, ma'am."

With another cop holding his arm, Ted stumbled out,

sweaty, eyes heavy in that still-drunk way, his right hand swollen.

"Jesus, Ted." Reagan shook her head, waved for him to follow her and turned to go. "This'll be a nice memory for the baby book. 'Things happening the year you were born.'" She sighed, then stopped: "Is there a back way out of here, closer to the parking lot, so we don't have to walk around the building?" she asked the lady cop. She could only imagine a press secretary would be too happy to inform the media that he'd been slugged by a guy from the other team and had him arrested.

The cop pushed open the back door and a light shone in their face, a camera. Grant Foxhall.

She felt the shock register, then put on her game face.

"Grant, hey, what brings you here?" She kept walking toward the car.

"Hey, Reagan," he said, his tone more apologetic than she would have expected. "Ted."

Ted nodded in his direction, then looked away again.

"Hey, Matt, how're Jenny and the boys?" Reagan asked Grant's longtime camera guy, smiling into the lens. They all kept walking as a unit, as if they made up an eight-legged animal.

"Hi, Reagan," Matt said from behind his equipment, sounding embarrassed by his role in this task. "She was just saying you guys are due for another lunch."

"I've been meaning to call," she said.

"So *I* got a call," Grant jumped back in, getting the train on track again. "And I wanted to confirm—has the Goodfellow campaign filed assault charges and a restraining order against you, Ted?"

"Grant, is this because Ted has been on MSNBC so much lately?" She tried not to show how much she wanted to punch him herself. She knew there was some reason they'd never gotten serious when they went out all those years ago.

Ted ignored it all. "Why do you always park so far away from everything, Rea?" he said into the air ahead of them.

"Maybe Grant will drive you home? You can give him an in-depth interview about whatever went on tonight." She smiled. She was annoyed with them both. She wanted to go home alone to her toddler girls who behaved better than these grown men. She wanted to watch something other than the news and eat ice cream.

The walk felt endless with the extra 320 pounds: these two idiots plus her twenty pounds of baby. She unlocked the car door.

"Guys, I'm fucking exhausted. Here's what's gonna happen. You're gonna ask one polite, nonattacking question." She pointed at Grant. "You're gonna give a thoughtful, remorseful answer 'this election has been emotional, I regret letting it get the best of me, blah blah.' And then we're so fucking out of here." She smiled again. "Good?"

As Reagan drove home, Ted watched the city pass by outside the window for a few minutes, then became engrossed in flipping through radio stations.

"I'm scared to look at my phone," he finally admitted.

"Yeah, you should be. Did you give people a heads-up to commence damage control?" she asked flatly.

"Yeah." He was quiet for several minutes. "I just made a mistake."

"You think?"

Silence again and then, "Why do I care so much?" he asked it sincerely, thoughtful.

"Generally speaking, that's not a bad thing," she said, more gently now. "But something's going on with you this cycle.

I don't know." She was glad to be driving so she didn't have to look at him.

"I just. I'm sick of failing. I need a win to erase two years ago. I can't keep losing."

She understood. This was what she loved most about Ted. He *did* care too much. He didn't have another speed; it was all or nothing.

"This is why people burn out and have heart attacks," she said, serious.

"I'm sick of being a failure."

"There's more to your life than whether your boss wins an election, whether you win an election."

"It just feels different this time. I'm an adult now—"

"Allegedly," Reagan said under her breath.

"Seriously, though, I'm supposed to be a *provider*," he said, beat down. "I've got a family. There's more riding on it this time. I can't fail."

"I know. But why don't you check your poll numbers at *home*? You still have a very high favorability rating with two very tough little girls." She said it firmly, trying to get through to him.

"Oh my God! Wait! Where are they?" he said frantic, as though just remembering that he did, in fact, have two children.

"They're home. They stayed up late again working in their meth lab." She rolled her eyes, but he didn't seem to find it funny. "Cady's there. They were sleeping when I left."

"Ugh, is she going to want to *talk*?" he asked, exasperated, the "soul-searching" and "introspective" portion of their discussion apparently over. "Why is she always so chatty?"

"Maybe because she's a nice person? And a good friend to me," she said, suddenly regretting having very briefly introduced them at the Arnold fund-raiser. "Or maybe you would've preferred to have our girls on CNN with you? Family night at the lockup?"

"Sorry," he said in a voice barely detectable to human ears. "What was that?"

"I said I'm sorry, okay," he bristled, a moody teen who had taken the car without permission.

She hoped whatever was going on with him was just a phase, and that it would be over soon.

When Reagan checked her email the following morning, she had a message from Grant's personal non-CNN account with a time-date stamp just thirty minutes after their run-in outside the lockup. Subject line: "I'm sorry"

Message body: Reagan, I'm sorry about tonight. Truly sorry. I know it won't matter but it was just business, exec producer on us these days, etc, you know how it goes.

She wrote back to him while the girls threw their bananas at breakfast: You are barely human. She wasn't sure why she had expected more from him, more compassion. It wasn't as if they were actual *friends*, but still, she *had* expected more. She had always thought maybe there was something greater in his character than he had shown when they first met way back when, that perhaps his arrogance had been an attempt to impress her and she had misjudged him. But, no, it seemed she had been right all along.

During a commercial break on his show, she received this response: Fair enough, it may seem that way when I do things like last night. But I am capable of being a good friend occasionally. Ask Buck Brandywine.

She didn't write back. She was still too disgusted and disappointed in him, in this entire situation, and she planned to feel that way for quite a while.

22

AIR FORCE TWO HAS A
MILE HIGH CLUB

★

Jay watched Sky drive off to rendezvous with Rocky and Co. at her hotel and then Andrews Air Force Base. Arnold had apparently offered Rocky a lift to the convention, and she was taking some of her reporters along. There was clearly a story coming, but Sky couldn't get anything more out of anyone yet.

Jay wasn't quite ready to return to his empty apartment, so he opted for a walk, the H Street corridor already coming alive. The strip was studded with memories, mostly of the early days of their relationship since they spent most of their time in Jay's neighborhood now: the sushi place from one of their first dates, the performing arts center where Jay had tagged along on some of Sky's early assignments. How lucky he had been that Sky had invited him along. He laughed at himself now, the uncertainty at the beginning about whether it was really all work. The thick July air was stagnant even at nearly eight in the evening; it had been a day of record-breaking heat and soupy humidity, the kind of weather that got everyone hot and bothered about how crazy George Washington had been to build his city on swampland. Even though factually, that wasn't true; it wasn't technically a swamp. Jay found this time of year exhausting, having to constantly set everyone straight.

Despite himself, Jay had done his best to convey his excitement as Sky had packed for another trip earlier. "Tell me everything! We'll do a piece on it. Like fun facts on Air Force Two!" Jay had said, lying on Sky's couch. "Take abundant selfies! And whatever pics you can! Like, pics of everything! Take souvenirs too, like if there's a blanket with a presidential seal or, like, bags of pretzels or whatever! So, you know, in short—play it really cool, just like I would." Sky had laughed, always generous with Jay's humor.

Lost in his thoughts he walked all the way to Union Station, over a mile. Just before Sky's expected takeoff time, Jay heard from him once more. Rocky isn't only one here—Carter Thompson too, Sky texted. staff. some white house pool. heard cnn guy whispering to producer that the decision is being made imminently! hear anything there? trying for more. taking off. xxxx"

Seated at a bench inside the grand lobby of the station, Jay forwarded Sky's notes (minus the xxxx) to Helena and the rest of the Politics Desk with the subject line: "Arnold vetting VPs now!"

Helena called seconds later. "That's awfully optimistic of Arnold," she launched in, no greeting, as soon as Jay answered. "Is Sky sure?"

"Well, maybe—" Jay started.

"Fascinating!" Helena cut him off, answering her own question. "He's neck and neck with those two and scared to lose the nomination, so—"

"If you can't beat 'em, join 'em?" Jay asked.

"Exactly," she agreed.

Cady was still at work and, noticing the time, texted Jackson just before he was due to take off: come back as a staffer for the next vp! good luck to carter! xoxox She didn't know how it had happened, but Jackson had come home the night before with hush-hush news that Carter Thompson was now on the short list to be Arnold's *vice presidential pick*. Jackson wouldn't say any more.

"So mysterious! I'm kind of loving this drama," she had

cooed, as she'd helped him pack. "And Carter would be cool with VP, right? I mean, who wouldn't? That ain't so bad." A few months ago, she never would have been so fascinated with Jackson's job. She was proud of how much she had learned about campaigns, how she had become part of his world.

"Oh yeah, it would be kind of perfect," Jackson said, eyes dancing. "There were so many reporters hanging outside the office today, more than ever. President was always going to be a long shot, but this, *this*, it would be like a dream team."

Ted nearly had to sit the convention out, thanks to his bar brawl. But a call came late in the day: there were decisions to be made *now*, strategies to fine-tune, and they needed him in on it. They were meeting en route to the convention, and they wanted him on the flight. Reagan got his text while at My Gym with the girls. By the time she wrote back, he was already in the air.

Cady got the alert on her phone: Fighter Jets Called to Escort Air Force Two. Just a headline, no story yet. She went looking for more and found only: Air Force Two Forced to Make Emergency Landing. Her heart fell. She called Jackson but, of course, his phone was off. She texted, emailed, left messages: Call when you get this, I love you.

Reagan had caved, feeling particularly exhausted and enormous after their afternoon at My Gym. (Stacy had the day off and therefore, Reagan had actually had to watch and chase the girls.) They were teething and wouldn't sleep, so she positioned the pack-and-play in front of the TV and was just searching for their favorite bedtime show on Sprout when she caught the headline. She called Ted but got no answer. Maybe Jay would know something.

★ ★ ★

"I'm fine, there was this turbulence, like something big hit the plane." Sky phoned Jay the minute he landed. "We're somewhere in Delaware. The plane was inspected. It must've been a bird that rammed itself against the plane's wing. Arnold is still going ahead with the meetings, right here. The press and staffers are just hanging out until another aircraft arrives, or a bus or something. We were all standing around outside, but it started pouring rain so the pilot gave the okay to let us back on and wait, said it was safe." Sky promised to text when he had more.

Pretty fucking crazy, Ted texted Reagan when the plane touched down. An eagle, they think. We were in Arnold's quarters meeting with Haze—she's probably out. Staying here for a bit—looking like Thompson will get it, IMO. Love you and girls. Don't worry, fine, promise.

Cady didn't understand why Jackson wasn't writing or calling. The aircraft had landed somewhere, and it seemed everyone else had been able to contact loved ones. Reagan and Jay had both heard by now and let her know that Ted and Sky were fine, and from what they knew there were no life-threatening injuries. A few reporters and staffers just had bumps and bruises, maybe one concussion. She pictured Jackson being the one person who hadn't been okay and wished she could just hear *something* from him. She wouldn't be able to move or breathe or think until she did. She waited, his phone still off with calls going straight to voice mail, no returned texts or emails. She searched obsessively for news, more details, any sign that there might be injuries that hadn't been reported yet. All she managed to find was one major press break from *Capitol Report*:

REP. CARTER THOMPSON TO BE ARNOLD'S VP PICK

By Willa Sedgwick, *Staff Writer*

Capitol Report has learned exclusively that Iowa Representative Carter Thompson will be John Arnold's pick for vice president. Story developing.

EYES ON THE PRIZE: ROCKY HAZE REPORTEDLY TURNS DOWN VP

By Sky Vasquez, Staff Writer, *The Queue*

The path to the presidency has been a dramatic one, but nothing could compare to the scene on Air Force Two Monday night. After severe turbulence forced an emergency landing near Wilmington, Rocky Haze had a change of heart. Sources say presidential hopeful Vice President John Arnold had all but offered Haze the job as his running mate, when she reportedly took herself out of the running.

"What happened on that plane shook me up, gave me some time to think about what I really wanted," Haze said after the landing, though she still hasn't issued a formal statement.

Only Haze and Arnold were in the meeting, no advisers, no press, but sources say what happened is the stuff of legend and folklore. "They had a great vibe, they talked about their families, about how hard it is to be on the trail, how intense the primaries were," says the insider. "Arnold said Haze was a good pick because her skeletons are all out there, no secrets, no

AIMEE AGRESTI 203

lies. Everyone knows her troubles, her past, how she cleaned up. Arnold offered it to her. She was polite and gracious, said it was the kind of opportunity she never expected would present itself to her. But that she needed a minute."

Haze returned to her seat to think it over, putting in her earbuds, closing her eyes. "This was when the turbulence began," says another source. "She was so calm, other people were freaking out. People's stuff was flying all over, hitting other people in the head." When the plane landed, got checked out, Haze met with Arnold once more. An adviser in the room this time described the scene like this:

"Haze says to Arnold, 'I want you to listen to this new track,' she cues up this song on her phone, says it was inspired by the Southern states she visited, it had a country twang, it was cool," says the source. "Then she asks him, 'How many fiddles do you hear there?' And Arnold says 'One?' like he's not sure. And Haze says, 'That's right and that's because I don't believe in playing second fiddle. And I can't start now. I'm sorry, I appreciate your offer more than you could know but I'm going to try to do this my way.' She shook his hand and smiled and returned to her seat."

Haze's camp will only say they intend to go forward with the contested convention. "We want to see where we stand."

Sky had texted just before the story posted: obvi: between you and me, haze is the "source," just not ready to go on record yet. totally unrelated: was superscary when everything happened, then everyone relieved, bonding, celebrating etc, after it was OK. but then everyone was working, sleeping, quiet. Except me (you know I can't sleep on planes) and a couple

others I noticed: I think air force two has a mile high club...
Swear I saw reporter girl go into restroom, followed by guy few
minutes later. Jay, it looked like Cady's fiancé :-((((((Hoping I'm
wrong, but I don't know. Looked like him. Might explain why
Cady didn't hear from him right away?

Jay wanted to unread this, just like he knew Sky wanted to
unsee it. Jay didn't know what he was supposed to do with this
information; did he have a moral obligation to tell Cady? He
would consult the best advice columnist he knew. She would
have all the answers. He texted:

What do we do???? along with a screenshot of Sky's damn-
ing text.

Reagan wrote back immediately: I'm on it, standby.

Thx. No way for Ted to corroborate, right? Jay tried, but knew
the answer from their previous texts: Ted had been with a few
staffers in the front compartment of the plane in the enclosed
cabin that served as Vice President Arnold's office.

I wish, she wrote. Amazed Ted even noticed the turbulence.

It was true, Jay had seen Ted in hyper-work mode. Reagan liked to joke that if he was in the *zone*, he would tune
out everything around him so intensely it was like he was in
some kind of sensory deprivation tank.

Seconds later, Reagan sent a screenshot of an exchange
between her and Cady. Jay groaned reading Cady's message:

you'll think I'm insane—on my way to Philly!!! just needed to be
with him, you know? Kinda freaked out from today.

And then Reagan's best advice to Jay:

ugh. :(we gotta let it play out now. let you know when I hear
from her.

23

OHHH, I'M SORRY, IS THIS
A WORK FUNCTION?

★

Cady got the last seat on the Acela. It had been impulsive, but she couldn't just sit around, waiting to hear something, and she had exhausted all of her sources. According to Reagan, Ted had been in the private office meeting with Arnold, and Jay said Sky had been with press in back. Jackson apparently would have been in the front with staffers. Jay had even asked Sky to look for him, but they had to remain seated and he hadn't gotten a good enough view. So she had cabbed straight to Union Station.

Her mind had taken her down so many dark paths while waiting to hear from him. She had instantly felt sick about every argument they'd ever had—of which there had been many lately—every time she could have just let things go.

To halt the steady flow of bad thoughts, she forced herself to focus on the good: the day they met, the start of it all. So much electricity and promise. After an interview about preparations for Times Square festivities on New Year's Eve in New York, the mayor had invited Cady to watch with his staff, front row seats without having to wait outside all day either. She had ended up next to Jackson, and after talking all evening, he had kissed her at midnight, completely unexpectedly, his lips warm against the freezing cold. She couldn't feel her hands or feet, but she didn't care.

The train ride felt impossibly slow, torturous, until finally, a full hour and a half after the news, when she was nearly to

Wilmington, Jackson's name at last popped up on her phone. This sweet comfort coming via text: All good here, just frightening moments. OK now. Official: Carter going to be announced as VP pick!!! Still going to convention tonight.

He was okay. She read it over and over, hand to her heart in relief, as the train rumbled on, the lights of Wilmington shining outside her window. This, a text, still wasn't enough though. She still needed to spend the night wrapped in his arms to know he was all right.

She arrived just after nine, catching a cab to Jackson's hotel. The front desk gave her a key to the room, no problem, when she told them she was his fiancée. *It probably shouldn't be that easy*, she thought, but for her purposes tonight, she was glad. She had texted that she had a surprise for him but hadn't heard anything since. He had probably gone to bed early after the whole ordeal.

She smoothed her hair and her dress outside the door, then knocked a spirited *bonkbonk bonk-bonk bonk*, putting her ear to the door for any sign of movement. She heard nothing, so she inserted the key and crept in very slowly.

"Helloooo," she whispered, stepping into the pitch-black room. She heard only a moan in response, someone waking up. "It's me! Surprise! I thought a near-death experience warranted—" She turned the corner into the room and someone screamed, followed by the thump thump-THUMP of someone falling out of bed, the crash of a lamp knocked over, another light flipped on.

Jackson stood there, naked, his perfect abs taunting her. "CADY! What the—!" he called out at her, tripping, trying to grab something to cover himself as though she hadn't seen it all before.

"Ohmagod!" Cady blurted. In the fluffy bed, sheets just the right kind of disorderly as though art directed for a photo shoot, a blonde stared back at her, plump pout agape. She looked like she could have been a lingerie model except she wasn't actually wearing any lingerie at the moment. Cady's hands flew up to cover her eyes. She felt as she had when he had proposed, like she was watching the scene from above.

"What are you *doing* here?" he asked, like she was the one who had done something wrong.

"I was freaked out after your flight. And not hearing from you... So I got... I wanted to see..." She was having trouble putting sentences together.

"It's not what it looks like," he said, barely trying.

Her mind now having fully processed the scene, Cady's anger set in. "It took way too long for you to say that." She opened her eyes, but looked away. Picked up the satchel she just realized she'd dropped. "This *looks* like a cliché. I can't believe you're really this...*typical*. Who is this anyway?"

"Willa," the girl said, meekly.

"It's just, it's not, it's, I mean, I don't know, it's, she's from *Capitol Report* and—we've sort of been working together and—" he stammered.

"Ohhh, I'm sorry, is this a work function?" She smacked her palm to her forehead, mocking.

"No, I just mean, we almost died today, or we could've died today, I could've maybe almost died," he tried, half-heartedly, for sympathy.

"Congratulations," her voice cracked.

"No, I mean, we drank too much, after we didn't die—"

"After you didn't die."

"From that flask—the one that YOU gave me."

"So this is my fault, for giving you a fucking engagement gift. My bad. I can't even..." She had to get out before any tears came. He didn't deserve them. She tripped on her way to the door but didn't fall, thank God. She threw the door open with such strength it hit the wall, and trembled as she ran down the hallway, ungracefully, in her heels.

"Wait! Cady!" he called after her.

She heard a crash and glanced back: the door had swung shut, closing behind him. He was in the hallway, completely nude, his hands rushing to cover the part that had gotten him into this trouble in the first place. She kept running and flung her key card over the ledge, letting it flutter down to the lobby below.

He caught up with her just as the glass elevator doors closed. Their eyes locked, and she whipped around, turning her back before the first tear dropped.

On the train back home, she couldn't stop that scene from playing and replaying and replaying in her head on an endless loop. The bed. The girl. The parade of nudity. The inner battle to not cry. And then her mind ticked off their many recent tiffs and offenses: him missing the majority of their engagement party, him being absent the day she moved in, with nowhere to put any of her stuff. But then some of the good stuff trickled back in: that night they met, the Hay-Adams, the proposal, him whisking her around their engagement party as a team, as a unit. She was a mess.

She tried to figure out how things had changed so drastically. How had they gone from that to *this*? Should their beautiful history outweigh it all? She sure as hell didn't know. She felt sick, her stomach knotted, her eyes sore from holding back tears as best she could. She didn't want to be that person sitting alone on a train in the middle of the night having a breakdown. She didn't want to be alone at all.

It felt like her life had exploded, and now she had to sort

through and determine which parts were still viable. She didn't want to think about him or see him ever again. And she really didn't want to go home to that apartment that looked like him, smelled of his cologne, had the TV tuned to whatever channel he had left it on. She made a call.

24

THIS IS TINDER FOR NERDS

★

Reagan picked up on the first ring without even looking.

"Reagan, darling, it's Birdie, and you will *never* believe where I am," Birdie launched right in. She paused for dramatic effect, expecting Reagan to take a stab, apparently.

"Umm, I would guess the convention." Reagan stifled a yawn. It was nearly eleven, but her rapidly growing bump—what was it now? The size of a cantaloupe? She had stopped reading those weekly baby emails—kept her awake. For some reason this pregnancy seemed harder than carrying the twins, but maybe it was just because she was also chasing after the girls while cooking up this new creature. She was fucking *tired*. And the evening's Air Force Two drama had further exhausted her.

"Oh, darling, no one who's anyone is even seen there until Tuesday night. My event isn't till Wednesday. No."

She sounded a little tipsy, but with Birdie it could be hard to tell.

"So! I am at the one and only Madison Goodfellow's stunning pied-à-terre."

Ohhh boy. Reagan felt nauseous—and not from the baby. She hadn't spoken much about Ted to anyone. They had heard and seen his clip with Grant, which made the rounds, but they had all been respectful enough not to ask her about it and instead just let it run its course through the news cycle, passing like a kidney stone. Birdie had texted her simply: Ted has done us all a great public service. Jay had come over with a bottle of sparkling cider, feeling terrible that he'd slept through Reagan's text that night of Ted's arrest and feeling even worse that she couldn't actually drink at a time like this.

"It must be beautiful there," Reagan said, not sure where this was going.

"Of course it is, but I didn't call to brag. What are you doing *right now*?"

"You know, typical Monday night rager."

"Excellent, hop in a cab and come over."

Reagan looked at the other end of the sofa: her mother snuggled in a blanket, snoring softly. She had come in from San Francisco the day before Ted left, ostensibly to help out while he was away at the convention. But really, Reagan suspected, her mother felt that the full iciness of her glares at Ted couldn't be adequately communicated over FaceTime. Mama was not happy.

It was the last thing Reagan felt like doing. But the idea of Birdie and Madison potentially discussing her—and her family—while she wasn't there proved a powerful motivator. She had to be there to defend Ted's actions, to set things right. He wasn't perfect, but he was passionate about his job, about this country, about Arnold's vision. And though sometimes that kind of intensity could boil over, it came from a good place. "Sure," Reagan said, trying her best to sound like she wasn't heading into a firing squad.

The second they hung up, she called Jay.

"Ohmagod! Is Ted in jail again? I'm there!" Jay started in as soon as he picked up.

Reagan sighed. "No. Not this time. Put on something cute and be ready in twenty minutes. Details forthcoming." She didn't have time to answer all the inevitable questions. But she sure as hell wasn't going in there alone.

She threw on a tank dress and flats, woke her mom gently. "You said I should have more fun, and the girls want to take me out for a late drink, nonalcoholic of course," she said.

Mama gave her a look, eyebrow cocked, not entirely believing it. But then she nodded anyway, giving Reagan a kiss on the cheek and taking the baby monitor from the coffee table and setting it beside her.

On the way to Jay's, Reagan called the Ritz and arranged to have two bottles of champagne and a plate of cookies for her and Jay to bring up. She was *not* arriving to this thing empty-handed.

Jay was waiting curbside and hopped in. "You are *so* mysterious lately," he said.

"Birdie called. We're going to Madison Goodfellow's place."

"Ohhhhgod," Jay said. "For real?"

"Yes, sir."

"What? How? I feel like some *Real Housewives* shit is gonna go down. In which case—" He threw his hands against the window, pretended to try to escape.

"We'll see!" she said faux perkily. This had, obviously, occurred to Reagan. She certainly hoped she wasn't facing a reality-TV-style ambush. Much as she enjoyed those shows, she didn't want to be *in* one. But she trusted Birdie, felt that she wouldn't lure her over there just to have Madison Goodfellow wipe the floor with her for Ted's fisticuffs with that press secretary.

"If I'm your backup, you're in trouble—that lady can work a fire baton like nobody's business," Jay joked.

The door to the penthouse opened: Madison, wearing the perfect casual separates, wide-legged embellished denim pants and a short-sleeve lacy top, which Reagan was fairly certain were both Chanel. Her photographic memory placed it in

Vogue, a resort-wear pictorial, from her pre-Iowa-party reading frenzy.

Madison didn't say a word, so Reagan introduced Jay and said, uncomfortably, "We come bearing gifts?"

The woman looked into Reagan's eyes, expressionless for a long, painful moment, and Reagan braced herself, prepared to defend her husband despite his Neanderthal-like behavior that night. In the background, she could hear Birdie singing along to a Rocky Haze song.

Madison finally spoke. "I was just talking to Birdie about this terrible thing that happened and how I needed to talk to you. And she said she could just call you right now so we could get this out of the way."

Reagan tensed up, preparing possible responses in her mind to what might come next. But before she could say anything, Madison nodded once and hugged Reagan, squeezing her tight in her strong, slender arms. When Madison let go, she still held Reagan's hand in hers.

"I am so glad, so very glad, to meet you," she said in her drawl. "And I am so sorry I didn't send a car to take your husband home that night."

"Excuse me?" Reagan said, confused.

Birdie came to the door, a small plate crowded with sushi. She nodded and pointed to Madison as if to say, *Get a load of what this one's about to lay on you.*

Madison guided her inside, still holding her hand. "I was with Hank when he got the call from Mike," Madison explained, "our press guy, about what had happened. So Mike says he ran into a man from the other campaign and thought it would be fun to get him all worked up. And he *did* and then got the man to hit him so he could tell the press how crazy the other campaign—the Arnold people—are."

Reagan couldn't believe what she was hearing, and who

she was hearing it from. Ted still shouldn't've taken the bait, but she felt for him now.

"I grabbed the phone from Hank, yelled at Mike—I never liked that guy." Her drawl flared up now, her eyes teary. "I'm sure they all thought I was just madder than a wet hen, but I didn't care. It wasn't right, and it's not right. A lot of the things Hank's been doing and saying... I've had about enough. So I went over there and bailed him out, your husband. And I'm just so sorry about this all."

The landline rang, and Birdie answered, making herself at home. "Cady Davenport is here?" she asked, pleasantly puzzled.

Reagan had forgotten to mention that. "Oh! I invited her," she said. It had been selfish—not to mention a flagrant etiquette breach—but Reagan had wanted to have as many people as possible there on her side.

"She's having kind of a rough night," Jay came to the rescue, offering an explanation. "Her engagement is, like, *over*."

Birdie shook her head knowingly. "Send her up."

"Well, it's a good thing you all brought more of this." Madison grabbed one of the champagne bottles and a towel and set to work.

Madison answered the door and without a word gave Cady a bear hug. "They're all terrible in their own way," she said comfortingly.

Then came Birdie, champagne flute in hand. "Come, self-medicate, darling." She handed Cady the drink and threw her arm around her. "Reagan filled us in. We're all up to speed."

Cady absorbed the scene. Reagan and Jay, deep in conversation while typing on their phones, sat perched on Madison's sleek white sofa by the floor-to-ceiling windows overlooking the city. Rocky Haze music played; an impressive array of sushi was laid out on the kitchen island. Cady still couldn't believe she had taken Reagan up on the offer and come over here straight from the train. She just couldn't bear the thought of the apartment.

"Aww, sweetie, you look so pretty," Jay said.

"This was supposed to be my 'I'm-so-glad-you're-alive look,'" she said, pained.

"Well, your heart was in the right place," Jay said.

"A million guys would love to get a surprise convention booty call from you," Reagan said with sweet sympathy.

"Just apparently not this fucker," Birdie said. "But you do have options."

"You know, when Hank did this, it was after Henry was born, and I was miserable," Madison said, sipping her champagne, perched on the sofa arm. "I mean, we were high school sweethearts, college sweethearts, I *loved* that man. We split up and married other folks, this is all, you know, pretty much common knowledge by now, but we still loved each other, and when he divorced that gold digger that was his second wife, I set out to make him *sooo* jealous. It worked, because honestly, men are pretty easily manipulated when you set your mind to it. And then we got together again, and this time it worked." She spoke in the open way of someone with a healthy amount of confidence but few female friends. "We've been going strong ever since." She tilted her head back, draining her champagne. "Until now, I mean. But this time he's just in love with power, which oughtta be an easier problem to fix than an affair, but who knows."

"Wow," Jay said softly, sitting on the edge of his seat.

"The question," Birdie began, "is whether you want to stay or go and how you want to go about that."

Cady could barely formulate a response. "I don't know. I

don't even know what I'm doing here. Not here—" she gestured to the apartment, adding "—this is lovely."

"Aww, thank you." Madison squeezed her hand.

"But I mean, here, in this city. What am I doing? I'm thirty
years old and my life is self-destructing. How did this happen
to me? This isn't how I...*operate*. I just, I don't know." She held
her head in her hands, speaking as if the only one in the room.

"Listen." Birdie knelt on the floor in front of her. "You can
start over. Everything changes in this city every eight years,
sometimes every four. Everything shakes up and rebuilds and
starts over. So you can do it too." She said it so easily, shrug-
ging, as though it were no big deal at all, just something that
needed to be done, like brunch on Sunday afternoons. "Now's
when we find out what kind of woman you are."

Cady looked away a moment and then back at Birdie, holding back tears. "Maybe I don't know who I am," she whispered, defeated.

The others remained silent, not even breathing, it seemed.
Madison smoothed Cady's hair like she was a lap dog.

"Ugh. Please," Birdie said, not having it. "Yes, you do. You
did the minute you set foot on the set of that crappy show and
turned the whole damn thing around. So just be that ball-
buster in your personal life. Okay?" Birdie said, looking in
Cady's eyes.

Cady nodded, exhaled. They expected her to man up and
seemed sure that she could move on, restitch her rapidly unraveling life. So she would have to, pure and simple.

"Okay then." Birdie nodded too. Then continued, "So,
onward—your options. Inciting jealousy is always a fine way
to go, in my book. These two have been doing some oppo."
She gestured to Reagan and Jay.

"Oppo?" Cady asked, pulling herself together now.

"Opposition research," Reagan clarified. "On Willa Sedgwick."

"It appears that this was her debut on the *The Hill*'s Annual
Hottest in DC list. She's with a rag called *Capitol Report*," Jay
said, scrolling through his phone. "But she appears to be really a terrible reporter—a staggering number of corrections
have been issued and the stories she does write, well, look like
they may have been largely borrowed—"

Reagan coughed, "Plagiarized." *Cough*.

"From other sources," Jay continued.

Cady didn't feel better though. "She's not our problem,"
she said. "The fact that he let this happen is our problem."

"Very well. I admire that we're not pointing fingers," Birdie
agreed, taking a different tack. "Drink, drink, and let's look
for our candidate, someone to inspire jealousy and also deliver
some...instant gratification. That's a win-win." She grabbed
the remote to Madison's enormous TV and dimmed the lights
as though they were about to screen a movie.

Madison served the cookies Reagan had brought—on a
gold-rimmed platter that probably cost more than a month
of Cady's salary. She smiled as Cady took one.

"These also go well with silk scarves." Madison winked
at her.

Birdie clicked through the channels, reaching her destination: "Bingo," she said. On-screen a panel of lawmakers sat
behind microphones looking serious, while equally stone-
faced staffers sat against the wall behind them.

"Are we seriously watching C-SPAN right now?" Jay asked
quietly.

"We're going to find Cady a rebound," Birdie said, matter-
of-fact. "We're going to hit Jackson where it hurts—"

"All right, get him in the—" Jay started.

"Legislative branch," Birdie said.

"Right," Jay said under his breath. "Not where I was going but okay."

"So *this* is C-SPAN?" Madison asked, watching excitedly.

"We just need a good hearing. Reagan, darling, what do you say?"

"I'm with you." Reagan leaned in, considering. "What's on C-SPAN 2 and 3? Let's see the options."

"'House ways and means. Senate intelligence. POTUS immigration speech from the rose garden,'" Birdie read.

"Hank tried watching this once, months ago," Madison said to Cady, sipping her champagne. "But he turned it off immediately. He said it was like soccer, not enough scoring. I didn't mind it, but I just prefer shows with more women. Then I can relate better."

Cady smiled. Madison wasn't wrong on that last count.

"My gut tells me, Senate. It's more intimidating since it isn't Jackson's world," Reagan reasoned.

"Brilliant, and intelligence committee is sexy," Birdie agreed, tuning in. "They know all the secrets. Okay. Cady, love, gather round. I'd like to draw your attention to that row of staffers sitting behind the senators." She pointed. "They are young, passionate, smart. And, this is a small town. Between the four of us, we can probably get to any of them. Start browsing! This is just what you need—"

"This is Tinder for nerds," Reagan said.

"This is Tinder for nerds, yes," Birdie repeated.

Cady sighed. She wasn't much in the mood. She would've been fine just drinking until she passed out, but she didn't want to be a bad sport. "Okay, um—" she guzzled her glass of champagne, then looked again "—that guy. Blond. Seated behind—who is it?" She squinted to read the name placard. "Behind Senator Tallon."

"Nice!" Jay said in approval.

"Yeah, yeah, we wrote a speech for Tallon once," Reagan said, snapping her fingers, then called out like on a game show. "Bryce Smithson! Engaged. Sorry."

"Figures," Cady said, her glass magically refilled as Madison topped everyone off.

"Oooh, him!" Jay called out, pointing. "I know him."

"Talking to McAfee?" Birdie asked of a brunette whispering in the senator's ear. "Cute."

"Matt Gorbanski!" Jay blurted. "Sky's friend from school dated him. I think he's single now."

"On it," Reagan said, focused on her phone.

"What about that one? He looks sweet and smart." Madison pointed to a man with glasses, a serious expression, with a huge stack of papers in his arms. "He looks like he would be so nice."

"Madison, darling, yes, but we can do better," Birdie said gently. "This isn't a charity hookup situation."

"Cady isn't a 501(c)(3)," Reagan joked.

"Cady is a gorgeous, whip-smart woman who just happened to have been wronged," Birdie said, speaking as though Cady wasn't actually in the room.

"No, oh, I know, I'm sorry." Madison grabbed Cady's hand. "I was just looking for someone real nice for you since it sounds like you haven't had someone real nice."

"You guys are great to do this, but maybe this isn't the right time. Or...hearing," Cady said, appreciating the effort. She was beginning to feel woozy.

"I wasn't going to tell you this but that Willa hussy posted an Insta of her, Jackson and a couple other people next to Air Force Two," Reagan said, waving her phone at Cady.

She grabbed Reagan's hand, getting a closer look. It felt like another kick in the gut. "Is it getting hot in here, do those windows open?" Cady pushed the hand and phone away, tossed back her champagne, then curled up on the buttery leather sofa, fanning herself. She felt shaky again—and livid. "Fine, so what do we know about that Matt guy?" she asked.

"Might be in a relationship," Jay said, scrolling on his phone.

"Let's also check that 'hottest list,' just to be sure we're covering all the bases," Birdie said.

"On it," Jay said.

"Does party affiliation matter?" Birdie asked.

"I don't know, no," Cady said, unsure.

"Good. You can kick this Carville-Matalin style, that's sexy," Reagan said.

"Ohhhkay," Cady said, not sounding very optimistic.

"Wait, wait, wait." Reagan hit the sofa, perking up. "You know who's cute and used to be on the Hill? Emo guy, from the bar?!"

"Yesss!" Jay said.

"Emo guy?" Cady asked.

"Broken heart, broken arm, you know, the one who's always talking about his feelings—"

"That's cute," Jay said, encouraging.

"What's his name, Parker," Reagan said. "And he's super into you."

"I think he's just friendly," Cady said.

"Good enough," Birdie said, switching among the news networks, all rerunning footage from the convention.

"No, it's more than friendly. I'm good at this stuff," Reagan said.

"We can go there tomorrow night," Jay proposed.

"If nothing else, stake your claim to that bar so Jackson doesn't get it in the breakup." Reagan shrugged.

"It did seem like a fun place," Madison said. "Hank and I never go to places like that anymore. Reminded me of the greasy spoon we worked at in college."

"Really? I can't even picture that. You two," Birdie said.

"I know. I keep telling you, the Hank out there now isn't the guy I married."

Cady was barely listening. "I'm suuuuper sleepy," she yawned. She tried to sip the rest of her champagne—was it her third or fourth glass? Who could say? But she was still lying down and only half got in her mouth, the rest splashing onto Madison's immaculate couch.

Birdie gasped "Roche Bobois!" and yanked Cady upright.

"Fuuuck, I'm sorry. Don't know what's with me tonight," Cady slurred.

"It's fine, sweetheart," Madison said, hand on Cady's shoulder. "You've had a night. And this'll come right out."

"This is some crazy champers," Cady said, holding up her empty glass. She shook her head, but only very slowly. She *never* referred to champagne as "champers." Her jaw felt slack like she'd been shot with Novocain. Her brain seemed to be working at normal speed but her body in slow motion. She tried to say, "Either my defenses are down and this is a psycho-somatic response to the emotional annihilation of my day, or there's something else going on here." But to her ears all that came out was a low, moaning demon voice, "Psychooooemo-tionannnnihilationnnnn."

"Fuck! Birdie, what did you do?" Reagan asked, kneeling in front of a flopsy Cady. She could hear them, it was just taking some time to lift her head. She tried to give a thumbs-up.

"It's just a little something I thought would be helpful. A pick-me-up. It's like ecstasy but legal…ish, legal-ish. It was supposed to make her *happy*. Huh. CADY," Birdie said loudly. "YOU'RE GOING TO FEEL AMAZING. VERY SOON."

"I'm fiiiine," Cady mumbled, face flat down against the sofa. "Justtiredbuthappy."

"See?" Birdie said, vindicated.

★ ★ ★

By the time they put Cady in an Uber home, with many hugs and kisses, she had begun to feel a surge in energy. When she protested that she was fine, she could stay, they all packed her into the cab anyway. Jay and Reagan both fought to accompany her home but she wouldn't allow it. "No, no, I'm fine," Cady said, feeling at ease. So they waved goodbye from the curb, the party over. She felt her heart rev back up, a jolt coursing through her veins. She felt free—sloppy, as though she couldn't totally control her limbs, which wanted to flail and dance to the music playing in the cab—but *free*. Her phone displayed a string of texts from Jackson that she refused to read and at least four missed calls.

She rolled down the window to let the warm night air whip through her hair.

"Sir!" she called to the driver, as though he were miles, not feet, away. "I have a crisp—" She went through her wallet, found only one twenty-dollar bill. It made her sick. "A Jackson, of course, that fucker."

She tried again. "I've got twenty bucks extra if you take me somewhere else."

Anxious to purge all Jacksons from her life, she flung the bill into the front seat with a flourish.

The cabdriver just looked over his shoulder, confused. "I'll take you anywhere you wanna go, that's my job. But I don't need this, it all goes on your Uber account, you know? Are you new here?"

Of course, she still wasn't quite thinking clearly. Well, Jay or Reagan, whoever had called the cab for her, would be paying. She would reimburse them whenever, but right now, she had more pressing matters. "Take it anyway, sir! You're so nice and isn't it just a magical night?!" Feeling winningly loopy, she gave him the new address.

25

I'M GETTING CUSTODY OF THIS BAR!!!

★

Cady flung open the door with a crash and stomped in. "I'm getting custody of this bar!!!" she shouted, still slurring.

Parker looked over as she clomped down the stairs, nearly tripping in her very-high heels.

"I was here first!" she barked, righting herself.

"Yikes," Parker said, leaping over the bar and darting across the crowded room—full of Hill denizens watching the convention post-show—to get to her. "Well, that could've been a lot worse." He laughed, grabbing her arm. "I'd get you your drink, but it looks like you've been cheating on me."

"What?" she nearly spat at him.

"Looks like you've been drinking somewhere else I mean."

"Oh. Yeah. Sorry. But not at another bar," she said, mumbling.

"Oh, good, just at home, then." He guided her to a bar stool. "I'm cutting you off. Buddy, a water over here?" he called to the bartender as Cady began to slide off the stool. He picked her up and held her around the waist. "Make that to go, Buddy!"

"*Those*—" she pointed to the bar stool "—are *very* dangerous."

"Yeah, well, so are you," he said. "You're scaring my customers, so let's call you a cab from my office where the furniture is less hazardous."

On wobbly legs, she let him pull her around the other side

of the bar and through a door with a STAFF ONLY sign. As the door swung shut, her heel tripped him and they landed in a heap on a beat-up old corduroy sofa.

He jumped to his feet, handed her a bottle of water and pulled out his phone. "Let's get you that cab," he said, tapping his screen.

She tried to drink but spilled it all over her dress. "WOW that's cold." She gasped.

"Ohhh, boy, I meant for you to drink that, but that oughtta sober you up fast at least," he said, grabbing the only thing on the coatrack: a tuxedo jacket. "Here." He held it out.

She pulled herself off the couch, shimmied on the jacket and stumbled around the room. "This is cozy," she said, opening the closet, which even through her haze she noticed was full of clothes.

"Thanks." He shut the closet door. "I like it here. It's a short commute to work," he said. "Your car is arriving in four minutes."

She plunked down in his desk chair and began opening and closing each of his desk drawers. "Looks like you spend a lotta time here."

"HEY!" He swooped over, slamming shut the bottom drawer.

"Jeez! So secretive," she said.

"Jeez, you're a very rude guest."

"No, you are."

"No, pretty sure I'm not a guest here." He looked at his phone. "Three minutes. You're a handful."

"You've said that before," she said, brow furrowed.

"That's because it's abundantly true."

"Thank you."

He shook his head. "Not really a compliment. What's with

you anyway? No offense, but you're—" he paused, arms up
"—not really yourself tonight."

"Jackson cheated on me," she said nonchalantly, spinning
around and around in the chair fast, faster, fastest.

He stopped her, both hands on the arms of the chair. "Wait.
What?"

She propped her dizzy head on her hands. "Yup."

"What an asshole," he said. "I mean, I'm sorry. I know
what that's like. Are you okay? I'm sorry, that's a stupid thing
to say. Are you—"

She flopped her head to the side; it still felt like she was
spinning. "You. Are. Cute."

"Uh, thanks?" he said.

"No. You. *Are.* Cute," she said again, as though making a
discovery then confirming her findings: "Cute. Hot-cute."

"Okay?" he said, standing upright now, ruffling his hair,
checking his phone.

In a quick sweeping motion, she charged at him, her body
hurling itself, arms around his shoulders, lips landing on or
near his mouth; she couldn't quite tell, the exertion leaving
her depleted.

"Whoaaaa there," he said, catching her messily and depos-
iting her back on the couch.

She didn't remember much about finally getting home.
Just that he helped her open her apartment door and then said
good-night once she was safely snuggled onto her sofa.

PART III

ELECTILE DYSFUNCTION

26

AND THE GENERAL ELECTION STAAAAARTS... NOW!

★

AFTER NARROWLY MISSING NOMINATION, HAZE ENTERS RACE AS INDEPENDENT

By Sky Vasquez, Staff Writer, *The Queue*

The underdog fights on: with delegate voting and negotiating still in high gear, Rocky Haze took to the podium on the convention's third night and made the game-time decision to freestyle. According to Haze insiders, the musician bagged a more formal speech that had been crafted by the party aimed at keeping the peace while delegates were still casting votes. Instead, Haze used her time to express gratitude for her supporters while also declaring her break from the party, rebranding herself an independent.

"If you still believe in me, like I do in you, join me as I continue our journey as an independent candidate for president," she told a stunned hall that quickly erupted into cheers. Wasting no time, Haze welcomed to the stage New Hampshire Governor Frank Fisher, naming him, "my running mate and your next vice president."

As the audience roared, seemingly thrilled at this hijacking of the convention, music cranked up and Haze announced,

"We call this one, 'Taking the Party With Me.'" She began her newest fight anthem.

"This is getting ugly, the party needs unity,

I'm out for now, don't pout, this process just ain't my cuppa tea

Starting something new, hope you'll come with me too

Been independent since birth

Goin' it alone, know my self-worth

Gonna hang tight, keep up the fight, do this right

Tonight: still got hopes for this country and dreams, not ready to leave this scene, not saying goodbye, just taking the party with me."

She might have continued, but the sound system went dead, stage lights turned off and the voice of an announcer overtook the auditorium: "Due to technical difficulties, today's session will be ending early. We hope to have matters resolved by the start of tomorrow's events. Thank you."

As attendees filed out of the convention center, two hashtags took the top trending spots on Twitter: #breaktheconvention and #rockyhazeforpresident...

Jay took a seat at the far end of the conference room and proceeded to look busy on his phone. Though the rest of the office had settled into that annual end-of-July summer slumber—folks taking vacations and long weekends, deadlines loosened—the Politics Desk churned on. The prickly Helena had called a meeting of the Poli Team now that the conventions had wrapped and the reporters were briefly back from the field. Everyone around the table all appeared so at home, catching up like old friends, laughing, smiling, trading war stories. Yet Jay still didn't feel quite like he fit in, even though

Sky's stories had been outranking everyone else's. It would've been easier if Sky had been there. He'd almost come home the day after Rocky's speech, but instead continued on with the Haze crew to her first appearances in New England with Fisher as her running mate. Even Sky hadn't anticipated her striking out on her own.

Helena whooshed in with a notebook, her various devices and her usual air of importance.

"And the general election staaaaarts…now!" Helena said, kicking off the meeting. "Welcome back to the faces we haven't seen in a while…" After running through the site numbers and stats, page views, new visitors, all the ways *The Queue* had benefited from this unusually zany primary season, she started down another road. "Obviously you've all done stellar work," she said. "Round of applause for yourselves." She let them clap for two-and-a-half seconds, then cut off the celebration: "BUT, as you know, the field has narrowed down considerably from a ridiculous twenty-eight candidates to three. Which means we'll need to do some restructuring to be sure our resources are being utilized to the fullest po-tential. We'll be tripling up on the candidates who are left." She laid out a rotation schedule with three reporters assigned to each candidate. When she was finished, Jay couldn't help but notice that Sky had been left off. Entirely.

"So these three subsets, I'll be meeting with you individu-ally to work out the coverage through November. The rest of you—"

Jay raised his hand, polite and respectful. He was not called upon. Helena just kept talking. Finally he shouted from the opposite side of the room: "HELENA!"

She paused. "Yes, Jay, you're free to go if you'd like."

"No, actually, that's the thing," he said. His blood began to boil, and he centered himself. He had felt so off-kilter these several months as though he was method acting what it would be like not to have Sky in his life anymore, how he would handle it if Sky left him. But they had been *all right.* They had made it work, hadn't they? He didn't want to live in fear of what might happen anymore, all that mattered at this moment was making sure that Sky got to keep doing the job he loved.

"NO!" Jay stood up, surprising himself. All eyes focused on him. "We're *good,* we don't need the extra help on Haze."

"It wasn't really a request, it was more a directive, to stand down on this," she said, frosty. "We've got more seasoned reporters—"

"I'm not going to sit here and let you take this away from Sky, who is *killing* it. Sky, who delivered this news break to you in the first place, who has had a perfect record of number one *Queue* stories and whose work has been flawless." He leaned in her direction, slamming his hand on the table for emphasis.

"Jay, look, you guys were new to the political team, you did a great job," she said. "But this is just how things work in this department. It's different from the Culture portal. Here, there are constant reassignments. It's business, not personal."

"From a business standpoint, I guarantee you won't get the access Sky has gotten if you put someone else on Haze," he said, firm.

"Jay," she snapped. "That's enough."

"No," he said. "You know what? I'm gonna hijack this meeting until you agree." A switch flipped. "I'm going to *filibuster.* I'm going to keep talking about Sky until I have your promise he continues on the beat he has been kicking ass on." He took out his phone, brought up *The Queue* app; searched for Sky's bylines.

"I'm going to have to ask you to leave—" Helena started.

"Let's take a trip down memory lane and read his work, shall we?" Jay said, ignoring her and the snickers from the others. "I'll start with the first one. There are probably, let's see, at least one or two a week since the end of January, at least thirty? 'Life of the Party,'" he began to read, projecting in a grand voice.

They tried to talk around him. They asked him to leave again. They glared. Until finally Helena put her head in her hands. "FINE! Make this stop!" she said. "We'll keep you guys on, just *stop*."

Jay smiled, sat down. Didn't even say thank you. You don't thank a thief for giving back something that was yours to begin with, he thought.

He vowed not to tell Sky. Sky finally had the confidence to do this work. Jay wouldn't let anything erode that.

The week of the convention marked a painful few days for Cady, emotionally *and* physically. If she had not completely embarrassed herself at Preamble, she might've called over and begged them to deliver some hair of the dog to her office the next day. She had woken up on her couch, still in her clothes from the day before, not sure where she was and unclear about just how much of the past twenty-four hours had been a dream.

Horrifically, she realized, it had all been real.

She considered calling in sick to work but, like a person grieving, she needed to keep busy doing the things she always did. To have some bit of normalcy and stability. Today Madison Goodfellow would be showing the viewing audience how to make a Southwestern salad using one of those kits from the supermarket with the sour cream, tortilla strips, cheese and dressing already portioned out in little Baggies and then placing it in the kind of pricey sterling silver bowl that resembled the one given to female Wimbledon champions.

Madison gave Cady one of her signature bear hugs when she

saw her, and told her to call later if she needed anything. Hank was coming to town, so she had to get back to their condo.

Cady called Reagan as soon as the show ended. She picked up right away:

"Cady, how are you?"

"Uhhhhh," Cady groaned, head in her hands.

"I was afraid of that," Reagan said. In the background the twins chanted "MomMY MomMY MomMY more cookie more cookie more cookie!"

"Shh-shh, sweeties, Mommy's talking to Aunt Cady. Aunt Cady had a bad night." The twins chanted "baaa nigh baaa nigh."

Cady loved Reagan but wasn't sure she could handle these noisy background vocals with such a hangover. She cut to the chase. "So I did something last night after I left you guys and I need you to make me feel like I don't need to enlist in the Witness Protection Program and disappear."

"One night stands are not that bad. Who was it?" Reagan said, maternal.

"No! It's not *that* bad."

"Okay. Sorry. Shoot."

Cady outlined the events, to her best recollection, after leaving Madison's place. "And so then I may or may not have thrown myself at Parker, still a little hazy on details," she said.

"What's the problem? He's supercute, have some fun, good for the soul," Reagan said, then paused. "Ohhh, wait, was he *catching* what you were throwing?"

"Um. Negative," she whispered, embarrassed.

"Ohhh. Well. I am shocked. I thought he would be all over you. Shit. Maybe I've been a mom too long, my instincts are off," she said. "Well, maybe you *thought* you were being for-ward but you were *actually* being too subtle. I could see that happening with you."

"Yeah, no, I think I was pretty clear."

"Ouch," Reagan said, not quite comforting enough. "Okay, nip this in the bud, get out in front of this—text him and just tell him you'd been drugged. It's actually true. Which is a bonus."

"Good thinking," Cady said.

She hung up and proceeded to do absolutely nothing but hope it hadn't actually happened.

27

MAYBE RELATIONSHIPS SHOULD HAVE TERM LIMITS?

★

On Friday afternoon, four long days since the implosion of her personal life, Cady found herself gazing out her office window across the river at Washington's sun-soaked skyline when she should've been reviewing the lineup for next week's shows. All the adrenaline that had kept her working like a machine all week, and had steadily stoked her fiery anger, was finally running out. It had been a good week at the show at least, and it had been comforting to throw herself into work. She didn't care what people said; sometimes, a job *could* love you back, especially when you were feeling like a blowtorch had been taken to your personal life.

The latest 'Kitchen Hacks with Madison Goodfellow' had once again been picked up everywhere. *Best Day DC* continued to be the only show getting any time at all with Madison. Cady had, of course, discovered that was because the Goodfellow campaign's punched-out press guy had been attempting to keep Madison out of the spotlight. But lucky for Cady, Madison had been determined to sneak away to keep taping her segments. "I like you, Cady, all of you all here," she'd told her. "I like that you just let me be me."

Cady knew that Madison had much more going on than anyone in media—or in her husband's camp—was giving her credit for. She could have played the perfect First Lady Hopeful if she'd wanted to. At some point, Cady would figure out the reason behind her behavior. In the meantime, she would

just revel in the attention the show received and in this unexpected friendship.

She tried again to focus on the upcoming Olympics-heavy
schedule: pretaped packages with hometown athletes prepping
for Rio, tips and recipes for viewing parties. Friday's show
would tape on location at The Grill From Ipanema, that Bra-
zilian place in Adams Morgan, where she and Jackson used to
get drunk on caipirinhas when he'd first moved to town and
she would visit on weekends. Those early trips had felt like
minihoneymoons: they spent their days in bed with no plans,
no ambition beyond getting *reacquainted*, and emerged in their
Saturday night finest for dinner and cocktails, sometimes with
groups of his friends and colleagues, always at the latest and
greatest spots. Thinking back, she had felt more a part of his
life then, more woven into his fabric, more a team, than she
had since moving in with him in January.

She grabbed her bag, hoping a coffee run would get her
through the afternoon, when her phone pinged twice in rapid
succession. Jackson: can I come home? And: guess we have stuff
to talk about? She sighed and collapsed back down in her chair.

The apologies had stopped coming by Tuesday night and
his messages had shifted to this more utilitarian: hello?

are you getting these?

did u change number?

where are U?

U in dc now? She had ignored them all.

Stuff to talk about? She shook her head now and typed
back, ya think? saying it out loud as she did, but then quickly
deleting it. "Ugh, enough with you," she said to her phone,

chucking it at her desk just as the new, nervous intern materialized with her mail. The girl looked stricken. "Not you, sorry," Cady said. "It's just… Never mind. Thanks. You're doing a great job," she added hastily. The girl skittered out.

Cady tried to declutter her desk, tossing the couple of magazines, invitations and a poster tube into her inbox, as if doing so could also help clear her mind. She returned to her cell phone. It was just too overwhelming, trying to craft the perfect response. The schizophrenic ups and downs that had been going on in her heart and her head since Monday were too complicated for this form of communication. Yet she also felt sick to her stomach when she considered what it would be like to have to *talk* to him. And *look* at him.

Sighing, she tried again and typed, whenever. i haven't changed the locks. yet. She was kidding but liked that he probably wouldn't know for sure. She hit Send. Then felt bad and sent: kidding. Then felt like she was being too nice-borderline-doormat and sent for now. *Stop*, she told herself. No more. She wasn't good at this. She didn't have a flair for the dramatic. She had always been the kind of girl guys would break up with, and she'd calmly accept, or actually, more commonly, they would just ghost her. That was even easier.

Why did it feel that in the six months since her move they hadn't actually had any *fun* together? What had they been *doing*? When she stopped to take stock—an exhaustive undertaking she had been doing involuntarily nearly every hour of every day since that train ride home from the convention— it seemed that things had actually been *worse* since the move. If she were to task the graphics department at work to chart her and Jackson's joy quotient, it would be a steep and steady decline from the night of that proposal until the rock bottom of Black Monday, as she referred to it. What had changed? It couldn't all be blamed on his constant travel. They had been long-distance before and managed much better than this. She had questions but, still, her head cautioned her heart that the answers probably weren't going to make her feel better.

He wrote back thx.

Seriously, he couldn't even spell the word out? She at least deserved a properly spelled *word*. Now she was *angry*, the adrenaline pumping again.

She sent a group text: 911: he's coming home tonight. advice? xo.

Reagan came first: have your talking points ready, type them up and print them out maybe? be tough, get answers, leave nothing unsaid.

Then Birdie: yes and book emergency appt at drybar gtown and a mani, tons of good places near there—looking grt is best revenge.

Then Jay: set the mood—for an ass-kicking—make a playlist with your fight songs. you are boss!!!!!! xx.

And finally, even Madison: just say what's in your heart.

Her nerves and anger receded and in their place, love bloomed. She sent a thank you all so much, spelled out in *proper English*, and a you're my heroes. She felt raw from this week and to have this crew swoop in to help, her own personal pep squad, it touched her. They understood her. It meant a lot to her, especially since she still didn't feel she could talk to any of her old friends about this upheaval. She just felt like they wouldn't get it, they were too far removed from this world.

With a renewed vigor, she scheduled her appointments, caught up on emails, typed up notes for her Jackson tête-à-tête, organized a playlist on her phone and then caught a cab to Georgetown.

Cady didn't mind that the salons couldn't take her until after eight and that Friday night Georgetown traffic made the trip back to the apartment even longer. She'd secretly hoped he would already be home when she arrived adequately glammed for her showdown. Let him feel what it's like to *not* have her at home. Let him notice the empty space in the closet where her dresses had hung. (She had already moved them into a garment bag Wednesday night in a fit of pique, watching Carter speak at the convention. Jackson didn't deserve to be having the best week of his life when she was having the worst of hers.) Let him see his dishes from the morning he left on his trip still unwashed in the sink (she had cleaned only her own). Let him put the TV on and have it immediately tune to Channel 8, *Best Day DC*'s station. Let him find the DVR stuffed full of episodes of *her* favorite shows, his SportsCenter deleted.

She listened to her playlist (consisting almost entirely of Rocky Haze songs) the whole way home, in her own world. When she finally returned to her building, unlocked the door, she found it almost impossible to ignore the jitters: she really should've factored in time for a glass of wine somewhere along the way.

The apartment was pitch-black, silent.

"Hello?" she said into the abyss, already knowing she wouldn't get an answer. She hated him even more now. Why wasn't he here yet? She went straight to the kitchen, their sparsely populated wine rack. No, she could do better than that. She opened the fridge and found it: the bottle of Veuve Clicquot gifted to them for their engagement. It was really nice, the kind of champagne that deserved to be saved for something important. Like tonight.

She unwrapped the seal, popped the cork neatly and poured a generous amount into a *Best Day DC* coffee mug. She settled in on the sofa, draining her mug, keeping her shoes and dress on: whenever he came home she would tell him she had only *just* gotten home herself. She was busy and important too, and had been out having fun and living her life, and look at all that he would be missing by leaving her. Just look.

When she woke up, Seth Meyers was on TV, the apartment still desolate. "Hello?" she called out. She almost expected her voice to echo back, it was that empty and lonely. Her phone showed no signs of life, save for Reagan two hours earlier: how's it going????? Cady wrote back, blood boiling: I've been stood up. To get dumped. But my hair and nails are on point. Great.

She didn't sleep well, in fits and starts, tossing, turning, thinking too much. Cady's anticlimactic night brought one bit of clarity: she really liked the idea of *not* being around when Jackson arrived. At six in the morning, she was already dressed and shoving things into a bag. She wasn't sure where she would go or how long she would be away, just that she wanted to be in control. To be the one that *he* had to put effort into seeing if he wanted to "talk." She didn't want to be the one here, waiting around.

Ted was home for a few days, so she wouldn't burden Reagan. But Sky was probably still on the trail with Rocky Haze, and Jay might be up for company. She'd wait until a decent hour and call. In the meantime, she collected her most frequently worn items into a suitcase, her makeup, hair dryer, the essentials. As she began tackling the shoes, the door rustled. *That can't be him, he would never come home this early. He never could get himself anywhere before seven on a weekend.*

He pushed open the door, suitcase wheeling in first. "Cady?" he called out, his voice deflated.

She didn't speak, just sped up her packing as though this movie had been put on fast-forward. The very sound of his voice made her furious, brought her back to that hotel room, that hideous, beautiful Willa creature that he had probably been shagging nonstop for the duration of the convention.

She had had a *plan*. Why had ALL of her plans been completely upended lately? She had *planned* to be gone, or at the very least here, looking amazing, Rocky Haze's "Notes from the Underdog" cranked up, bags packed. This wasn't how it was supposed to go down. In her ripped jeans and old white T-shirt, that stain from her iced coffee. She knew she shouldn't've made that morning Starbucks run. Where were her talking points? Why had she only printed them and not emailed them to herself? Why were they on her computer at *work*?

"Cady?" he said again; it sounded like he was in the kitchen.

The anger couldn't be absorbed anymore, it bubbled up, seeped out.

"Yeah, still here, but on my way out so you'll be free to hook up or whatever." Her voice came out like a toxic spill. "Hey, leave a tie on the door so I know if it's not cool for me come back for the rest of my stuff, okay?"

He appeared in the doorway of the closet in jeans, a sport coat and a button-down shirt open at the collar. She hated how attractive he was. She wished he had somehow become instantly repugnant-looking the moment he'd cheated on her, completing the metamorphosis from prince to horny toad.

"Hey," he said cautiously, as though waiting to be stabbed with the stiletto in her hands.

Madison's words came to her first. She took a deep breath, looked away, her heart spoke. "I can't talk to you right now." She said it firmly, zipped up her suitcase. Hopped up to her feet, slipped on the first pair of flip-flops she saw, worn-out and beat-up, not her best, oh well.

"Are you going somewhere? Now?" he asked, confused.

She pushed past him. "I can't do this now."

He followed her through the living room. "I had been wanting to talk to you, but there wasn't a good time," he said to her back as she kept walking to the door.

"That's because there's never a good time to talk about bad stuff, so you fucking make time," she said, more controlled than she had expected, proud of herself. She pulled open the door. "Or else I guess you just find someone else and figure it'll work itself out. Look, I gotta go, I can't—" Without finishing, she walked out, started down the hall. She meant she couldn't handle this right now. She didn't want to do this. At all. She didn't even care about anything he had to say; looking at him now she realized she couldn't be with him anymore. She just kept seeing that hotel room.

He followed her down the corridor.

"I didn't mean for it to go this way," he said, passing their neighbors coming back from a jog, glistening and cheery. "Don't go, let's just talk for a minute."

She kept walking to the stairwell; she always hated that there was no elevator here. She didn't want him to watch her struggle with her suitcase so ungracefully on the stairs, so she distracted him with a question: "We were apart for thirteen months. What was going on then?"

"Nothing, just you," he said. "This other thing was just the one time… Willa."

"I don't want to hear her name," she blurted out.

They'd reached the bottom of the staircase.

"Sorry," he said.

"So why was it so hard to be with me when I was *here* if you could be with me when I *wasn't*?" she said almost to herself, thinking out loud as she shoved open the front door. It closed on him.

"I don't know," he said, pushing through the door a second later.

"What do you mean you *don't know*?" she asked, sweating from the stairs. She stopped at the corner, hand in the air for a cab.

He stood in front of her, tried to look in her eyes, but she kept turning away, searching for a cab. "I don't know, maybe it's because I proposed."

"Well, who told you to go and do that? Not me. Not. ME," she said, seething. A taxi pulled up, but she was so fired up she forgot to open the door and get in.

"We're good," he said, smacking the back door and the cab took off.

"Fuck," she said. "Why won't you let me just get the hell away from you?" She set off walking, no clear destination. "What I need is a cab. Not a ring." She had worn it to work to avoid having to talk to anyone about what had happened but had taken it off last night, leaving it on top of Jackson's pristine dresser. She had already made the teary calls to her parents and brother during the week, which she tried to cap at ten minutes per call, but had still somehow amounted to a full-on ugly-cry festival that had left her feeling emotionally spent. She would just email her friends the news, at some point when she could do so without a modicum of emotion.

"I thought you wanted that."

"I didn't need that to happen the minute I got here. Especially if it was under duress like you were some kind of hostage," she said, eyes straight ahead as she walked toward Dupont Circle. The morning sun already blazing, her T-shirt sticking like flypaper in the thick humidity. Her pulse raced. She wasn't going to let this go. "I never said a word about getting engaged," she spat. Early-morning joggers began to notice their quarrel, glance at them and look away. Sure, she had hoped one day they would get engaged, you could be an independent woman and still hope for stuff like that. But it wasn't as if she had harassed him about it.

"Maybe I thought I would be a better boyfriend if I proposed?" he said.

"How'd that work out for you?"

"I don't know, maybe it's not my fault. Maybe there should just be term limits or something."

"What?"

"For relationships. Term limits."

"That's great. You're an actual caveman. That's basically just a fancy way of saying you don't believe in monogamy. Which, aside from being a totally boring excuse for what you did, is also a conversation we should've maybe had *before* you asked me to move in. And marry you. You didn't run on an antimonogamy platform."

He shook his head. "Can we just talk?"

She crossed the street, running into the park at the center of Dupont Circle. The wheels on her suitcase squeaking like they might fall off. He followed her, cars honking and almost hitting him.

"We're talking *now*. We've been talking for like, half a mile, while I walk in fucking circles. And I'm enjoying this even less than I enjoyed surprising you in Philadelphia." She still didn't know where she was going. She just cut through the center of the circle past the fountain, its mist cooling her down, past where people lay on blankets reading, where they did yoga, walked dogs, sipped coffee, all trying to politely ignore this traveling soap opera.

"Don't you want to, like, sit for a minute?"

She glanced back and was pleased to see he was sweating. She kept on.

"I just don't even know what I'm doing here," she said.

"I don't either. Where are you going?"

"No. *Here* here. Why am I even here, in Washington? Why did I fucking move here if we're not together?"

"What? You said you didn't move here just for me."

"I was *lying*! Of course I fucking moved here for you."

"Well, why'd you do that?"

She closed her eyes, squeezed her fists; it was all she could do not to scream in the middle of Dupont Circle. "I should've known it was a bad sign, like, cosmically, when you dropped the ring."

"Well, I guess," he said, hesitating. "I mean...I never *actually* dropped it."

She stopped walking finally, faced him, sure she had misheard. *"What?"*

His eyes shifted, looking everywhere but at her. "No, I mean, I was having, I guess, second thoughts? Before you got there? And—"

"Then why did you propose?" she yelled. "Why didn't you just *not* do that?"

"I... I don't know... I...don't...know... I just...maybe I thought the cold feet would go away or something? I mean, I was there and I had planned it out and all, but then all of a sudden I was dry heaving—"

"Gross—"

"And leaning over the edge, and I thought if there was no ring, then maybe it wasn't so much like a real, official proposal and I could just ease into the idea and then give you the ring later."

"You're insane, certifiably." She could barely contain herself.

"So I just put it back in my pocket."

"The ring. In your pocket," she repeated. She couldn't believe this.

"But then those guys made it into this whole thing at Rose's Luxury that night—"

"Jay and Sky. This is *so* not *their* fault—"

"No, but then it seemed okay again. It was exciting and I was good with it."

"With being engaged." She shook her head.

"So I hired a guy on Craig's List to walk the ring into the office."

"Into your office? Are you——I mean, you're, like, a sociopath basically." She realized she was still standing there on the street corner and crossed Connecticut Avenue. The sign for the Metro, an oasis.

"I just wasn't ready, and, and, and, I guess," he said, flailing as though understanding time was running out to make his case. "And I was working a lot. And then I guess you were working a lot too, which made things kind of hard, like when you just had to go to that fund-raiser and other things and I kind of was spending a lot of time with Willa, you know, as a source for her articles, but we were just friends until Air Force Two and—"

"Whoa." She stopped just before that endless escalator down to the Metro platform. A couple behind her wove around them with a nasty look. But Cady couldn't move. She thought back to how hot and cold he had been these past months, the Arnold fund-raiser he hadn't wanted her to cover, all the times he had belittled her work.

"Is this really because—" she almost couldn't say it, like she was giving herself too much credit. "Because I'm actually kind of doing well here?"

He looked away, squinting in the sun. "No, that's crazy, now you're the crazy one," he said. "Willa just was there and, you know, she respected my work and all the things that have been happening for me with this election."

"Oh, okay, sure."

"She was impressed, and you've just been too busy to—"

"Too busy? You mean, busy doing my job well?"

"Too busy to—" He seemed unable to find a single word to defend himself.

"Too busy to what? To fawn over you like some kind of groupie? To stroke your ego? Is that what this relationship was supposed to be?"

"I don't know. You just didn't look at me the same way. I wasn't as big a deal or whatever, and she made me feel—"

"I'm so not listening to this." She had heard more than enough. She stepped onto the escalator, didn't say goodbye or storm off, just one light step and it took her down. She closed her eyes to keep from checking to see if he was watching.

28

THERE'S A MOLE IN SHEEP'S CLOTHING?

★

It wasn't until after Monday's show and subsequent planning meetings, that it occurred to Cady to tackle some of the many tasks she had let slide last week, what with all the inner turmoil. She began sorting through the slim stack of mail now, much of it duplicates of things already lurking in her email. Even though she had Metroed to the office, suitcase in tow, directly after her weekend fight with Jackson, she certainly hadn't done anything resembling work that day. She'd had plenty else to keep her busy like reading through the list on her computer confirming that she had addressed several of her talking points with Jackson. (Even if she had failed to deliver the various zingers she had worked so hard to craft.)

When she finally called Jay, he had extended the invitation instantly: "We are presently accepting emotionally wounded refugees," he had said kindly. She insisted on buying him dinner as a thank-you, and when he dictated that they order in and watch movies instead, it was like he'd read her mind. She knew Sky would be returning the following week, so she would have to figure out somewhere else to stay then, but for the time being, she was grateful for the couch.

Inbox cleared, desk in order, she finally got to that poster tube that had been hanging around. She popped open the top, slid out a rolled poster and found a note on Preamble stationery.

Cady,

You may or may not remember (probably not actually) dropping by Preamble the other night. Just a note to say that these words helped me when my world exploded. Independence can be a good thing. Pursue your happiness. The founding fathers had it right.

Yours, Parker.

PS: Okay, ulterior motive here: you still have my only tuxedo jacket. Not that I need it anytime soon. But it lives here at the bar, on the coatrack in my office. It's like a pet or a plant that I'm just used to having around. Thanks.

The jacket. She had forgotten all about it, but could picture it now, crumpled in the corner of the closet. She would have to go back to the apartment for it when Jackson was out. It was already too late today, she couldn't risk it, but she could leave work early tomorrow on a rescue mission.

She unrolled the poster: the Declaration of Independence, the kind they sold in so many of the museum gift shops, but with the words "pursuit of happiness" circled grandly in silver spray-paint. The same words she had seen as graffiti on the wall of Preamble. She grabbed a roll of tape from her desk, balanced on a chair and stuck it up on her office wall right above the TV so she would look at it all the time.

With your blessing, I shall leak this today. Conventions are over, this can dominate the news cycle, the email greeted Madison first thing that morning. It's go time.

I trust you. Let's go for it, Madison typed back as she hopped on the elliptical machine in the mirrored gym of their Upper East Side town house. I'm ready to do my part. It'll be tough but

I can get it done in time. She felt a little queasy, but she needed to put on her game face now. Like any fire baton twirler worth her weight in lighter fluid, Madison believed strongly in the mantra Go Big Or Go Home. Or, as it had been declared by one of her key donors the night she had crashed the Arnold fund-raiser: great risk brings the potential for history-making rewards. She also believed she might as well get paid handsomely for something she was already planning to do for free, challenging as it would be.

As she finished her five miles on the machine, CNN already had it. The banner on the screen read: Anti-Goodfellow Super PAC: $7 million and Counting.

She turned up the volume to hear Grant Foxhall. "There's been plenty of *talk* surrounding the notion of an anti-Goodfellow movement, with little evidence of an organized effort," the handsome anchor began. "Until now. Suddenly nonbelievers have put their money where their mouths are. A Super PAC called Up To No Goodfellow has surfaced claiming to already have accumulated $7 millon to invest in preventing Hank Goodfellow from becoming the next commander in chief. The group claims on its newly launched website, it may use donations to 'support Goodfellow's opponents, fund attack ads or find new and novel ways to chip away at the grossly underqualified candidate.' It also boasts a mole inside the Goodfellow camp. In coming weeks we'll be anxious to see if this has any impact on the candidate's so far steady poll numbers."

Madison felt the guilt seep into her skin like a chemical peel gone bad, and switched channels to escape it. A sudden flurry of activity came from upstairs: conversation, stomping, something shattered, phones ringing. Members of the Machine, no doubt hearing the same news. She froze in place, turned down the volume: Hank's voice, muffled by the distance but also ranting and raving. "There's a goddamn mole in here? Who is it? Who's the goddamn mole?"

"That's the problem, sir, we don't know," someone said, probably Mike.

"So you mean to tell me there is a mole in sheep's clothing?" Hank said. He always had trouble with metaphors.

"Um, yes," Mike said.

"All these years I've never dealt with more lyin' cheatin' lowlifes," he said, and she could just picture him shaking his head. "I've gotta know who I can trust. I am all about trust. You know that. I know that. I need the American people to know that."

Deep in her heart, Madison knew she was doing the right thing, but it did not feel good. Kind of like the time she had tried the Master Cleanse, but much, much worse. Hank was a good man. But she knew him better than he knew himself these days. And he refused to listen to her when she told him this might not be the right *business venture* for him. All she had to do was think of their son, Henry, that call he'd made to her back in the beginning of the year. "What's going on with Dad, Mom? Why does he sound so hyped up all the time? He talks about invading countries and stuff, but I kind of feel like he doesn't understand what's happening in the world sometimes," Henry had said in a whisper, as though speaking this way was treason. "We've been studying a lot of this in class, US foreign policy through the years, and it's heavy, complicated stuff. Does he know what he's talking about?"

She couldn't lie to Henry and had told him simply, "I don't know, sweetheart." But she *did* know that this could be bad for business in the long run. This could threaten to destroy all he had built for himself. The company, the sports teams, these were what mattered to him. The rest had just been a power trip. In the oil world and the sports arena, Hank had been in his domain and branded himself a charming-Southern-playboy-with-an–occasional-wild-streak turned family man. He had never paid much mind to politics. Sure, his associates would make the offhand suggestion a few times a year when strong quarterly reports would come in for the company: "What *haven't* you conquered yet, Hank? Are you gonna run for president one day?" It had clearly gotten to his head, as can happen when you're a person who is generally successful at everything you try, as Hank was. So she had taken a deep breath and said to their beloved boy, who was so much wiser than either of them, "The next few months may look a little…odd…for our family, but I'll sort this out for us all. Have the kids at school been giving you any trouble about this?"

Henry had hesitated just enough, then, "It's okay. A couple of them are assholes—"

"Language, sweetheart."

"But, whatever. Those guys are like that with everyone about something, so it's no big thing," he continued. "And everyone else is pretty cool, the guys on the team and all, they know it's not me up there."

She was instantly grateful that Henry was not only a smart, levelheaded young man with solid friends to count on, but also a gifted lacrosse player, who was already being recruited by the Ivies. Talent could protect and insulate you against the world in some ways, she had always thought. She had long wished to have some skill that truly commanded respect. Beauty was the polar opposite, but you work with what you've got.

"Keep studying and playing hard, sweetie, okay? This will get settled, sooner or later," she'd said, wishing she could be more comforting. When he was about to hang up, she stopped him. "Henry. You know, sometimes people need to be saved from themselves and sometimes the only way to do that, and to reach them, is by hitting them over the head with things, sort of."

"Okay, Mom" was all he had said.

Madison took the elevator upstairs to avoid running into the Machine. The plan with her donors had been to let him get the nomination, then talk him out of it, leaving the field wide-open for Arnold to win the election. By then it would be too late for Hank's party to put up a replacement candidate with any hope of winning, and Madison knew no one much cared for the likely choice, Hank's VP pick. Even that, Hank had gotten wrong. A political lightweight state senator who had once been a baseball player. He should've picked the girl.

Figuring out when to strike would not be easy. Madison had barely had any alone time with Hank in weeks. She peeled off her gym clothes—from her own line developed for that chain a few years ago, now discontinued. They didn't wick away the sweat as much as she had hoped but had been a good price point and she still took pride in wearing them nonetheless— and stepped into the shower, hoping to wash away this feeling of dread.

Dear Motherfucker,
As a mom, it seems hard to get positive reinforcement or confir-
mation that you're not completely fucking up. Do you ever feel
like the day is somehow often a series of fails no matter what
you do?
Asking for a Friend

Dear Friend,
Please, the last time I got any kind of positive job performance
review was during labor when my doc told me I was a good
pusher and asked how much yoga I'd done during my preg-
nancy. I'm expecting again, ask me how much yoga I'm doing

now— None. (Though I am wearing yoga pants every day.)
I receive this question in some form every week, and yes, as a
mom, the days are manic depressive with highs and lows—your
kid ate a vegetable: score!; your kid took off all their clothes and
ran out into the front yard: fail!—but as long as you're giving
them love, then everyone's winning. When I'm feeling down,
I steal extra hugs, I squeeze their plump, pinchable thighs, kiss
their chubby cheeks and I feel better. And a glass of wine after
bedtime doesn't hurt. By the way, let me tell you what no one
else will: you're doing great, keep up the good work, Mama.

Reagan finished her column during the twins' nap time
(rereading it she was reminded yet again of how much she
had changed since they'd come into her life, how they had
softened her edges, how she hadn't understood how delicious
babies were until she'd had them), and then she did the unthinkable: she sat down for a few minutes, put her swollen
feet up and turned on the TV. She flipped between the news
networks and stopped at MSNBC: footage from the requisite
trip to DC's own Ben's Chili Bowl. John Arnold stood smiling as he ordered at the counter of the famous eatery, then,
sleeves rolled up, he dug into what the general viewing audience might call a messy chili dog—but what she knew to be
the Original Chili Half-Smoke—and gave a thumbs-up for the
camera. Over his left shoulder in the background, Ted stood
in profile, tapping away on his phone. The nostalgia washed
over her, and she had an idea. It didn't look like it was a live
shot, but she wanted to try anyway.

Unearthing her phone from between sofa cushions, amid
a treasure trove of spilled Cheerios, she texted Ted: Having a
craving, are you still on U Street???

The craving wasn't so much for chili as it was for their first
date, those early, fizzy days and months and years of their

relationship when they used to swing by the famous spot tipsy, always their last stop during a night out.

Two minutes later she received a photo of what appeared to be the inside of the fridge at the Arnold campaign headquarters with a Ben's Chili Bowl take-out bag front and center: already on it... he wrote.

Did I mention I love you?

me too—and I don't mention it enough. Did I also mention the secret ingredient: nutmeg.

it's a curry. She had always been confident.
cinnamon. He never really purported to have any idea.

curry!

kumquats.

She laughed out loud. He was in a good mood today. She wrote back: yuzu?

you who?

ras el hanout?

rhubarb?

This had been their ongoing debate on their very first date: trying to guess the secret ingredients in Ben's Chili. As that night had worn on, and the drinks had flowed, and they had fallen for each other (she still remembered being transfixed by that stunning contrast of his jet-black hair and brows against

his ice-blue eyes), the suggestions had become more outland-
ish. It became a long-running inside joke in the years since
then. It made her smile now to think back.

She was already asleep when he got home, but she enjoyed
her own Original Chili Half-Smoke for breakfast.

29

I'M DEFRIENDING YOU—RIGHT NOW

★

Mercifully, five o'clock was way too early for Jackson to have been home from work, so Cady let herself into the apartment and found it empty. Just three days since their fight and already the place had ceased to feel like home. She quickly located the jacket just where she thought it was—it wasn't in such bad shape, though she wished she had actually hung it up instead of just tossing it on the floor of the closet. But she obviously hadn't been her best self that night, what could you do?

She Metroed to Preamble, not bothering to tell Parker she was coming. She kind of hoped it would be busy enough there that she could just leave it with one of the bartenders and then disappear. She just wasn't feeling particularly social.

The place was in full swing, so many Hill staffers and even a congressman or two swigging beers and watching the TVs oscillate between news and sports. Still, somehow, amid the happy hour ruckus, he seemed to spot her the minute she walked in.

"One Sour Suffragette coming up—unless this is the end of another pub crawl for you," he called out.

She tried to smile, embarrassed. "Nope, not drinking to-night," she said, but it came out a little too sour indeed, so she added, "There's a first time for everything, right?"

"Just don't make a habit of that, last thing a bartender wants to hear." He smiled as she approached the crowded bar.

"Thank you for this," she said, handing over the jacket. "I think it probably looks better on you, so I'm returning it."

"Nah, I'd have to disagree. You're welcome to borrow it anytime."

"I'll keep that in mind." She wanted to laugh, but feeling that her spirit was dulled, looked away a moment, noticing the spray-painted mantra on the far wall as she did. "Oh, almost forgot. Thank you, also. For the poster. You'll be happy to know it's hanging proudly in my office." She said it all just a little too flat.

"Anytime," he said, squinting at her like a cop who wasn't buying a suspect's alibi. "Although, it looks like you're still not living up to Thomas Jefferson's dream."

"Huh?"

"Thomas Jefferson? Pursuit of happiness?" he said, a little impatient.

"Exactly, got it, that's—" she started to defend herself.

"What's goin' on here?" he cut her off, waving his hand. "Your whole...energy...or something...is off."

"Oh, yeah, no, I'm about to pursue my happiness, any minute now. I just had other stuff to do today. You know, emails to return, groceries to buy, exes to evade—it was not easy going back to get that." She gestured to his formalwear.

"I appreciate your sacrifice." He smiled kindly. "So, no drinking, got it. You know, don't tell the others but we actually do serve nonalcoholic beverages too."

"Thanks, I think I'm good today. Next time." She waved, turning to walk away.

Jay had been kind enough to give her a key, so at least she could get in to his place if he was still at work. She thought she might even walk for a little while. But in a few steps Parker was by her side again.

"You know what?" He stopped her.

"Whoa," she said, startled. "Hi. Again."

"I don't think you're good today."

"Well, that's not very nice to say."

"As a bartender, who was also a psych major, I think you have what we in the business call...the blues."

"That's a scientific, medical term?" she asked, still walking to the door.

"And I don't know where you're going right now," he said, following her. "But it's probably not as fun as this place."

"For a walk. And then Metro."

"Yeah, that sounds terrible."

"Thanks."

"Can you at least go do something, anything, better than that if you're determined to *not* be here?"

"I don't know."

"I can think of a thousand places you could go to get a jump on pursuing your happiness."

"I told you, I'm going to put that off just, like, one more day."

He held the door open for her. "Okay, how about if I put you in a cab and send you somewhere, and then you can get to your pressing matters of walking and taking public transportation?" His arm flew up to hail a cab and somehow, instantly, one arrived.

"It never works like that for me," she said to herself.

He opened the door and closed it behind her. "Hey there," he said to the driver. "She's going to..." He paused to think. "Natural History Museum."

"I don't like dinosaurs," she called from the back seat, like a grumpy child.

"The dinosaurs are under construction, you're safe. No, go to the second floor, butterflies." He paused for a moment, just as the driver nodded and hit the gas. "Wait!" he yelled. The cab stopped, and Parker yanked the door open. "Move over."

"You're very bossy today."

"I don't trust you. I'm coming with you."

The ticket area for the butterfly pavilion was empty, the cashier pointing to a sign to explain why: they had just missed the last viewing of the day. Cady didn't mind so much, she felt like she wasn't the best company right now anyway. She still couldn't believe Parker had come along.

"Look, Chris," he said, reading the cashier's name tag. "I didn't want to have to bring this up, but she just got dumped."

"Thanks," she said.

"And, metaphorically, she needs to remember how to fly again, you get me?"

Cady gave Parker a look, not appreciating his commentary.

"I was a poetry minor. Very minor, I wasn't very good," he explained.

Still, the cashier agreed to speak to the butterfly wrangler and in no time they were standing in the vestibule, just waiting to be let in for their own private session.

"Trust me, it's impossible to be pissed off in here," Parker said.

The wrangler arrived, and they stepped into the humid room lined with so many plants and trees. A puff of water-misted air pumped in, and the butterflies that had been lounging on the leaves and flowers, hidden among the vegetation, spread their wings and took flight, swirling around the two of them. Suddenly the winged creatures were everywhere. Cady watched them fly and laughed as they touched down on her bare arms and then flitted away again.

"Don't move," Parker said, taking out his phone and snapping a picture: a monarch had landed in her hair, perched there like a beautiful barrette.

★ ★ ★

"You know what's almost worse than the emotional shit after the breakup?" he asked, taking a bite of his ice-cream cone. Parker had insisted they patronize the ice-cream truck outside the museum. "The practical shit. Like, 'Oh, thanks, now I have to find a new place to live.' 'Great, what do I do with all my stuff now?' Who has time for all that? We're busy people with busy lives!"

He didn't say any of it bitter or angry, but in a funny way that made her smile.

"Ugh," she groaned dramatically, licking her ice cream. "I forgot that I even *have* stuff. Like real baggage not just the emotional kind."

The sun had set and the sky was just beginning to dim. The Mall still hummed with the activity of early August: joggers, tourists trickling out of museums, staffers on recess taking the scenic route home.

"I know, it sucks," he said. "But I've got a great storage unit in Alexandria. Supercheap. And there's plenty of room if you want." He shrugged.

"Eek, I feel like that's maybe where I went wrong," she said with a laugh. "Maybe my stuff shouldn't cohabitate with anybody's stuff anytime soon. What if your stuff got sick of my stuff and just kicked it out one day with no warning?"

"My stuff is very friendly. I don't think that would happen. But I respect your decision, very levelheaded."

They cut across one of the paths, walking the width of the Mall to the opposite side, and stopped before the carousel. Patriotic music filled the air. A few kids were still riding before it closed for the night.

"We're going on that," Parker said, tossing the rest of his ice cream in the trash and taking hers to do the same.

"Hey!" she said, but he was already buying tickets.

"We have to get the sea dragon," he explained, bolting as soon as the gate opened and yanking her hand. They ran halfway around the carousel until he finally stopped at a turquoise serpent.

"I saw you glare at that child." She laughed.

"Gotta do what you gotta do," he said, gesturing for her to take a seat on the sea dragon as he climbed onto a nearby horse.

"It *is* pretty cool," she admitted, petting the dragon, then leaping up to ride sidesaddle. An attempt to be ladylike since she hadn't expected to end up here when she put on her dress and heels that morning. Maybe she should have been more embarrassed, but being there, it was just so ridiculous. She kind of loved it. Besides, they weren't the only adults unaccompanied by minors.

The music cranked up, and they set off with a boom. She laughed, almost kicked off her serpent. "I've got a feisty one," she said.

They began spinning, wind whooshing through her hair as the sea dragon glided. She watched the Mall pass by, surprised to find her mind was finally at peace.

She had expected to head back to Jay's after the carousel, but Parker said there was one more place to see and hailed another cab. "It's near your apartment anyway," he said.

Curious, she decided not to tell him she was staying in an entirely different neighborhood.

The cab dropped them off where 22nd Street dead-ended. In the dim streetlight, nestled in among trees, mysterious steps led to a fountain flanked by two curved staircases. It felt like a secret hideaway, tucked in this nook so close to the bustling center of Dupont Circle.

"I give you, DC's version of the Spanish Steps." He gestured. "You're welcome."

She followed him up to the fountain, where the statue of a lion stared back at them.

"I never knew this was here, and I've been living just a few blocks away all this time," she said, taking it in.

"I know. That's what's so great about it," he said. "I used to live near here and found it by accident one day, and I wondered why no one had told me about it."

"Probably because everyone who knows it's here wants to think they're the only ones who know," she said.

"Exactly. But, you know, secrets don't keep that long in this town," he said.

They climbed the staircase to the landing above the fountain, which connected to S Street, and sat on a ledge overlooking the lion's head.

"So anyway, my point in all of this is, there are plenty of distractions here, no matter how messed up you feel," he said, staring out into the darkness.

"Point taken," she said.

"Have you done the purge yet?"

"The what?"

"It's pretty key, for your well-being. Gimme your phone." He held out his hand, shook his fingers. "C'mon, you'll thank me."

She dug her phone from her bag and relinquished it.

"Let's delete him," he said, all business.

"Seriously?"

"Delete him and block him or just delete him?" He didn't wait for an answer. "You know what? We'll go easy for now, just delete." Parker fiddled with her phone. "I'm all over this. I just did this stuff. I'm like the Geek Squad for Breakups now."

"Thanks?" she said, unsure.

"I promise, you'll be glad. Then you won't be tempted to call, and let's face it, no good can come of us calling these people. He's not blocked though, so you know, nothing that can't be undone."

"Oh, it's okay. I think it's done," she said quietly. "I mean, I know it's done. I guess."

"It won't always feel this bad," he said, tossing pebbles into the fountain below.

She watched them fall. Several long seconds passed, so many that she forgot for a moment that Parker was there beside her. Her mind was all over the place, sorting through and trying to make sense of things, a jumble of conflicting impulses. Finally, she was drawn back to the present, her voice lower now, more cautious, as she spoke.

"I find you kind of annoying," she said slowly, just stealing a quick glance at him. She liked how his lips seemed to curve into the slightest smile, even at rest.

"Possibly not the first time I've heard that. But what's *your* reason?" he said.

"Why are you handling your breakup so much better than I am mine?" She had vowed to move on, fast, not be one of these sad sacks with plenty of other good stuff in their lives but with their self-worth tied up in a guy.

"Me? Are you kidding?" His tone just a shade darker than it had been. "I am a complete disaster."

"You don't seem that way," she said, almost accusatory. "Aside from the broken arm a while back, you seem all healed, overall. I'm sure you're meeting babes at your bar every night, no problem, living the good life."

"Well, I appreciate that you have this warped idea of me. I probably should just agree with you, yes, that is exactly how it is to be me. It's awesome. But seriously, I'm a mess. Still. And just because I'm a nice guy, I'll tell you all about what a fuckup I really am so you can feel better about yourself."

"Oh, good," she said, cheerful.

"Yeah, settle in, there's a lot. So. Despite all of the great press, all orchestrated by you, I might add—thank you—"

"Anytime."

"—we are still barely breaking even, which freaks me out. I heard that Melanie moved in with the guy she left me for. Which I totally don't care about because I'm done with her, but she's allegedly *fully* moved on. *And* has a new place. Meanwhile, I am living in my *office* at the *bar*. No joke. Sleeping on the sofa."

"It *is* comfy," she argued.

"Yeah, well, not every night."

"And some congressmen do that, stay in their offices."

He continued. "I can't get those guys from my old office to stop coming in and harassing me."

"This isn't sounding *so* horrific."

"My arm is still messed up and my elbow stiffens up—" he held his arm out, studying it "—and, like, won't bend when it's about to rain, which is practically every fucking day in the summer in Washington."

"Okay, true. That kind of sucks."

"And even though it's gross, I saved my cast after they sawed it off, and I have it in my desk because it was signed by the girl I'm kind of, maybe, completely in love with even though she probably thinks I'm just a friend, with the exception of when she's drunk, which doesn't really count. And it's probably not smart to be in love again yet. But—"

Cady felt the blood in her veins run green, envious. "Wait." She looked at him, disappointed. "I thought I was the only one who signed that cast."

He was quiet for a moment, throwing endless pebbles into that fountain. "You are." He sighed.

Her heart beat too loudly in her chest, and for a second she remained frozen.

But then she felt a gravitational pull, a rip current. It swept her, and she didn't want to fight. She leaned into him.

"Jeez, it doesn't help when you look at me like that," he said.

"Like what?" she asked, unsure, taking a breath.

"Like that. With your *eyes*."

"How else am I supposed to *look* at you?"

"No, with your eyes all deep and whatever. That messes me up. It's not a nice thing to do." He looked away again.

"Really." She said it as a statement.

"Yeah, really," he said, meeting her eyes again, focused.

"Then you're definitely not going to like this." She inched toward him, her lips finally landing on his and finding them willing participants this time. His hand gripped the back of her head, pulling her closer, while his other arm held her firmly against his body. Her arms wound their way around his neck.

"I don't know why you think I'm your friend." Her words came out just breathless enough, her eyes locked on his. "I don't *want* to be your friend," she said, just now fully understanding it herself.

"Say that again," he whispered into her lips before kissing her again.

She breathed him in. "I am defriending you. Right. Now."

"Me too," he said softly into her ear, tightening his arms around her, kissing her again, lowering her along the ledge as he did.

Each breath he took she could feel in her own chest. She felt a good kind of dizzy, like that other night, but not from any drug this time. His hold on her the only thing keeping her from sliding, it was a considerable feat they hadn't fallen down into the fountain by now. But she couldn't think of that. Only physical; only him.

She thought the siren was in her head at first, some kind of internal flare telling her to take another breath. But then he pulled away too, and they both jumped, startled. They turned back as a police car raced down S Street, followed by another, to a destination unknown.

He grabbed her hand and pulled her as they took off running, not stopping until they reached her block.

"I don't know why I ran." He laughed as they slowed their pace to a stroll.

"Seemed like a good idea at the time," she said, their fingers still entwined.

"It's not like they were looking for us, right?" he joked. "Worst thing I've done in months was bounce a check, and it was just the one and there were extenuating circumstances."

"Hardly the stuff of police car chases," she said. She was still drunk on him, not paying attention as he stopped in front of her building.

"I have to tell you—I wanted to kiss you the night you showed up at the bar, but I've always had this policy about not kissing girls who won't be able to remember it."

"That's a good policy," she said. "I have to tell you, I'm kind of not living here right now."

By the time they finally arrived at Jay's U Street apartment, she was feeling as she had before the sirens; she didn't want Parker to leave.

"I hate that I kind of don't really live here," she said into the golden flecks of his eyes.

He answered her with another kiss and then, "I hate that you kind of don't really live here too."

"You should—" She was about to say come up. He should definitely come up. Now. Maybe Jay was out. Or else she could just kick Jay out. Of his own apartment. Or something. She would figure it out during the elevator ride between here and there.

But Parker ruffled his hair, in that shy way of his, and said, "I should probably quit while I'm ahead—I mean, I'm ahead, right?"

"Yes," she said. "You're definitely ahead."

"For the record, I'll regret this as soon as I get back to the bar," he said, like it was a promise. "But as mistakes go, there are worse, right?"

Mischievous smile, hands in his pockets, he turned and walked away.

30

I THOUGHT WE WERE A TEAM

★

In his heady, blissful prereunion haze, Jay had little focus left for such mundanities as editing, so he turned on the TV. "The fascinating thing going on with the Haze movement—and I think we can safely call this a movement at this point—is that this is a person who's told us that character and loyalty are important," Buck Brandywine told Grant Foxhall and a panel of strategists on CNN's morning show. No matter that Jay's office TV wasn't HD, he could see there was no ring on Buck's left hand. "She's not using the playbook we're used to. This unity ticket is shocking enough. Two parties, one ticket, God love her for trying this. She told us labels don't matter, and now she's showin' us that."

"And let's talk about that running mate," Grant said. "New Hampshire Governor Frank Fisher is safe, but he's also from the only state she doesn't need help winning. Again, loyalty and character in that decision?"

"Absolutely," Buck said, adding with a laugh, "Not the kinda thing we're accustomed to seeing in the political landscape— loyalty and character. But Fisher was first in line with his endorsement. He legitimized her campaign. It seems she likes to reward those who've been good to her. We'll see how far she can take this. Fun to watch, that's for sure. Can't get much more antiestablishment than this."

"Your wife still listening to a lotta Haze?" Grant asked in that glib way of his.

Was he blind? What was wrong with him? Jay wanted to email Birdie, but they weren't that kind of close. He still felt the distance that came with reverence and respect. And she hadn't said a word about it that night at Madison's, a natural time as any for her to have brought it up.

"She's always had great taste in music, as in everything," Buck quipped. "Except maybe men." They laughed.

Jay flipped back to MSNBC, not wanting to kill his buzz by thinking about his favorite couple on the rocks. There was too much joy to revel in: Sky would be coming home today, a pit stop for a few days since Rocky was campaigning in the area. He touched down at one thirty and would be coming straight to the office. Jay had been too excited to sleep, staying up late talking with Cady after her impromptu date. He was lucky Ted was back in town, otherwise Cady would have been staying with Reagan instead, and he'd needed the reminder of what it felt like to have someone want to be with you. He had fallen in love with how he felt around Sky and how he felt about himself around Sky, but had been desperately clinging to the feeling. He only hoped Sky had been too.

He had finally gotten through a theater review—the Woolly Mammoth had already staged a send-up of the election, they sure worked fast—when he heard the knock. Jay looked up and felt his eyes and heart leap from his body. Sky opened the door, amber eyes glowing, looking like a hipster newshound in black jeans, a vest and short-sleeve button-down.

"Never thought I'd say it, but I missed this place," he said, swinging the door shut behind him and dropping his bag on the floor to embrace Jay tightly.

"Almost forgot what you looked like," Jay said. "Almost." Sky kissed Jay's cheek, and then his pillowy lips were full, firm and fast on Jay's, taking him by surprise. It was their first kiss in the office, but Jay had stopped caring; they had earned it.

Sky collapsed into the chair in front of Jay's desk, and Jay took his seat again. They watched each other a few seconds; Jay wished they were at home, his, Sky's, anywhere but here. But he would take what he could get. "Tell me everything," Jay said.

"Oh my God, Rocky has been—"

Jay cut him off. "Everything that I haven't already read in your copy and reporting files."

For half an hour they caught up in rapid-fire bits and pieces, so much to fill each other in on.

"Wanna hang with the press pool tonight? Oh! So, Paz and Steve are like, a full-on, thing now. Be prepared. They're not even trying to hide it. It's almost unprofessional, gotta say," Sky said, slouching in the chair, scrolling through texts and emails.

"Wow, good for them," Jay said, unsure if they were supposed to be supportive of this or wary of it. He still didn't know Sky's campaign friends well enough to have formed an educated opinion.

"But Rocky's whole campaign vibe is so loose. I mean, you know, I totally have to write about this today, but we took her jet here. She's upgraded us from the buses."

"Seriously, write it up," Jay said.

"She said now that her candidacy is cemented and all, it makes sense. And remember when Rihanna had that party jet we covered? It feels like *that*. Rocky was handing out drinks and snacks *herself* and answering everyone's questions, like, nothing off-limits, and she had this acoustic jam session. It's a long way of saying I wish you were there."

Jay's phone rang: "Helena," he said with reflexive dread.

"That's my cue for sure," Sky joked.

"No, it's okay," Jay said, not wanting him to leave so soon. He wasn't ready to share Sky with the newsroom.

"Better get to my desk, look busy." He smiled and let himself out.

★ ★ ★

Not even an hour later, Sky appeared at Jay's door as he went over edits with a reporter on a profile of Dave Grohl pegged to his upcoming show at the Black Cat. ("We need more on life now, family, et cetera et cetera. Everyone knows he didn't graduate from that high school in Alexandria, no one cares. He's like the best ad ever for dropping out.") This time Sky just barged right in, hands on his waist, concerned look in his eyes. Jay jumped off the phone abruptly.

"Hey, you okay?"

"Why didn't you tell me they wanted me off the campaign?" Sky asked and folded his arms across his chest in a way Jay did not like to see.

He felt like he'd been knocked out. "What do you mean?" Jay said, instantly regretting it. Sky's reporting was always solid.

"You know what I mean," he said. "I'm sitting at my desk and Sophie comes up and tells me there was this whole thing in a meeting. She says your speech has become 'legend.'"

"Well, I don't know I would go that far," Jay said, secretly flattered that people were still talking about it. Sometimes it was good to shake things up, especially if you had a nice-guy reputation. The way he saw it, that speech was one of the greatest things he had done for his career since accepting the Arts editing gig over that Opinions section job in the early days.

"Well, it seems kind of like a big deal, maybe you would've at least mentioned it in one of the millions of texts or calls in the past week."

Jay took a breath. "First of all, if Sophie spent a little more time writing and a little less time trying to audition for a gossip reporting job that isn't available, then it would be better for everyone." He was getting tired of Sophie. She hadn't even been in that meeting.

"This doesn't really have anything to do with her."

"Okay," Jay said, shaking his head. "I was acting as your representative here, your agent, your coach sort of, you know? I wasn't going to let any of the drama *here* get in the way of you doing what you do on the playing field." He liked sports metaphors even though he wasn't much of a fan. "I was protecting you and your work. I don't see how it's a bad thing. You should've seen this meeting. It was completely unfair."

"Maybe you should just be my editor and tell me what's going on," he said. "I don't need you to treat me like a child."

"I wasn't, I'm sorry. It's obviously exactly the opposite of what I wanted to have happen." Jay stood now, upset at how this was going, unsure how to turn it back around. "I had the best intentions."

"I don't like secrets," Sky said.

"No, I know, me neither," Jay said.

"I thought we were a team."

"I know, we are. I made a mistake, I'm sorry."

But Sky just walked out. Jay followed to the door, where he watched Sky stride past the cubicle colony and keep going.

Jay sat down in his chair, like he might be having a heart attack. Yes, that's exactly what it was: it was a broken heart attack. He felt the same as everyone who found themselves ambushed, engaged in a fight that made no sense to them. Pure misunderstanding. He had mounted no defenses; he hadn't thought he'd need any.

He didn't see Sky the rest of the day, despite passing his empty desk three times and shooting daggers at Sophie as she left the yoga studio. He texted Sky on his way home: I'm sorry Sky, not sure what happened today.

He got a call back, and Sky launched in as soon as Jay picked up: "Look, Jay, the election has made me crazy. I feel like a vet from a really weird war on, like, another planet trying to reacclimate."

"I understand," Jay said softly.

"No, you mean well, but you don't. You can't," he said, controlled, weary.

That hurt Jay more than anything. It had always been his fear that the time apart would somehow change them and make them not fit together in the same way.

"I'm sorry, listen, I'm just exhausted," Sky continued. "You're the person I love most, so you're the easiest target. I don't know, maybe I'm at a place where I wouldn't mind a break, like a couple days off."

His chest squeezed, but he was able to get out two words. "A break?"

"From the campaign, Jay."

"Oh!" He was speechless.

"Maybe the idea of sharing this beat would've been nice. This schedule is rough."

It occurred to Jay that he had possibly overcorrected, gone from wanting Sky home to nearly banishing him. His mind worked in extremes and absolutes; he didn't know why. "How about if I bring over Busboys and wine?"

"I think I just want to crash tonight, if that's okay," Sky said.

"Sure, of course," Jay said, but he was anything but sure. No matter what Sky said about just wanting time off from the campaign, to Jay, it still felt more personal than that.

31

I'M NOT HUNGRY, I MADE A MISTAKE

★

Just before noon, two days after that kiss at the Spanish Steps that she couldn't stop thinking about, an email popped up in Cady's inbox.

Subject: "what's for lunch?"

Not sure what the proper amount of time is to get in touch after a date—was that a date? not being presumptuous, but definitely the best date/non-date/whatever I've ever had—anyway: hey there. Not stalking you, however, wanted to make sure you were aware in case you're looking for exciting new lunch options: the Preamble truck is at Wilson & N. Pierce Tuesdays and Thursdays 11:30 till 2:30. (And if I'm not mistaken, today is, in fact, Thursday.) I feel like you're not the food truck type—except I guess for formal events (too soon for that joke? Sorry. Never mind.)—that's cool, no pressure. But, you know, there's a special going on today: free meals for all TV show producers named Cady…
Yours, Parker

It was so him, she had to smile. It was true; she had never once visited the strip of food trucks around the corner from her office, but there was a first time for everything. She wrapped up some work, then dabbed on more lip gloss, smoothed her hair and went out in search of lunch.

She found a long line of people braving the oppressive, steamy August heat outside the Preamble truck, and suddenly felt like she was waiting outside the stage door for a band to emerge after a concert. Like a groupie. Not her favorite feeling, but still exciting. Eventually she made her way to the front. A man inside the truck had his back to her, flipping a burger on the grill, but he didn't look tall enough to be Parker. Then someone popped up from below the window.

"Hi! What can I get for you?" a woman said perkily. She had high cheekbones, perfectly pouty lips and bodacious bouncy caramel hair that was more appropriate for a shampoo commercial. Frankly it should have been tied back. Cady was looking for faults, she knew, and that was all she could find. The woman had the kind of curvy figure that made the Preamble T-shirt look like it was designed for her and made Cady instantly disappointed with her own boobs in a way she hadn't been since middle school. She was certain that this was Melanie.

For a moment, she was too shocked to speak, and then the truck's side door opened and Parker appeared.

He slapped the man on the back. "Hey, man, I'm clocking in—" He stopped, looked at Melanie. "What are you doing—?" Then he noticed Cady. "Cady—"

Cady finally found her voice. "I'm not hungry." She squinted, trying to process what she was seeing. "I'm not hungry. I made a mistake." Then she backed up and began to walk away.

"Cady, wait!" She heard him say.

And then Melanie said, "How do you not know if you're hungry?"

Cady tuned it out and sped through the snaking lines of patrons, nearly jogging, just trying to keep it all together until she turned the corner to her building. She just hoped he wouldn't try to follow.

She typed a text once she made it safely into the elevator.

911: the ex was in the food truck. With him. She's WAAAAAY cuter than me. She didn't bother sending it though. She had run out of steam. She was done with disappointment.

Jay had been happy to throw himself into work. He hadn't seen Sky in the couple of days since their fight, and that seemed significant in a very bad way. Luckily with so many editors on vacation, there was plenty to keep him distracted and in a comfortable state of denial for the time being. He began editing the daily gossip column and was sorry to see that Sophie had preyed upon one of the assistant editors enough for a shot at cowriting. Jay was also immediately sorry he had been so generous with that assistant editor. Gossip had never been the site's strong suit, but these pieces were particularly bad, running the gamut from cheap shots to total absurdity: two items about reporters from other publications—he never liked throwing stones at the competition, it was just bad form, and he cut both—one item on Carter Thompson supposedly talking marriage with that national news anchor—they were gorgeous and would make hot babies, but honestly, Jay was pretty sure it was just a showmance for the campaign audience—and then a final item that absolutely had to be false. He hoped. It was too ridiculous. He texted Sky first.

Hi, I have a crazy work-related question: there isn't anything going on with Rocky and Buck Brandywine, is there? Thanks. In other news: I love you and miss you.

The response came instantly: Not that I know of, but the pool has been off for a few days. Haze people just said "personal matters" and back on Monday. I know you won't believe me, but I've literally just been sleeping and doing laundry. Xo.
Before Jay could even begin to sort through his feelings

for Sky, he had to deal with the other part, the newsy part. He couldn't see any way around it: he was going to have to call Birdie. He would kill the item now. But that was only a Band-Aid. If it was true, someone else would soon discover it, and they might not be so diplomatic.

Cady's phone pinged as soon as she got back to her office. She had managed not to cry and decided to just go straight to the angry stage of grief. Mild progress.

A message appeared from PARKER APPLETON. She was confused. She was positive she didn't have his number saved in there, hence why they were always emailing each other.

She considered not reading the very large block of text that came next, but she couldn't avoid her problems anymore.

hi, it's parker, i put my number in your phone the other night when i deleted your ex. i wish i had told you that before, because now it's just another weird thing to have to explain when i have a bigger weird thing to have to explain: i wanted you to know what happened today. i'm angry and don't know where to start so i'll start with the most important thing: there's nothing going on with melanie. (that was melanie in the truck.) i haven't talked to her since she broke up with me. she showed up today, she wasn't invited. chip was working the early shift on the truck but was going to leave early for a doctor's appointment so i was going to go take over for him. i emailed you on my way over there. chip said she just showed up to surprise me and made it seem like she was invited, but she wasn't. he's an idiot. i love him, but you know what i mean. anyway, i made her leave and told her not to come back, we're over, etc. i guess she got dumped and decided to try to come back, but cady, i'm not interested in that. at all. she is the past and i didn't realize how messed up that relationship was until i got to hang out with you. and that's even before this week, though this week was pretty great (until today, but you know what i mean). it was the first time we met and then when you interviewed me and when you did that thing where you tied up your hair with that pen? and it was kind of falling out but not all falling out and just really pretty. so anyway i'm really hoping you understand. god, this is a really long text. i'll let you go now but if you can just forget about today and start over with me, i'd really like that. just shoot me an "OK" or "it's cool" or something if we're good. i'll leave it up to you.

She definitely wasn't going to write back right away. She wasn't sure if she would bother at all. She read the note again. It seemed sincere, but what did she know at this point? Look at Jackson. Parker wasn't Jackson. She knew that. But she felt so beat-up and beat down and had to get off this roller coaster. Maybe she just needed a break from all of it.

Someone knocked at the door and she half expected to see Parker. But instead Jeff appeared, a nervous, agitated look in his eyes. He threw himself into Cady's chair and started talking without waiting to be asked in: "Gotta go over some things with you."

She set her phone down. "Is this about that gardening segment? I didn't realize the Weedwacker had that much horsepower. It sounds like Gracie's leg is going to heal in a flash," she explained. There had been a little mishap testing out some new tools; still, they had gone to a commercial break and there had been very little blood, at least.

"No, I don't care about that. She can take one for the team." He rolled his eyes, flitted his hand. "No, I need you to find ways for us to buzz it up for the sake of our show."

"I know Madison's hacks have gone well. I'm trying to get

her back, but she's had trouble getting away lately. It's like she's under house arrest."

His eyes lit up: "Seriously? Should we stage some sort of prison break? Intervention?"

"No, I was just—no, it's not, like, a hostage situation. She's just been stuck on the trail, which isn't her favorite place." The campaign was probably trying to keep her off the show actually, which made Cady feel important though she knew she wasn't.

"Oh, well," he said, disappointed. "Well, keep thinking, okay?" He got up, brow still furrowed, eyes dark, very unlike him and troublingly so.

"Hey, Jeff, when you say 'for the sake of our show,' how bad is it?" she asked.

"We're doing the best we have in years, but it's not enough. We're gone after the election unless we figure something out."

She felt knocked out.

"Like rebrand again. I dunno. I'm gonna go drink in my office and update my resume."

32

WANT TO BE MORE THAN
A SPERM DONOR?

★

Birdie perhaps shouldn't have been *so* surprised: she had, after all, been on guard against this sort of thing ever since it happened the first time. But this story just sounded so...unexpected. Yes, unexpected. She wouldn't have guessed Buck would choose someone so high-profile. She would have imagined someone more...*disposable*. Certainly not anyone even more well-known than he was. Something felt off about this. But at the same time, it was true that she hadn't seen him coming or going next door for several days. And she *had* been watching. The fall semester wouldn't start for another week or so, late August, and his summer schedule had been far more relaxed. He had been on board to lecture for some of the classes, but not regularly, from what she gathered.

"Thank you, Jay, I appreciate your telling me," she said into the phone, peeking out the window into another warm and sticky evening as though Buck might appear at just that moment. "And it was incredibly kind to kill that for me."

Cady's eyes bugged.

Birdie shook her head, telling her not to worry. It wasn't that kind of kill. Though Birdie had been enjoying the company up until now, she did wish she hadn't had to take this call with her houseguest in the room. But she had been there for Cady's Very Bad Night, so Birdie would just have to accept Cady viewing a bit of her own unraveling too. That was friendship, wasn't it? It just wasn't Birdie's style, if she were being honest. She was fine helping when *others* had come undone, but she would rather be alone when it was her. She preferred keeping up illusions, with everyone, across the board, no matter how much of a kinship she felt with them. Still, Jay, himself, after all, had been the person who had arrived on her doorstep on a very fragile day months ago. She had had no choice, really, but to let him in. And now, at a moment like this, she was glad she had.

"Absolutely, Birdie. But, my worry is that if we have it, then someone else probably does too," he said, ominous. "Or they'll get it."

"I understand." And she did; she intended to get some answers. "You said it checks out?"

"Yes, I'm afraid, or at least that one part of it. I called the Watergate and they confirmed that Buck's staying there. The rest we're still not sure of. Sky isn't due back on the campaign until next week."

When they hung up, she told Cady simply, "I have to make one quick call," and disappeared upstairs into the bedroom.

To Birdie's great surprise—the second of the night—Buck picked up. "I know it's not my business what you do or who you do it with until November 9," she launched right in. "But you should know that there's been some chatter. I'm mostly just puzzled why you would choose to stay at the Watergate instead of enjoying the fine accommodations of our multimillion-dollar home beside this multimillion-dollar home."

"I have my reasons, Birdie," he said easily, almost playful, which she didn't know how to interpret. "But I'm just not at liberty to discuss them at the moment. But nice talking to you." He said it perfectly congenially, then hung up.

Now she was angry. She marched downstairs, where sweet Cady was trying to appear like she was absorbed in whatever show was on; Rachel Maddow, it looked like.

"Could you get us a camera or two?" Birdie asked, arms folded as she threw herself into her favorite Herman Miller chair, the one that looked like a coconut slice.

"Sure. I do work at a TV show."

"Yes, but I mean those tiny ones that could be hidden in corners, that kind of thing."

Cady paused. "I have a better idea."

Reagan wasn't sure what was worse: having Ted home or having him away. At least there had been no run-ins with the law this time. But, when he wasn't at the office, Ted mostly just roved around the house muttering into his Bluetooth, leaving laundry for her from the suitcase he'd abandoned in the middle of the living room for reasons unknown (she left it there as a matter of principle, and the girls filled it with dolls and wooden blocks), and then occasionally letting the girls climb on him like he was a jungle gym. That, of course, made up for all the time he had spent away, in their eyes.

When Birdie called asking for a favor on this rare weekend Ted was in town, Reagan signed on immediately, without even knowing the details. "We're just going to need your baby monitor for a couple days. I hear it's top of the line."

Ted claimed he would be glad to watch the girls, spend some quality time home on a Friday night, so Reagan found herself in a sedan (dispatched by Birdie) pulling up to the Watergate Hotel, baby monitor tucked into her Hatch diaper bag, at 7:30 p.m.

Apparently, Birdie—who booked her own accommodations at the hotel in order to have "an on-site war room, just in case"—had managed to finagle a key to Buck's $500-a-night suite on the 10th floor, overlooking the Potomac River, in record time. From what Reagan could gather it had involved a lot of subterfuge and some flirting. It seemed Birdie's assistant, Abbie, had charmed a hapless male front desk attendant and, using Birdie's room key as a decoy, fed him a story about how her boss was staying there with her husband but the boss's key wasn't working. Could they please give her a new one for Buck Brandywine's room? "And I totally wasn't thinking and I didn't write down the room number, could you remind me? She'll kill me if I call to ask her another question today, you know how it goes," Abbie had gone on and on, smiling sweetly.

In Birdie's words, it had been absurdly easy.

Cady was there to meet Reagan in the lobby: floor-to-ceiling 1960s retro fabulousness meets modern-day luxe, a wonder of curved metal, woodwork and marble. Reagan hadn't been there since it had reopened earlier in the year, and while she wished her business at the historic spot was slightly less sordid, she was just glad to have been able to get out of the house.

"Abbie called Buck's book researcher and found out Buck's at a dinner from seven till ten tonight," Cady greeted her with a status update. After a beat she added, "And, gotta warn you, Birdie is a little intense today."

"That's a surprise, because I've got a baby monitor in my bag and I'm here to rig it up in her husband's hotel room," Reagan said.

They both laughed as they waited for the elevator.

"How's Ted?"

"We'll see, half an hour and no phone call yet, that's gotta be good." She gave Cady a look. "Enough small talk—what's the deal with Parker?"

"What do you mean?"

"I mean, I'm not usually one for giving someone a break,

but I do think he was telling the truth, in that text, about what happened."

"*I* just need a break. It's kind of a lot of drama condensed into a short time frame. Maybe it was the universe trying to tell me to be on my own a little bit."

"Or it was the universe telling you that this guy has a thing for brunettes." Reagan tugged at Cady's very light brown hair. "So, game on. Why would he invite you there to hang with him and his ex-fiancée though?"

"Why is the sky blue? My life is just sucking now, it's a given, incontrovertible truth."

The elevator door opened, and Birdie stood inside in head-to-toe black lululemon and a black fedora. "There you are. Come," she said, tugging each woman by the arm.

"I definitely missed a memo," Reagan said. "Were we supposed to dress like sporty cat burglars?"

Birdie ignored her. "I want to do this fast. You never know with him. Sometimes he isn't in the mood to socialize and he'll leave a dinner party early just to appear eccentric. He's such a diva. You know *I'm* the one who got him into TV in the first place. *I* pushed him, *I* made a call for him those years ago, *I* told him, 'No, no, a face like that demands to be shared with the world.'"

Cady gave Reagan a glance as though to say, *See what I mean?*

The elevator opened again. "She's our lookout." Birdie nodded toward Abbie, who gave a thumbs-up from the stairwell doorway. "We've got an intern in the lobby too."

In no time they were inside Buck's room. Since Reagan's belly had grown exponentially more voluminous since she last saw them, she took Cady up on her kind offer to do the necessary climbing. So Cady now stood atop the smooth-edged wooden desk fastening the camera above the window treatments.

Birdie supervised. "Where do you get something like this? The Spy Museum? CIA gift shop?"

"Do they have a gift shop?" Cady asked.

"Buy Buy Baby," Reagan said as she loaded the app onto Birdie's phone that would allow them to access the camera remotely. "The night vision is great on this so you'll see, you know, everything there is to see," she said, regretting her choice of words instantly. "I mean, not that there'll be anything interesting to see. But, you know."

Birdie looked over Reagan's shoulder at her iPhone screen. "So that's it, there we are."

"Get ready for your close-up," Reagan said, zooming in.

"This is so amazing it almost makes me wish I'd had babies," Birdie said. *"Almost."*

Reagan and Cady exchanged glances.

Birdie must've noticed the looks. She snatched her phone from Reagan.

"Just remember, it's not recording so you need to actually watch," Reagan said, collecting the instructions and extra wires into her bag.

"Oh, I'll remember," Birdie said and sighed. Then she hopped back up to the camera as if to triple-check the connections, though she clearly had no idea what she was doing. "I know you think I need to be fitted for my straitjacket today, but... I'm just having flashbacks of this time in my life that wasn't particularly enjoyable, and I'd rather not have to live through the same thing again just with a different leading lady."

The two women knew well enough to keep quiet, remain frozen.

Birdie didn't look at them as she climbed back down and

lay on the bed, checking her phone again. "I deserve better than this. With Gracie Garfield, I was young and stupid. I would've missed it entirely if he hadn't flat-out *told* me. But at least I had enough of a competitive streak to use it to light a fire under me. I thought, 'He embarrassed me, he made me feel like I wasn't worthy of *him*? Never again.' I wouldn't have been half as successful if he hadn't made me so miserable doing what he did. I wanted them to say, 'Buck Brandywine is married to *her*, how did he get *her*?' But like anything, then it's not enough."

The sun had set and the room was dark now. No one made a move to turn on a light lest they should break the spell.

Birdie continued, speaking to the ceiling as though her words could evaporate up into the air. "I wanted to even the playing field. I wanted *him* to feel like the widow. I wanted to be the one in demand. I wanted him to wonder how much fun *I* might be having and with whom. Even though it was all for show. No matter what anyone may have said, I only cheated the one time. Immediately after he told me about Gracie. It didn't make me feel better. It was only the illusion of having these other men that ever felt good. In case anyone was wondering."

Without a word, Cady crept from the desk she had been sitting on and lay down next to Birdie, held her hand.

Reagan followed her lead, on the other side, then with great effort rolled to face Birdie. "Sorry, gang, I'm only supposed to lie on my left side," she said in a soft voice. "I'm clearly carrying a giant sea turtle at this point."

Cady was first to giggle. Then Birdie.

A phone rang underneath one of them. Cady found it: "Abbie." She handed it to Birdie.

"He's in the lobby waiting for the elevator," Birdie relayed.

They grabbed their bags and were out the door and in the stairwell by the time they heard the elevator doors open.

Reagan felt a newly invigorated love for Ted when she got home: he wasn't perfect (she wasn't either), but he wasn't the type to cheat, to let something happen, to slip up. It just didn't seem to be in his DNA, and for that she was grateful.

She walked into a quiet, albeit ransacked house—remnants of dinner all over the kitchen, dishes in the sink, dirty diapers on the floor—and went looking for him, anxious to tell him about Birdie. They had known only bits and pieces of that story, cobbled together from years in the rumor mill.

"Finally," he greeted her before she said a word. "I didn't realize you were going to be out all night."

"It was, like, three hours. Maybe four."

"Well, it sure felt like longer."

"Welcome to parenthood." She said it upbeat and thought he would hear that in her voice.

"What's *that* supposed to mean?" he asked, apparently not in the mood for upbeat.

"No, nothing," she smiled. "It just means it's not easy, it's harder than, like, sitting at a desk or strategizing a presidential campaign," she actually wasn't kidding. "I mean, it's more fun, for sure. But it's exhausting. My bosses are probably tougher than yours." Again, she thought she was being funny, referring to the girls this way. Sometimes she needed to maybe *not* try to be funny. Like now. But these were the words that had come out.

"And what's *that* supposed to mean?" he asked again, sounding offended.

"Never mind, forget it. I just meant, it's, you know, tougher than it looks. Especially if you want to be more than just, like, a sperm donor." She realized as soon as she said it that it was not going to be an applause line.

"Oh! Okay then, so we're doing this," he said, ready to fight.

"No," she sighed. "Look—"

"This sperm donor is also the breadwinner, last time I checked."

"Look, I'm enormous and exhausted and hormonal. Let's just stop talking. Now. Not, forever. Just for, like, ten/fifteen minutes."

He took a deep breath and exhaled, then with a nod but not another word he turned around, walked silently to their bedroom and closed the door. She knew he was on edge between the election and the baby, she hadn't intended to wage any battles tonight. She curled up on the sofa, a feat that took several minutes to accomplish, and switched on the TV. Their old baby monitor—just sounds, no picture, like radio before the invention of film—hissed static on the coffee table.

Cady pulled on her pajamas and snuggled into the cushy bed. She had packed her overnight bag, reluctantly taking Birdie up on the very generous offer of the room at the Watergate for the night. Flipping through TV channels, Cady puzzled over the evening's events: a piece of Cady didn't want to live that way, keeping score, after what Jackson had done. But she couldn't stop comparing her situation with Jackson to what she had learned of Birdie and Buck. How was she, Cady, any different from Birdie? She understood why Birdie had stayed, but she also felt Birdie and Buck's foundation might have just been stronger to begin with. It was impossible to know what went on in anyone else's relationship, but perhaps there was just a greater feeling between Buck and Birdie that they were still a team that could overcome something so damaging after all these years. Maybe there was an extra level of commitment or effort. Whereas with Jackson she felt more like this had been a sign that they just weren't right, a signal that he had changed and he just didn't want the same things she did anymore. She stopped at PBS, a special about the restoration of the Capitol. The camera crew snaking up that same spiral staircase she had taken into the dome on one of her earliest days in the city. As much as she longed for that night, now that she thought about it, maybe her relationship with Jackson had been like the Capitol Dome: beautiful on the outside, but quietly crumbling inside, in need of a massive overhaul in order to not completely fall apart. She turned off the TV, then the lights. She would start looking for an apartment in the morning. It would have to be small, a studio, for her to be able to afford it, but it was time.

Secretly Birdie liked the idea of being home alone tonight after her day. So she poured herself a glass of wine, turned off the TV and watched Buck's room on her phone from the comfort of her couch. She had seen him arrive minutes after they'd left and watched him undress, shedding his suit for his favorite joggers and a Georgetown T-shirt she was sure was new. She had had to take a few calls, send a few emails, and had missed some footage from earlier, but when she returned to this very slow-developing show, she found him lying in bed, alone, the glow of the TV filling the room. And a text on her phone: Birdie, I left a note for you on the bed.

A sweet combination of shock and thrill overtook her. She raced upstairs to their bedroom. Had he dropped by during the day? Their housekeeper had been here much of the afternoon and hadn't said a word. Maybe it was while she had been at the Watergate? She found nothing on top of their Frette comforter so she shook it out, then peeled back the blanket and sheet, even looking beneath the puffy pillows (he always said there were too many pillows). Still, she found nothing.

Finally, she wrote back: Very intriguing, but I'm afraid I can't find anything. Did you sneak in here today?

He texted: I'm not the one who did the sneaking. Check your monitor...

She felt her blood go cold. She brought the camera up again: the lights now on in his room, Buck waved right at the camera and gestured to the foot of the bed, where he had written in very large letters on many sheets of paper, "Hi Birdie Breaking + Entering = your new talent?" He smiled right into the camera.

I know you were in here, your perfume is all over this place, he texted. Then I found the camera. Very clever. Not sure what you're looking for but don't think you'll find it here.

She didn't respond at all, what could she say? She had never felt quite so caught.

You should be flattered, she wrote, giving up.

I suppose I should.

But not too much: all of my shows are in reruns, one has to do something.

Goodnight, Birdie.

Goodnight, Buck.

He turned off the light but didn't bother disconnecting the camera. Birdie watched him until he fell asleep, then she dozed off on the sofa, clutching her phone.

33

JUST TELL ME WHAT I'M SUPPOSED TO BELIEVE

★

ROCKY HAZE STAFFING UP: STAR STRATEGIST BRANDYWINE JOINS CAMPAIGN

By Sky Vasquez, Staff Writer, *The Queue*

A spokesman for Rocky Haze announced today that legendary political strategist Buck Brandywine has been acting as political director for the campaign for the past month.

"They wooed him," an insider says. "Haze and Brandywine spent a couple of weeks off the grid, hammering out a plan, prepping her for upcoming debates, and formally nailing down her platform." Sources say Brandywine had been unsure of Haze's depth of knowledge on the issues but "was completely won over" during their vetting process. "He was impressed with her United Nations work and came away from their time beyond confident in her ability to lead and to formulate foreign and domestic policy. She's no lightweight. He feels a Haze administration would bring the right kind of change to Washington."

Early on a crisp September morning, Jay sent the story to Birdie to preview before posting it. His note read simply: "Mystery solved..."

The hottest summer on record had wound to a close, and Sky had returned to the trail, after the worst homecoming ever. They had barely seen each other at all, and having so little time together created even more tension as every minute ballooned in importance. Maybe Sky really had just been overworked and in need of rest. Jay kept going over it in his mind. Jay always had trouble bouncing back from even the slightest bump, so he could acknowledge that, yes, maybe he had acted a little awkward the rest of Sky's time in DC.

Still, since he had left, Jay had become increasingly irritable, angry, and yet shockingly efficient at work. It was amazing how fast he could get things done now that he wasn't concerned with others' feelings. He had always prided himself on being that easygoing editor, ruling his section with a velvet glove, not an iron first. Now he was like an iron fist inside a very thin velvet glove. But his page-views were through the roof. Too bad he was miserable.

He finished his notes on the Jared Leto profile he was editing: "We're getting the crazy passion but none of the fun—Jesus, why doesn't it look like there's any fun? I need more color from your bike ride around the city with him. I want this back in thirty minutes."

Madison stretched her arms up, twisted her neck side to side, yawned and returned to her phone, flipping through emails as she attempted to tune out Hank's red-faced histrionics at the podium. "More Syria? Can we talk about something else, for chrissakes?" he barked at his team.

"We can move on when you've got the position set, sir," his new senior adviser said flatly.

"I don't know, what am I supposed to say again? Just tell me what I'm supposed to believe."

It was too painful to watch. So she focused on texting

Henry. Soccer season (his second best sport) was just getting under way: Good luck at the game! Go Big Blue! And Gemma: Hi sweetie! Did you see any butterflies or squirrels on your walk today?

The first debate, from what Madison had gathered, had not gone well. Hank had insisted on winging it. He had tugged at his tie, grimaced and repeated, "I'm just gonna change it all, gimme a chance, you're gonna love me!" enough that even she could tell it wasn't the strongest showing. So now they were "doing this the old-fashioned way," according to the Machine. Which meant spending hours sitting in this hotel ballroom in downtown St. Louis watching Hank roll his eyes while being fed answers to questions he didn't bother to understand. Madison had attempted to leave St. Louis for New York the night before, but Hank had claimed he needed her; the debate had him jittery.

Mike burst up from his chair at the front of the ballroom, running to Madison like there was a fire in the building, "I NEED YOUR PHONE! NOW! MADISON!"

"Mike, what in God's good name are you doin'?" Hank asked.

The weary Machine, seated at their long table, sighed at the interruption.

"Is everything okay, Mike?" she asked innocently.

Madison had been watching a video their nanny had taken of Gemma doing cartwheels across the rooftop of their town house while singing the new Justin Bieber song. It made her smile and long for home even more.

"You've been hacked!" Mike, perspiring in his suit, yanked the phone from her hand, as though she had been caught texting in class. "Your Twitter. Facebook. Instagram. Snapchat. EVERYTHING!"

"What? How do you know? What do you mean?" she asked calmly, vacantly.

"Have you seen this?" He pulled up her Facebook page. "A post from early this morning reads, 'Climate change advocates, protectors of our country's vast natural resources and fellow naturists.' NATURISTS!" Mike said, eyes bulging. "'I urge you to join me on October 9 at the Presidential Debate in beautiful St. Louis to demand that our candidates address our growing environmental concerns. Global warming is an epidemic. Show your support in raising awareness of these key issues by shedding your clothes for the cause. #backtonature #goodfellow2016.'"

"Ohhh, naturist, is *not* a nature lover," Madison said, smirking. "Wouldn't that be funny to see?" Observing that Mike was not amused, she went on. "No, that's not from me. My last post was the picture of that chubby cat near the big arch from yesterday. It got 55,000 likes. You know? This one isn't from me."

"Fuck me, now we've gotta give him a position on global warming too," she heard one of the advisers say, more loudly than he should have.

"Where are you on global warming, Hank?" another one asked.

"I don't know, where am I supposed to be?" Hank said, annoyed at the question. "Shut this down, Mike," he called out. "We gotta get back to it up here."

"Let's get back to the Middle East," one said.

"Nowhere I'd rather be," said another sarcastically.

Hank and the Machine continued their discussion of foreign policy talking points while Mike typed furiously at Madison's side, speaking aloud. "Hello Goodfellow supporters, my sincerest apologies. My Facebook, Twitter, Instagram and Snapchat accounts have been hacked. Today's posts have not come from me. We appreciate your support while we are investigating this breech. See you at the polls! Fondly, Madison Goodfellow." He looked at Madison. "Hold off on social media until I give you the green light and some new passwords."

Whiplash sidled up, pulling Mike away, and Madison returned to her home videos, trying not to smile. Then she opened her email—the secret account she had set up that Mike had yet to discover—and wrote to Birdie Brandywine: Hope you saw my pages before my warden took the posts down. I put out the call for disrupters. ;-) Love, Maddy PS: Going to try talking to him tonight.

She left her seat, pulled Mike's assistant, Kimberly, aside. "Can you get me a coffee, please?"

But as soon as Kimberly left the room, Madison followed, catching her privately. "You have access to Hank's schedule, right?" she asked. "Book him for thirty minutes at nine o'clock tonight."

"That's dangerously close to bedtime," Kimberly said, protective.

"I know, I know, just do it. The location will be our hotel suite."

The call came at 9:29 p.m. from Whiplash. "What is it?" Hank barked into the phone. "I hate it when you all plan these meetings right before my shut-eye. Where?"

Madison, listening in from the living room of their suite, put her glasses on and knocked on the open bedroom door. "It's with me, your appointment," she said.

"Never mind, Whiplash. Night, son," he said and hung up. "Since when do you get on my schedule?" he asked, hands on his waist.

"Since never, which is why I had to make a formal appointment," she said firmly. "Sit down, Hank," she instructed.

To her shock, he did as he was told and folded his arms across his chest.

She leaned against the bureau, hoping to imply a sense of control over the proceedings. "You remember when you told me to tell you if you were getting carried away?" she asked, slow and cautious. "You're past carried away. This hobby has gone on long enough. Let's get back to what you're good at and enjoy life again. I don't think you really want the prize that you're competing for."

He looked at her and made his pitch. "But I can win."

"It's not supposed to be about that. Do you honestly want to do this job? Because I think it'll destroy you. Doesn't give me joy to say that, but I don't see you wanting this. This feels like the hockey team. You could win and you could figure out how to do this, but you will be miserable. Leave this to someone who wants it. Bow out on your terms. Get back to your philanthropy, your company, your baseball team, your basketball team, the things that bring you happiness. You've already proven you can do this."

He sighed, stared down at his feet, shook his head.

I have him, she thought. She knew it was all the thrill of the chase for him, and she didn't want them to give up the next four years, risk doing actual harm to the country, just because he wanted to prove he could attain something.

"Madison," he said, looking her in the eyes. "This is how you feel?"

"It is. You know that I'm right about this," she said gently. "We can find an easy way out, blame it on the family, how you realized this would be disruptive to us all, to the kids." She could have told him about Henry taking some heat at school, but she wanted to protect the boy.

"Well, all right," he said. He picked up the hotel room

landline, presumably to call the Machine: "Yes, hi there, this is Hank Goodfellow. I'm gonna need another room…"

She perked up, shocked, standing now as the rug was pulled out from under her.

"…no this one is fine, I mean an extra room—additional room—a suite, something nice, anything that's not here on the top floor," he continued.

"What are you doing?" she asked, taking a step forward.

He shot her the briefest, most lethal look. "And you can bring that key up to me?…Thank ya so much." He hung up. "You're not welcome at this thing tomorrow."

"The debate?"

"Yep, that's right."

"I'm not leaving this room."

"You don't have to, I am. It would take ya too damn long to pack your shit up and I don't have the time. In case you haven't noticed, I've got an election to win. But you can take your pretty self back to New York tomorrow. We don't need ya on the trail if you're not on board with the mission here. Shoot, Maddy." He shook his head. "I don't know what your problem is. You're getting all kinda attention, and they all sure seem to like *you*. None-a this should surprise me. We never did see tit for tat on things—"

"Eye to eye, you mean—"

"What?"

"And it's not even true," she said. "We usually do, but this whole thing has changed you, and I don't think you're giving the world your best Hank right now. I think you know this job isn't for you."

"That's about enough outta you." He raised his voice.

She rolled her eyes. "Don't talk to me like I'm one of the kids." She swept her Chanel makeup bag into her Louis Vuitton tote as a knock rattled the door. "Simmer down, Hank," she said. "Think about what I said. I'll come back in the morning for the rest of my things."

He liked to act like he was going to divorce her whenever they fought, but she considered this conversation just the start of negotiations. He should know that, businessman that he was. She opened the door to find a smiling concierge with a new room key on a silver platter. She swiped it and walked out without saying goodbye.

34

I'M NOT JACKSON, IN CASE THERE WAS ANY CONFUSION

★

They had weeks, *weeks*, to turn things around at the show. If she lost her job on top of everything else…she didn't even know how to finish the thought. She would go back to New York? She would find another line of work? Well, she would stay here at least for another ten months because she had boldly signed a yearlong lease at the end of the summer (worst-case scenario she could always sublet, though she hoped it wouldn't come to that) and moved into a (very) cozy little studio in Columbia Heights, not far from Jay's office.

She had missed a call from Madison that morning while meeting with Jeff to go over their dismal numbers. "I wanted to run something by you," Madison had told her voice mail. "It's kind of crazy, but, well, just give me a holler when you have a sec."

Cady was just punching the phone number when her cell pinged. Hi. Just a friendly reminder that I'm Parker. Not Jackson. Just in case there was any confusion there. She hung up the landline, slouched in her chair, stared out the window across the river at the city.

Ever since the food truck debacle of early August, Parker had taken to texting Cady weekly, like some sort of newsletter she hadn't signed up for. The texts had become shorter, much like the days as summer stretched into midfall. It was now October, but still these missives arrived, and still they managed to make her smile. She occasionally wrote back a quick, Hi, Parker. She secretly dreaded the day they might stop.

She thought of those kisses daily, as though they had happened in an alternate reality or an especially good dream. She missed him, dropping by the bar, how he would greet her there, their easy dynamic—she had taken all that for granted. How had she not realized sooner, those sparks? She had tried to ignore them: she was engaged; that's what you do. But now, it was getting harder and harder. And here he was, still texting her. It may not have been logical, but she needed to stay away, to focus on herself.

Parker was right, of course. He hadn't actually done anything wrong. She just wasn't ready to put herself in the position to be hurt again, so she had taken herself out of the game. She stared at her iPhone longer than she should have, debating whether to write back, what to say. The Declaration of Independence poster still hung there in her office above the TV. She'd nearly shredded it the day of the food truck incident, but she actually liked it and decided to grant the poster itself a pardon. Finally, she typed: Hi, Parker. I miss...my namesake cocktail... That was all she could bring herself to say, for now.

It was a Thursday, and at lunchtime the receptionist called her with a delivery: at the front desk she found a to-go cup and a straw with an envelope. Inside, on Preamble stationery, it said simply, "Cheers.—P." She took a sip and smiled.

Madison almost didn't watch the debate, she was *that* angry with him, but as with any potential train wreck, she felt she couldn't look away. It was both her civic and her wifely duty, in this case. So she had the nanny put Gemma to bed, poured herself a glass of Cabernet—and grabbed the rest of the bottle, why not?—and went up to their bedroom.

It felt like a sporting event. The tension in her muscles and bones, pulling for a difficult outcome. She wanted him out of this race, but not in this way. She knew the minute they began, the moment the camera's wide shot showed him tugging at his tie, making that grimace like he might be suffocating. She knew even before the index cards or the barking. She saw it in his *eyes*, all the spirit drained. And then she was sure of it at the end, when, before leaving the stage, he took his tie *off*, rolled it around his hand, forming a wheel, and shoved it in his inside pocket.

FINAL DEBATE BRINGS FIREWORKS AND TENSION (BUT NO NUDITY)

By Sky Vasquez, Staff Writer, *The Queue*

Nothing could top the October 9 debate for sheer entertainment value. Or so we'd thought. That event, intended to have been a town hall forum, was infamously shut down within minutes of beginning when hundreds of noisy, nude protesters descended on the Athletics Complex of St. Louis's Washington University, shouting, chanting and bearing signs, banners, plants and even animals to raise awareness for environmental issues. The group had been rallied by, of all things, messages posted to Madison Goodfellow's social media accounts by hackers. A number of the rowdier demonstrators storming the stage were later escorted out of the hall by police and forced to spend a (very cold) night in jail.

If that event will be remembered for its lack of proper attire, tonight's debate was marked by its lack of decorum as Vice President John Arnold and opponent Hank Goodfellow were left visibly rattled by independent Rocky Haze. The musician-turned-political newcomer also delivered the biggest bombshell of the night after moderator Grant Foxhall of CNN inquired of the three candidates: "Politicians are often accused of campaigning more than leading as they approach an election year. Fast-forward to 2019, you're president, how will you balance doing the job while also working to secure a second term?" Haze answered last. "I'm just running for this term. I don't want the worries of reelection to get in the way of me doing the best job right now. I'm going to dig my heels in for four years, do everything I came to Washington to do, and then let someone else have their chance."

The hall fell silent, then burst into applause and cheers. Even Foxhall appeared flummoxed as he stumbled over a follow-up question: "Um, seriously? Why?"

Goodfellow had a shaky start, flinging a stack of index cards onto the floor and going off script when he became frustrated with questions surrounding his economic policy. "How many times have I gotta tell ya, we're gonna work this all out? Get the deficit down without raising taxes? We've got plans in the works, and they're really good ones. But, Jesus, would you demand to know the end of a movie before buying your ticket? The world just don't work that way." Meanwhile, later on as discussion turned to international politics, Arnold sniped, "I'm just going to lay out the facts of my foreign policy platform, I didn't realize we were at a poetry slam," when following Haze's off-the-cuff rhymes.

Indeed, Haze received cheers and chants and showed a serious side, speaking (rather than rapping) her mind much of the time. "On my website, we have our detailed plan for balancing the budget. It's not the lightest reading, but it's there, here are the basics…"

The crowd, which included a small, but vocal contingent of university students, seemed overall most engaged by Haze. They clapped along as she began her platform, which she called "Four-year Outlook: Watch for Haze":

"You might be surprised, maybe falsely surmised,

what the world looks like seen through my eyes

I've got a plan too and here's a preview, what's in my purview…"

Then Haze stopped, looked into the audience for a few long seconds and said simply, "You know, I'm going to listen to Vice President Arnold and not hide behind my music. Let me tell you what I have planned if you grant me the chance to lead." After laying out her key policy initiatives, she made an impassioned plea, again in spoken word, rhythmic as those words were:

"Voters young and old, fresh and bold, tried and true or new at the polls,

I urge you, speak up, use your voice, consider the future and make a choice."

Just days from the election, the latest polls have the three candidates in a statistical dead heat…

Jay couldn't sleep. He was too occupied poring over Sky's last text before turning in for the night: We'll get everything back on track after this.

"Back on track," he repeated out loud. He had barely edited a word in Sky's story—Sky was that good these days—but Jay wished he could edit the hell out of that text.

★ ★ ★

The call came just a day after the debate. "Maddy, do you got a minute?" Hank said in a shaky voice as soon as she answered. He never asked that, ever. He always assumed it was a fantastic time for everyone to talk whenever he phoned.

"Um, sure, what's going on, Hank?" She sighed, temporarily halting her plans and taking a seat on the stone ledge before the seven-foot-high metal fence. She leaned her signpost against her legs. "Isn't it past your bedtime?"

It was nearly 10:30 p.m. and pitch-black and empty where she was. She wore all black—her old athleisure line—and a matching black baseball cap, her ginger hair pulled through in a ponytail.

"Yeah, I dunno, I think I'm having a heart attack, Maddy."

"Why do you think that, Hank?" she asked, unconcerned.

"I'm sweatin' and havin' trouble breathin' and my heart just won't stop beating, it's so dang fast." He sounded upset—and very Southern, which happened when he was upset—but not in actual danger. This had happened before, when he'd bought that damn hockey team.

"Well, if your heart is *beating*, then you're probably not having a heart attack, but I'm not a doctor," she said calmly. "Maybe you should call a doctor."

"No, I wanna talk to you. Keep talkin', I'm starting to feel better."

She sighed again. "Ohhkay, well, what were you doing when this all happened, Hank?"

"I was lookin' at this Halloween mask of my *face*," he said. "It is one ugly son of a bitch, this thing."

"Oh, Hank, throw that thing away right now."

"And I was thinkin', why would someone *do* somethin' like that? Put my face on one of them creepy rubber masks like something from a horror movie?"

"I think maybe you're having a panic attack. Why don't you sit down and breathe into a paper bag or something?"

"Who would do something like that? Make a mask of some- one's face, like you're some kinda joke?" he asked.

She opened her mouth to answer, but she was at a loss.

He went on. "And then I thought, well, people wouldn't *make* this sucker unless they thought there were enough people out there who'd want to *buy* this. What is wrong with people, Maddy? I don't think I like this."

"I don't think you're supposed to."

"This isn't what I signed up for."

"I think you did, Hank. I mean, I think that just comes with the job. Just one of those things," she said. "There are some sick puppies out there, Hank." She knew this wasn't entirely about the mask. The media, which had enjoyed him up until now, called him things like "folksy," had been scathing about his performance at the most recent debate. This Is Your New Leader? one headline had read, and then the sentiment had been slapped with a hashtag that was now trending.

"There are," he said, exhaling. And then, apropos of noth- ing, "Awww, Maddy, and, you know, I don't know a god- damm thing about the Middle East." He whispered it, a great secret.

"I know." She smiled. She couldn't help but love him.

"Or the economy."

"I know."

"Lord knows I know how to make money, that's for damn sure, the stock market, running a corporation, all that. But the actual economy? Policy?"

"I know."

"I could learn. All of this stuff. People would love me, hell, they already do. And I could do this, like anything else, if I worked at it."

"I know."

He was quiet for so long she thought the call had dropped.

"This could be a goddamn disaster for me," he said softly. "Hell, I don't know if the fallout would be worse to win and screw up or to... It could be a goddamn disaster. Even if it's the right thing."

She knew what he meant by "the right thing"—dropping out. This was delicate, so she proceeded with great caution. "Listen, Hank," she said slowly. "There are so many easy ways out of this. And I know people who can plan the whole thing, make it go off without a hitch. It doesn't have to—"

The phone went dead. She was talking to herself now. But this call had been progress. She gazed back over her shoulder at the north portico of the White House, illuminated and glowing. *Might as well carry on*, she thought. Thank goodness they hadn't raised the height of this fence yet—it was due to double in size apparently—she was fairly certain she could climb it at its current height. She had been a remarkable tree climber growing up, shimmying up that grand oak in their yard in bare feet and gingham dresses.

Of course, if this went bad, it would go very bad.

She turned on the digital camera again—it had just seemed like the video might come in handy sometime—and positioned the tripod right outside the fence. Henry had shown her how to work the thing two Christmases ago before their annual family trip to the Alps; she had gotten some great footage of him snowboarding.

She slid her signpost through the bars of the fence. Not a soul around to see her. Then, standing on the rocky ledge, she grabbed the bars, jumped and slithered up like a cat. She pushed herself over the top of the fence and then dropped down on the other side, landing on the grass on one foot and one knee. Ouch. Something had crunched in her leg, but she shook it away and kept going, the adrenaline coursing through her. She grabbed her sign and ran toward the White House. Midway across the lawn she staked the signpost into the ground.

"HEY!" came a man's angry voice. "Stop or we'll shoot!"

She took off running, flinging herself back over the fence again just as the Secret Service came into view. She grabbed the tripod, camera still attached on top, and ran through darkened Lafayette Park. She didn't stop until she made it to the Ritz.

Birdie saw it on every news show and blog the following morning: someone had placed a sign featuring a giant photo of Hank Goodfellow's face in a circle with a line through it —as in No Hank Goodfellows here—on the North Lawn of the White House. She texted Madison: You have got to be kidding me. You've outdone yourself.

Birdie got this reply: I must be losing it because this is all starting to seem like fun.

A sure sign that you truly belong here, Birdie typed back. As I always suspected!

Reagan could be wrong about the letter. The email address, of course, was random and anonymous, but the email itself was too telling:

I've recently become, for lack of a better phrase, a stay-at-home dad while my wife pursues a dream. It has been an exhausting process for both me and our child. Financially, we are fine, for which I'm grateful, but the rhythm of our family unit has been disturbed with so much travel and so little time at home. And I am even more concerned that, if this actually worked out for my wife, life as we know it would change so drastically, we would have to carve out a new normal. Do you have any advice on how to face these potential changes and keep us all steady?—Out of Tune

She typed up her response. Every day feels this way when you're a family. There's a constant fear of shaking things up. Just as you establish a routine, something always comes along to disturb it whether on a grand scale or small one. I applaud you three for not being afraid and for creating the type of environment where one of you can pursue dreams headfirst and heart first. Every day as a parent is a wild card. Just keep communicating, checking to see how everyone is absorbing these changes. It sounds like important opportunities are on the horizon for you all. What's good for one of you is good for all of you. Be strong and supportive and loving and as fearless as you can. You'll get each other through.

She sent her column along to Jay "OMG, have Sky check. I swear this letter is from Alchemy…"

Jay welcomed any excuse to reach out to Sky these days, and any exchange that didn't involve editing and didn't require them to talk about their relationship was a rarity, so he was only too happy to forward Reagan's column along. Just curious, does this sound like anyone we know? If you're not at liberty to say just blink twice.

Sure enough, Sky sent back the emoji happy face with its eyes closed, twice, then wrote: Wow, Reagan is good. You didn't hear it from me, but Alchemy and I have become pals. Other day we were watching Rocky at a town hall and he had been quiet all day and finally just shook his head and said, "She could actually win this and I'm not even sure what that means—it's a whole new life for us, Harmony, our family. I just don't even know." Never seen him like that, you know? Worried, dejected almost. Not like him. I didn't know what to say so I just said why don't you talk to someone and he said he didn't trust anyone. I said, what about anonymously? So we sent it in. It was the only thing I could think of. OK, now delete this! PS: Miss you J.

Jay savored that postscript, reading it over again and again.

And Jay wasn't the only one feeling better. When Reagan's column posted on the site that week, Sky texted: Reagan's answer was perfect. Alchemy said that was all he needed, just to have someone tell him it wasn't crazy to feel like he was feeling. Tell Reagan thanks…and to never tell!!!

35

HAVING THE MOST HORRIFYING HALLOWEEN

★

Reagan almost wished Ted hadn't gotten the tickets, terrible as it was of her.

"You won't be there? Are you sure? We can meet you there," she said, phone to her ear.

"Reagan, I'm not even on the *East Coast* today. It's a week to the election, it's like a parade of fucking swing states," he said wearily. He sounded completely exhausted.

She'd thought he was coming back today. She never knew his schedule. Polls and predictions still showed John Arnold locked in a near tie with Goodfellow, and Haze not far behind. Ted seemed to be rapidly imploding, always one extreme or another: either entirely beat down like today or the opposite, manic as a college kid hopped up on Adderall during finals week, trying to save his GPA. Except he wasn't twenty-two, he was forty, and she worried he would give himself a heart attack with all this freaking out. She wanted to remind him to take a breath, that there would be plenty of people to hire him even if Arnold didn't win—he knew this whole town, and even if their party got knocked out of the White House and was in the minority in Congress, there would still always be a place for him *somewhere*. That was the one luxury of having worked like a dog for so many years. She didn't say any of this though; he wouldn't want to hear it right now.

"The girls will love it. It's the White House, it's Halloween.

Believe me, I'd rather be there than wherever we'll be today,"
he went on.

"I know, of course, it'll be a blast. We'll just miss you."

On the sofa, Natasha and Daisy squealed, hugging and wres-
tling, and she couldn't tell if their game was happy-go-lucky
or hostile. It changed by the minute. No tears yet though.

"I miss you guys too. And don't forget to take some pictures!"

She knew, absolutely, it was a great privilege to get to do
something like this. How many kids could say they got to
trick-or-treat at the White House? But she would be lying
if she said she wasn't at least slightly terrified by the idea of
going there alone with Natasha and Daisy at the appointed
time, which happened to be their afternoon nap time.

Some switch had flipped and the terrible twos had taken
hold with a vengeance. They no longer sat in any high chair
or booster seat but would only eat meals while walking around
the living room, as though at some kind of toddler cocktail
party. Getting into the car seat required bribery—"Bri-breee!
Bri-breee!" they both chanted, requiring cookies or electronics for a simple drive to the grocery store—and the stroller
was a crapshoot; sometimes they were content, sometimes
they viewed it as a torture device.

But still, with hope and cautious optimism, she got the girls
into their little denim shirts with their little red-and-white-
polka-dotted bandannas, rolled up their sleeves and taught
them how to flex their arm muscles. Then she loaded her two
mini Rosie the Riveters into the car along with the stroller
that had been outfitted with a We Can Do It! sign, and she
drove them downtown.

She had packed enough snacks and drinks to feed a tiny
army, she had her phone and iPad fully juiced and loaded with
new apps; she was fucking prepared. They were angels waiting

in line for nearly an hour, smiling and waving, making friends with other children, perfectly content to suck their thumbs in their stroller and take in the festive ambiance, all these costumed families revved up for their visit to 1600 Pennsylvania. She had almost decided not to dress up herself, but she was glad now that she had found that Mother Earth costume online, a drapey toga-sort-of getup, covered in faux flowers and leaves with a picture of the globe strategically placed to cover her pregnant belly. She even put some flowers in her hair. They were going to get at least one decent Instagram shot of the three of them, goddammit. She was determined.

At last the line moved past that monument of General William Tecumseh Sherman on horseback across from the Willard Hotel, and snaked onto the sprawling emerald green South Lawn. The late October air just crisp enough without being chilly, the sun shining bright in a blue cloudless sky. She took a deep breath, grateful for her sweet girls, wishing that Ted could be there to enjoy one peaceful family moment.

But then something happened as soon as they passed through security, as though the metal detectors had activated the Crazy Chip in their little brains. A wonderland of overstimulation greeted them instantly. Circus performers juggling! Clowns walking on stilts! Acrobats flying on a trapeze! Costumed characters handing out candy in boxes embossed with the presidential seal! So many people everywhere! And Natasha began squirming. "Go, Mommy! I go! Down! Down! I want GOOOO! Now!" she cried out. And then Daisy, quietly contorting herself, trying to Houdini out of the stroller straps, twisting and arching.

"No, no, sweeties! We have to try to see the president and then we go-go," she said in the extra cheery voice she used when surrounded by parents who seemed more successful at parenting than she was. She patted the girls' heads, gently easing them back down into their seats. Hustling now, she wove around groups of dawdling families with children happily riding atop their parents' shoulders. She positioned the stroller with the White House in the background and snapped a quick picture, both girls grimacing, screaming as though being held against their will.

A joyful mom of serene twin storm troopers, who looked to be a mature seven or eight years old going on thirty offered to take a picture of the three of them. Reagan posed, then jogged away before being asked to return the favor— she had to get to the exit at the opposite side of the grounds before these two completely expired. She whipped them past the endless line directly in front of the White House where the best candy and best photos could be had. "Me get out! Out, Mommy! Out, Mommy!" they both screamed now, crying, faces red and wet as they thrashed, trying to stand in the stroller. She pushed them faster, her gargantuan belly so heavy she thought the baby might just fall the hell out. Winded from climbing the long hill, she ran out of steam and couldn't push the stroller anymore—what was wrong here? She slowed her pace, shaking the stroller; something had jammed. One wheel was stuck, her long, flowy costume caught in the spokes. She yanked it out, ripping the cheap fabric in the process, and that was all it took.

In that split second, Daisy slunk out through the stroller straps and bolted across the lawn toward the West Wing, like some kind of tiny captive animal returned to the wild. There were no guests over there, only Secret Service: a sure sign that this area was *not* intended for play today. Reagan ran after her—pushing the stroller, where Natasha remained tangled in her straps. "Daisy! No! Daisy! Stop! Now! You're supposed to be the easy one!"

She tried to steady Natasha as they ran, but the girl stood

up in her seat as though surfing. And then she leaped. Some-how, Reagan abandoned the stroller and caught her midair, running while holding the kicking, hysterical child. Ahead, she watched a burly, stone-faced man in a boxy suit with an earpiece lunge for Daisy, swooping in and grabbing her up into his arms in one swift motion. Expressionless, he walked toward Reagan, handing over the crying toddler as though she were a feisty fawn.

"Watch her," the Secret Service agent said in a command-ing, gruff voice.

"Sorry, sir, won't happen again," Reagan said, still pant-ing from the exertion—that had been the most exercise she'd had in months. She held one child in each arm, barely man-aging to speak between breaths. "This is the way out, yes?" she asked, pointing down a hill.

He nodded.

She set Natasha down for a moment, holding her arm with one hand while trying to get Daisy into the stroller with her other. Still completely stoic, the Secret Service agent scooped up Natasha and buckled her in seconds. Meanwhile, Daisy did her best impersonation of a wooden doll with no hinges, com-pletely rigid, refusing to get into the seat. With great effort, Reagan finally shoved her in and got her fastened.

It wasn't until she had wheeled them back outside the gates near the Eisenhower Executive Office Building that she real-ized how bad she felt, and not just normal exhausted-pregnant-mom bad: Were those *contractions*? "What the fuuuuck," she said out loud, not caring about the passersby glancing. "Three fucking weeks early? *Now?*"

She called Jay, laid it out in one long sentence. "Having the most horrifying Halloween here and I *might* be having a baby can you come meet us and take these maniacs I think I should probably go to the hospital I'm sorry, this is, like, a really inconvenient time for this shit to be going down. We're chilling behind EEOB."

"OHMAGOD, Rea! I am coming RIGHT NOW!" he said.

"You are my hero," she said.

She looked and found the girls had somehow fallen asleep. She leaned against a giant planter and called her mom until Jay arrived.

Back on the Upper East Side, Madison was swiping thick black liner along Gemma's upper eyelashes and winging it out—"You're going to be the prettiest Cleopatra anyone's ever seen!" she said, kissing Gemma's freckled nose—when her phone rang.

"Maddy, remember last time we talked? What you said?" Hank asked by way of greeting.

She could hear the TV on in the background. Where was he? Pennsylvania again? Like the rest of the country, he had seen the signpost on the White House lawn. For some reason that didn't bother him so much, according to an interview she'd seen of him on Bloomberg. "Look how damn close I'm gettin' to the White House. I'll always have that," he had said when ambushed after one of his rallies. She had been oddly encouraged, as though he was still mulling over their conversation, the possibility of bowing out.

She froze now. "Yes, Hank, of course I remember."

"Mommy, I need my hair," Gemma said.

"One second, sweetheart." She patted Gemma's head, her long fine ginger locks snuggly wound in small flat spirals to fit beneath her sleek black wig. "What is it, Hank?"

"It's all this. I'm getting a little tired of all this, Maddy," he said, like a child who had grown sick of his Saturday morning Little League.

She knew he hated to admit this so she didn't gloat.

He was quiet a moment. "It's just not what I like to *do*. I'm not sure I want to *do this*. I'm not sure I like the prize enough to keep competin' for it. Maybe you were right."

She didn't say a word, just listened.

He sighed. "So how in the hell do I do this?"

"I know someone who could work it all out, put just the right, what's the word? The right…spin…yes, the right spin on it." She was sounding so Washington, she almost didn't recognize herself.

"You really think so?" he asked.

"I promise. This'll be something we laugh about one day, like that time you took up hang gliding and ended up in the middle of the East River and got fished out by that nice captain from the Circle Line tour boat."

"Those were the days!" he said, coming back to her.

"But if you don't bow out, I don't think we'll be laughing. And I don't think anyone in the country will be laughing. So we'll do this, I'll make a call, okay?"

"Yeah," he said, giving in. "Hey—why are you always right?"

"Someone's gotta be," she said, warm.

"Ever since high school," he said, wistful, as if recalling the past. "Wait, now, one last thing: I may be crazy for askin' but Mike was talkin' and, honey, you don't have anything like a Super PAC, do you? There's this thing out there, and Mike seemed to think—"

It would do no good to lie at this point. "Oh, Hank, you do have sources everywhere, don't you?" she said lightly. "I did have one. But I didn't mean to, it just happened." She had needed to put all the money from those Arnold donors *somewhere*. Now she'd have to decide what to do with it. These were good problems to have.

"Magnolia, you are full-a surprises. That's what I love about you."

★ ★ ★

On a chilly November morning, one week before the election, Hank Goodfellow gathered his running mate, his most trusted advisers, a crowd of thirty, into the banquet room of his Upper East Side town house. He plied them with drinks before he set foot inside, so they could've been forgiven for assuming it was some kind of very, very early celebration.

When he arrived, in a button-down shirt, sleeves rolled, no tie, Madison at his side pretending to look grave, he laid it all out. "Look, you all know me and you know, better or worse, I follow my gut and my heart and that's how I got here. And, sorry to say, but that's how I'm getting out of here too. Plain and simple, this just isn't for me anymore."

No one moved, no one breathed, for so long that Madison wondered if they had even heard. Then, a delayed-reaction gasp and "WHAT?" swept the room. Someone dropped a glass, another person threw one. "You've gotta be fucking kidding me," someone blurted.

"I know, I get it, you're pissed off at me and y'all got a right to be, but this is what I had to do," he went on. He pushed his silent running mate forward. "Remember this guy? Well, he's still runnin', so you all have still got jobs and if you get him to win, even better. I'm gonna be pulling for him too. And let's face it, he's a hell of a lot smarter than me."

Hank put his leg up on the banquet table, leaning forward as if he was about to tell a secret, and promised to throw his money into ads in every state reminding voters that a vote for Goodfellow now meant a vote for his VP pick, since ballots had already been printed. "I don't expect you to like this, but I'm hoping in time you'll forgive me. I still love y'all."

Hours later, the news already trickling out, he stood on the steps of his town house, grinning like the perfect salesman before a group of reporters.

"I've thought long and hard about this and decided I can have a greater impact on our country, help folks more, by just doin' what I do, just givin' my money away. I'll let the other folks do the business of 'leading.'" He made air quotes around the word as though this was a newfangled kind of occupation. "With this behind me, in the coming months you'll hear about a whole buncha philanthropic projects—ones that took a back seat when I began pursuing *this* dream. This country's big enough for a lotta different dreams and a lotta different ways to make the world better."

As he read Birdie's words verbatim—or more precisely, Birdie's crisis-managing-prose made shiny smooth by Reagan—Madison stood by his side, beaming, proud for the first time since that interview before primary season. She even allowed Gemma and Henry to be there.

Linking arms, the foursome walked back toward the door of their home together. Hank patted Henry on the back and scooped Gemma into his arms playfully. The girl turned and waved over her father's shoulder one last time.

The text came as Cady was on her way, with Jeff, to the meeting of her life with the station owners. She would find out the fate of a pitch she had made, for a new show, of all things. Hustling down the hall to make it in time, she glanced at her phone and couldn't help slowing her pace to read.

Parker: So I'm catering this party on the Mall. Election night. I know, I know, it sounds cold and miserable but apparently there are these things called tents and heat lamps. It'll be near the carousel, can't miss it. I've got a full catering staff so I'll just be standing around looking pretty. Please come. I miss you, actually. Maybe a weird thing to say since it's not like I've known you super long, but there it is. Putting it all out there. You've got my vote. If you want it.

"Yeah, I'm on fucking bed rest," Reagan said on the phone to Cady.

The doorbell rang, and she heard her mom answer it.

"False alarm, just stress, who the hell knows. But my mom is here now until Ted's back, and my dad's coming this weekend too."

Her mom opened the bedroom door, handing over a package the size of a shoebox and a cup of decaf Earl Grey tea, the girls trailing her.

"Thanks, Mom," she said. "Hi, sweeties."

Reagan's mom fluffed the pillow behind her head, gave her a kiss, then grabbed the girls' hands and closed the door behind them.

Reagan took a sip of tea and studied the package, confused, then tossed it on the bed. "It's not the worst, I've gotta say. It's like a spa day, you know, but without any of the fun treatments."

"Well, that sounds like a good time, kind of," Cady said, then changed the subject. "So, not to take away from all that you've got going on, like almost having a baby," she kidded. "BUT I got this text from Parker…"

"Oh my God, what's your deal?" Reagan sighed. She had become even more impatient and cut-to-the-chase since being stuck on bed rest.

"It's just—"

"I know, you moved here for a dude who ended up being an asshole, and then you weren't sure you belonged here, you don't want to just run into something with another guy because I get it, you're not really a rebounder. Shit has meaning with you, which I love about you, Cady. But, without even knowing what's in that text, I would say—it's been a while now. He's still hung up on you. If you're into him—and no offense but I know that you are and honestly he's adorable and allegedly a great fucking kisser—"

"True—"

"So go for it. You belong here. You've got your own life going now, you're allowed to try again." Her voice softened just enough. "I'm sorry, my mom is making me lie in bed 24/7 and I am so fucking bored and just happy to have human contact right now. She's taking care of the girls, which is awesome, but I haven't bossed people around enough today."

Cady laughed. "You're pretty good at it."

"It's like the one part of my parenting that I have confidence in." She laughed.

When they hung up, Reagan opened the box. A note on Brandywine stationery read: "Been meaning to send this for a while, apologies—Buck Brandywine."

Beneath it, nestled in bubble wrap, she found her video baby monitor. She had Buck's email address somewhere and too much time on her hands, so she searched her inbox, then wrote:

Hi Buck,
Thank you so much for the monitor. (My apologies too.)
On an unrelated note, a funny question for you: we have a mutual acquaintance in Grant Foxhall. He mentioned that I should ask you to verify what a good friend he can be. It's a long story, but I was curious. Best of luck on November 8…
All best,
Reagan

The response: Hi Reagan, Yes, Grant is a friend of mine. Without boring you with the background, I will say that I asked him to help me out the night of Birdie's Iowa party. I had to be out of town and heard that one of the party guests had an eye on my wife. I'm not especially proud, but I asked Grant to find the man and, if possible, push him into the pond in our backyard. Not the most gentlemanly thing to do, but it's how we settle things where I'm from. If I'd been there I woulda slugged him but I couldn't and I wasn't about to ask Grant to do that much dirty work for me. Luckily the pond wasn't frozen over. Hope this helps. Best to you and the family, Buck.

She couldn't help but smile. She started a new message, not even bothering with a subject line or greeting, just typing this to Grant: Talked to Buck. Glimmer of humanity in you after all.

The response could not have been quicker: I appreciate that, Reagan. More than you know.

36

YOU'VE GOT MY VOTE

★

It was a crisp, sunny November morning and Birdie voted—at the church where JFK and Jackie used to go—right after SoulCycle. Every campaign season tended to feel like great foreplay before four years of lousy sex: the new administration usually never quite as exciting as it had seemed before taking power. But casting this ballot, she actually felt things might be different.

On the way home, she headed to Café Milano, greeting the owner with a hug and a kiss ("Franco, how *are* you, darling?"), to prepare for the party. She could have been in New Hampshire on duty for Rocky Haze's event, but she'd sent Abbie instead. Birdie had committed to *The Queue*'s party long before, and it was the larger of the two events, so her presence would be more vital there. At least, this was how she defended the choice to herself, her mind running over the past many months as she did a walk-through of the Georgetown restaurant. Was she trying to avoid Buck before their D-day? Maybe, she could admit. But Abbie could handle the Rocky event just fine and besides, Rocky had kept her plans exceedingly modest. If she ended up winning, it would look more like a high-school student-government celebration than a presidential one, but what Rocky Haze wanted, Rocky Haze got.

Buck would, of course, be there. Birdie didn't know, literally, what tomorrow would bring with him. How this would go. Would they *talk* about things? Had Buck made up his mind in some way that wouldn't be swayed? She tried to push it out of her head for just one more day, as she'd been pushing it with varying degrees of success (and occasional complete failure) since February. She knew what she wanted, but she didn't know if it was possible. And now, she had one last party to pull off this election season, and so she would.

The twins refused to nap, as they had the past several days, suddenly deciding the morning nap was passé, so Reagan loaded them into the car, with her mom's help, for the rare doctor-sanctioned excursion: to the girls' future elementary school to vote. She wanted them with her. "I remember you always taking me," she said as they drove through the narrow streets of Bethesda.

"You always liked to pull the lever," her mom joked. "You liked to be in charge."

Plied with the usual snacks and electronics, the girls stayed in the stroller the entire time, but when Reagan got into the voting booth with them at last, expecting this to be the quickest, easiest part of their adventure, she paused. Obviously Arnold was their guy. But now, she stood there and really thought about it, as if she hadn't been so predisposed, as if she had just been watching this election play out like the rest of the country, without being tangentially involved. Without her two degrees of separation from this candidate. She studied the ballot on her touch screen. A woman's name there: a woman who had started out seeming like a lark and turned out to be a heavyweight and something new. She looked at her girls, behaving so well today but with their strong, troublemaking spirits that would serve them so well in this world. Even if it might make it more exhausting to parent them.

She made her selection and kissed their foreheads.

On the way out, she freed them from their stroller and let them cover themselves in I Voted stickers, head to toe.

Jay had voted early over the weekend. Rocky Haze had been campaigning in nearby Virginia, even though everyone in the Haze orbit advised her she would never win John Arnold's home state, so he and Sky had been able to vote together.

After, they'd gone for a very early brunch at Busboys and Poets, like old times. Sky, always the more gregarious of the two, the one who had brought Jay out of his shell when they began dating, had seemed distracted; there was a general dreaminess about him that Jay hadn't been sure how to read. Was it sleep deprivation or his love recharging?

Though Sky had stayed at Jay's apartment, Jay had still felt something hanging over them, holding them back. A sense that they couldn't speak too freely because there was too much to say and there wasn't enough time to properly delve into it all. No time to unpack it, much like Sky's suitcase in the corner of Jay's apartment. Still, Jay had gone on working hard to keep the conversation light, easy. He knew there would be a state-of-their-union discussion coming, but for once he'd tried not to mourn in advance. Get the election behind them, let them start being *them* again, see where Sky's head was and then deal with the realities of whatever was going on, he'd coached himself.

Now election day was finally here, and he knew tomorrow things would be different. He just didn't know which way the wind would blow.

Absentee ballot mailed in weeks before, Madison pulled on her bold cerise Tory Burch jumpsuit—ideal for a party hostess, impossible *not* to be seen in something like this—and dusted shimmering powder along her décolletage. She stepped into her sky-high strappy heels and gave her bouncy locks one more fluff and shake, reglossed her lips. Done and done. Her team had flown in from New York to prep her: she wasn't just hosting *Best Day DC*'s election party, she was unveiling clips of her new show and needed to look the part.

She kissed Hank's forehead. He'd agreed to appear at the soiree later on to support her. Until then, he was holed up in the office of their West End apartment, prepping his announcement of a multimillion-dollar donation to help fight kid's poverty in the DC area. Earlier in the day, he had been caught skinny-dipping in the lap pool of the Equinox gym at the Ritz. All was right with the world.

She skipped out, then hopped in the arriving sedan headed for the Rock & Roll Hotel—which apparently was not a hotel at all but, in fact, a nightclub—in a part of the city called Northeast. There were four quadrants in Washington, she'd learned, and she had only ever been in Northwest. She looked forward to exploring them all now that she would be spending more time here.

The dress was a blue-and-red color-block sheath by The Row with tasteful diamond-shaped cutouts at the waist. "You'll look *amazing*," Reagan had told Cady on the phone after she'd ordered it for her. "And you're going because I'm starting to think you're just afraid of this, and you're just punishing yourself at this point. Time to have fun again, you earned it. It's okay to fall for this guy."

Cady understood why Reagan had done so well as an advice columnist. She didn't quite *feel* amazing though. She felt a little sick, like she had been running for days and couldn't stop, her nerves pulsing and trembling, muscles quivering. She told herself it was all just over the debut of the first episode of

Madison's new show, which would be occupying the former
time slot of the third hour of *Best Day DC*.

She had left work early to vote and now, thinking again
about punching that choice, about another woman pursuing
the life she wanted, going after the unattainable, she felt em-
boldened. Maybe she *should* just take everything she wanted,
try to have the elusive *all*, and not be held back by anything or
anyone. With one more look in the mirror, she grabbed a cab
outside her building and was off to the Rock & Roll Hotel.

It didn't feel much like a party when you knew you'd have
work to do, but at least it gave Jay an excuse to be engrossed
in his cell phone and not have to make too much small talk.
Café Milano burst with every bold-faced Washingtonian not
on a campaign, foreign dignitaries and a healthy smattering
of the LA and New York set. Earlier he had helped a very polite Sarah Jessica Parker secure a drink and was introduced to
Kerry Washington by a publicist friend, only to be shocked
when the actress complimented Sky's reporting. He'd immediately texted Sky, who wrote back: #mindblown thank you for
that, love her!!! but you're still my favorite cheerleader. Copy
coming in 10 min. It had made Jay smile.

Jay stood in a corner, sipping his Pinot Noir and watching
the party swirl, rereading his text under the guise of waiting
for Sky's story: it would be an update of the few states already
projected and color from the scene of Haze's gathering, held
at that bed-and-breakfast in Manchester, New Hampshire. So
far, precincts had been reporting such tight margins, networks
had projected winners in only two states. New Hampshire
would be coming in soon, the one safe bet for Haze.

The flat screen set up near the endless windows at the front
of the restaurant now showed a scene from Haze headquar-

ters. Jay looked up, searching for Sky, and didn't have trouble finding him beside Grant Foxhall, reporting live.

"We should be projecting any minute now New Hampshire," Grant said, holding his earpiece. "Yes, New Hampshire goes to Rocky Haze!" Cheers erupted behind him on screen. "The night is young but a solid victory in the home state of this independent candidate. We have here Sky Vasquez of *The Queue*, really the first reporter to break the story when Haze entered the race. How has Haze evolved through this process?"

Jay wasn't even paying attention, he just stared at the screen, so proud. Sky had grown throughout these months, becoming an authority, a true political reporter. Watching him now, Jay felt inspired by how Sky had tackled this new world, and Jay felt grateful to have gotten to be there to watch him conquer it.

Someone shook Jay's arm, and he snapped out of his daze to the discovery that much of the room was looking at him, grinning and cheering.

"What do you say?" Sophie asked, pointing madly at the screen.

"What?" he said, listening now. Sky was in the middle of some sort of soliloquy. "...so, Jay, I don't know if you're watching this, you're probably waiting for my story, but if you're watching, I'm hoping when I get back, that you'll marry me."

"What?" Jay blurted out. "What's he doing?"

"I love you, and I've been away so long. I just, I need to know you're mine, okay?"

"Ohmygod, yes!" Jay shouted at the screen.

Birdie, suddenly by his side, opened his jacket, pulled the phone from his inside pocket and handed it to him. "Call the man for God's sake," she said, in her way.

On the screen, Sky pulled his phone from his pocket, hand to his ear to listen as he wiped a tear from his eye.

"That looks like a yes," Grant Foxhall said.

The crowd inside Café Milano hooted for Jay, even Helena. And Sophie, who paused her celebration only to note, too loudly, "OMG, Buck Brandywine is here! Shouldn't he be in New Hampshire?"

Both floors and the roof deck of the Rock & Roll Hotel were packed, so many bodies you couldn't pass through without spilling your drink on someone. Jeff was wearing a suit for the first time since Cady had known him. "I'm thinking we need to throw more events," he said just before the screening of the trailer for Madison's new show. "If everyone here watched *Best Day DC*, we would be in first place."

As Jeff took his place over by Madison, the footage projected against a wall: Madison Goodfellow strolling down the National Mall. "I'm Madison Goodfellow and I love a good challenge as much as I love pitching in wherever I can do some good. In my new show, we get to make a difference together. You come up with the challenge for me—should I scale a building? Should I jump off a bridge? Should I convince someone I love *not* to run for president?—and then you let me know the people and places across the country that could use some help. I'll do the challenge if you pledge enough money to help the cause of the day. And then I'll show you that money being put to work. Donate, tune in, and we'll make dreams come true together. Let's do this, let's change lives."

Cady and Jeff had pitched it like Kickstarter TV. You get to see your money put to work with the added bonus of watching Madison, a personality people seemed to love, doing zany things. The syndication deal was already in the works.

Madison had had the first kernel of the idea when she'd noticed that her foundation saw a spike in donations every time she did anything seemingly un-first-lady-like. And then there was all that Super PAC money to sort out. She'd also promised *Best Day DC* an exclusive about how she had helped Hank decide to drop out of the race. Hank, according to Madison, was fine with it all and had moved on; that was how he was. Cady decided those two might have the best relationship she had ever witnessed.

Afterward, Jeff returned to her side, tossing back a drink. "To Madison Goodfellow," he raised his glass.

"To 'Madison Goodfellow's Mad Money,'" she corrected. "A title we're keeping as long as we can, Jim Cramer be damned."

"Exactly." He laughed. "Enough business. Our hostess, who is also our boss now, sent me over to tell you to leave immediately," he said calmly.

The shock swept through Cady slowly, and it took her a second to respond. "Wait, what?"

"She said you had a prior engagement—somewhere you had to make an appearance—and that she would fire *me* if I didn't make sure you left."

"Ohhhh." Cady looked at Madison in the distance, talking to reporters and partygoers, all aglow, as though she were the first lady—or perhaps commander in chief—of Washington TV.

Madison caught her eye and smiled, waving her hand in a shooing motion.

That was all she needed. Cady flew down the stairs, out into the chilly, starlit November night and into the first cab she could find.

She texted Reagan on the way: I'm going. Thx for styling help.

Reagan responded immediately: Having a baby—for reals this time.

OMG! I can come to hospital or watch girls!

Reagan called, and Cady started talking as soon as she picked up. "Ohmagod you're calling me while you're having a baby?"

"It's cool. I've already got the drugs in me, just waiting for this thing to happen. My mom is here, and my dad is with the girls. Just called to say, you're not using me as an excuse. You're not invited here—get over there."

"What about Ted?"

"He's at the Arnold party, but the returns are coming in slow. I'm gonna call him, but he may not be able to leave."

Ted only missed Theo Jr.'s arrival—T.J. for short—by four and a half minutes. He burst into the room, met his son and wept.

"I know you don't need me, but I want to be around. More. Okay?" he said, squeezing Reagan's hand. "A workaholic who's around a little more."

"And, who knows, maybe I'll be a momaholic, who works a little more," she said. "Not right this second, though, because you're too frigging cute to be away from," she said to the baby. Then, since she hadn't actually called in time, she asked, "How'd you—"

"Cady," he said, apologetic. "She's my nominee for godmother, by the way."

"I second it." Reagan smiled.

"That's my last political advising for a couple weeks," he promised. "I'm looking forward to spending time with my three—make that four!—favorite constituents."

37

IS THIS A VICTORY PARTY?

★

Birdie couldn't hide her shock when she saw him walk in the door. She froze and watched him make his way to where she stood, headset on, iPad in hand.

"Aren't you supposed to be in New Hampshire?" she asked as he approached.

But Buck just put his arm around her waist and planted a kiss on her lips. And then, as though business as usual, he explained, "I guess, technically, I am. And I was there. Hell, you're the reason I was there at all. You knew Haze was the real deal before *I* did. Anyway, but what do they need me for tonight? I can wait around and watch TV anywhere, so thought I'd do it here."

Birdie smiled. "I'm not sure you're on the list."

"That's the thing. I'd like to be. If that's all right with you. This has been the worst election season of my life."

"That's not my problem," she said, turning inward again, scared to let him back in to her heart too easily.

"Well, actually, it is, Birdie. Because I missed you."

Looking into his eyes, she saw the man she had met on the Hill decades earlier, the man she still loved and who she was sure still loved her. "You know, I never did anything. Only the one I told you about, when I was hurt and angry," she said softly, more Roberta than Birdie now.

"I know. And you had every right. I went wrong. You're allowed to be angry as long as you want. But I just wish you wouldn't. I wish you knew I was young and stupid, not think-ing, caught up in my first campaign and got carried away. It meant nothing, as I said then, and I'll spend the rest of my days making it up to you if that's what you need."

Then he whispered, playful, "What I really need is to take you home right now, but I know well enough than to try to pull you away from the second biggest party of the season." He winked. "I'm gonna stay and watch you work, and I'll be here to walk you home when everyone has left and the sun's come back up."

These were just the words she had longed to hear. Yes, she could live with that.

Cady walked the dirt path to the expanse of illuminated tents down the center of the Mall, the Capitol Dome shin-ing in the distance behind them, the chatter of TV cover-age, voices, buzzing from the party. She didn't really know how this was going to work out. News trucks surrounded the string of tents on every side. Layers of security at every pos-sible entrance. She texted him, worried she might not get a response. Maybe she should've told him, before right now, that she might be showing up, after all.

So, hypothetically speaking, how might one crash a party like this?

Then the answer came, swift and reliable: It's like a maxi-mum security prison in here. I'm making a break for it. Hang on. Meet you at the carousel.

She made her way to the carousel, dark and still at this late hour, and took a seat on the nearest park bench, folding her arms across her chest in the chilly night air. She had raced out of her party too fast and had forgotten her coat.

She heard his voice first.

"I'm not sure, but New Hampshire might be the better bet tonight." He said it as a joke, but there was something cautious, held back, in his delivery. He wore a suit but no tie, his hands buried in his pockets.

"Best I could do. Couldn't get there in time," she said, shivering either from the temperature or the nerves. Likely the nerves. She could barely form complete sentences. "What do you think, is this a victory party?"

"It is now," he said, taking a seat beside her.

"What?"

"You're here. So this—" he pointed to her and then himself "—is a victory."

She smiled, looked away, then back at him again. "Sorry if I've been a little—"

"Difficult?" he offered.

"I was going to say…reclusive—"

"Ohhh. That's what it was," he said, nodding.

"—while I figured stuff out."

"Guys call that *'space,'*" he said with dramatic emphasis.

"So, that's what they always meant. Now I get it," she said, sarcastic.

He stood up, took her hand and yanked her to her feet. "C'mon, I think we can get the sea dragon."

He took off jogging, and she waited a moment before following.

After climbing the gate to the carousel, he held out his hand, but instead she grasped the top of the gate and leaped over herself, heels and all. *Adrenaline, not just nerves*, she thought to herself, *that's what this was*.

"Wow, okay then," he said. "Bet you used to run hurdles or something. That's how you got away from the truck so fast that day."

They strolled along the perimeter of the dark carousel. All the leaping horses silhouetted, their quiet audience.

"Oh, that," she said.

"I don't want to think about that day again, ever," he said, sharing her unspoken sentiment as he hopped onto the carousel platform. They moved slowly in the pitch-black, grabbing for the horses to guide their way. "But I hope you finally believe me about all of that." He stopped to look at her, as though to be sure she heard him and understood.

"Yeah, I do," she said softly, sorry she had given him a hard time.

"Because I just want to really start over. I'm Parker." He held his hand out to shake hers, and she took it.

"Cady."

"Great, let me tell you about me, Cady," he said, walking again. "I own this bar that is not doing so bad actually."

"I'd say." She gestured to the party.

"And contrary to what's been previously reported," he went on, "I'm not living in my office—anymore—"

"Oh?"

"Just moved in with Buddy. In Adams Morgan."

"I'm in Columbia Heights."

"Nice. We're getting our acts together."

"It seems so." She smiled.

"What else about me? My favorite show is *Best Day DC*."

"An excellent choice."

"And if I'm being fully honest—and why not?" He stopped walking again. "Then I should also say, I've had a crush on their senior producer probably since February."

"February?" she asked, surprised.

"I could've given anyone those sliders," he said, then added more thoughtfully, "And Melanie and me, we had been rocky for a while."

"Interesting," she said, taking a deep breath and leaning against the horse behind her. "Well, I guess if we're sharing here, which is not something I generally do much of, then I would say, I might have had a crush that I ignored for...*a while*." This was true. She had always been drawn to him in that safe way, with that healthy distance of someone firmly committed to someone else. But once the cracks had truly started to show with Jackson, once those first ripples of the impending quake could be felt, she'd started to view Parker differently: in a dangerous way, a way that scared her because he'd become important to her. The engagement party, it had taken great effort to keep him relegated to the friend sector of her life after that.

Cheers erupted in the distance, presumably a state projected for Arnold, and they looked toward the glowing tents.

"What's going on in there?" He turned his gaze back to her, tapped her head, smiling.

"Too much," she whispered.

The golden flecks in his eyes picked up the streetlight, and she wondered if he felt the way she felt watching him: something intense, all-consuming, combustible. His lips curved in that way, that smile of his, and suddenly she wasn't cold anymore. It felt like the night of that kiss over the summer, at the fountain. And that current flowed through her again, the same one that had also overcome her earlier in the night when she'd imagined what it would feel like to see him again. But stronger now, enveloping her, so electric that she almost expected to see a spark if he touched her, when he touched her. *When.*

"Too much," she said again. Too much to say, and he had to know: she was here. "And you? What's going on? In there?" She tapped his chest, his heart.

He looked away a moment and then: "Just this," he said, his lips on hers, gently at first, pulling her close, one hand in her hair, one at her waist, his palm burning against that small cutout where her skin peeked from her dress. He stepped toward her, against her, until she was backed against the carousel sea dragon, the only barrier keeping them from tumbling.

Finally, after months of fighting her feelings for him, months of closing herself off while she sorted herself out, put herself back together, she let herself get lost in him.

He kissed her neck and whispered in her ear, "Do you still need space? I'm hoping not. I'm not giving you any, at the moment."

"No, I'm good," she said as he kissed her neck again. And then, just for herself, for her own clarity, "For the record, I don't need you...I *want* you."

"Works for me," he whispered lightly, that broad smile, his eyes bright. "But, you know, I'll say whatever I have to in order to get your vote."

"You've got it."

He celebrated with another kiss.

EPILOGUE

★

January

CROWDS FLOCK TO CITY, HAZE INAUGURAL EXPECTED TO SET ATTENDANCE RECORDS

By Sky Vasquez, Staff Writer, *The Queue*

It was the closest election in history, with results delayed until absentee ballots had been counted and recounted in a number of battleground states. But now the country is ready to celebrate the dawn of a new administration…

Reagan swanned into the Jefferson Hotel, waving as soon as she saw her: Alex Arnold, already seated for afternoon tea at the best table in the room. Their favorite old-school extravagance, perfect for a snowy winter's afternoon just days before the inauguration. Reagan had jumped at the chance to see her friend and help her drown some sorrows. But Alex didn't look like a woman whose husband had just missed the presidency by a few hundred votes.

"So sorry I'm late," Reagan said, handing over her coat to the quick-arriving server with a thanks.

Alex, elegant in winter white pants and a cozy cashmere sweater, rose to give her a warm hug, setting down the magazine she had been reading: the new issue of *GQ* with Alchemy. The cover line: America's *First* First Gentleman Loves His Job By Sky Vasquez.

"I thought it was hard leaving Ted with two kids but with three, it's nearly impossible."

"You look amazing," Alex said, taking her seat again, sipping her tea. A waiter materialized instantly to take Reagan's order, probably assuming she must be important to have kept the wife of the former veep waiting. "Don't tell me you're just chasing the kids."

"I'm just chasing the kids. That can be some serious cardio— the twins are in constant motion and T.J. is already very busy."

"Fine, don't tell me your secret," she joked. "But, whatever you're doing it's working."

"You too. Not winning the election seems to have agreed with you," Reagan said gently.

"Ah, well, there are worse things," she said, folding her hands in front of her. She squared her shoulders, serious now. "So *I* know that *you* know I'm going to ask you this question."

"What do you mean?" Reagan tried but mostly failed to feign ignorance.

"You're going to make me beg. Okay." She laughed. "So if Haze is serious about this one-term thing, then I'm doing this. It's my turn. I did the Senate, I did Treasury. I'm giving this a go. I'm running."

"For president," Reagan said. "Not in a half-marathon or something, just to be clear."

"For president, yes," she said, leaning back in her chair. "And I need you working for me. I want Birdie fund-raising, you speechwriting and communications, and anyone else you know that I need, think about it. Give me names. I want a dream team."

"I've got a few ideas," Reagan said, mind racing.

"So, you're in?"

Reagan exhaled, even though she had known this was coming, and cocked her head. "20/20 vision, baby. I'm in."

Cady and Max took a swing by the Capitol after taping a
segment with the youngest freshman congresswoman—just
twenty-five years old, brilliant Rhodes Scholar fresh out of
her Harvard PhD program—in her office in the Longfellow
building. Since the congresswoman was rushing to a meeting,
Cady and Max had decided to shoot some B-roll of National
Statuary Hall to fill out the piece. They had their work cut
out for them too. Between *Best Day DC* and Madison's show,
the schedule was madness…and Cady loved it.

Tourists swarmed inside the Capitol, so many in town for
the inauguration. As groups were being herded through, the
crowd momentarily parted, and across the room she saw a
ghost: Jackson. She hadn't spoken to him since she had moved
her things out of his apartment at the end of the summer.
But it was a small town, and she'd heard that he was doing
this now, giving Capitol tours. Because of an Iowa law pro-
hibiting a person from running for more than one office at a
time, Carter hadn't been allowed to run for his congressional
seat once he'd become the vice presidential nominee. Now
he was out of a job altogether, as was Jackson. They would
both land on their feet soon enough, not that Cady was losing sleep over it.

Cady had taken this tour before. Parker had continued in-
sisting she hit all the tourist sites, and he had been more than
happy to guide her. It was their favorite weekend pastime. *"I'm
doing you a favor. You're a local show producer. How bad would it
look for you to not know this stuff? You're welcome."*

So she knew, from experience, that Jackson stood at the
very spot in Statuary Hall where the half-dome above threw

the acoustics wildly. She knew what he was telling his tour group as he bent down to the ground: "If I whisper something into the floor here, it bounces off and can be heard all the way across the room over there." He pointed in Cady's direction. Then he whispered, and she heard his message, clear as crystal: "Cady, I'm sorry."

She turned her head, nodded to him, blissfully indifferent. It didn't matter anymore. She never would have expected to be able to look at him, accept his apology, feel no tug, no pang, no longing in his presence. She felt liberated by this lack of feeling for him. He would just be a footnote in her history.

"Your lunch date is here," Max said. "See ya back at the office."

Parker nodded, strolling toward her, flakes of snow on his coat. "Hey you," he said. He kissed her as though he hadn't just woken up next to her that morning. "Got what you needed?" he asked, referring to the interview. His arm around her shoulder, they walked out the Senate side of the building, in the direction of Preamble.

She nodded, smiled. "I did."

★ ★ ★ ★ ★

ACKNOWLEDGMENTS

★

Just as the Widows had each other to lean on, I'm so lucky to be surrounded by so many truly amazing people. Thank you, thank you, thank you so much...

To Stéphanie Abou, agent extraordinaire, laser-sharp reader and dear friend: you are the very best and I adore you! With an extra thank-you to the great gang at Massie & McQuilkin.

To Melanie Fried, brilliant editor: thank you for your tremendous guidance, patience and encouragement along the way. You are wonderful! Huge thanks also to Lisa Wray, Pam Osti and the fantastic team at Graydon House, Harlequin and HarperCollins. And to the lovely Elena Stokes and the Wunderkind team. I'm so grateful to you *all* for your work championing this book; you are incredible!

To Eddie Gamarra for helping this book to expand its reach.

To Margo Lipschultz for discovering this book!

To Richard Ford for your wisdom and inspiring words.

To the best squad a girl could have—you all know who you are!—with an extra shout-out to: Rachel Paula Abrahamson, Jami Bjellos, Jenny Laws, Ryan Lynch, Poornima Ravishankar, Anna Siri, Jennie Teitelbaum and Kate Ackley Zeller.

To my amazing family and cheering section: fabulous parents Bill and Risa, awesome sis (and beloved first reader!) Karen. And supersupportive in-laws Steve, Ilene, Jill, Lauren, David and Gabrielle.

To Brian—of course!—for the love and endless encouragement (and millions of political chats), and for watching our wild, adorable boys while I disappeared into my office to write. And to sweet Sawyer and Hardy for sneaking your beautiful artwork and Lego sculptures onto my desk when I wasn't looking.

And finally, thank you, dear reader, for devoting your time to these Widows. I so hope you've enjoyed reading their adventures as much as I've enjoyed writing them!

CAMPAIGN
WIDOWS

AIMEE AGRESTI

Reader's Guide

GRAYDON
HOUSE

1. How does Cady's arrival as the new girl in town bring the Widows together? In what ways does she become the glue uniting them?

2. Though the Widows all lead very different lives, they quickly become each other's shoulders to cry on. What are the turning points in their friendships? Think about your own friendships. What are some of the moments that have solidified those bonds?

3. How is the campaign itself a character? What effect does it have on each character's relationships? Think about your own relationships. How have they been tested, and what made them succeed or stumble?

4. Discuss how each Widow evolves over the course of the story. How do the bumps in their romantic relationships make them stronger as individuals?

5. In what ways do the Widows end up influencing the election, despite being on the periphery of the campaigns?

6. Do you think Rocky Haze will be a good leader, and if so, why? Would you have voted for her?

7. Discuss the current of girl power running through the story. How are many of the women underestimated at different times in the novel? How does each overcome obstacles and rise above the naysayers?

8. What would each Widow have to say about the idea of "having it all," the notion of successfully balancing personal and professional lives? How does this theme relate to your own life?

9. How is the theme of independence woven throughout the novel? What type of message does the story send about believing in yourself and taking chances?

10. Which Widow did you most relate to? Which Widow would you most want to be friends with and why?

11. Discuss the tone at the end of the novel. How did you feel about the way the author chose to conclude the story?